wonderful children, and she and her husband even tried ranching exotic birds (ostriches, emus and rheas). Ask her, and she'll tell you what it's like to go toe-to-toe with an angry three-hundred-and-fifty-pound bird! Elle loves to hear from fans at ellejames@earthlink.net or www.ellejames.com

Lena Diaz was born in Kentucky and has also lived in California, Louisiana and Florida, where she now resides with her husband and two children. Before becoming a romantic suspense author, she was a computer programmer. A Romance Writers of America Golden Heart® Award finalist, she has also won the prestigious Daphne du Maurier Award for Excellence in Mystery/Suspense. To get the latest news about Lena, please visit her website, www.lenadiaz.com

Discover more at millsandboon.co.uk

SHOW OF FORCE

ELLE JAMES

SMOKIES
SPECIAL AGENT

LENA DIAZ

MILLS & BOON

First Published in Great Britain 2019
by Mills & Boon, an imprint of HarperCollins*Publishers*
1 London Bridge Street, London, SE1 9GF

Show Of Force © 2019 Mary Jernigan
Smokies Special Agent © 2019 Lena Diaz

ISBN: 978-0-263-27415-8

0519

Printed and bound in Spain
by CPI, Barcelona

SHOW OF FORCE

ELLE JAMES

This book is dedicated to my mother, who has always been there for me, my sister and brothers. When my father was deployed to other parts of the world, she was the one who held down the fort at home. She's beautiful, talented and determined. She encouraged us to follow our own paths, wherever they might lead.

I love you, Mom!

Chapter One

Just after four o'clock in the afternoon, Riley Lansing slipped in through the back entrance of the Marriott Marquis hotel in downtown Washington, DC. She wore a stolen employee badge and one of the dresses required of the female waitstaff. With her dark hair tucked beneath a blond wig, she passed for the woman in the fuzzy image sufficiently enough to make it past the security guard.

She carried a large purse and smacked chewing gum. When the guard asked to search her bag, she made certain her less-than-sexy panties and feminine products were on top to discourage him from digging deeper and discovering her second costume of the night.

Her trick worked. The guard waved her past the checkpoint.

Riley sailed through and entered the employee locker room. Instead of ditching her bag, she carried it through to the door on the far side that led deeper into the hotel's service area.

Riley's heart pounded against her ears, and her pulse

thundered through her veins. She'd trained most of her young life for this. Her mother and father had drilled her daily on her responsibilities and loyalties. But Riley had hoped and prayed she would be forgotten, shuffled into the far regions of some paper file that had never been converted to digital data.

All the years she'd immersed herself in the American life her parents had created for her, with their own false identities and her legitimate birth certificate, were about to be blown wide open. No one she'd come into contact with over her lifetime knew her as anyone but Riley Lansing, daughter of Linda and Robert Lansing. Her parents spoke perfect American English and appeared to be the finest of upstanding citizens of the good old US of A.

Only they weren't. She wasn't. Her life had been one big lie, leading up to what she'd been tasked to do that evening.

Why now? Why, after the deaths of her father and mother in an auto accident five years earlier, had they come back to call her to service? Riley had hoped her parents' handler had forgotten their daughter and her little brother even existed.

She'd pushed her secret life to the back of her consciousness for so long, she almost believed it was all a weird dream made up from a child's wild imagination.

Until that morning, when she'd received the electronically distorted message from an anonymous voice initiating her call to action. "Baryshnikov has risen."

At first, she hadn't recognized the code words. When they sank in from the years her father had repeated them, a chill raised the hairs on the back of her neck and rippled down the length of her spine.

"You will find instructions at the luggage storage area at the Metro in downtown DC." The voice left an address and locker number. "And to guarantee your compliance, we have a little insurance policy."

A moment later, little Toby's voice came through the receiver. "Riley?" he said, the one word catching on a sob. "I'm scared."

"Oh, Toby. Sweetheart," she said. "It's okay. I'm coming for you. I'll find you and bring you home."

Her little brother sobbed once more, jerking at Riley's heartstrings.

"Toby?" Riley cried out.

"Do the job tonight and the boy will be returned to his home," the voice said. "Fail and you will never see him again."

Clutching the large bag close to her side, she hurried through the maze of corridors she'd traversed the day before, familiarizing herself with the layout of the kitchen, the staff elevators and the ballroom where the evening's event would take place. She'd even identified an electronics closet where she could hide until the event began, ensuring she'd be past the security guards who would be posted at every entrance and exit checking identification against invitation lists.

The second worst part of her plan was the two hours she'd have to wait until she could initiate the operation.

The absolute worst part of her plan was the crux of the operation and what she had to accomplish to satisfy her handler and get her little brother back alive.

To succeed at her mission, she had to kill someone she not only knew but admired.

Her hand shook as she slipped a file into the keyhole and jimmied the lock on the door to the electronics closet. It clicked, and she pulled the door open. She'd played with locks from an early age and could open just about anything requiring a key. This skill had come in handy during college when she entered her dorm past curfew and the doors were locked.

Once inside the electronics room, she closed the door and locked it from the inside to keep anyone from randomly walking in looking for something or someone.

For the next two and a half hours, she waited. The security detail would have swept the ballroom and surrounding cubbies, restrooms, hallways and anterooms. Guards would have been positioned at all corners, equipped with radio communications devices and handguns.

Her target would have no fewer than four bodyguards in attendance. Having had an attempt made on her life recently, she wouldn't take any chances. Not even at a gala with the prime purpose of raising money for sick children.

During the two hours Riley waited, she went through her proposed actions in her mind, the steps she would take and how she would maneuver her victim out of the ballroom and into one of the anterooms or the ladies' restroom. Once there, Riley would aim her small handgun at the woman and force her to take a small pill. She slipped her hand into the voluminous purse and curled her fingers around the HK .40 caliber handgun that fit snugly in her grip. She knew how to fire it. Knew where to hit her target to ensure a quick and painless death. But she wouldn't fire the handgun unless absolutely necessary. The poison would do the trick much more quietly. All she had to do was make her take it, and Toby would be set free.

She couldn't think about the woman she'd been sent to eliminate. Toby was only six years old. He deserved a chance to live. If it meant taking the life of an older woman who'd had her chance at living, so be it. Riley couldn't let anything happen to her only living relative remaining on earth. As far as she knew, Toby didn't know what her parents and she herself had been recruited to do.

No one knew, except Riley and her handler. And Riley had no clue who her handler was. When her parents died, she'd taken on guardianship of her little brother. She should have known hiding him in the Virginia countryside with a paid nanny wouldn't be enough to keep him safe. When her parents had passed away, she should have moved as far away from DC as she could get. At least then the Russians wouldn't have been able to find Toby and use him as collateral to collect on their investment.

As the time neared, her breathing became more erratic and her pulse raced. In less than an hour, she'd have to put her skills as an assassin to use on an innocent woman who had gone out of her way, spent her money and engaged her employees to help Riley. She'd betray the woman's trust and the trust of her new assistant, Riley's best friend and roommate, Grace Lawrence.

Riley swallowed hard on the bile rising up her throat. She'd never asked for this assignment. She'd spent her life training with the misguided belief she'd never have to use that training. If asked to do something she didn't like, she'd always imagined herself refusing.

Until they'd kidnapped Toby. Toby was her Achilles' heel. She'd do anything for her little brother.

Even kill?

The alarm on her watch vibrated, letting her know the time had come. She had to get ready and make an appearance at the gala. Her target would recognize her and welcome her with open arms. She might even wonder how Riley could have afforded the plate price to get in. Riley had a lame excuse to cover long enough to get her quarry alone. She'd take her someplace where she could be assured they wouldn't be followed by the woman's bodyguards. There, she would do what she'd come to do.

Riley removed the blond wig, slipped the maid's dress over her head, released the clasps on her bra and slid the straps down her arms. Naked but for a pair of silky black panties, she wrapped a small amount of C-4 explosive to her inner calf with an Ace bandage and tucked the detonator affixed to a hair clip into her long dark hair, pulling it back behind her right ear and letting the rest of her hair fall over her left shoulder. The C-4 and detonator were courtesy of her handler, from among the items she'd found in the locker he'd sent her to in the train station.

Once she had her diversion devices secured, she dug a long black dress out of the bottom lining of her purse and shook out the wrinkles. She'd purchased the dress while shopping with her friend, intending to wear it to a less expensive charity event later that summer.

She almost laughed at the thought. That was when she was still an innocent American female who had nothing more to worry about than riding the Metro to and from her work as an aerospace engineer. The irony of it all was that she'd been recruited by the FBI to help them capture someone stealing government secrets from the corporation where she worked.

They'd come close but hadn't nailed the bastard. What was so ironic was that thief might have been working for the Russians. Just like she was.

She pulled the dress over her head, settling the halter strap around her neck and letting the silky gown slide down her torso and over her hips. Riley and her roommate had both loved the dress. Though it had been a little pricey for her budget, she'd purchased the garment, excited to wear it to a ritzy DC function.

She no longer was the child easily molded and trained by her parents. That little girl had grown into a woman with a mind of her own. All the propaganda her parents had used to shape her beliefs had been replaced by the readings and research of an inquisitive mind. She had no desire to work as a spy or an assassin for a country for which she felt no affiliation. She was an American, despite her parents' home of birth.

She wanted the American dream, the American life-style, and the right to pursue happiness and love. And she'd hoped to accomplish some of that pursuit in the dress she'd purchased with her roommate.

Riley tucked the murder weapon into the bra of her dress. A tiny plastic bag containing one small pill that only had to touch the victim's tongue to do the job. The pill would dissolve before anyone could do anything to help her, and the damage would be done. She'd die within just two minutes, her body hemorrhaging internally.

Pulling a small mirror from her purse, she examined her makeup and the dress in an entirely different light from that of the happy young professional engineer she'd been when she purchased the item. In that dress, her life would change forever.

To Riley, the dress would always be what she'd worn when she committed murder.

"ARE WE HERE?" Charlotte Halverson asked as the limousine pulled up to the curb outside the Marriott Marquis hotel in downtown Washington, DC.

Mack Balkman had the lead on the bodyguard detail for his new boss. "Yes, ma'am."

"And don't call me ma'am," the woman said. "It's Charlie."

"Yes, ma'am—Charlie." Mack choked on calling his new boss by her first name. His years on active duty made him want to address his boss with the utmost respect. And if that wasn't bad enough, his parents had insisted he address women older than him by their surnames. Calling Mrs. Halverson by her first name didn't sit right in his books. But she was the boss, and if she wanted him to call her Pookie while standing on his head, he'd do it. She'd given him a job when most others wouldn't have given him the time of day.

"Are my men in place?" Charlie asked.

"They are. We've got you covered." He touched his headset. "All clear?"

Mustang, their point man who'd arrived on a motorcycle ahead of them, replied, "Ready as we can be. This place is crawling with people here to see the red-carpet show."

Augustus "Gus" Walsh climbed out of the passenger seat of the limousine and opened the back door.

When Charlie started to slide across the seat, Mack touched her arm. "Normally, I'd say ladies first, but not tonight."

"Right." Charlie settled back and waited for Mack to exit the vehicle.

He stood, straightened the tuxedo she'd arranged for him to wear and patted the nine-millimeter SIG Sauer P226 tucked beneath his jacket. Under his white shirt and cummerbund, he wore a bulletproof vest. He'd already cleared his men through the service that had been hired to provide security for the annual gala. All they had to do was show their identification and they would bypass the metal detectors that would make all kinds of noise if they found guns or knives on those who passed through.

He held out his hand for Charlie and helped the older woman from the back of the limousine. Gus closed ranks, moving in on the other side of her. He used his body as a shield against any potential threat.

They couldn't be too careful. Less than two weeks prior, an attempt had been made on Charlie's life. Two vans full of bad guys had cornered her limousine on a busy DC street. They'd killed her previous bodyguards and attempted a kidnapping. Thankfully, former Force Recon marine Declan O'Neill, Mack's old team leader, had been there to save her. She'd rewarded him by hiring him and his team to provide security for her or anyone she deemed in need of assistance.

"You gentlemen don't know how safe it makes me feel to have highly qualified, loyal men protecting me." Charlie patted his arm. "I can't tell you how happy I am that Declan agreed to come on board and bring his team with him."

"Ma'am—" Mack started.

"Charlie," she said.

Gus smiled. "I don't know about you, Mack, but I have a hard time calling her Charlie myself. She could be my mo—"

Charlie held up her hand. "Don't say it."

Gus clamped his lips shut.

Mack hid a smile.

"Don't say I'm old enough to be your mother. I feel old enough as it is. But my mind is still sharp and I feel like a twenty-five-year-old, thanks to Edwardo, my personal trainer." She lifted her chin. "And this dress makes me feel like a million bucks." She sighed. "My husband would have liked me in it."

"You look amazing, Charlie," Mack said. "But I'd

feel better if you looked amazing inside the hotel. Not out here on the streets where anything can happen."

"Right." Charlie forced a smile to her lips and stepped out on Mack's arm.

He knew he appeared to be more a date than a bodyguard, but he didn't care, as long as he had room under his jacket for a weapon. He scanned the crowds of people standing on the other side of a barricade. Photographers snapped pictures and bystanders watched as vehicles pulled up one by one, discharging well-dressed men and women onto the red carpet.

Mack and Gus eased their charge along.

Charlie smiled and waved at the reporters and the people like a celebrity on a walk of fame.

From what Declan had told Mack and the other men of his team, Declan's Defenders, Mrs. Charlotte Halverson was a kind of celebrity in her own right. The rich widow of a prominent philanthropist, she'd rubbed elbows with some of the most influential people of the century, from Hollywood movie stars to the leaders of many countries, including the president of the United States.

Charlie stopped and waited her turn to have her official photograph taken in front of the gala's backdrop. Ahead of her was a younger couple, the woman wearing a fancy silver gown with sequins and a diamond necklace that probably cost more than what Mack had made in a year as a marine.

He didn't envy the woman her jewelry or the money it took to buy it. Instead, he cringed at the amount of money wasted on jewelry that could be given to the charity the gala was raising money for.

But he wasn't there to judge the people attending; he was employed to keep Charlie safe.

When it was Charlie's turn to have her picture taken, she insisted on Mack standing with her.

"Wouldn't you rather have one of your friends pose with you?" Mack asked.

"These people are acquaintances. Besides, you're much better-looking than they are. I'd love to make them all jealous." She smiled up at him. "But if it makes you uncomfortable, you don't have to be in the picture."

"I'd prefer to stay close," he said.

"Good. Then it's settled." She led him to stand in front of the backdrop. Once they were there, photographers snapped their pictures.

The flashes temporarily blinded Mack. He touched a finger to his headset. "Keep your eyes peeled," he said softly.

"No worries," Gus responded. "We've got Charlie covered while you're playing the model."

Mustang chuckled. "Nice tux. Didn't know you could clean up so well."

"Damned monkey suit," Mack muttered.

"I heard that," Charlie said between her teeth as she smiled for the camera.

"Sorry."

"Don't worry. My husband hated to dress up as well. But the gala for the children was one of his favorites.

He wouldn't miss it for the world." Her smile faded. "He would have loved being here."

Mack realized he didn't know much about the Halversons, other than what had been printed in the tabloids. He wondered how long they were married and whether they'd had children.

"You see, my husband and I weren't blessed with children." She hooked her arm through his and left the photographers' circle and continued on toward the hotel. "We tried, but it wasn't meant to be. All the money we would have spent raising and educating one of our own went into scholarships, research and a new wing on the children's hospital. My husband didn't live to see the wing complete."

"Did they capture your husband's killer?" Mack asked.

Charlie shook her head. "No. And that's part of the reason why I decided to hire your team leader. The police force is too overwhelmed with work to find all the bad guys. I figured I could help, if only just a little."

They entered the building and moved with the flow of people toward the main ballroom.

The crush of guests all dressed in glitz and glamour surrounded Mack and Charlie. Mack's first instinct was to grab Charlie and back away. How would he keep her safe in a room as crowded as it was?

He gripped her elbow and slowed her to a halt.

Charlie frowned. "What's wrong?"

"There are far too many people in this room," he said.

Her frown easily turned into a smile. "The more the merrier. The charity will get lots of donations."

Mack grunted. "I'm more worried about your safety. You need to hang out on the fringes where we can give you better coverage."

"Oh, pooh." Her smile slipped. "And my safety isn't as important as getting the money needed for the research that could provide cures for children with life-threatening diseases. My husband was a big proponent of this particular aid group. I won't hide behind my bodyguard when there are children in need of cures." She shook her arm loose of Mack's grip and marched into the middle of the ballroom, smiling like a Valkyrie declaring victory.

"What's wrong?" Gus asked. "Why is Charlie alone in the middle of the room?"

"I think it was easier facing the Taliban than working for Mrs. Halverson," Mack muttered. "The woman has a mind of her own, and she doesn't like following orders."

"I'm not liking it," Mustang said into Mack's ear. "We can't protect her if she's not willing to protect herself."

"You're telling me," Mack said, and pushed his way through the throngs of elegantly dressed people until he arrived at Charlie's side.

"Well, darn," she said, and smiled up at Mack, the lines at the corners of her eyes crinkling with mischief. "I thought I'd lost you."

"Please, Mrs. H—"

She raised a finger. "Uh-uh."

Mack sighed. "Charlie, don't go running off. I can't protect you if I'm not at your side."

"I want you to keep me safe, but I can't take you everywhere."

Mack straightened to his full six foot three inches. "Where you go, I go."

Charlie raised her brows. "I'm sorry?"

"If you want my protection, you have to follow my rules."

Charlie crossed her arms over her chest and raised her salt-and-pepper brows. "Not to the ladies' room, I should think."

Mack frowned deeply. He hadn't thought about areas off-limits to men. Perhaps they should have hired a female bodyguard just for that purpose. For now, he'd have to make do. "I'll clear the room before you go in."

Charlie patted Mack's cheek and smiled. "Sweetie, that won't be necessary. I can manage a trip to the restroom on my own."

If he was going to do the job right, he had to know exactly where his charge was at all times. Disappearing behind a closed door was not something Charlie could do without having him or one of his men check the facilities first. He'd cross that bridge when they came to it. For the moment, he kept busy chasing the wealthy widow around the ballroom.

An hour into the night's festivities, Charlie exclaimed, "Oh, look who's here."

Mack glanced in the direction Charlie was looking.

A dark-haired woman in a long black dress stood next to a man in a white tuxedo. She nodded, spoke to the man, made him laugh and then looked up. A moment later, she was walking toward Charlie, a smile spreading across her face. "Mrs. Halverson, I didn't know you'd be here."

"My dear, wild horses couldn't drag me away. This is the one charity event I can't miss." She clasped the woman's hands. "Mack, you remember Riley Lansing, don't you?" Charlie squeezed Riley's hands and let go, then turned to Mack. "She was the woman who led us on quite the wild chase a couple weeks ago. In fact, it was her roommate's concern for her that made me consider spinning up Declan's Defenders."

Mack remembered Riley. "I'm sorry. I barely recognized you."

"That's okay." She smiled. "I guess I clean up well."

Mack couldn't keep his gaze from traversing the length of the black dress from her neck to her toes. The fabric clung to her curves like a second skin.

"I'm so glad to see you," Charlie said. "For two reasons."

Riley raised her eyebrows. "Two reasons? That sounds pretty specific."

Charlie laughed. "You'll understand in a moment. Number one, I'm glad you're okay. For a while there, we didn't know what had happened to you when you went missing. And two, I couldn't convince Mack to allow me to go to the ladies' room on my own. But I'm sure if I go with you, he won't insist on accompanying me." She gave Mack a challenging lift of her brow.

Mack frowned heavily. "I still think you need me to clear the restroom before you go in."

"Fine." Charlie's lips pressed together. "I'll tell everyone to leave so that my big bad bodyguard can inspect each stall." She shot a glance at Riley. "Do you mind coming with me?"

Riley gave Charlie a tight smile. "Not at all."

Mack studied the younger woman. Something wasn't quite right about her response.

Her hands clenched into tight fists, and a slight glow of perspiration coated her fair skin.

"Miss Lansing, are you feeling well?" he asked.

She jerked her head around to stare up at him. "Yes. Why do you ask?"

He shrugged. "You seem nervous." He tipped his chin toward her balled fists.

She laughed, uncurled her fingers and pressed her palms together. "No. I'm not nervous," she said quickly. And then sighed. "Well, maybe just a little. I don't normally wear fancy clothing or attend expensive galas."

"Speaking of which," Charlotte interrupted, "how did you manage to get a seat at the event? I thought it had sold out within thirty minutes of going up online."

Riley gave a brief smile. "I won the ticket on a radio talk show."

Mrs. Halverson clapped her hands. "What a gift. This event is one of my favorites. I hope they have the children's choir sing as they have in the past."

"Children's choir?" Riley's eyes widened.

"Yes. They always do. There they are, lining up now." Charlie bit down on her bottom lip. "I'd like to make a trip to the ladies' room before they begin." She reached for Riley's arm. "Do you mind accompanying an old woman? I promise not to make any strange noises." The widow winked and held up her fingers like a Boy Scout. "I swear."

Riley darted a glance at the children lining up near the raised dais where the band had set up earlier. "I suppose I could." She nodded as if making up her mind and turned to take Mrs. Halverson's arm. "Let's get this over with."

Charlie smiled over her shoulder at Mack. "Happy? I have someone looking out for me so you don't have to."

"I'd still like to clear the room before you go in."

"I'll ask people to leave," Riley offered.

Mack informed his other two team members of his intentions and then followed the women to the hallway where the ladies' restroom was located. His gut was tight and roiling just a little. Like the time just before the mission that had ended his marine career. He'd had the same feeling then as he had now.

Charlie waited with Mack outside the restroom while Riley rounded up the occupants and ushered them out. When she returned, she nodded. "The room is clear."

Mack entered, checked each stall and looked for any other doors leading in or out. When he was satisfied no one else was in the room, he returned to Charlie and Riley. "Okay, the room is clear."

"I could have told you that," Riley said. "But I guess you had to see it for yourself."

He nodded and checked his watch. "Five minutes tops. If you're not out by then, I'm coming in."

Charlie smiled. "I can barely get my lipstick out of my purse in five minutes." She patted Mack's arm.

"Don't worry. I'll be out by then. If not, please come in and get me. I might be stuck." She laughed all the way through the door.

Riley glanced back as she followed Charlie inside. A frown dented her forehead and gave her a worried look.

Mack opened his mouth to ask what had her concerned, but she disappeared behind the closed door before he uttered a word.

The next five minutes stretched before him like a chasm. His pulse pounded, and his heart banged against his ribs. Why, he didn't know. He'd checked the room and every stall. No one but Riley was inside the restroom with Charlie. So why was he worried?

Chapter Two

Riley waited for Charlie to enter a stall before she extracted the small plastic packet containing the pill from the bra of her gown. She pulled the clip from her hair and set it on the counter in front of her. Once she administered the poison, she'd set off the small explosion and make her exit in the confusion.

She hadn't counted on Mack being there and so attentive. Her gut clenched, and she closed her eyes, mustering the strength she needed to do what she had to in order to save her brother's life. Toby was only six years old. He deserved the chance to live to a ripe old age. Charlie was in her sixties. She'd lived, loved and traveled the world.

And saved your life by offering the services of Declan's Defenders. She didn't deserve to die any more than Toby. But her death would be much less painful than what her handler would do to Toby if Riley didn't complete the mission.

With her eyes closed, Riley could see Toby's face the last time she'd visited him in the Virginia countryside. He'd been so happy to see her and sad when she'd had to leave. Margaret, the nanny, had smiled and held him like he was her own. The woman was like a grandmother to both Riley and Toby. Riley had known the woman her entire life.

Riley hated leaving but knew she had to go back to her job at Quest Aerospace Alliance that Monday or she'd be missed. Throughout her life, her parents had warned her she would be called on to perform for her mother country one day. The tasks were yet to be determined. She'd assumed spying of some sort. Not assassination, though she'd been trained with a variety of weapons and in both defensive and offensive maneuvers.

Within hours of leaving the country house, Riley was back at her apartment with her roommate, Grace Lawrence. In the middle of the night, she'd received the text. Knowing she couldn't confide in her roommate, she'd kept the text to herself and lain awake the remainder of the night until morning. Then she'd had to act as if nothing were the matter. She'd contacted the nanny, who had just woken up and discovered Toby missing.

Thankfully, Margaret, who'd been her nanny when she was a little girl, hadn't been harmed in the abduction. But Toby was gone. Explaining to Margaret that she couldn't call the police had been difficult. But she'd calmed Margaret and prayed she'd have the strength to hold off calling the authorities when Riley wanted to do the same.

If she had called the cops, what would she have told them? *Hi, I'm a Russian spy. I don't want to be, but I'm tasked with assassinating a wealthy widow in order to save my brother.*

She'd be locked up faster than she could say *seriously.*

And Toby would be absorbed into the Russian spy machine, tortured and brainwashed until he didn't know right from wrong.

Sweet heaven, she had to go through with the assassination. She couldn't abandon Toby to Russian machinations.

A hand touched her arm, making Riley jump.

"Riley, honey, what's wrong?" Mrs. Halverson stood behind her, wearing a silver gown that complemented her silver hair. The slim woman still appeared beautiful despite the lines and wrinkles on her face. And the frown she wore was soft and worried. About her.

Riley stared into her clear blue eyes for a very long moment, the tiny plastic bag burning her hand. All she had to do was open it, shove the pill into the older woman's mouth, and it would all be over.

Her hand shook. Trembling started at her knees and rippled all the way up her back. "I can't," she whispered. "I'm so sorry, Toby. I just can't."

The tiny plastic bag dropped from her nerveless fingers and drifted to the floor.

Mrs. Halverson bent to retrieve it.

"No!" Riley tried to grab the bag from the woman, but Charlie held it out of her reach.

"What is this?" the widow asked.

"Nothing. I was just going to flush it down the toilet." She reached for the bag. "Please. Let me have it."

"Is it a drug?" Charlie's gaze captured hers. "Are you taking drugs?"

"No. Of course not," Riley answered automatically.

"Then why do you have it?"

Tears filled Riley's eyes and trickled down her cheeks. "I'm sorry. I'm so sorry."

"For what, my dear?" Charlie pulled Riley into her arms and held her.

"Why did you have to be so nice?" Riley muttered between sobs. "This wouldn't have been so hard if you weren't so good to me."

"What wouldn't be so hard?" Charlie held Riley at arm's length and stared into her eyes. "Tell me what's bothering you. Perhaps I can help."

"Oh, it's no use," Riley shook her head, more tears falling down her face. "The only way you can help is for you to die."

Mrs. Halverson's eyebrows rose on her forehead. "Sweetie, whatever do you mean?"

"The only way to save my brother is for me to assassinate you." Riley nodded toward the plastic bag. "The pill is poison. One touch on your tongue and you'd be dead in seconds."

Charlie's eyes widened, and she held the plastic bag up in front of her. "You wanted to assassinate me? Why? Did I do something to make you mad?"

"Oh, Mrs. Halverson, no. You did everything to help me."

Her forehead wrinkled. "Then why would you want to kill me?"

"They're making me. They have my brother, Toby.

If I don't kill you, there's no telling what they'll do to Toby. I'll never see him again. They could kill him, or worse."

"What could be worse?" Mrs. Halverson asked. Then her eyes rounded. "Torture?"

Riley nodded. "And brainwashing. I can't let that happen. He deserves a better life. He's just a child… only six years old."

"Oh dear." Charlie stared at the little bag, shaking her head. "Whatever can you do?"

"Nothing. I can do nothing. My brother will disappear, and I'll never see him again. He'll think I've abandoned him. They'll tell him I never loved him. They'll make him a weapon to use against others in the future." Riley broke away from Mrs. Halverson. "I can't let that happen."

"There's nothing else you can do, then, is there?" the older woman said softly.

Riley stopped pacing and turned to frown at Mrs. Halverson. "What do you mean?"

"You'll have to kill me." The wealthy widow held up the bag. "I'll take the pill and die. Your brother will be safe, and all will end as it should." She started to open the little bag.

Riley dived toward her. "No!" In her effort to stop Mrs. Halverson from doing the dastardly deed, she knocked her to the floor and straddled her.

Mrs. Halverson let out a squeal and grunted as she landed hard on the marble tile.

The door to the restroom burst open. Mack charged

in. "What the hell?" He grabbed Riley around the waist and yanked her up off Mrs. Halverson.

"Let go of me!" Riley fought to free herself of Mack's grip, but his iron band of an arm held her tightly against his chest.

"Charlie, are you all right?" Mack asked.

The older woman sat up, still holding the little plastic bag. "I'm okay. Miss Lansing was only helping me to take this pill. It will relieve the headache I'm getting."

"No! Mack, don't let her take that pill. Please, let go of me. She can't take that pill."

"Fiddle. Of course I can." She tilted her head to the side. "It's what you wanted, wasn't it?"

"No," Riley cried. "I never wanted it. Don't do it. Please, don't take that pill." She struggled against the arm holding her around the middle, tearing at Mack's tuxedo sleeve with her fingernails. "Let me go. You don't understand. Please. Don't let her take that pill." Tears poured from her eyes to the point she couldn't see clearly. She blinked rapidly, trying to clear them, trying to see what Mrs. Halverson was doing. Praying she didn't go through with the instructions Riley had been given.

"Mack. Let the dear girl loose." Mrs. Halverson pushed herself to her feet. "I'm quite all right. And for the record, I'm not going to take the pill." She held the packet up. "But we can't just flush it down the toilet. If it's that potent, it could harm someone else."

"What are you talking about?" Mack asked, still

holding Riley around her middle. "Is this woman really a threat to you, or not?"

Charlie smiled. "She's not. She just proved she doesn't have it in her to kill."

Riley sobbed. "No, I don't. I've failed Toby. Oh, sweet heaven, I've failed him."

She went limp against Mack, her heart breaking into a million pieces. She'd failed her little brother. What horrible things would happen to him now?

MACK HELD THE woman in the black dress against his chest as she sobbed into his jacket. "Could someone please tell me what's going on?"

"Let me lock the door first." Charlie hurried to the door and twisted the lock, blocking anyone else from accidentally barging in on them.

When she turned to face Mack, she lifted her chin. "We have a situation."

"Do I need to call the others in?" he asked.

Charlie held up a hand. "Not yet. I have a plan on how we can remedy the trouble, but I need your complete cooperation."

"Mine?" Mack shook his head. "I have no idea what you're talking about."

"You will, soon enough." She nodded toward Riley. "Did you know that Miss Lansing was a Russian sleeper spy?"

Mack stared down at the dark head of the woman crying her eyes out into his expensive tuxedo jacket. "Seriously, what's going on? Why is she crying?"

"She's crying because she failed to assassinate me," Charlie said.

Mack shook his head. "Come again?" Had the woman had too much of the champagne flowing freely throughout the ballroom?

"You heard me." Charlie tipped her head toward the other woman. "Ask Riley."

Touching a thumb beneath Riley's chin, he tipped her wet face upward. The tears on her cheeks made his stomach clench. He wanted to hold her close and chase away whatever was troubling her. "What's Charlie talking about?"

Riley sniffed twice, and then her face crumpled. "She's right. I'm supposed to assassinate her. I'm a Russian sleeper spy, sent to kill Mrs. Charlotte Halverson."

"And if she doesn't, she'll never see her little brother again," Charlie concluded. "I can see no other way to solve this problem but to take the pill she brought to do the deed with and die. Do you?" She tilted her head and stared at Mack.

Mack's jaw dropped. "Are you out of your mind?" He grabbed for the little packet.

Charlie held it out of his grasp. "No, no. Hear me out. In order for Miss Lansing to have time to find her brother and get him out of the clutches of his kidnappers, I have to die."

"Charlie," Mack said in a slow, even tone, though his heart was hammering and his muscles bunched, ready to make another grab for the tiny plastic bag the woman held in her hand. "You didn't hire me to stand by and watch you die. If Miss Lansing is threatening to kill you, I can take care of her. Now hand me the bag before someone gets hurt."

"Don't you understand? The only way to help Miss Lansing and her six-year-old little brother is to have me die. If not permanently, then for a short amount of time. Enough to give you and Riley a head start figuring out who has her brother and getting him back."

Refusing to release Riley, Mack faced the woman footing the bill for Declan's Defenders. Her heart was in the right place for most things, but defending a woman out to kill her was just plain crazy. "I can't let this woman go. If what you're saying is true, she came here to kill you." He frowned down at Riley. "How could you? This woman is responsible for saving your life."

Riley nodded. "Don't you think I know that?"

"Then why would you want to hurt her?" he asked.

Her shoulders sagged. "I had no other choice."

Mack shook his head. "There are always more choices."

"Not when it comes to her little brother," Charlie said.

"Since when do you have a little brother?" Mack's eyes narrowed. "You never mentioned a little brother."

Riley lifted her chin. "You don't know me well enough to ask."

"Does your roommate Grace know you have a little brother?" Mack asked.

Riley shook her head. "I don't advertise that part of my life. I thought I had him hidden away. I didn't think they would find out about him." She threw her hand in the air. "Hell, I thought they'd forgotten I even existed." She stared down at the arm clamped around her middle. "You can release me. I can't kill Mrs. Halverson. I just can't."

"Charlie," the older woman corrected. "Call me Charlie."

Riley gave her a weak smile. "See? How could I kill someone who is as kind and generous as Charlie?" She held out her hand. "Please, let me have the pill. I can't let it get into the wrong hands."

"Oh, but you've put it in exactly the right hands. I'm going to die tonight. And you're going to save your little brother," Charlie said.

"You are out of your mind." Mack released Riley and lunged for Charlie.

She backed toward the door, a frown pulling her brows together. "Listen, you two. We don't have much time."

Riley glanced at the watch on her wrist. "Time. Damn. I forgot. They gave me C-4 to set off as a diversion. I'm supposed to kill Mrs. Halverson and set off the explosive to create a diversion and allow me to escape. They're expecting the explosion."

"Good." Charlie smiled. "That will give us time to get my dead body out of the hotel and off to the morgue." Her smile faded. "As long as the explosion doesn't hurt anyone else."

"It shouldn't. I didn't use a lot of the explosive and I set it in a storeroom surrounded by other empty rooms.

No one was there, and it was empty. No one should go back there."

"Wait a minute." Mack held up his hand. "I can't possibly be hearing this correctly. You can't set off explosives in a crowded hotel. It will start a stampede. Even if the explosion doesn't bring the walls down, the guests will rush for the doors and crush the people in front of them." Mack shook his head. "No. No. No. This is insane. Besides, I can't let you take that pill. If it's poison, what antidote is there? We don't even know what it is."

"I'm not going to take the pill, silly. I'm only going to pretend I did. You'll call for an ambulance. They'll wheel me out. Riley will escape and you'll go with her to help her find Toby, her little brother." Charlie drew in a deep breath and looked from Riley to Mack and back. "You see? All I have to do is lie dying in a hospital long enough for you two to find Toby and get him back."

Riley's eyes narrowed. "The instructions said the poison was fast-acting."

"So I didn't take all of it."

"They'll wait to give me Toby until they know for certain you're dead," Riley said.

"Money can buy just about anything," Charlie pointed out. "Even a fake death certificate."

"But they'll come looking for the body."

"So we'll give them one in the morgue."

"You seem to be forgetting something," Mack said.

"Am I?" Charlie frowned. "What am I forgetting?"

"You're not dead. You don't belong in a morgue until you are."

"Then you'll just have to find the boy while I'm lying on my deathbed in the hospital." Charlie crossed her arms over her chest.

"I don't like it," Mack said. "Why don't we go to the authorities and get them to find the boy?"

"The people who have him are Russian," Riley said. "They're not going to let the authorities find them or my brother. They'll move him out of the country. If they do, I'll never find him. As it is, I don't know where to begin looking. I don't know who my handler is." Riley's shoulders sagged. "Some Russian spy I am. I can't even take care of my own brother."

"Don't worry," Charlie said. "Follow my plan. Poison me, set off your explosion, let me play the dying matriarch and see what happens from there. What could it hurt? You get a few days' grace, and I get a rest in my husband's wing of the hospital. I can't see where this could possibly go wrong." She waved toward Riley. "Go ahead. Set off your explosion. You'll see."

Mack wasn't quite as sure as Charlie. And he'd rather have brought his men in to discuss what was going to happen, but Charlie had it in her head that her plan would work long enough for him and Riley to save her brother. She wouldn't be deterred.

"Where's the detonator?" Charlie asked.

Riley pointed to the ornamental hair clip lying on the counter near the sink. "But—"

"The longer you wait, the more suspicious your handler will become," Charlie pointed out. "Just do it and we'll take it from there."

"I don't know." Riley worried her handler would see through the plan.

"Have you worked with C-4 before now?" Mack asked.

Riley nodded. "But it's been years. Back when I lived with my parents. Before I went to college."

Mack gaped. "As a teen?"

Riley frowned. "I told you. I was trained to be a Russian sleeper spy. My parents prepared me for just about anything."

"I thought you were just an engineer…" He clapped a hand to his forehead. "Selling secret blueprints to your comrades?" He shook his head. "You were the one selling the top secret data to the Russians from Quest Aerospace?"

"No, of course not. I thought I was in the clear. That when my parents died, their handlers would forget about me." She snorted. "I was just another loyal American, trying to do good. Well, they didn't forget about me. They drew my number and tasked me to kill Mrs. Halverson."

"Charlie," the widow corrected.

"Charlie," Riley echoed. "They're using my brother as an insurance policy. They didn't give me a choice."

"Are you sure about the amount of plastics you used?" Mack asked.

"Pretty." She drew in a deep breath. "It should make a loud noise and shake the walls but not cause too much damage or a fire."

"For the record…" He caught Charlie's glance. "I don't like any of this."

"So noted." Charlie gave him a mock salute. "But you're going to go along with it?"

Mack nodded and touched his hand to his headset. "Guys, be ready to lead the guests in an orderly exodus from the hotel," he said.

"Did you say what I think you said?" Gus questioned.

"What are you talking about?" Mustang asked.

"Can't say," Mack said. "Just be ready." Then he nodded to Charlie. "Assume the position."

Charlie grinned and sank to the floor in her expensive gown.

"You can't smile if you're dying," Mack warned her.

The smile disappeared from her face and she closed her eyes. "Ready."

"I'm calling the ambulance," Mack said, and dialed 911. He turned to Riley, not sure he should trust her, but knowing it was what Charlie wanted and possibly the only way to get the woman out of the hotel safely if others were gunning for her. "As soon as they say the fire department is on its way, let 'er rip."

Mack reported a woman down to the dispatcher. Once he was assured the ambulance was on its way, he nodded toward Riley.

She lifted the ornamental hair clip and activated the switch on the back.

A thundering *bang* rippled through the heavy doors of the restroom.

Muffled screams sounded.

"The guests are moving toward the doors on the west side," Gus reported.

"And on the north and east," Mustang confirmed. "So far, they're moving swiftly without panic. The security staff are facilitating their efforts. Where are you and Charlie?"

"In the ladies' restroom on the southern end of the ballroom," Mack said. "If the exodus is moving well, Mustang, I need you here to take over for me. When the ambulance arrives, Gus, lead them into the restroom to collect Charlie."

"What happened? Is she all right?" Mustang asked.

"No." Mack stared across the room to where Charlie lay on the floor with her eyes open. "She's been poisoned. I have to leave, but I need you and Gus to stick with her like glue and keep her safe. Someone wants her dead. If she lives through the poison, they might not let her live to leave the hospital."

Chapter Three

"Riley, you need to leave the restroom before anyone arrives," Charlie said.

Mack's eyes narrowed. "I don't know that I trust her to leave without me. And I can't leave until Mustang gets here to protect you."

"I'll wait for you inside the doorway near the end of this hallway," Riley said.

"How do I know you won't take off?" Mack said.

"I have to find my brother, and I need help doing it. But I don't want you to leave Charlie alone, either. She's done so much for me already. I couldn't live with myself if someone finished what I was supposed to start."

Mack's lips thinned. "I don't trust you. But more than that, I won't leave Charlie." He jerked his head to the side. "Go. I'll catch up with you."

He didn't have to say it, but he meant he'd catch up to her whether she waited for him at the end of the hallway or not. His tone said he'd hunt her down if he had to.

Riley shivered at the killer glare Mack gave her.

Though she knew how to stop a two-hundred-fifty-pound man dead in his tracks and could cripple her foe in one easy sweep of her leg, her knees turned to jelly at just one look from the tall, dark-haired marine. He frightened her more than her mysterious Russian handler. And it wasn't so much Mack's demeanor and strength. It was the way he'd made her feel when he wrapped his arm around her waist. He made her feel feminine and vulnerable. She couldn't afford to feel vulnerable. Not when the stakes were so high.

If she were the only one at risk, she wouldn't be as concerned. But Toby depended on her to find and rescue him. And Charlie…the woman who'd helped her so selflessly on more than one occasion. She owed the woman more than her life. She owed her loyalty and respect. Whoever wanted her dead wouldn't stop until the wealthy widow was six feet in the ground.

Why?

Mack moved to the door and peered out. "The hallway is empty. If you go now, you won't be seen."

Riley didn't have time to contemplate all the questions roiling around in her head. She had to get out of the restroom before Mack's buddies descended on him to discover why he'd given them such cryptic instructions in anticipation of an explosion. They had to be filled with questions he wouldn't have time to answer.

Riley eased up to the door and stood beside the big marine.

He smelled of aftershave and seemed larger than life in his black tuxedo with the crisp white shirt peeking out from between the jacket's lapels. Beneath the fancy clothes, the man was handsome in a rugged way that made her heart flutter.

He jerked open the door. "Go."

Riley startled and rushed through. The hem of her dress caught on the door and ripped the side seam farther up her leg. She grabbed the fabric and gave it a quick tug, freeing it from the corner of the door. Then she lifted the folds in her hands and ran as fast as she could in three-inch heels. Racing down the hallway, she ducked into the room she'd found during her reconnaissance a day earlier.

The room had two doors. One leading out into the hallway, the other leading toward the kitchen and the service elevators. If she'd done what she was supposed to do and actually killed Charlotte Halverson, she'd be sprinting to get out of the hotel, out of DC and back to her Virginia apartment, where she'd pretend she'd never left.

Her roommate had indicated she'd be with Declan O'Neill, Mack's team leader, for a mini vacation to the Outer Banks of North Carolina. Lucky her, she'd fallen in love with the man who'd helped her find and protect Riley when her brief stint assisting the FBI nearly gotten her killed. She still couldn't believe that her Russian handler had called her to action on an assassination, not on the data she'd developed dealing with a revolutionary aircraft design. She'd have thought they'd demand the design in exchange for her brother.

Perhaps the assassination was their way of compromising her so much she'd be forced to hand over the blueprints for the special project she'd been working on at Quest Aerospace Alliance. She wouldn't have a choice if they threatened to expose her to the authorities.

Was that it? Was her handler someone she knew at Quest? Was that where her search should begin?

She waited for two, maybe three, minutes for Mack to appear. The time stretched, feeling like half an hour instead of the few short minutes. If she didn't leave soon, and her handler was watching for her exit, he might begin to wonder about her success.

Riley glanced at the pretty watch on her wrist and realized it had only been two minutes since she'd left the ladies' room. She'd give Mack one more minute before she had to leave. Soon, the entire building would be locked down, with police and firefighters swarming over the structure. They wouldn't have the opportunity to leave at that point.

She eased the door open and nearly screamed at the face appearing in front of her.

"Come on, we have to get out of here," Mack said. "The police are coming through the lobby now." He took her hand and tried to lead her back the way she'd come.

"No. This way." She dug her heels into the carpet and dragged him into the little room and across to the door on the other side.

"Do you know where you're going?" he asked.

"Yes. Through the kitchen and out to the loading docks."

Mack followed, still holding her hand as he let her take the lead. "I didn't think you'd wait."

"I almost didn't," she whispered. "Now, shh." She raised her free hand to press a finger to her lips. "There's a camera located at the rear entrance. I came in this way as a blonde. I'd rather not have the camera catch us leaving."

"Can I reach it?" Mack asked.

Riley gave him a measured glance. "Maybe."

He pulled a handkerchief from his inside pocket. "With this?"

She tilted her head and shook it. "There's a breeze. It'll blow away if you try to throw it over the camera lens."

Mack glanced around the loading dock and took off. "I'll be right back." He made a beeline for a shop sink in the corner, wet the handkerchief and returned. "Let's do this. We don't have much time."

Riley stepped aside. "Go."

Mack peered up at the camera located on the wall over the back door to the loading dock. It pointed at the door and the loading bays where trucks backed in to discharge the supplies needed to keep a hotel as big as the Marriott in business.

With a flick of his wrist, Mack slung the wet hanky up over the camera. It caught, covering the lens.

Riley released the breath she hadn't realized she'd been holding. Without another word, she led the way from the hotel out onto the pavement and pushed through the bushes into the back lot of an office building.

"Where to from here?" Mack asked.

"I parked my car two blocks over."

"You really thought this through, didn't you?" His tone held an edge to it.

"I had to. My brother's life depends on it." She didn't wait for him to follow but took off, walking fast. Part of her wanted to leave him behind. His tone held judgment. She deserved his scorn but didn't want to deal with it. "We don't have much time. My handler will likely discover Mrs. Halverson isn't dead and demand I finish the job or Toby will pay the price. The sooner we find my brother, the sooner we can get him out of danger."

"And once you have your brother, your handler will allow you to walk free?"

Riley snorted. "No way. I'll have to take Toby and go into hiding somewhere far from here."

"Seems to me we need to put a stop to your handler as well as find your brother."

"Agreed, but most importantly, I need to find my brother." She stepped through another bush, her dress catching on the branches.

Mack helped her untangle the fabric and pushed through behind her. They came to the back of a building that appeared to be abandoned. A small charcoal-gray four-door sedan was tucked between a stack of pallets and a trash bin.

Riley reached beneath the second pallet in the stack, extracted a key fob and hurried toward the vehicle.

When she pulled the handle on the sedan, the doors unlocked.

Mack climbed into the passenger seat as Riley started the engine. He was putting his safety belt on when she pulled out from behind the building and raced out onto the street.

"Get a speeding ticket and you draw attention to yourself," Mack warned.

Riley eased up on the accelerator. "I don't know where to start. I have no idea who my handler is and how I can find him," she admitted.

"Start from when you received the message with the instructions."

She drove toward her apartment, not knowing where else to go. At least there she could change into more appropriate clothing for finding another Russian spy.

Hysterical laughter bubbled up her throat and threatened to escape. What did one wear when searching for a spy?

Mack whipped his head around. "You just ran a red light. Do you want me to drive?"

Riley pulled to the side of the street, got out and rounded the car to Mack's side.

He stepped out and held the door for her.

As she sank into the passenger seat, silent tears spilled down her cheeks.

Mack didn't say a word, just got in and drove. He knew where she lived from when Grace had invited the team to the apartment to celebrate their little victory.

Victory, hell. Perhaps Riley's little venture with the FBI had brought her back to the attention of her parents' handler. If she hadn't gotten so entrenched in her American life and started thinking she'd been forgotten, she might not be in her current situation, and Toby would be safe in the country cabin with his nanny.

Mack pulled into the parking lot of Riley and Grace's apartment building and turned off the engine. For a long moment, he sat beside her, letting her gather herself.

A hand reached out and touched her arm. "We should go inside."

Riley nodded. "I'm not usually so weepy," she said, and sniffed. "Only when it comes to my family. I love my brother. He's such a good little boy." She looked across the console at Mack. "He doesn't know who we are or what the Russians will want from me. He's just a little boy who plays with toys."

Mack nodded and held her gaze for another moment. Then he reached out and brushed his thumb across her cheek, wiping away the tears. "We'll find him."

"How?" she asked, her voice catching on a sob.

"There has to be a trail. We'll follow it. But we can't do it dressed like this. Go. Change and then we'll hit my apartment long enough for me to get out of this monkey suit. Then we'll get to work sifting through the clues." He unfolded his long frame from the driver's seat and rounded the hood to open the door for her.

Riley had the door open. When she stepped out, her heel caught on her dress, and she pitched forward into Mack's chest.

His arms came up around her and held her steady until she could work her heel free of the hem. She straightened, still in Mack's embrace, and looked up into his incredibly blue eyes. A streetlight shone down, making his dark hair glow a silvery blue. "Thanks."

"My pleasure," he replied. Still, he didn't release her. "How does one become a sleeper spy for the Russians?"

She gave a short, sharp burst of laughter. "You're born into it, and your parents raise you with their beliefs."

"But you attended American schools and speak perfect American English."

"I'm American, through and through. I didn't sign on to be a Russian spy. I thought when my parents died, I was off the hook. Their handler wouldn't remember the little girl they gave birth to shortly after their arrival in the US." Riley rested her hand on his chest and stared at the crisp white shirt beneath her fingertips. "I never wanted to be a Russian spy."

"But you learned about C-4 explosives," Mack prompted.

Riley sighed. "And weaponry, guns, hand-to-hand combat and how to pick locks. Every skill a spy would need to survive."

His lips twitched. "You're scaring me."

"My father was with the KGB before he brought my mother to the States. He knew all the tricks."

"But your little brother is only six years old? That's a big age gap between you and him."

"He was a late surprise to my parents in their forties. I'd just begun working for Quest when my mother told me she was pregnant."

"Where are your parents now?"

"They died in an automobile accident when Toby was only one year old."

"Which left you to raise him," Mack concluded.

"Only, I didn't want the Russians to know about him. Any more than they did. I moved him to a cabin in the country, and hired a nanny to live with him full time. I visited him as often as I could. I'd just started working on the Special Projects team at Quest. If I left, I was afraid anyone watching me would follow me to Toby." She snorted. "Apparently I wasn't careful enough. They found him anyway."

Riley led the way to her town house apartment. The damaged doorframe and broken window had been replaced from when the apartment was invaded by an intruder searching for her research memory card two weeks prior. She held the door for Mack, but he stopped inside the threshold, with the door open.

"Are you going to stand there, or come in?" she asked.

He leaned close and whispered in her ear, "If someone is watching you, you need to convince them I'm not a threat."

She frowned up at him. "And how do you intend to do that?" she asked, matching his low tones.

He nuzzled her neck and breathed into her ear, "They need to think I'm supposed to be with you."

She tipped her head back and closed her eyes, all the while keeping her voice down. If she was being watched, they might also be employing some kind of listening device. "We don't want them to think you're a bodyguard or coconspirator, do we?" She shook her head. "They know I don't have any other siblings, and I've never known any cousins."

"What about a boyfriend?" Mack suggested, running his hand up beneath her hair. "Are you known to have a boyfriend or lover?"

Butterflies erupted in Riley's belly at the touch of his hand on the back of her neck. "No. I haven't had time to cultivate a romance. I've been too busy living two lives to add another to the mix."

He leaned back and smiled down into her eyes. "Then let's set the stage for anyone watching."

"What do you mean?" She stiffened, her insides trembling, her body warming with excitement.

"Meet your new boyfriend."

MACK TOOK HER hand in his and gave it a gentle tug. If, like he suspected, her handler had eyes and ears posted wherever Riley lived or worked, they had to convince the watchers they were an item. Otherwise, why would he be at her apartment that late at night?

She came to him, rested her hands on his jacket and raised her face to his. "Like this?"

"Uh-huh," he whispered. "Only closer." He slipped an arm around her waist and pulled her ever nearer until he couldn't tell where her body ended and his began. Her breasts pressed against the lapels of his jacket, and her hands fluttered against his chest. The back of her gown dipped low, and his hands met warm, bare skin.

With one hand on her back, steadying her, he used the other to tip her chin. Then he lowered his mouth to just above hers. "We need to make it convincing."

"Okay," Riley said, her voice barely a breath. Then

her tongue swept across her lips, making them shine in the light over the door.

What had started as a show for anyone watching had taken on a life of its own. Mack couldn't look away from her shining lips any more than he could drop his hold. He was destined to kiss this woman who could be a national spy. Hell, she'd come to the charity event to kill the woman he worked for. Why would he be drawn to an assassin?

But he was, and he had to kiss her.

Cupping her cheek, he bent to brush his lips lightly across hers. They were soft. Like silk.

She gasped, and her mouth opened, giving him all the invitation he needed.

He swept his tongue past her teeth to claim hers in a long, sensual caress that made his insides ignite and his groin tighten.

Her fingers curled into his shirt, bringing him closer, deepening the kiss. Her hips pressed against his, his erection nudging against the soft folds of the dress covering her belly.

Mack groaned and lowered his other arm, crushing her to him. When he was forced to breathe again, he reluctantly loosened his hold enough to allow air in their lungs.

He inhaled deeply and pressed his forehead to hers. "That should do the trick," he said, wondering at the tremor in his voice.

She closed her eyes and pressed her lips together. Then she straightened and stepped back.

Mack dropped his arms from around her waist,

planted one in the center of her back and entered the apartment, kicking the door closed behind them. He would never admit to Riley that the kiss had shaken him as much as it had. He wasn't with her to start an affair. He'd been tasked by his employer to help Riley find her brother. The sooner they did, the sooner he'd be on to his next assignment.

Chapter Four

Mack waited in the living room of Riley's apartment while she changed out of the dress she'd worn to the gala.

She left the door to her bedroom cracked open a little—to continue their conversation or to keep an eye on him, Mack wasn't sure.

He searched the apartment for any signs of listening devices or cameras. Just when he thought he was chasing shadows, he found something in one of the lamps sitting on an end table. He was reaching for it when Riley came out of the bedroom pulling a light sweater down her torso. "You know, I think I know where we should start."

Mack spun toward her, grabbed her arms and pulled her into his embrace. "I know exactly where we should start." Then he sealed her mouth with his lips.

"What—" Riley tried to say as his lips moved over hers.

She stood stiff in his arms until he softened the kiss and swept his hands down her back.

After a long, incredibly delicious moment, he lifted

his head, pressed a finger to her lips and led her over to the lamp. He pointed to the small electronics device positioned on one of the wires holding the shade in place. Then he pointed to his ear. "I think we should start with a kiss," he said softly, but loudly enough for whoever might be listening in on their conversation.

Riley's eyes widened and then narrowed. She tilted her head toward the bedroom. "Maybe we should take this into the bedroom," she said in a sultry tone.

Riley took Mack's hand and led him into the bedroom, where they performed a thorough search of every nook and cranny.

Another electronic device turned up in the lamp on her nightstand and one more on the light fixture in the bathroom.

Her lips thinning with each step, Riley marched to the closet, grabbed a suitcase and stuffed it with clothing.

Mack couldn't blame her. Her space had been broken into before, but this was even worse. Someone had been spying on her with every word spoken. He checked behind the paintings on the walls and on the bookshelves just in case he found a video camera. He even stood on a chair and looked in the overhead light fixtures. Thankfully, there weren't any camcorders lurking. But he might have missed one.

When Riley was dressed in jeans and tennis shoes and had a bag packed with clothes and toiletries, she led the way to the door.

Mack opened it for her and they exited the town house.

"You want to drive?" she asked.

Since he still had the keys, he nodded. As soon as they were out of the parking lot, he turned toward his apartment. "I just want to change into something a little less confining than this." He waved a hand toward his tuxedo. "I have to admit, this is my first time in a tux."

"Really?" She tilted her head and studied him. "You wear it well."

"Thanks. But don't get used to it. I'm a jeans and T-shirt kind of guy."

"My preference," she said.

"In guys, or clothes?" he asked.

Riley smiled. "Both."

They accomplished the trip to his apartment in relative silence. After discovering three listening devices in her apartment, Mack didn't trust her car, either. When he arrived in his parking lot, he held the door for Riley and helped her out of her sedan, handing her the keys.

"You aren't driving from here?" she asked.

"Not in yours." He cupped her elbow and led her toward his apartment. Once they were out of listening range of her vehicle, he relaxed a little. "I think we'll take my vehicle from here."

"You think they had bugs in my car as well?" She grimaced. "Did we say anything that would lead them to think we weren't on the up-and-up?"

"I don't remember. But we'd do well to keep our conversations down to a whisper when we discuss the plan."

"We have a plan?" She looked up at him, her eyebrow cocked.

"We will," he said. "As soon as I get out of this suit."

"Right."

She followed him into his apartment, her gaze sweeping across the furniture and bare walls. "Are you one of those minimalists?"

He smiled. "No. I just moved in. Since I'm new to the area, I'm not even sure this is where I want to stay."

"It's an okay neighborhood, from what I could see in the dark."

"I prefer the countryside to city life. But my work with Charlie brings me to the city."

"How long have you worked for Charlie?"

He twisted his lips into a wry smile. "Two whole weeks."

"And before that? Were you one of Declan's teammates in the military?"

He nodded.

"What's the deal with you guys? Grace said you were basically kicked out."

Mack shut the door and twisted the dead bolt. "She's right. Dishonorable discharges."

"Seriously? Don't you have to be like the worst of the worst to get one of those?"

He shrugged. "I guess we are."

"What did you do to warrant dishonorable discharge?"

"We didn't follow through on our orders. The man we were supposed to kill got away and killed some important people because of it."

"Still…seems pretty drastic to get kicked out."

"We made a decision we could live with." If he had to make the same decision again, he'd do so.

"Did you think it would get you kicked out?"

Again, he shrugged. "No. But politics were involved."

"So you took the fall for someone higher up?"

"Maybe. Or maybe refusing a direct order was enough." Mack agreed, but what was done was done. Someone needed scapegoats. Their team took the fall. They were out of the Marine Corps, and life went on. "If we hadn't been kicked out, I wouldn't be here with you now. We can leave it at that."

"Okay." She walked to the window overlooking a park.

Mack left her in the living room and went to his bedroom to change. His gaze took in the sparse furnishings from Riley's perspective. He hadn't made the apartment his home. In fact, since joining the military, he hadn't made any living arrangements like home. He didn't stay in one place very long. The Marine Corps had a way of moving you often. Why put down roots and hang pictures on the wall when you'd just have to pull the nails out and move to another station or be deployed for half a year or more?

"You know, it might be a little late to ask, but are you married or anything?" Riley asked from the other side of the wall.

"I wouldn't have kissed you like I did if I was," Mack said. He pulled the jacket off and laid it across the end of the bed. Then the shoulder holster he'd worn beneath with the P226 handgun. "Call me old-fashioned, but if I were married, I wouldn't kiss another woman."

"Even if it was part of an undercover operation?" Riley asked.

"Even then." Maybe he wasn't cut out for undercover operations. If he ever married, he'd have to stick to bodyguard duties and leave the undercover shtick to the other members of the team.

"I'm impressed," Riley said. "My father would have insisted I do whatever it took to keep my cover. Even if it meant sleeping with the enemy."

"And have you?"

"This was my first assignment. And I didn't want it in the first place. If not for Toby, I wouldn't be in this situation. I'd have refused."

"Do the Russians allow you to refuse?"

She didn't answer for a moment. And then her voice came back softly. "I don't know. According to my father, we had no other choice. I'm beginning to believe him. I just wonder what they held over him. He seemed happy in his American life. Like he'd fully embraced the life, liberty and justice of the American dream. He had a good-paying job with a local factory, using his skills as an engineer to make parts for tractors and combines. If you'd met him, you'd never have known he was KGB. He had no accent that gave him away."

Mack shucked his white dress shirt, changed out of the tuxedo trousers into a pair of dark jeans, and stepped into the bedroom doorframe. "What about your mother?"

Riley looked up, her eyes widening. She swallowed

hard and swept her tongue across her lips before replying, "Also Russian, but raised by an American au pair." As if tearing her gaze away from his bare chest, she turned back to the window. "My mother must have taught my father how to speak American English."

"And yet she let him train you to be a sleeper spy?" Mack slipped a black T-shirt over his head and tugged it over his shoulders and torso.

"Maybe she thought since we were in the States, they wouldn't be called on to complete any missions. That was my hope, too. Especially after my folks died. I thought they'd forget I existed and leave me alone." She looked back over her shoulder with a weak smile. "I guess I was wrong." Her eyes were glassy with unshed tears. "And Toby is paying the price for my mistake."

Mack padded across the carpet, wrapped her in his arms. If she didn't want him to hold her, she could have taken him down like the professionally trained spy she was. Instead, she leaned her face against his chest and let the tears slip down her cheeks.

"My father would be so very disappointed in me right now," she said, and sniffed.

Mack brushed his lips across the top of her head, reveling in how soft and silky her black hair was. And it smelled of wildflowers. He inhaled deeply. "We'll find him," he promised. He wasn't sure how they'd do that, but he'd do his best to make good on that vow. He wanted to help this woman. She was a stranger to him, but he felt a connection that had nothing to do with the job.

RILEY'S HEAD SPUN in a thousand directions as she thought hard about where to start looking for Toby. The enormity of the effort threatened to overwhelm her. The hard muscles beneath Riley's palms strangely reassured her, like a rock in a fast-moving stream. He grounded her. This man had promised to find her little brother. They were smart people. Together they would figure it out.

For a long moment, she let herself lean on him, allowed her tears to flow while absorbing his strength.

He tilted her head up and stared down into her eyes. "We have to think through your life. There has to be someone in it who has been monitoring your every move. Possibly someone close to you."

She drew in a deep breath and nodded. "I thought it was my supervisor at Quest. But he's dead, killed by the people who wanted the data from my special project."

"Does anyone else at Quest hang around you a lot? Do you have any friends who seem really interested in you and your life?"

Riley didn't move from Mack's arms. Instead, she stared at her hands on his black T-shirt and thought through all the people she came into contact with on a daily basis. None stuck out more than the others.

"What about your roommate?"

"Grace?" Riley frowned. "No way. I met her my first year at Georgetown University."

Mack's brows rose. "And you were together for the entire four years?"

Riley's frown deepened. "Yes, but she's with Declan

now. And she got Mrs. Halverson involved in finding me. She's too nice. She couldn't be a Russian spy." She shook her head. "No, it wasn't Grace. My gut tells me no."

"And you trust your gut." Mack nodded. "My gut has saved me on more than one occasion."

"I need to talk with Margaret Weems, Toby's nanny. She might have seen something. And we have a security system at the house. I want to review the footage. I usually have access from my cell phone, but the connection has been interrupted. I have to find out why."

"You're not due back at work until Monday."

"If Mrs. H. hasn't died by then, it might be too late for Toby."

"Then we have to hurry through the leads we have." Mack set her at arm's length. "Are you okay?"

She snorted softly. "Do I have a choice? I have to be okay in order to find Toby. I'm all he has."

"Now he has me, too." With his thumb, he brushed away a tear. "Let's do this. Where is this cabin? Sounds like we need to make a trip there."

Riley checked her watch. "It's two hours outside the city in the Virginia countryside. With the amount of construction on the roads between here and there, by the time we get there, it'll be morning. Margaret will be beside herself. I haven't contacted her since the abduction."

"Then we start there. Just you showing up will help her."

"I doubt it. She blames herself for his disappearance. She thinks she should have heard the intruder."

"Let's get out there. We can question her."

"It's a small town. If a stranger came through, someone might have seen him."

"And someone might have security cameras on their shops. We could ask to see them."

Riley nodded. "It's like sifting through a haystack looking for one specific strand of straw."

"All it takes is that one," Mack said. "We just have to find it."

Mack disappeared into his bedroom and reappeared a few minutes later wearing boots and a black leather jacket. The bulge beneath it indicated he was wearing more than a shirt under the leather.

Once again, his presence gave Riley hope.

He held out his hand.

Riley placed hers in his. "Why are you doing this?"

"For one, it's my job."

"Is that the only reason?"

He shook his head. "Let's just say I had a little brother once. I would have done anything to save him."

Riley walked with Mack to a big black pickup. He helped her up into the passenger seat and then rounded the hood to the driver's side.

She gave him the address to the cabin. He punched it into his GPS and soon they were on a highway leading out of Alexandria into the countryside. As she settled back in her seat, she thought about what he'd said about his little brother. "You said *had*. You had a little brother." She glanced across the console at the man behind the wheel. "What happened to your little brother?"

His lips thinned into a straight line. "He didn't make it past six years old."

Riley drew in a sharp breath, her chest squeezing tightly. "What happened to him?"

For a long moment, Mack didn't answer. His face grew even darker in the light from the dash. "We were waiting at our rural bus stop when he stepped out in front of a logging truck."

"Oh my God." Riley cover her mouth with her hand. Her stomach roiled at the image conjured by his words. "And you saw it happen?"

"I was standing next to him one minute," Mack said. "The next minute he was gone."

"And you thought it was your fault," Riley said. She could see the truth in the way his hands gripped the steering wheel so tightly his knuckles turned white. He blamed himself for his brother's death.

"I should have held his hand. But I was older and didn't think it was cool."

"You couldn't know he'd dart out into the street."

"It doesn't matter now," Mack said. "Nothing I can do now will bring Aiden back. But I will find Toby for you. We will get him back. Alive."

Riley sat back, her heart hurting for Mack's little brother and the young man Mack had been when he lost him. The miles passed.

Riley must have fallen asleep. The smooth road turned bumpy, shaking her awake. She opened her eyes to the gray light of dawn pushing the darkness out of the sky. In front of her was the little cabin she'd rented when she moved Toby out to the country with his nanny, Margaret. The idea was to keep him hidden from her potential handlers. Now she wondered if she'd have been better off keeping him in the city, close to her. At least then she would have had a chance to fight off his kidnapper.

As they pulled up to the house, Toby's nanny, an older woman with graying hair, appeared in the door. She stared out at them, her eyes narrowed.

Riley climbed down from the truck. "Oh, Margaret."

The woman's eyes widened, and she cried out. "Riley!" She ran out on the porch and down the steps.

Riley met her halfway to the house and was wrapped in the older woman's huge hug.

"Oh, Riley," she sobbed. "I'm so sorry. I don't know how it happened. I've been beside myself since Toby disappeared. Please tell me you know what's going on. Tell me he's all right." She backed away far enough to look Riley in the face. Her lips trembled, and tears spilled from her eyes. "You haven't heard from him, have you? Oh, sweet heaven. My little guy is gone."

"Margaret." Riley cupped the nanny's cheek. "We'll find him. But we came to see if there's any images on the security system and to ask questions. We hope to find some clues."

"Why don't you contact the police? I've lifted the phone a hundred times and put it down." She wrung her hands. "We should call them. They'll know what to do."

Riley bracketed the woman's face between her hands. "Margaret, we can't call the police. The kidnapper will hurt Toby if we do."

"What does he want?" she said, her tone like a wail. "It's not like you're rich."

"He wants me to do something I don't want to do."

"Do it," Margaret urged. "Get Toby back."

"I can't talk about it. You have to trust me. I'm doing everything in my power to find Toby."

Margaret pulled a tissue out of her pocket and pressed it to her nose. "I just don't understand how this could happen."

"I'm going to check the cameras and the recordings. While I do that, talk to my friend Mack. He's here to help. Answer his questions, if you can. Anything you might have seen could help us find Toby. No matter how insignificant it might seem."

"Okay." Margaret looked from Riley to Mack. "Ask away. I hope I know something that will help."

Riley nodded to Mack. "I'll be inside looking through the footage."

"We'll join you," Mack said. "We can look and ask questions at the same time."

Mack followed the women into the cabin. He paused for a moment on the threshold and stared out at the woods surrounding the little house. Then he turned and joined the women around a computer monitor at a small desk in the corner of the main bedroom.

Riley wiggled the mouse and waited for the screen to come alive. When it didn't, she turned the screen on, then off. Nothing.

Then she turned the computer off, then on. Nothing happened; the motor didn't kick on and the fans that usually hummed inside were silent. The computer was dead.

"How long has the computer been dead?" Riley asked.

"I was online the morning before Toby disappeared. I haven't touched it since. I searched the entire house and the yard. I even went into the woods along the paths we usually walk. I thought he might have wandered away."

"He didn't wander away, Margaret. He's definitely been taken. The man who took him put him on the phone to prove it."

Tears welled in the nanny's eyes. "Poor baby. He must be so scared."

Riley's heart contracted at the trauma her little brother was experiencing. She hardened herself to the inevitable. She couldn't take that away from him, but she could bring him back. "Tell me about the day before Toby disappeared. I need to know where you went, who you talked to, anyone different you might have run into in town."

"It was a regular day. Toby had school in the morning. I took him, dropped him off and went to the store to pick up a few groceries."

"Did you see anyone in town that you hadn't seen before?" Mack asked.

Margaret frowned, her eyes narrowing as she thought back. "I can't remember seeing anyone different. It's such a small town, you'd think I'd notice. If anyone would know, it would be Janice at the convenience store. She's where everyone goes for the local gossip, since the store is at the center of town and you have to pass it to get anywhere in or out of Havenwood. You should ask Janice."

"We will," Riley said. "And I'll take this computer with me in case I can find someone who can fix it."

Margaret touched Riley's arm. "Please, find Toby. I'm completely lost without that child. He's such a ray of sunshine. I can't imagine anyone wanting to hurt him."

"We will," Riley said. She prayed she was right. She'd hoped the trip to the cabin would yield some small clue. But so far, nothing, and their time was running out.

Chapter Five

Mack reached across the console and grasped Riley's hand as they left the cabin and drove into the little town of Havenwood. "We'll find him," he reassured her, though he wasn't feeling as confident as he had when he drove up to the cabin.

"How can we find him when we have nothing to go on?"

"We'll talk with this Janice woman. She has to have seen something."

"And if she hasn't?" Riley stared through the windshield, her hand squeezing his tightly.

"Then we ask someone else." He entered the town, passed a diner that had cars parked outside. His stomach growled, reminding him that they hadn't eaten breakfast. In fact, he hadn't had anything to eat since lunch the day before. He would bet Riley hadn't had anything since she'd gotten the message from the kidnapper. After they talked with Janice, they'd stop in at the diner and have a bite. Waitresses always seemed to have the scoop of what was going on in town.

Mack pulled up to the gas pump at the only convenience store in Havenwood. Riley went inside while he filled the truck's tank.

Once he was finished, he entered to find Riley in deep conversation with the woman behind the counter.

"Yes, we do get people passing through occasionally," the woman said.

Riley turned to smile at Mack. "Janice, this is Mack, my…boyfriend." She turned back to Janice. "Janice was just telling me how nice it is to live in such a small town. She knows everyone, and everyone knows her."

"I've seen Riley here just about every weekend, but she never said anything about you." Janice eyed Mack, her gaze sweeping him from head to toe. "I wouldn't forget a good-looking guy like you." She held out her hand, her cheeks growing pinker. "Nope, I wouldn't forget you."

Mack took her hand and gave her one of the smiles he reserved for pretty girls at the bar. "Nice to meet you, Janice." He gripped her hand with a firm handshake.

"Ooh, and his hands are so strong." Janice grinned at Riley. "You're one lucky girl to have him as your guy."

Riley touched Mack's arm. "I know." She faced Janice. "I bet from your location you see all the people who pass through Havenwood."

The store owner nodded. "I do. I can tell you every vehicle that goes through this town." She tapped a finger to her temple. "I have a photographic memory. And I like to play games with the license plates. It helps me to remember them. Like just three days ago, an out-of-towner came through with Maryland license plates that spelled WMD 495."

Mack tensed. "You remember that?"

She nodded. "What does WMD stand for to you?"

"Weapons of mass destruction," Mack answered.

Janice frowned. "I guess it could be that, too, but I thought *what Mama does*. And 495 is my niece's birthday. April 9, 2005. So, you see, the game helps me remember plates. You never know when you might need to identify them for the police. Knock on wood." She knocked on her skull.

Riley leaned on the counter, giving Janice all her attention. "I bet you can remember every type of car with the license plates that have passed through Havenwood in the past three days."

"Sure can." Janice crossed her arms over her chest. "Go ahead, try me."

"Three days ago, WMD 495 came through. What kind of vehicle was it?" Riley challenged.

"Silver Toyota Prius. I remember because I thought it was a silly car. My mother wouldn't have driven it. It wasn't big enough. She likes driving big boats of cars."

"Do you remember the driver in the vehicle?"

Janice frowned. "If he hadn't gotten out and come in, I couldn't have told you. The windows were heavily tinted." She closed her eyes. "And there was a bumper sticker on the back. I think it was for one of the car rental companies."

"Any others come through?" Mack asked. "Your memory amazes me."

"A bright red Mustang convertible with an older

couple in it." Janice tipped her head. "Virginia license plate KNT 552. I think of KNT as *knit* and 552 as five-feet-two-inch girl like me. See how easy it is to play?" She gave them a triumphant smile.

"Was that all that came through that day? What about the day before?"

She tapped a finger to her temple and stared into the corner of the store. "We had a delivery truck from Maryland stop on its way to the next town, and one of those smart cars that was so tiny it could have been a child's toy. I remember it because it had the same colors as my favorite hockey team. Green and white."

"So, the driver of the WMD vehicle got out of his car?"

"Actually, he did. He came into the store. He had wavy dark hair and heavy eyebrows." Janice clapped her hands. "I can prove it. I recently had a security system installed. Got a deal from Henry last month. Got the whole thing put in for under five hundred. Wanna see? It's the coolest."

Riley gave a casual shrug. "Sure."

Inside, Mack would bet, she was shaking with excitement. This could be a clue they'd been looking for.

Janice turned a monitor around so that they could look at the images as she worked the keyboard. "It's the easiest thing to do. All I have to do is slide the bar back to the date and time I want and voilà!" She pointed to the date and time on the bottom corner of the screen. "See? Three days ago, around four in the evening. There's the car, just like I said, with the license plate WMD 495." Janice pointed to one of the images. "And there he is entering the store." She enlarged the image of the man. "I remember thinking he could use a haircut."

"Do you mind if I take a picture of the screen? I'm thinking of installing a security system and I like this one," Riley said.

"Go ahead." Janice waved toward the monitor.

Riley held up her cell phone and snapped a picture of the man in the image and the license plate of the vehicle in the other image.

"Janice, you have a good memory," Mack said. "I'm impressed."

The store owner blushed and shrugged. "That was all I had before this fancy-schmancy security system. That and the height gauge on the side of the doors." She nodded toward what appeared to be a measuring tool on either side of the door, indicating the height of those who entered and left. "You can't be too careful these days."

"No kidding."

"By the way, how's Toby?" Janice asked. "He usually comes in with you."

Riley didn't miss a beat with her answer. "He's visiting a relative."

"He's such a good little boy when he comes into the store with Margaret. Such good manners. They were here the same day as that man I described." She moved the slide button to a few minutes later. Toby and Margaret entered the store. Toby ran to the candy aisle ahead of Margaret.

"He likes chocolate. Margaret gets him a little bite of something every time they come in."

Riley's smile slipped, and her jaw tightened as she watched Toby.

Mack studied the little store and noted that the man with the dark hair from the car with the WMD license plate stood at the end of the same row as Toby. He stared at a display of snacks, but he didn't take anything.

Mack's hands clenched into fists. The jerk was watching the kid.

Margaret came up behind Toby, selected a candy bar from the rack and led Toby by the hand to Janice, the cashier.

"My, my hair was a mess that day," Janice said. "I'm surprised I didn't scare anyone." She patted her hair and turned the monitor back to face her behind the counter. "Anyway, you didn't come in to learn all about me and my monitoring system. What can I help you with?"

"Nothing really. I just never stop and chat when I come through," Riley said. "However, I would like one of your iced drinks." She removed her wallet from her purse. "What do I owe you?"

Janice filled a cup with ice and the soda of Riley's choice and rang up her purchase. "I'm glad you stopped by. We don't get too many visitors stopping for longer than to fill up their gas tank."

"Did the man with the WMD license plate come back through again?"

"I thought he was just passing through, but he must

have stayed nearby. I was looking through my record-ings the next day, playing with the date-time feature, and noticed he came through again late that night." Janice shrugged. "Must have been visiting one of our residents to be leaving that late. Or early…depending on how you look at it."

"What time of the night or morning was it?"

"Around three o'clock. I wouldn't have noticed, but nothing else moved on the street shot until that car went by." She tilted her head. "I'm still trying to figure out who he was visiting around here." The bell over the door rang and Janice looked past Riley and Mack to the newcomer. "Rocky. I've got your quarts of oil you asked me to order." She glanced again at Riley. "Don't be a stranger. It gets boring around here, and I love to visit."

"Yes, ma'am. We'll be back." Mack cupped Riley's elbow and led her out of the store.

"Do you think it was him?" Riley asked as soon as the door closed behind her.

Mack pulled his cell phone from his pocket and pressed Declan's number.

"Yo, Mack. What's up?"

"Sorry to bother you on vacation, but I could use some contacts."

"For what?"

"I need to run a license plate and find out who it belongs to."

"I can help you with that," Declan assured him. "Charlie gave me some names in the DC police department and a contact her husband had with the FBI. I'm sure one of them will be able to help."

Mack gave him the license plate of the dark-haired man and added, "It's urgent that we find out whose car it is as soon as possible. I'll fill you in later. I might need the team's help."

"On it. I'll get back with you as soon as I hear anything." Declan rang off.

"What can your team help with if we don't find our guy?" Riley asked.

"We're going to find him," Mack said, his jaw hardening. "And when we do, we'll need help extracting the boy. I'm sure they won't just hand him over." He anticipated a fight and hoped the boy wasn't collateral damage. "Right now we're getting breakfast at the local diner."

RILEY DIDN'T WANT to waste time eating when the minutes and hours were ticking by so quickly and they still hadn't found Toby. But she knew she couldn't operate without fuel for her body. What good would she be if she didn't have the energy to fight for her little brother?

Mack drove his truck to the diner and parked.

Before she could alight, he was there opening her door for her. She liked the gesture, but she didn't want to get used to it. Having been an independent woman all her life, she found it difficult letting a man treat her like the weaker sex. Especially knowing she very well could take him down in a few of the moves her father had taught her.

Her body heated at the thought of tossing Mack to

the ground and pinning him between her thighs. He'd put up a fight, but she'd hold him there until he begged for mercy.

Or kissed her.

Her lips tingled at the memory of his previous kisses. She wanted more but didn't know quite how to ask for them. With her brother still unaccounted for and her handler possibly watching her every move, or that of Mrs. Halverson, she couldn't let her focus divert.

They entered the diner and chose a booth in a far corner.

"Hi, I'm Maddie. I'll be your server." A waitress with long, straight blond hair pulled back in a pony-tail stopped beside Mack. "Our special this morning is two eggs any way you like them, bacon, hash browns and toast."

"I'll have the special," Mack said.

"Me, too," Riley echoed, her stomach rumbling loudly. When she thought back over the past three days, she hadn't had more than one meal since getting that message from Toby's abductor. She didn't feel right eating when Toby might not have been fed.

Mack reached across the table and covered her hand with his. "You have to keep your strength up to help Toby. When the time comes, we might have to fight our way in and out to get to him. You can't do that without fueling your body."

Riley nodded. "I know. I just can't help wondering if Toby is being taken care of. I hope they're feeding him. The boy can pack away some groceries. He's growing again."

The waitress returned with glasses of water and orange juice. "You two are new in town, aren't you?" Her brow dipped as she studied Riley. "Though I think I've see you before."

Riley nodded. "I come occasionally."

"That's right." Maddie smiled. "You come in once or twice a month with Toby. He's such a good little boy. He's polite and well-mannered."

"Thank you. I'm proud of him." Considering what all he'd gone through, having lost his parents when he was a baby and living with his nanny and the occasional visit from his sister, he was growing up to be a very well-behaved young man.

"Will Toby be joining you?" Maddie asked.

"Not today," Riley answered.

Maddie left the table and returned a moment later with a coffee mug for each of them and a pot of coffee. "What brings you to Havenwood? Well, besides Toby."

"Actually, we were trying to track down a man who might have come through here a couple days ago," Riley said. "I believe I left something in the rental car he's driving, and I want to retrieve it."

Mack thought Riley's story was a little weak, but the waitress seemed to buy it.

"Oh yeah?" Maddie tipped her head. "What does the car look like? Chances are I've see it."

"A silver four-door Prius sedan."

Maddie smiled. "Dark and four-door describes a lot of vehicles that come through the parking lot. Got anything more than that?"

"It has the license plate WMD 495."

"Oh, that car." Maddie snorted. "If it weren't for the license plate, I wouldn't have remembered that one. But WMD makes me think, *what would Mother do?*" She laughed. "My mother wouldn't be working in the diner, that's for sure. The man in the silver sedan pulled up in the parking lot like he was going to come in for something to eat. But he sat in the vehicle, facing the road, and then left a few minutes later. I thought maybe he was talking on his cell phone or something." She shrugged. "We were slow at that time. I could have used the tips. But whatever."

"Oh, well. I guess I'll keep looking," Riley said.

"I'd go back to the rental car company and see if they recovered your item," Maddie suggested.

"You're right," Riley said. "I'll do that."

Maddie disappeared into the kitchen and came back a few minutes later with their plates of food. "Can I get you anything else?"

"I don't need anything." Mack glanced toward Riley.

Riley shook her head. "Looks we have it all here. Thank you."

Once Maddie left them alone, Riley stabbed her fork into the eggs. "What do you think our mystery man was doing in the parking lot?"

"If he was facing the road, he might have been watching for Margaret and Toby to pass by."

"And then followed them out to the cabin." Riley's stomach roiled. But she shoveled food into her mouth, determined to be ready when the time came to fight for Toby's return. "We really need to know who owns that car."

Mack's phone vibrated on the tabletop. He glanced down at the screen. "It's Declan. Maybe he's got something for us to go on."

Riley leaned forward, her gaze on the phone. "I hope so. Answer it."

Mack already had his finger on the button to answer when she urged him to respond.

"Mack here," he said, and then listened in silence. "Okay. Send it to me in a text. We'll follow up." He ended the call and met Riley's gaze.

Her heart fluttered in her chest. "Well?"

"He got a hit. The car was rented by an Alan Durgan. He lives in Arlington. Declan is sending me his address."

Riley started to rise. "What are we waiting for? Let's go find him."

"Finish your food, and then we'll go."

"I'm full," Riley lied. Though she wasn't full, she couldn't eat another bite when her stomach twisted and churned.

"I need energy. I'm finishing, and then we'll leave." He touched her hand. "I'll hurry."

Riley sat across the table, trying to contain her impatience as Mack shoved his eggs and hash browns down his throat.

She even ate a few more bites as she waited. Less than five minutes later, Mack washed the food down with coffee, threw some bills on the table and stood. "Let's go."

Riley leaped to her feet and hurried out the door in front of Mack.

Once they were in the truck, she had to contain her excitement for the long drive back into the city. Since it was a weekend, the traffic wasn't as horrible as a workday, but it was steady and thick.

Riley cursed how slow the traffic moved. Finally, they reached their turnoff. Her heart beat faster as they neared the street address. They pulled into an apartment complex with peeling paint on the walls and run-down cars parked in the lot.

"Maybe you should stay here," Mack suggested.

Riley raised her eyebrows. "Really? I don't think so."

"Suit yourself. Just be ready. I don't have a good feeling about the neighborhood."

Three men in old jeans and faded shirts sat on the steps leading up to the building, smoking cigarettes.

Mack walked up to them.

Despite her bravado, Riley wasn't excited about passing the gauntlet of men in ragged clothing and smoke. But if the man inside the building had Toby, she'd do anything to get him out. Throwing back her shoulders, she followed Mack up the stairs, giving the men on the steps as much room as possible.

When she thought she'd made it past without incident, a hand reached out and gripped her ankle. Instinct took over. She turned the leg he held on to and shoved with all her might. The man fell off the steps backward, losing his grip on her ankle as he tumbled.

The other two men laughed at their friend.

Riley hurried up the steps after Mack before the man on the ground could recover.

Once inside, they climbed to the third floor and walked down a hallway that smelled like a dirty locker room to the fourth door on the left.

Mack raised his hand to knock. When his knuckles touched the door, it swung inward. The lock had been broken, and the doorframe was splintered.

Riley's heart plunged into her belly. She pushed past Mack and ran into the apartment, calling out, "Toby? Toby!"

No answer.

A moan came from a room to the right.

Riley started to enter, but Mack grabbed her arm and held her back. He pulled his handgun from beneath his jacket and waved her to the side.

Because he was armed, she let him take the lead, though it cost her to wait.

"Riley," Mack called out.

She ran into a bedroom containing a bare mattress and bloodstains on the wall.

Mack knelt on the far side of the bed. "We found our mystery man, but he's in bad shape."

Riley ran around the bed and stared down at a man with a hole in his chest, lying in a pool of blood. He reached up to clasp Mack's hand. Mack took it and held on as if he could keep the guy from dying by the strength of his grip.

"Where's the boy?" Mack demanded.

The man opened his mouth and coughed, and blood trickled from the corner of his lips. "He paid…me…" He coughed again, his chest rattling with fluid. "Paid me…to follow."

"Alan, who paid you?" Riley asked. "Does he have the boy? Did he take Toby?"

The man's gaze shifted to Riley. "Yes."

"Who is he? Please, tell me," Riley begged.

"Cash deal." Durgan coughed and closed his eyes.

"Alan Durgan, don't you die on me," Riley said. "That's my brother he has. Where did he take him?"

"Didn't know," Durgan whispered.

"Can you tell us anything about him?" Tears filled Riley's eyes and spilled down her cheeks. The man was going to die without telling them who had Toby.

"Badge. Had a badge."

"What kind of badge? Was he a police officer?"

"No. Worker badge…dropped when…paid." Durgan coughed, the rattle in his chest worse.

"Did the badge say where he worked?"

The man lay with his eyes closed, his breathing fading. He gasped, drawing in a rattling breath and letting it out with one word Riley could barely hear: "Quest."

"What did he look like? What was his name?" Riley grabbed the man's collar and shook him. "Don't die on me. Toby is all the family I have left."

Durgan didn't respond. He lay still, his chest no longer rattling, rising or anything. The man was dead, and with him went the knowledge of who had Toby.

Chapter Six

Mack placed the call to the police. While they waited for the authorities to arrive, they left the apartment and descended the stairs to the ground level.

Of the three men who'd been there when they came in, only one was left. The one Riley had shoved onto the ground. And he didn't look all too happy.

Mack lifted his chin and stared at the man, studying the tattoos on his arms. One stood out from the rest. "That's a Marine Corps emblem on your arm. You earn that or pay for it?" he asked.

"Both. Seven years, two deployments to the sandbox and a bum knee." The man's eyes narrowed. "What's it to you?"

"Did twelve in the corps." He held out his hand.

For a moment, the man stared at the hand. Then he took it and pulled Mack into a quick hug. "Thank you for your service, man."

"And you yours," Mack responded. "Name's Mack Balkman."

"Joe Sarly," the man introduced himself. "Who's your girlfriend?"

Riley started to open her mouth, but Mack answered before she could. "Riley."

Joe snorted. "Got a helluva kick." He nodded to Riley. "I deserved it."

"Damn right you did." Riley glared at the man.

He rubbed his chest and grinned. "You looked like a woman on a mission. I couldn't resist poking at you." He glanced up at the apartment building. "Who ya visiting?"

"Alan Durgan," Mack said.

Joe frowned. "The PI?"

"PI?" Riley asked.

"Yeah, he's a private investigator. Most of the time he's taking photos of men cheating on their wives or wives cheating on their husbands. What's he done to you?"

"He provided information to a man who kidnapped a child."

Joe's eyes widened. "No kidding? The dirtbag deserves to be shot."

"He got what he deserved," Riley muttered.

Joe looked at the building again. "What do you mean?"

"Someone shot him." Mack turned toward the sound of the sirens wailing a couple of streets over. "The police will be here shortly."

Joe shifted on his feet, his gaze on the entrance to the parking lot. "Damn. I didn't really mean it about him deserving to be shot."

"How long have you been sitting on these steps?" Mack asked.

Joe shrugged. "A couple of hours."

"Did you see anyone besides us go into the apartment building during that time?"

"The lady who lives on the second floor came and went." Joe scratched his head. "And some guy delivered a package to one of the units inside."

"Do you know which floor?"

"I didn't follow him, if that's what you mean. But I could hear his footsteps for what sounded like a couple of flights of stairs." Joe's eyes got rounder. "You think the delivery guy offed Durgan?"

"We don't know, but I'm sure the police will want to ask the same questions." Mack nodded to the police car pulling into the parking lot.

As much as Mack didn't want to stick around and answer questions, he felt that if they left without speaking with the police, they'd appear guilty.

An hour later, Riley was pacing the parking lot, ready to leave. Declan managed to contact one of Charlie's contacts in the police department who cleared the way for them to leave as long as they dropped by the next day to sign a deposition about what they'd found in Durgan's apartment.

Mack held the door for Riley to climb into his truck. When she was settled in the seat, he rounded the hood and slipped into the driver's seat. They were on their way soon, weaving between the emergency vehicles that had gathered in response to Durgan's murder.

"The guy who has Toby works at Quest," Riley said, staring out the windshield, her fingers digging into the armrest so hard her knuckles turned white.

"We don't know that. He might have stolen a badge to get inside and spy on you."

"When badges are stolen, they don't go long before they are reported. The only reason he'd still have that badge is if he is on the inside."

"Do you think this has something to do with what happened a couple of weeks ago?" Mack asked. "Do you think the people who were stealing the secret project plans are paying you and Charlie back for interfering?"

Riley stared across the cab at Mack. "If that's the case, he could be one of four thousand employees in that building. How do we narrow the search down to one man? And how do I do that before the weekend is over? Surely he'll want to know Mrs. Halverson died before Monday. He's expecting a quick death. And if I didn't do it right, he might step in and finish the job."

"My guys will be watching over Charlie. They'll make sure he doesn't get anywhere near her."

"Can you be certain?"

He held up one hand, the other firmly on the steering wheel. "They can be trusted to protect her."

"But I got to her when you were supposed to be protecting her."

Mack's fingers tightened on the steering wheel. "I thought you were one of the good guys."

"And I thought I was, too." She stared down at her hands. "Sometimes we do things we don't want to do to protect those we love."

"I failed Charlie this time." He'd been surprised the widow had let him stay on with Declan's Defenders after he let her into the restroom with an assassin. "My guys won't let it happen again."

"I need to get inside Quest. Maybe the man who has Toby is connected with the folks who were stealing secrets."

"I thought the only one in Quest who was helping with that was your old supervisor. And he's dead."

"Yes, he is, but there might have been more."

"And how will you be able to single him out when most people are at home for the weekend?"

"I don't know. I just think the answer is at Quest."

"Can you get me in?"

She shook her head. "Not through the front door. Declan got in last time by sneaking in via a delivery truck."

"The chances of that happening on a weekend are slim to none."

"Then I'll have to go alone."

"What about the cleaning crew? Does Quest have a service?"

Riley's eyes narrowed. "Yes. They come in after hours and on weekends when there aren't many people in the building. I remember working on a Saturday and Sunday and hearing the sound of the vacuum cleaner on my floor."

"All I have to do is slip in when they do."

"There are security cameras throughout the building."

"Then I have to look like I'm cleaning. Easy enough."

Riley's brow wrinkled. "You hardly look like the cleaning crew."

"I can disguise myself. You can get in on your own ID and I'll find a way in via the cleaning crew."

"Okay." Riley nodded and focused on the road ahead. "Then what?"

"We track down who your supervisor had contact with. You might also check your desk for bugs and your computer for Trojan horses. Someone might have a backdoor into your computer at work who is monitoring your communications."

Riley shook her head. "I'm very careful about changing my passwords."

"If there's a listening device or camcorder recording your movements, it doesn't matter how many times you change your password. Someone could be recording your changes as you make them." Mack brushed her arm with the backs of his knuckles. "You could be doing the right things and still be giving away secrets."

"Damn." She ran a hand through her hair. "If he wants the data I kept him from getting, why ask me to kill Charlie?"

"Apparently, he knows Charlie was behind the foiled attempt to secure the data. That and if you killed Charlie, he had that over you to make you do whatever he wanted. All he had to do was threaten to expose you."

"And use Toby as his leverage if that didn't work." Riley closed her eyes. "He has no intention of giving Toby back to me."

"Which makes it all the more imperative we find the child and get him back."

Riley nodded and bit her bottom lip. "That poor kid has to be traumatized by all this. He can't help who his parents were and who his sister is. Why can't they leave him alone?"

"Because they know he's your weakness," Mack reminded her. He reached for her hand and held it. "But if you're going to have a weakness, it's a good one to have. It shows you have a heart."

She tightened her fingers around his and held his hand the rest of the way to the building where she worked.

Mack liked the way her fingers felt, supple but strong. He could imagine how they'd feel sweeping across his naked chest and lower. He admired her strength and her commitment to her brother. If he'd had a chance to save his brother, he'd have taken it. He knew how it felt to lose someone you love, especially someone who had his entire life ahead of him. Aiden had barely begun to live. Mack refused to let anything happen to Toby. That kid was like the little brother Mack had lost all those years ago. They had to find him. He had to live. For Riley. For Aiden.

RILEY STARED THROUGH the windshield at the street ahead, her mind going through all the possibilities. Who at Quest had been watching her besides her supervisor? Who would have paid a PI to follow Toby and the nanny? Who had bugged her apartment?

All those questions remained unanswered as long as she sat in Mack's truck. She needed action, and she felt that she'd find the answers at Quest.

When they approached the building, Riley had Mack circle the block. A van stood at the rear of the building near the loading dock. The writing on the van indicated it was from the cleaning agency that serviced the building.

Three women left the Quest building, walked to the van and climbed inside. They pulled out of the dock area and drove out onto the street.

"Follow them," Riley said. She glanced at her watch. "It's noon. They might be going out to get something to eat."

Mack gave the van a sufficient lead before he turned onto the street behind them.

After several turns, the van stopped at a pizzeria and the three women entered the establishment.

Mack pulled into a parking lot at the Thai restaurant one building over from the pizzeria. "Be ready to roll. I'll be right back." He opened the driver's door and dropped down from the truck.

Riley slid across the console into the driver's seat, her heart pounding. "Where are you going?"

"Into that van."

She waved toward the vehicle in question. "But it's out in the open."

"If those women are hungry, they aren't watching the van. They're watching the guys inside making pizza." He walked across the parking lot as if he were going to pass the back of the van. As he came abreast of the back door, he tried the handle. The door swung open and Mack disappeared inside.

Riley held her breath, her gaze going from the van to the pizzeria. What if the ladies came out early? What if they caught Mack in the back of the van? Would they call the police?

A moment later, the door of the pizzeria opened and the three women came out carrying two boxes each of pizzas. They were laughing and smiling as they walked toward the van.

One entered through the sliding side door at the same time the back door opened and Mack slipped out, carrying a bundle. He eased the door closed and hunkered low, waiting for the side door to close and the other two women to get into the van.

Then he made his move, walking out from behind the van as if he were passing by. Only he walked away from where Riley sat in the truck.

The ladies in the van pulled away from the pizzeria and back out onto the street.

Riley whipped the truck into Drive and went around the other side of the pizza place, where Mack stood with his bundle, grinning.

"What did you do?" Riley asked as he jumped into the passenger seat and slammed the door closed.

"I got my ticket into Quest." He held up a security badge and a jumpsuit with the name of the cleaning company embroidered on the front along with a woman's name. Eudora.

"You're going into Quest dressed as a cleaning lady?"

He nodded. "I am. Didn't Declan get in as a package delivery guy? I figure if he can do it, so can I."

"One big drawback." Riley stared at the badge and at Mack. "You don't look anything like Eudora."

"I'll wear a baseball cap."

Riley shook her head. The idea of the big marine dressing up as a cleaning lady was ludicrous. "You think you'll fit in that jumpsuit?"

He nodded. "It's big."

"Yeah, but you're tall. That thing will barely go past your knees."

He slipped out of his shoes and shoved his feet into the legs of the jumpsuit. "It'll do to get me past the gate and the security cameras."

"And if it doesn't?"

"Then I'll run like hell and come up with another idea. At the very least, you'll get through the door and I'll provide a little distraction while you poke around your office."

Riley drew in a deep breath and pressed her foot to the accelerator. "You're crazy, Mack Balkman. You know that, don't you?"

"We do what we have to do to get the job done." He shoved his arms into the sleeves and dragged the jumpsuit up over his broad shoulders. As he said, the jumpsuit was very large. Eudora must be a big woman.

Even so, he had to strain to get the front zipper all the way up. The fabric stretched taut over his muscles, and the legs of the suit didn't cover his ankles. Thankfully, his boots covered the rest.

"You could do with a shave," Riley muttered. "Unless Eudora is also prone to facial hair."

"I've got that covered." Mack reached in the glove box and pulled out a battery-powered razor. Moments later he'd removed most of the stubble from his chin, neck and cheeks.

Riley reached into her purse with one hand and rummaged around until she found a tube of lipstick. "Use this. It can't hurt."

Mack made a face but uncapped the lipstick and pulled the visor down to look at his reflection in the mirror. With an unpracticed hand, he applied a coat of fire-engine red to his lips and rubbed them together. When he was done, he clapped a cap on his head and grinned.

Riley laughed out loud. "For such a good-looking guy, you're an ugly woman."

"But will I do?"

Riley studied him briefly before returning her attention to the street. "You'll do." She gave him the location of her office. "I'll watch for you and let you in when you get there. Only authorized personnel are allowed back there, but I know some of the cleaning staff have been cleared to enter for housekeeping purposes only."

Mack glanced down at his name tag. "Hopefully, Eudora was one of them."

Riley's lips curled for the rest of the drive to the Quest campus. Mack dressed as a cleaning lady was too funny to not see the humor in the situation. She wished she could take the time to snap a picture of him. His buddies would give him hell.

Two blocks from the building, Riley pulled into an empty parking lot, parked the truck and nodded to Mack. "I'll go first."

"I won't be long behind you."

"*If* you get in."

"I'll get in," he said, smiling with his bright red lipstick. "Just watch." Then he winked.

Riley got out of the truck, clipped her badge on her shirt and slipped her purse over her shoulder. The way she saw it, her time was running out. If she didn't find something inside the walls of Quest, she didn't know where she'd look next, or if she had time.

Hang in there, Toby. I'm trying.

Chapter Seven

Mack waited until Riley entered the gate at Quest before he left the truck and made his way to the same gate. He checked his stride, hoping to imitate the way Riley walked with the natural sway of her hips and the much shorter steps. He had to look ridiculous in the jumpsuit that was too short and too tight. But it didn't matter as long as he got through the gate using Eudora's badge. Once inside, he'd find his way up to the floor where Riley worked.

Hunching over a little, he tried to make himself as small and short as possible, which was hard to do for a man over six feet tall. At the gate, he slid the badge through the card reader and waited for the light to turn green and the gate lock to click. For a second, he thought the card wasn't going to work, but then the light flickered to green. He pushed through quickly and strode across the campus to the entrance.

As he passed the guard at the front desk, he averted his gaze and hurried toward the elevators.

"Hey!"

Out of Mack's peripheral vision, he noticed the guard rising from his desk.

Pretending he didn't hear, Mack punched the button for the elevator going up and counted his heartbeats until the door slid open.

"Hey, you!" the guard called out again.

"George, what are you doing on Saturday shift?" a female voice called out.

"Hey, Lois, long time no see," George said, his voice not nearly as loud.

The elevator doors slid open. Mack stepped in and turned to punch the button for the floor where Riley worked. Then he hit the button to close the elevator door. He glanced across the floor to where George stood talking to Lois.

George looked over Lois's shoulder at Mack. For a moment, the guard's eyes narrowed.

Then the elevator door closed, and the car moved upward.

Mack let out the breath he'd been holding, willed his pulse to slow to normal and watched the floor numbers blink on and off until he stopped at Riley's floor.

The door opened, and Mack stepped out.

Just outside the elevator stood a cleaning cart.

Mack looked both ways but didn't see a cleaning person. He grabbed the handle of the cart and pushed it down the hallway toward the sign over the door that read Special Projects.

As he reached the door, it opened.

For a split second, Mack froze.

Then Riley poked her head out and waved him toward her. "In here."

Mack pushed the cart through the door.

Riley closed it behind him.

"Remember to look for bugs or hidden cameras," he whispered to her.

She nodded and held up a small electronic device that had been smashed. "Found this attached inside the receiver of my desk phone."

"I'll dust my way around the overhead light fixtures and see what I can clean out."

"Good. In the meantime, I'll be working my way through my desktop computer."

Their conversation was whispered. Riley barely moved her lips as she spoke.

Mack wanted to bend down and kiss those incredibly pretty lips he knew to be soft and pliable beneath his. Then he recalled how ridiculous he looked and wondered if a woman like Riley would ever want to kiss him after seeing him dressed as he was, wearing red lipstick.

"By the way…" Riley glanced up, a wicked gleam in her eyes. "You're cute in that getup." Before he could respond, she turned and walked away.

Pushing the cart in front of him, Mack followed Riley into the realm of the Special Projects unit. He unloaded the small vacuum cleaner from the cart and plugged it into an electric socket. Then working his way from one end of the aisle Riley had gone down to the other, he vacuumed and dusted, checking the overhead light fixtures as he went. At one point, he climbed onto a stepladder he found affixed to the side of the cleaning cart to dust the fluorescent light that illuminated Riley's desk. Inside the fixture he found a small device the size of a single throwing die. He swept the duster across it and trapped it in the microfiber, then dropped it into a trash bin, covering it with a wad of paper towels.

Riley barely acknowledged him. She worked at her computer, her head bent toward the screen, her fingers flying across the keyboard.

Mack emptied trash bins from beneath each of the desks surrounding Riley's, checking through the discarded papers. He looked at the items on the desks, photographs and notes, hoping to find some anomaly. Most of the desks had photographs of family members or pets. Except one. The nameplate on the wall outside the cubicle read Steve Pruett.

Mack committed the name to memory. He'd ask Riley about Pruett when they were out of the building and somewhere it was safe to talk.

Dusting his way down the aisle on the far side of Riley's cubicle, Mack paused when he thought he heard the door to the area creak open.

"Hello?" a female voice called out.

Mack ducked low and moved toward the end of the corridor to get a better view of the person who'd just entered.

Riley poked her head above the five-foot-high walls of the cubes and answered, "Can I help you?"

"Sorry to disturb you, ma'am, but I seem to have

misplaced my cleaning cart. I don't suppose you've seen one around here?"

"Bridgett, is that you?"

"Oh, hi, Miss Lansing. Why are you here working on a weekend?"

"I had some catching up to do, since I was out a few days," Riley responded. "I haven't seen your cleaning cart, but then I haven't been looking for one. Have you tried the area on the other side of the hall?"

"I have. It wasn't there. I went down to supply for some window cleaner, came back and the cart was gone. Do you mind if I look?"

"No," Riley said. "Go for it."

Great. Mack listened for the sound of footsteps, gauged the direction they were coming from and went the opposite.

Just as he slipped around the end of the row of cubicles, he heard a gasp.

"Ah, there it is," the cleaning woman said.

"You find it?" Riley asked.

"I did. I don't know how it got in here, but it's okay. I'll get out of your hair and come back later to clean this area."

"Thank you," Riley said.

Mack hid in a cubicle on the other side of the wall from where he'd left the cleaning cart. He carefully controlled his breathing so the member of the cleaning staff didn't hear him or come around the end of the row to find him lurking in his borrowed jumpsuit, with his purloined badge and red lipstick.

The cleaning woman wheeled the cart out of Special Projects, closing the door behind her.

Mack waited a full minute before he worked his way back to where Riley worked.

"That was close," Riley said. "Find anything?"

"Other than the camcorder in your light fixture… no."

"Camcorder?" Riley shivered. "I can't believe that even in this area, someone was able to get in, plant devices and get out without being noticed."

"Have you found anything?"

"I was able to get into the shared drives and into my old supervisor's stored emails. He wrote some cryptic emails to one of the department heads that made no sense."

"The emails or the department head?"

Riley's lips twitched. "The emails."

"That department head ever act weird around you?"

Her brow wrinkled. "I don't think so. Though I don't think Bryan Young liked me much. He always had a scowl on his face like he'd eaten something that didn't agree with him."

"When you were trying to figure out who was selling secrets, was Young ever on your list of maybes?" Mack asked.

Riley lifted a shoulder. "I guess he was. But my contacts with the FBI never found anything on him."

"Who else were they monitoring?"

"Mr. Moretti, my supervisor, and Tracy Gibson, his secretary."

"What happened to Tracy when Mr. Moretti didn't come back to work?" Mack asked.

"She was laid off. No one wanted to take her on, knowing Mr. Moretti was one of the insiders helping to sell secrets."

"Do you think she was as dirty as Moretti?"

"Hard to say. She might only have been in the wrong job with the wrong boss."

Mack stared down at her. "What does your gut say?"

"After Moretti showed his true colors, I wouldn't have trusted her."

"She bears looking into. Whoever has Toby wanted Charlie dead. The rich widow could have been targeted for a number of reasons, one of which was hiring Declan to help find you, and in the process, exposing Moretti and the leak inside Quest."

"Do you think they want Charlie dead out of vengeance?"

"It's as good a motivation as any. And since you were involved in setting up the sting, what better way to dispose of Charlie than to force you to do it? And then you would be exposed for the Russian sleeper spy you were trained to be."

"Could my handler be that entrenched in Quest and possibly one of the traitors selling or even buying the secrets?" Riley shook her head. "There are too many coincidences. And if the person on the inside of Quest isn't actually my handler, how did he know the code word for my activation?"

"All good questions we won't know the answers to until we find Toby and his kidnapper."

"Then we better get started. I say we follow Bryan Young and see what he might know."

"Got an address?" Mack asked.

"I was able to hack into HR files." Riley pulled a sheet of paper off a pad and stuffed it into her pocket. "Got it."

"Get Tracy Gibson's, too," Mack insisted.

"Give me a second." Riley clicked keys and leaned toward the monitor.

"And while you're at it, Steve Pruett," Mack added.

She glanced up, her brow wrinkling. "Steve? Why him?"

"Just in case. His was the only desk with nothing on it."

"Steve tends to be overly particular about his things. I'm not surprised his desk is neat. But a Russian spy?" Riley shook her head.

"He's too neat. No indication of who he is. No personality, makes me think of a sociopath, in my opinion."

Riley brought up Steve's information and jotted down his address. "Got him and Tracy. Anyone else?"

"I didn't see any other desk that triggered my instincts."

Riley pursed her lips. "It's sad when all we have to go on is gut instinct."

"And your digging in the HR files."

"I hope they can't trace back to my hacking."

"If Quest learns of your Russian upbringing, do you think they'd let you continue to work for them?"

Riley sighed. "I don't think any American company would let me work for them."

"Then let's go." Riley pushed herself to her feet. The door to the Special Projects unit opened at the same time. She ducked low. "Wait, someone's coming," she whispered."

Mack dived into a cubicle and crouched behind a file cabinet. He didn't like that he couldn't confront whoever had come in, but he was the odd man in the room. Riley was the one who belonged.

RILEY SAT BACK at her desk and pulled up one of the drawings she'd been working on before everything had gone south in her life.

The tall, angular form of the head of the department, Bryan Young, stopped beside her desk. "Miss Lansing. I'm surprised to see you working on a weekend."

She glanced up with a forced smile. "Oh, Mr. Young, I could say the same about you."

The department head frowned. "I'm here quite often on Saturdays, or I wouldn't have made that remark."

"Oh, well… I was out a couple days and my work fell behind. I thought I'd come in and try to catch up. But I was just finishing what I was doing, and I'm about to leave. I have a few errands to run before I head home." She exited out of the drawing file and pushed to her feet. "Are you staying long?"

The man shook his head. "No. I just stopped by to check on a few things and collect a document I needed to read over before Monday. Then I'm out of here."

"Good. Weekends are for family," Riley said. Normally, she'd be out at the cabin, spending time with Toby. Her heart squeezed hard in her chest at the thought of her little brother. She prayed they didn't hurt him.

The man snorted. "Or a long to-do list," Young muttered. "Have a nice day, Miss Lansing."

"Thank you, Mr. Young. You, too." She gathered her purse and stepped around the department head.

"Oh, and Miss Lansing, Human Resources has decided to conduct a thorough rescreening of all employees since Mr. Moretti's untimely death and the ugly business of selling secrets to foreign countries. The FBI has asked to be involved." Young gave her a narrow-eyed glance. "I trust that you weren't involved in Moretti's dealings."

Riley tensed. "I assure you, Mr. Young, I had nothing to do with selling secrets to anyone. I work for Quest only." She could say that with truth in her heart. Though she worked with the FBI to help flush out all those involved in selling data and plans from the project she had been working on, Riley had given bad data for the transfers to keep the data thieves from getting the real data for the secret project. None of her hard work had made it into the wrong hands, unless Moretti had hacked into her files and passed on the information before he was shot and killed.

"Well, I'm done here," Riley said. "See you Monday." If she found her brother, and if she still had a job then.

Riley walked toward the exit door, her pulse racing.

Where was Mack? She prayed Mr. Young didn't decide to inspect every desk in the Special Projects unit.

Mack needed Young to leave the area so that he could get out without being seen.

Riley waited until Young was almost to his office before she hurried after him. "Mr. Young. I had a question for you about Mr. Moretti's replacement."

She made it a point to pass by the cubicle where Mack hid. As she passed him, she jerked her thumb toward the exit.

"What is your question, Miss Lansing?"

"Are you going outside the organization to replace him, or will you be promoting within?" She stopped beside the man where he paused with his hand on the doorknob to his office.

He twisted the knob and pushed the door inward. "Why do you ask, Miss Lansing?" The man stepped through the door.

Riley glanced back over her shoulder.

A shadowy movement assured her Mack was making his way to the exit. All Riley had to do was divert Young's attention until Mack cleared the unit.

"Mr. Young, I've been with Quest for over five years and moved up in ranks each year. I believe I could be the supervisor over Special Projects. I know everyone on the team and the work that is being done."

"I'll be sure to keep your name in mind when we decide to advertise the position."

Out of the corner of her eye, Riley saw the exit door open and close.

"Thank you, Mr. Young. I just want you to know I'm interested in the position. Have a good day."

"Same to you, Miss Lansing." Already, the man's attention had shifted to the contents of his desktop.

Riley backed out of the office and turned to leave.

She had just reached the door leading out of the unit when she noticed Mr. Young leaving his office and locking the door behind him.

The man hadn't stayed long and seemed to be in a hurry to get somewhere.

Riley had no desire to share an elevator with the man. When she stepped out into the hallway, she looked for Mack. He was nowhere to be seen. Instead of taking the elevator, Riley took the stairs down to the ground floor. When she exited the stairwell, she sought out Mack in his costume, but still didn't see him.

Hoping Mack had found his way out of the building, Riley left Quest and its campus and found her way back to the truck a couple blocks away.

Mack sat in the driver's seat, scrubbing the lipstick off his mouth with a napkin. He'd removed the jumpsuit and cap and looked more like himself.

"Did Young give you the job?" Mack asked.

Riley snorted. "I don't think it's completely up to him. The job will have to be advertised and posted so others can apply. They have to go through the motions, even if they have someone in mind for the position." She stared out at a vehicle leaving the Quest campus. "That should be Mr. Young. Now would be a good time to follow him."

"Did you get a feeling from him that he might have Toby?"

"I didn't, but why would Moretti have sent those memos to him in some kind of code?"

"I don't know, but let's follow him and find out what he's up to."

With his lips still brighter red than he liked, Mack pulled out onto the street and fell in behind Bryan Young, staying back far enough the man wouldn't be suspicious.

Young drove for twenty minutes, working his way out of town heading west into the countryside.

Riley sat forward in her seat, her eyes glued to the expensive car in front of her. "Do you think he has Toby?"

Mack didn't say it, but his gut wasn't feeling it. "I don't know." And if they spent too much time chasing Young and he turned out to be the wrong man, they'd have wasted time they could be using to go after someone else. Mack pulled out his cell phone. "Call Gus. Ask him how Charlie's doing."

Riley found the right number and hit the call button.

"Hey, Mack," Gus answered, his voice coming over the truck's sound system. "How's the hunt for the little boy going?"

"Not well. We don't have a lot to go on."

"Sorry to hear that. We've had a little excitement here at the hospital."

"What's happening?"

"Someone dressed as a nurse tried to slip past us in the middle of the night to get to Charlie."

Mack's fingers tightened around the steering wheel. "How's Charlie?"

"Fine. Getting a little antsy. But she's fine. Mustang wouldn't let anyone into Charlie's room. Not even the doctor on call. Charlie pulled some strings and has her personal physician checking in on her."

"Did you run a check on the nurse who tried to get in?"

"Mustang had the sense to snap a picture of the badge. We ran it against the hospital employees' database. That nurse reported a missing badge this morning."

"Were you able to detain the woman?" Mack asked.

"No, she left as soon as Mustang snapped a photo of her badge. Mustang wouldn't leave his post to follow her, and I was on a coffee run. By the time I got word, the woman was gone."

"Have Mustang send that photo of her badge and hopefully of the woman to me and Declan."

"Already sent to Declan. He passed it on to one of Charlie's contacts with face recognition software."

"Great."

"Snow and McCastlain are doubling up on shift. If anyone tries again, we'll have backup."

"Glad to hear it," Mack said. "Keep Charlie safe."

"We've got her covered," Gus said. "Question is, do you need help?"

"I've got Declan chasing down some leads via Charlie's contacts. Riley and I are following a lead now. Hopefully something will turn up. In the meantime, we're working against the clock. I fully expect Riley to get a phone call soon if Charlie doesn't show up in the news as having passed."

"We'll do our best to keep that from happening, but that doesn't help Riley get her brother back."

"Exactly."

"Stay in contact."

"Will do," Mack said, and ended the call.

"Mr. Young just turned off," Riley said.

The car in front of them exited the main highway onto a side road.

Mack slowed the truck, giving Young enough time to pull ahead.

By the time Mack turned off the main highway, Young had made another turn and disappeared.

"Damn." Mack pressed his foot hard on the accelerator.

"There!" Riley pointed down a street to the right. "He just turned left two blocks down."

Mack drove another block and turned right, sped past one block and was well on the way to the second.

"Slow down." Riley leaned forward. "He stopped at a house on the next street. Stop the truck. We can walk from here without alerting him to the fact that he's being followed."

Mack pulled the truck to a stop against the curb and shifted into Park.

Riley was out of her seat and dropping to the ground before he could round the front of the truck. Together, they ran between buildings. Mack could see the car Young had been driving pull into the back alley behind a yellow-and-white cottage.

Riley slowed to a stop behind a bush and parted the branches. "He's going in through the back door. He could have Toby in there." When she started to go around the bushes, he stopped her.

"Wait and let him get inside."

"But—"

"He could be visiting his mother for all we know," Mack reminded her.

As Young climbed the steps to the back porch, the back door opened, and a pretty woman with bleached-blond hair stepped out and flung her arms around Young's neck.

"I could be wrong, but that's not his mother," Riley said.

The woman wrapped her arms around Young's neck and kissed him.

"And I'd bet that's not his daughter."

"I've met his wife," Riley said. "That's not her."

Chapter Eight

Riley held back long enough for Mr. Young to get inside the house. Then she ducked around the bush and hurried toward the little yellow-and-white house. Apparently, her department head was having an affair. But did that make him a Russian spy? And did it mean he was the one holding Toby hostage? She doubted it, but they'd come this far; they had to be certain.

Mack caught up to her and got to the house before her.

Since he was taller, he could see in through the window without having to climb up onto the porch.

"See anything?"

"Just the two of them kissing."

"Any sign of Toby?"

"No." Mack moved from that window to another. Riley followed. "And the windows aren't completely covered. You'd think if they had the boy, they'd have him hidden."

"You'd think if they were having an affair, they'd hide it better. Any private investigator could have a field day snapping photos."

Making a semicircle around the house, Mack checked every window. "From what I can tell, there isn't a basement. I'm not seeing any sign of anyone other than Young and the woman. And they only have eyes for each other."

"Give me a boost," Riley demanded.

Mack cupped his hands. "Have a look."

Riley stepped into his palms.

Mack raised her to eye level with the window.

As he'd mentioned, Mr. Young and the woman were heavy into kissing and more. Clothes were flying off, and Mr. Young backed the woman against the wall.

"Good Lord, that's Rachel from HR." Riley jerked and knocked her forehead against the glass pane.

The couple stopped in mid-grope and turned toward the window.

Riley dropped down, her heart pounding. "They might have seen me. We need to get out of here."

"You feel confident they don't have Toby?" Mack asked as they ran around a thick stand of bushes.

"Positive."

"If you think there might be a chance they have him hidden in a closet, I'll go knock on the door. They don't know me. I could make up some story to get them to let me in."

"No. I think we're wasting our time." Riley stood still for a moment, afraid to move unless Young and his lover caught sight of her.

The back door opened, and the woman peered out. Mr. Young stood in the shadows behind her.

Riley held her breath.

The woman shook her head and turned, closing the door behind her.

Riley grabbed Mack's hand. "Come on, we have to check out the other two people on our list. I feel like we're running out of time."

A dog barked as they passed a fence, and someone yelled for it to shut up.

Riley broke into a run, a sense of urgency making her pulse race and her stomach twist. Mack opened the door for her and then hurried around to get into the driver's seat.

"Where to next?" Mack shifted into Drive and pulled out onto the street.

"Steve Pruett's place." Riley stared down at the map function on her cell phone where she'd keyed in Steve's address. "It's about twenty minutes from here."

"We'll make it in fifteen." Mack pushed down hard on the accelerator.

Riley stared out the window, despair eating away at hope. "I feel like we're on a wild-goose chase."

Mack reached across and gathered Riley's hand in his. He gave it a gentle squeeze. "As long as Toby's out there, we can't give up hope."

She nodded, her heart swelling at Mack's touch. He gave her strength in the simple contact. "I'm not giving up," she assured him. "But there has to be a better way to find him than chasing down impossible leads."

As if on cue, Mack's cell phone rang.

Riley lifted it and read the caller ID screen. "Declan." She slid her finger across the display. "Hey, Declan. Tell me something good."

"We had a hit on Steve Pruett."

"What kind of hit?"

"We found a police report about a domestic disturbance at his house a month ago. The neighbor called it in. When they arrived, his girlfriend refused to press charges, even though she had a busted lip. She swore she'd walked into a door."

"That doesn't mean he's a kidnapper."

"No, but we also found information on a debt collection agency. The man owes over $100,000 in credit card bills. Apparently, he likes to live at a level greater than his salary warrants."

"Motivation to sell secrets, but not to kill," Riley said.

"Unless someone is paying him to have you do the killing," Declan suggested. "He bears looking into. Grace and I cut our vacation short. We're back at Charlie's place with the computer guy who worked with her late husband. He's an expert hacker. We've got him digging into anything to do with Pruett."

"Good. We're on our way to Pruett's address. Anything you find in the next twenty minutes could help."

"Will let you know. And we didn't find anything on Bryan Young. Other than his wife recently filed for divorce. They're in marriage counseling, to mediate and salvage their marriage."

"Yeah, that's not going to happen," Mack muttered.

Riley's lips twisted into a wry grin. "Anything on Tracy Gibson?"

"The most we could find was that she's drawing

unemployment for now. No police record or rap sheet on her."

"So far, Pruett's all we have. If your hacker can get into Moretti's computer at Quest or his home, have him see what he can dig up."

"Will do," Declan said.

"We'll let you know what we find at Pruett's place." Mack ended the call with a touch to a button on the steering wheel. "What do you know about Steve Pruett?"

Riley shook her head. "That's just it. I don't know much about any of my coworkers. I was so busy working and spending time on the weekend with my brother. And when the FBI got me involved with finding the leak in our department, I was focused on Moretti. I didn't see anything in any of the others…because I wasn't looking." She clenched her hands into fists. "Too many secrets. I hate living a life of secrets. But how did Pruett find out about mine? No one knew but my parents' handler, as far as I know. Why would the handler share that information?"

"Unless he had an agenda of his own and needed to keep his identity secret."

Riley glanced down at the map on her phone. "We turn here. Two blocks over and turn to the right." Once again, her heart beat faster. If Pruett was their man, he could have Toby locked up in his house.

"Parking now."

Before he had the gearshift fully engaged in Park, she was out of the truck and running toward Pruett's address. Pruett had to be their guy. Toby could be yards away.

Riley's heart raced as her legs powered her forward.

A hand on her arm jerked her back.

"You can't go charging up to the house. He's not just going to hand over Toby." Mack brought her up short at the corner of a house three doors down from the target address and gripped both her arms, forcing her to look at him. "We have to take it slowly."

Riley nodded. "I know. I know. I just…it's Toby. I have to get him back. He's bound to be scared to death."

"If he's there, we'll get him."

Riley curled her hands into his shirt. "He has to be there."

"We'll soon find out." He swept his hand along the side of her cheek and brushed a strand of her hair back behind her ear. Then he bent and touched his lips to hers. "Let's do this." Mack took the lead and slipped behind the houses, following an alley that paralleled the street out front.

Riley shifted her gaze from the buildings ahead to her cell phone, tracking their progress since they weren't looking at the numbers on the curb or mailboxes. "This is it," she said, stopping short of the house. The backyard was surrounded by a chain-link fence. The one before it had a collection of old junk stacked in varying piles. Not Pruett's house. The yard was pristine. Absent of everything but neatly trimmed grass. He didn't even have bushes around the foundation.

"He has a basement." Riley pointed to a trapdoor with a padlock securing the outside.

"Let's see if he's home." Mack inched up to one of the windows and peeked inside.

"See anything?"

"No movement."

Riley eased around the side of the building to the garage and looked through the window into a one-car garage. "No car. He must be out. We can get inside and be out before he returns."

"That's breaking and entering."

"I don't care if I have to smash a window. I'm going in." Riley dug in her jacket pocket for the file she kept handy for just such an occasion. She climbed the stairs to the back porch and slipped the file into the lock on the door. Within seconds, she had the door open.

"One of your spy skills?"

"My father had me tinkering with locks from a very early age," Riley admitted. "I'm good at it." As she crossed the threshold into Pruett's house, she glanced back. "Stay outside. I don't want you taking the rap for breaking and entering. It'll be all on me, if I get caught."

"You're not going in alone." Mack followed her up the stairs and entered the house, closing the door behind them.

The house was old, with hardwood floors, crisply painted walls and not a cobweb or dust bunny anywhere. The hallway passed a small laundry room. Riley glanced through that doorway and moved on. Mack entered, checked it thoroughly and followed Riley into the kitchen.

A study in white, the kitchen was like the rest of the

house, sparkling clean with white marble countertops and white cabinets with chrome pull handles, polished bright. No fingerprints marring the smooth finish.

Riley lifted her hands, afraid to touch anything for fear of leaving evidence that she'd been there. A staircase led off the kitchen up to the second floor. Riley hurried up the steps. Two bedrooms were completely empty with no furnishings or wall hangings. The light fixtures were clean, and cobwebs wouldn't dare make an appearance in the rooms.

Mack led the way back to the ground floor and found a door beneath the staircase. Using the hem of his T-shirt, he opened the door and flipped on the light switch. A light hung overhead but only illuminated the staircase, nothing beyond.

Mack went down first.

Riley held her breath and followed.

Once they reached the concrete floor below, they had to turn to see into the rest of the basement. A shiny steel toolbox stood in one corner next to a workbench. Behind the workbench was a pegboard with tools hanging neatly. Each tool had an outline on the pegboard. Every tool had a place and every tool was in it.

Riley had the sudden urge to knock them all down and fling them across the floor in disarray. None of the tools had any dings, dirt or oil on them. They appeared to be barely used.

Mack made a quick inspection of the rest of the basement. "Nothing here," he said.

"No secret doors?" Riley made her own pass through the room. "No hidden rooms?"

"Nothing."

Her heart sank. "Where's Toby?" she whispered.

"I don't know, but we need to get out of here before Pruett returns and catches us."

"Where would he keep a little boy?"

"We don't even know it's Pruett who has him."

"What about the girlfriend? Can your friend Declan find her?"

"I hope so. Let's get out of here. This place gives me the creeps."

"Me, too." Riley climbed the stairs and had reached out to push the door wider when she heard a sound that made her blood run cold. The front doorknob rattled.

"Someone's at the door." Riley eased back, switched off the light and pulled the door almost all the way closed. The only light came from the gap between the bottom of the door and the floor.

Riley stepped down a step and bent to look through the gap.

As she suspected, someone was coming through the front door. All she could see was a pair of men's leather shoes moving across the floor. The crisp *tap* of heels on wooden floors echoed off the walls.

The wearer of the shoes paused in the hallway. A rustle of fabric sounded, and a garment hit the floor. From what Riley could see, it was a jacket and was quickly snatched up.

The shoes moved toward the door behind which Riley and Mack stood.

Short of stumbling down the stairs in the dark,

Riley could do nothing but freeze and pray the shoes didn't stop.

She held her breath and waited, fully expecting the door to burst open and Pruett to call the police. Bunching her muscles, she prepared to launch herself up out of the basement and run like hell. Though what good that would do, she didn't know. Pruett would recognize her, and she'd be charged with breaking and entering. What bothered her most was that Mack would be charged as well.

The shoes slowed on their way past the door but didn't stop.

Riley listened as the footsteps passed the kitchen and moved on to the bedroom on the main level. Moments later, the sound of water rushing through the pipes gave her hope.

"He's taking a shower." Mack touched her arm. "If we want to leave, now would be the time."

Riley eased the door open and stuck her head around the edge. The water rushing through the pipes suddenly stopped. Going out the back door would force them to pass the door to the main floor bedroom. Instead, Riley headed for the front door, opening it quietly and easing through the screen door.

Mack followed, closing the door carefully behind them.

Once she was out of the house, she walked down the steps as if she had just left a friend's house and turned away from the side of the house with the master bedroom.

Mack fell in step beside her, took her hand and held

it like a boyfriend going out with his girl for a stroll.
After a block, they turned and doubled back on the next
street, hurrying toward the parked truck.

As they approached the truck, a car whipped around
the corner from the direction of Pruett's house.

Riley grabbed the front of Mack's shirt and pulled
him into a tight embrace, rising on her toes to slam her
mouth against his.

Taking his cue, he cupped the back of her head and
turned her face away from the oncoming vehicle.

What started as a kiss to hide Riley's face became
something entirely different.

The car passed and turned the corner, disappearing
around the houses on the next street. But Mack continued to kiss Riley, and Riley kissed him back.

She liked the way his lips were soft, but firm. Liked
how hard his body was against her softer curves. Loved
how he made her feel more feminine than any other
man. She was familiar with every way to take a person
down but was almost certain she'd struggle to over-
power this man. And she liked that, too.

With one hand at the small of her back and the other
buried in her hair, Mack brought her ever closer until
there was no space between them. When he skimmed
his tongue across the seam of her mouth, she opened
eagerly, wanting to taste him, to caress him in that intimate way.

They might have gone on for a lot longer, but a car
slowed in passing and a teen yelled, "Get a room!"

Riley backed away, her cheeks heating and her
mouth throbbing from Mack's kiss. "Was that Pruett?"

she asked, her voice shaking. Her entire body trembled with her reaction to being so close to the marine.

"I don't know. I think so."

"We should try to catch up." She stared up at him, her legs refusing to move.

Mack nodded. "We should. But I think he's too far ahead."

"Right." Riley took a deep, steadying breath and climbed into the truck.

Mack got in beside her. "Tracy's place?"

"Yeah." She fumbled with her cell phone and keyed in the address.

They drove to her house in silence, neither looking across at the other. At least not blatantly. Riley watched Mack in her peripheral vision. He didn't turn to face her once.

It took all of the thirty-minute ride for her heart to return to a regular pace and for her to talk herself down from the raging desire she'd felt in that one kiss. She wanted so much more.

By the time they reached Tracy's apartment, dusk had settled over that corner of Virginia. Tracy's apartment was completely dark from the outside.

Mack walked up to the door and knocked. If she answered, he'd make up a story or pretend he'd gotten the wrong apartment. Riley waited in the truck with the interior lights off. When no one came to the door, Riley joined Mack at the door and worked her magic with the file. They entered Tracy's apartment and moved around using a penlight Riley kept in her purse. Unlike Steve Pruett's place, Tracy's was a disaster. Clothes littered the floor, dishes were piled in the sink and the bathroom looked like it hadn't been cleaned since she moved in. Tracy wasn't there, and neither was Toby.

Riley left Tracy's place discouraged.

As they pulled out of the parking lot, a dark older-model SUV sprang out of a side street and slammed into the passenger side of Mack's pickup.

Riley was flung sideways. The seat belt tightened across her chest, keeping her rooted to her seat though her head jerked hard on her neck.

The SUV backed up, the engine revved, and the tires spun up smoke as the vehicle came at them again.

At the last moment, Mack gunned the accelerator.

The SUV hit the bed of the pickup, spinning the entire vehicle ninety degrees to the right. When the SUV backed up to hit them again, they were nose to nose.

Mack shoved the gearshift into Reverse and spun the wheel, turning the passenger side of the truck away from the SUV and taking the brunt of the attack on the front left bumper.

The SUV hit hard. The driver's side airbag deployed, shooting a bag and white dust into Mack's face. The passenger side had been turned off, giving Riley a clear view of the vehicle coming at them yet again.

"Gun it!" she yelled, and grabbed the steering wheel, jerking it to the right.

Blinking the dust out of his eyes, Mack punched his foot to the floor, sending the truck into a spin.

The SUV clipped the back end and sped away.

Mack shoved the truck into Drive, but it limped forward, grinding to a stop.

"What the hell?" Mack jumped out and stared at the front bumper.

Riley got out and stood beside him, staring down at the fender bent all the way into the front wheel. The truck wasn't going anywhere but up on a tow truck.

Whoever had hit them hadn't had a license plate on the back of his vehicle. Nor had the lights been on. All Riley could say was that it was a dark SUV. Nothing really to go on. If it was the same person who had Toby, why would he want to kill them when Charlie was still alive? Nothing made sense.

Chapter Nine

Mack called Declan. Within twenty-five minutes, his friend arrived, picked them up and took them back to Charlie's place, where her computer guy was working late, trying to find some connection among Charlie, Tracy, Pruett, Moretti and Russia. With too many angles to pursue, the search could be endless.

"Why didn't we go to my place?" Riley asked.

"Charlie didn't think it would be safe," Declan said. "She has a security system set up all around her estate. No one is getting in without her permission."

"She isn't actually calling you, is she?" Mack asked. "Cell phones can be hacked, and people could be listening in on her conversations. They'd know immediately she wasn't in that bad shape."

Declan grinned. "She passes all information through Gus and Mustang. The reports coming from her doctor to the press are that she's in critical condition, not expected to live past the next twenty-four hours."

"I'm surprised the hospital is letting her stay," Riley said. "Is her doctor even allowed to practice in that hospital?"

"Money has a way of paving the way to breaking rules," Declan said. "I think she's promised to upgrade all the medical equipment in the emergency room and all of the operating rooms and build a new children's wing."

"I wish finding Toby was that easy." Riley sat on a white sectional sofa in a large den with cathedral ceilings and windows from the floors to the twenty-foot ceilings. The house was situated on a little bit of a hill, surrounded by at least ten acres of lush landscaping. The lights of the city sparkled all around, close but not too close.

"I expected to hear from Toby's kidnapper by now." Riley scrubbed a hand through her hair. "With reports of Mrs. Halverson still showing she's hanging on, I would have thought he'd threaten me again if I didn't finish the job."

"My mother told me never to borrow trouble." Grace entered the room, her hair up in a towel, looking fresh and squeaky clean from a shower. "Hey, roommate. I'm sorry about Toby. I have some extra clothes in my suitcase if you'd like to get a shower and freshen up."

Riley sighed. "I'd like to find my brother more than anything."

"Yeah, but while you're waiting, you might as well take advantage of that incredible shower." Grace held out her hand.

Riley placed hers in her friend's and let her draw her to her feet.

Mack stood as well and waited for the women to leave the room.

"What's the scoop on Riley?" Declan asked.

Mack stiffened. "What do you mean?"

"I understand she's Russian." Declan shook his head. "You'd never know by her accent."

"Because she was raised in America, not Russia." Mack's fists clenched. "She didn't ask to be a spy."

"But she was raised for that capacity?"

"Yes. But you can't always pick your parents. What's your point?"

Declan held up his hands. "No point. I just want to make sure you're okay helping her. Charlie was pretty adamant about us helping Riley find her brother. I can't believe Riley was sent to kill Charlie."

"And she could have," Mack said. "But she didn't."

Declan's brow dipped, and his eyes narrowed. "You like the girl?"

"I didn't say that. I just know she's all about rescuing Toby. He's the only family she has left. Hell, the kid's only six."

"Gotcha." Declan draped an arm over Mack's shoulder. "We'll do everything we can to find him and bring him home."

"I get the feeling we're looking for the wrong person. Even if Pruett or the Tracy woman is involved, they had to have gotten information about Riley from her handler. That's the guy who can make or break Riley in the end. What do we know about Russian agents in the area? Can we tap into the FBI or CIA? Does Charlie have any connections on that front?"

"She does. Or her husband did, and she does because of him. Come meet Jonah Spradlin. He worked with Mr. Halverson on a special project and still works for Charlie. He's amazing with the internet and anything computer. And he's prior military."

"Marine?"

"No, but almost as good. He was in the navy."

Mack followed Declan through the maze of rooms and corridors in the sprawling mansion. He stopped at a doorway with a hand scanner affixed to a panel near the doorknob.

Declan pressed his palm to the pad. A moment later a lock clicked, and the door swung open. He briefly glanced toward Mack. "Don't worry, the entire team will be set up to enter the war room when Jonah can get around to it. Right now he's busy working this case. He's barely stopped to eat since he started."

"Good to know someone is on it. We haven't made much headway chasing people."

"Jonah assures me he can find just about anything in the data."

They descended stairs into a basement with a large table down the middle of the room, computer monitors lining one wall and a huge whiteboard across another wall.

A man sat in the far corner in front of an array of six large monitors. He bent over the keyboard, typing away, his attention on the monitor directly in front of him. Every so often, he'd glance to one of the other screens.

"Jonah, Mack's here. You two should put your heads together on finding Toby. And when Riley gets down here, she might have even more insight into who might have her brother."

The man at the keyboard held up a finger. "Hold on." He keyed some more, stared at the monitor and frowned. "I might have something here." Jonah turned to Mack. "Declan said you went by Pruett's house?"

Mack nodded. "We did, but we didn't find anything there. He came home while we were hiding in his basement, but we made it out before he caught us."

Jonah held out his hand. "Which house did you go to?"

Mack frowned as he shook the computer guy's hand. "What do you mean?"

"Real estate records show that he owns more than one." Jonah released Mack's hand and turned back to the monitor. He clicked a couple keys and brought up images of two houses.

Mack leaned over his shoulder and pointed to one. "We went to that one."

Jonah pointed to the other. "He has this one on a lake in the next county. The bank has threatened to foreclose on it."

"I don't get it. The guy's other house doesn't appear too extravagant. What's he spending his money on?"

"I looked into his bank records. He likes expensive cars and vacations. He's been to Bora-Bora more than once in the past two years and to a high-end all-inclusive resort in the Caymans a number of times. And he doesn't go alone."

"Who is he taking?"

"I'm working on that. I couldn't get that information from his bank records, but I'm tapping into the resort databases, hoping to get passport data from the rooms he secured."

"Anything I can do to help?" Mack asked.

"You can go through his phone records and see if you find anything else. If you find a number he's used in the past couple days more than once, you can enter it here." Jonah pointed to another monitor. "It'll bring up who it belongs to, unless it's a blocked number. In that case, I'll have to do a little more digging. Is there anyone else we should be looking at?"

"What about the nanny?" Declan asked.

"I've met Margaret Weems. She's an older woman who seemed pretty upset that Toby was taken."

"In a lot of abduction cases, the child is taken by someone close to the family, if not a family member," Jonah pointed out. He made a note on a piece of paper. "Margaret Weems?"

"That's her name," Mack confirmed.

"I'll check on her," Jonah said. "In the meantime, you can get started on Pruett's phone records."

"I'm on it." Mack pulled up a rolling chair, sat at a computer keyboard beside Jonah and immersed himself in sifting through data.

"I'll see about getting some food brought down to you," Declan said.

Mack didn't hear him leave. He was so focused on the numbers and looking up who they belonged to that he tuned out all else.

Until Riley entered the room and stood behind him,

resting her hand on his shoulder. As he brought up the numbers, she commented when she recognized one.

"That's Paul Robles, our project leader's number," she said. "The man has three kids of his own and two adopted from fostering. He doesn't have time to kidnap another."

Soon she pulled up a chair beside him and leaned over his arm to read the names on the screen.

Declan delivered sandwiches, which they ate while poring over the phone records of Pruett, Young and Tracy Gibson. Nothing appeared out of the ordinary for a team of aerospace professionals communicating on a group project.

After midnight, Riley laid her head on the desk, blinking hard to keep from falling asleep.

Mack fought fatigue until he finally gave up and rose from his chair. "Come on, let's find a place to sleep."

Riley yawned but didn't lift her head from the desk. "I'm good right here."

"You two get some rest." Declan said. "I'm betting you've been going since last night."

"Up for over thirty-six hours," Mack confirmed.

When Riley didn't rise, he bent and scooped her up in his arms.

"Hey, I can walk on my own," she said, though her head lolled back, and she closed her eyes, snuggling into his chest. "But this is easier."

Mack strode across the room and climbed the stairs.

Riley roused enough to open the door but closed her eyes again when Mack stepped through.

Declan met them in the living room. "There's a room for each of you down the hall. Doesn't matter which you take. First two doors on the right. I think Grace left some clothes for Riley in the first one. And one other thing." Declan held out his hand. "Keep this on you, Riley. In case whoever set you up for this assignment decides to take you." He placed a small metal disk in her hand.

"What is it?" she asked.

"A GPS tracking device," Declan said. "We can follow where you go, should you get separated from Mack."

She frowned. "Are you afraid I'll run off?"

Declan smiled. "Not at all. It's more for your safety in case we can't get to you soon enough."

Riley slipped the disk into her pocket and leaned her head against Mack's chest. "Thank you for your concern over my welfare. It's more than I deserve."

"Thanks, Declan," Mack called over his shoulder as he turned and headed for the first door.

The spacious room had been prepared by one of Charlie's staff, the comforter turned back and the pillows fluffed. A powder-blue nightgown lay spread out on the white comforter.

"This one's yours." Mack lowered her legs, letting her body slide down his until her feet hit the floor. "I'll be next door if you need me."

She touched his arm. "Thank you for helping me."

"I haven't done anything yet."

"Yes, you have." Riley tilted her head to the right and then left. "If I'd been on my own in my car, that

SUV would have wiped me out." She tipped her head to the right again and winced.

"Are you pretty sore from the attack?"

She shrugged and grimaced. "I guess I am a little more than I thought."

Mack turned her around and rested his warm hands on her skin where her neck met her shoulders.

"Um, that feels good." She leaned her head forward and relaxed.

Mack gently rubbed the back of her neck and shoulders, carefully kneading the knots out of her muscles.

The more he touched her, the more he wanted to touch. His groin tightened, and he shifted to relieve the pressure.

"I'd better go," he said, and dropped his hands to his sides, afraid if he lingered any longer he'd want to stay the night.

Riley turned and wrapped her arms around his waist. "Thank you for all you're doing to find Toby." She pressed her cheek to his chest. "I don't know where I'd have begun without your help."

"Thank me when we get him back." He gripped her arms and set her to arm's length. "Now, I'd better go to my own room before I do something I'll regret."

Riley looked up at him with her big sleepy hazel eyes. "Like what?"

"Like kiss you," he said. And he did. He leaned forward with the intention of only brushing his lips across hers, ever so softly. But as soon as his mouth connected with hers, he knew he couldn't stop.

When Riley's arms circled his neck and brought him closer, he was a goner.

He clamped his arms around her waist and pulled her body against his. The hardness of his erection pressing into the softness of her belly. He groaned, knowing this wasn't the time or place.

His tongue darted out and met no resistance.

She parted her lips and accepted him in, curling her own tongue around his in a long, sensual caress.

Mack weaved his hands into her hair, loving how soft and thick it was against his skin. She was beautiful, strong and yet vulnerable.

When he brought his head up, he drew in a deep steadying breath. "I should go."

"Stay," she said on a breath of warm air that feathered across his chin and neck.

Mack moaned and fought his desire, knowing he couldn't take advantage of her when she was so worried about her brother. "I can't."

"Can't or won't?" she said. "I won't ask anything of you. Just stay with me. Please."

"If I stay, I won't be able to keep my hands off you."

Her eyes widened. "So?"

"So, I can't stay and not touch you." He shook his head.

"Then touch me," she said. "Because I want to touch you, too." As if to prove her point, she slipped her hands beneath his T-shirt and splayed her fingers across his chest. "Stay with me. I don't want to be alone tonight."

Mack was tempted. But the woman was an admitted Russia sleeper agent. If he slept with her, his loyalty to his country could be in question.

Ah, who was he kidding? He'd been dishonorably discharged from the military. His loyalty was already in question by others. But not to himself. He was still the same marine who'd give his life for his country and the citizens he'd sworn to protect and serve.

In his heart, he knew this woman wasn't one of the bad guys. She was a victim of her birth, of her upbringing. But she loved her little brother and would do anything to get him back.

And, like Riley, Mack would have done anything to save his brother, had he been given a chance.

They weren't all that different from each other. And she felt right in his arms.

Riley leaned up on her toes and pressed her lips to his. "If you don't want to stay, I understand." She cupped the back of his head and brought his mouth to hers in a long, warm and wet kiss.

It was his undoing. Mack scooped her legs out from under her and laid her on the bed. He climbed up to lie on the comforter beside her, deepening the kiss she'd started. What began as two mouths meeting soon turned into his hands exploring the curved surfaces of her body.

Riley sat up, pulled her shirt over her head and tossed it to the side. Then she reached for Mack's T-shirt, dragging it up over his head.

He raised his arms and took it the rest of the way, slinging it to a far corner. He lay beside Riley, trailing a finger over the curve of her breast, the indentation of her waist and the swell of her hip. "You're beautiful."

She traced a line from his collarbone, across his chest and down to one of the hard brown nipples, where she pinched it between her fingers and rolled it into a tight little bead. "You're not so hard to look at, you know."

"We don't have to do anything but hold each other," he said. "I'd be happy with that."

"You would?" she asked, looking up with a furrowed brow. "Because I wouldn't be nearly as satisfied." Her fingers trailed down his torso to his belly button and lower to the waistband of his jeans. "Be with me tonight. In every sense of the word," she whispered.

Mack gave up the good fight to remain unfazed by her touch and embraced all of what she offered. He gathered her close, pressed his lips to her temple and then her cheek. He trailed a path from her lips, across her chin and down the long, smooth line of her neck to the pulse beating wildly at the base.

Riley moaned and writhed beneath him, her back arching, brushing the lace of her bra across his naked chest. The coarse texture sent a thrill of excitement straight south, making him grow and harden.

Mack shifted on the bed, rising to lean over Riley. "Say the word and I stop here."

She shook her head and reached for the button on his jeans. "Don't stop. I want what you have. I need you to be with me. I need life to continue on." Riley flicked the button through the hole and lowered his zipper.

He sprang free into her palm and nearly lost himself

there. But he held back, determined to give her just as much pleasure as he was already feeling.

All his fatigue disappeared in a rush of adrenaline. He rolled off the bed, shucked his jeans. Then he leaned over Riley, unbuttoned her jeans and slid them down her legs. Once she was free of them, he trailed his fingers up the inside of her calf, knee and thigh to her hot center. Her panties were damp from her juices, making Mack want to tear them off with his teeth. Instead he hooked his thumb in the elastic and tugged them over her hips and thighs in a long, slow glide, following the path of her panties with his tongue.

Once the silk underwear cleared her ankles, she let her knees fall to the sides.

Mack worked his way back up her long, smooth legs, brushing his lips across every inch of her skin. He didn't stop until he reached her entrance.

"Protection?" she gasped, her breath hitching in her throat.

"Got it." Mack bent to where he'd shed his jeans, pulled his wallet from the back pocket and unearthed a packet. He held it out to her.

She took it, tore it open and rolled it down over his staff. "I want you, Mack. Now."

He smiled. "I want you, too. But first you."

RILEY WAS ALREADY so close to losing herself, she moaned her frustration.

When Mack slipped a finger inside her channel and swirled it around, Riley nearly came undone. Then he dragged it up to that bundle of tightly packed nerves at her center.

Riley dug her heels into the mattress and raised her hips to meet his assault on her senses. Every muscle in her body tensed, and tingling began at her center, spreading outward. She couldn't breathe and couldn't think beyond what he was doing to her. For a brief moment in time, she forgot about her worries, about Toby, about everything as she shot over the edge and rocketed into the stratosphere.

For what felt like forever and yet only a moment, she spiraled out of control.

When she drifted back to earth, she gripped Mack's shoulders and dragged him up her body.

He settled between her legs and touched his shaft to her entrance.

Beyond any kind of patience, she clutched his buttocks and pulled him into her.

He was hot and thick, filling her and stretching her in a long, delicious glide.

Riley rose to meet him thrust for thrust until they rocked the bed in rhythm.

He tensed, his body going as rigid as his shaft. Thrusting one last time, he buried himself inside her.

Riley held him there, her fingers digging into his buttocks. She'd never felt anything quite as satisfying as making love with Mack and suspected she'd never feel this way with any other man.

He collapsed against her and rolled them both to their sides without losing their intimate connection.

Riley snuggled close, pressing her cheek to his chest, inhaling the musky, male scent of the man.

Exhaustion pulled at her eyelids, and she gave in to sleep.

As she drifted off, his voice rumbled against her. "We'll find him. I promise."

Chapter Ten

Mack lay awake after Riley fell asleep, wondering how he would keep his promise to find her brother. He wanted to keep that promise more than anything. But they had so little to go on.

After a while, he gave up on sleep and returned to the door leading to the computer room.

"Couldn't sleep?" Declan padded barefoot in from the direction of the kitchen, carrying a steaming mug. "I made a pot of coffee."

"I could use some. Point me in the direction of the kitchen?"

"I can do better than that. This place is huge and can be confusing." He tipped his head. "Come on."

Mack followed Declan into a huge gourmet kitchen. Jonah sat at a massive table, eating a massive sandwich stuffed full of deli meat.

Jonah chewed what was in his mouth and swallowed before saying, "Not finding much on those names you gave me. Still looking for the exact location of Pruett's lake house. It shows up in court records as lots and plats. It's on a rural route, which to me says dirt road. When I have it, I'll get that address to you ASAP."

"Good. I've been thinking about it. You might also expand your search to anyone with access to Riley's office after hours at Quest. Only someone who came in after hours would have been able to set the camera in the light fixture."

"Will get right on it after I finish my breakfast, lunch and dinner." Jonah held up the sandwich.

Mack chuckled. "Fair enough. You have to fuel the body, even if you don't need sleep."

"You got that right." Jonah bit into his sandwich with a healthy growl.

"How's Riley holding up?" Declan asked.

"She's exhausted. I imagine the worry is eating away at her."

"I can't get over that she's a trained Russian spy."

Mack stiffened. "Riley's a product of her parents. She didn't sign up for it or want it."

"Still, there had to be some brainwashing along the way. The Russians are really good at raising their own secret agents. Are we sure we can trust her?"

Mack remembered how he felt inside her and the way she gave herself to him completely. "Can you trust every American you meet?"

Declan shrugged. "Not everyone. We have our own homegrown terrorists and zealots who've got a beef against our government. They'd just as soon shoot you as give you the time of day."

"Yeah, but a trained sleeper spy…" Jonah shook his head. "It's a lot to ask to trust someone who was sent to this country for the benefit of Russia. Their leader isn't above using every asset at his disposal to take what he wants."

"Yeah, he's a wild card," Mack agreed.

"As concerned as she is about her brother, I doubt she's a threat to us."

"Maybe not now. But what about when she finds Toby?" Declan asked. "She needs us now. She's not going to kill those who can help her, until they are of no more assistance to her."

Mack's instincts had been pretty spot-on for most of his career in the military. His gut told him Riley was one of the good guys. "Charlie trusts her."

Declan turned to face Mack, his eyebrows raised. "Yeah, but do you trust her?"

"I—" A noise drew Mack's attention away from the conversation. But when he turned toward the living area, no one was there. He might have imagined it, or the sound echoed off the wall close to where Declan was making another pot of coffee. He shook his head and tried to remember the question. "The fact that she didn't kill our boss says a lot. She could have done exactly what her handler wanted and gotten her brother back sooner."

"Or not."

"Either way, she didn't kill Charlie. In fact, I pulled her off Charlie."

Declan's eyes narrowed. "She physically attacked Charlie?"

"Charlie had the poison Riley was supposed to give her. She threatened to take it herself so that Riley wouldn't lose her brother. Riley fought Charlie for that poison. She wouldn't let her take it."

"Are you sure that was what she was doing?"

Mack nodded. "Positive. And Charlie would back it up. Riley went to the gala with the intention of doing whatever it took to get her brother back. But when the rubber hit the road, she couldn't do it. She might be trained as a Russian spy, with all the skills necessary to survive in that role, but she doesn't have the heart to kill an innocent woman."

Declan handed Mack a cup of coffee. "Sounds like you've made up your mind about the woman."

"I have."

"And it doesn't have anything to do with her being a knockout?"

"No. She's the real deal. I'd trust her with my life."

"I hope you're right." Declan frowned. "Because you might be playing with fire if you put your faith in her."

Mack's back stiffened. "I'll take my chances with Riley. I know I'm right about her."

Declan's frown cleared. "Can I get you something to eat?"

"No. The coffee is all I need for now. I need to get back to work. I'm not good with sitting around waiting for something to happen."

"None of us are," Declan said. "But we don't have a lot we can do until we know what we're up against. What's your next move?"

"We need to find Steve Pruett's lake house and pay it a visit." He hoped like hell they found Toby there. Time was running out for Riley and the kid.

RILEY HAD WOKEN to an empty bed. A glance at the clock indicated it was just past midnight. She pulled the sheet up over her naked breasts and stared around the room, lit only by the starlight shining through the window. Where had Mack gone? Did he regret making love to her?

She didn't regret it at all, though it complicated their working relationship and could only make it more awkward. Still, she couldn't regret having had the best sex she'd ever experienced. The man's lips were magic.

Her body heated with the memory, and she was deliciously sore. Riley moaned softly and ran her hand over her breasts and down the tuft of hair over her sex. She'd really made love to a man she'd only known a short time. What had she been thinking?

That she needed to hold someone and be held. When the odds were stacked against her, she had Mack to lean on, to help her find her way through the maze of clues. If anyone could help her find her brother, Mack was the one to do it.

She tossed the sheet aside, pulled on her clothes and tiptoed, barefoot, across the floor to the door. When she opened it, she hoped to find Mack on the other side, on his way back to bed with her.

He wasn't there. Curious now, she wandered down the hallway. Voices sounded from across the wide expanse of living area to another room Riley supposed was the kitchen.

Barefoot, her feet made no sound on the wooden floors. Not until she reached the entryway into the kitchen did she realize the men in the kitchen were talking about her.

More than once, Mack's friend Declan said the word *Russian.*

Riley eased up to the doorway and cocked her head to better hear what they were saying.

When Declan asked Mack if he trusted her, Riley froze in place. Mack hesitated with his answer.

Her heart leaped into her throat, threatening to cut off the air to her brain. Mack didn't trust her.

Her pulse pumped so hard against her eardrums she couldn't hear his response. Her chest hurt so bad she could barely draw a breath. Riley spun and ran from the living room back to the bedroom, where she grabbed her cell phone, called a car service and gave him the address of Charlie's estate.

Then she pulled on her shoes, hooked her purse over her arm and slipped out a French door onto a patio. Making her way around the house, she paralleled the driveway, clinging to the shadows as she hurried toward the exit. At the gate, she made note of the camera. So what if Mack saw her leaving? He didn't trust her anyway. He'd think the worst, that she was skipping out, maybe to complete the job of killing Charlie.

Well, he could think what he wanted. He probably only stuck to her like glue to keep an eye on her.

Why, oh why, had she slept with the man?

She stood still, staring at the gate without really seeing it. She'd slept with him because she'd felt a connection so deep she'd thought it was real. It had been...on her part. But apparently not on his.

Riley looked the gate over for a button to open the heavy iron bars but couldn't find one. Headlights turned onto the street and slowed as they approached.

Not wanting to buzz the house to let her out, she climbed up a tree beside the stone wall, looped her leg over the top and dropped to the other side.

The car slid to a stop.

For a moment, Riley thought it might be the person who'd tried to bash the hell out of Mack's truck. Bunching her muscles, she prepared to make a break for it.

The car stopped beside her and the passenger window slid down. "You the lady who called for a ride?"

"Yes," she said.

"Good. I wasn't sure about the address. Never been in this neighborhood." He stared up at the lights shining down on the massive stone gate. "Fancy place."

"Yes, it is."

Riley yanked open the back door and slid into the back seat.

Even before she had her seat belt completely fastened, the driver pulled away from the gate, heading toward her apartment.

She'd get her car and continue her search on her own. She didn't need the liability of someone who couldn't believe in her. In her heart, she knew she was one of the good guys. She couldn't kill an innocent person. She could kill, if she had to defend someone she loved, but not at the command of another just because that person had a grudge. If Mack couldn't see past Riley's upbringing to the person beneath her skin, he was missing who she really was.

In her mind, she circled back to the most important issue at hand. Finding Toby.

Steve Pruett had a lake house. All she had to do was find that house and find Toby. She didn't need a former marine to hold her hand through the process. She was a trained assassin and spy. She could handle anything anyone could throw her way.

MACK LEFT THE kitchen and returned to the bedroom where he'd left Riley sleeping. As soon as he walked through the door, he knew something was wrong. The bed was a jumble, the sheets half on the floor, the comforter pushed to the end of the empty bed. A quick glance around the room confirmed his fear.

Riley's clothes were gone, along with her purse. He checked in the adjoining bathroom but knew before he did that she wouldn't be there.

He ran back down the hallway to the kitchen.

Declan and Jonah glanced up.

"Riley's gone," he said.

Declan pushed himself away from the counter and set his mug down. "Are you sure?"

A lead weight sank to the pit of Mack's gut. "Positive."

"Hang on, I'll tell you where she is." Jonah touched the screen on his phone and brought up the security monitors. "She's jumping the front gate as we speak."

"Damn." Mack slammed his fist into his palm.

Declan glanced at the video. "Where do you think she's going?"

"I don't know," Mack said. "She doesn't have Pruett's second address." He paced the kitchen floor. "She could be going back to her apartment." He glanced up. "I'll go there and see if I can catch up to her. I hope she's all right. After the SUV attacked my truck, I don't think she's safe out there on her own."

"We'll get that address to you as soon as we find it," Declan said. "Did you give Riley the tracking disk?"

Mack nodded. "I did."

"Good." Declan's lips pressed together in a tight line. "It makes it easier for us to track her."

Mack's lips tilted upward. "She was happy we cared enough to give her one."

"Does she understand it's not for us to spy on her, but to keep her safe in case she ends up in the wrong hands?"

Again, Mack nodded. "Yes."

"Good." Declan tipped his chin. "You'd better get going. And take this truck." He handed Mack a set of keys.

"Thanks." Then he ran out the door and down the steps. He was in his replacement truck backing away from the house when a call came through his phone. He hit the talk button on his steering wheel. "Yeah."

"Mack, Jonah here. I went further back on Pruett's phone records and got a hit on one of the phone numbers. He placed several calls to a Tracy Gibson last month after hours. The calls ended about the time Moretti was killed and Tracy was laid off."

"Good to know. Thanks."

"Also, texting the address of Pruett's lake cabin. It's out there and on a dirt road. Not many houses show up in that area. If he's hiding the boy there, no one would know."

"I'll get right on it as soon as I find Riley."

"Gotcha," Jonah said. "In the meantime, I can get other members of the team to lead the investigation of Pruett's lake house."

"No. I'll get Riley and head that way. She'll want to go in. The boy will want to see someone he knows. Have the team gather and wait on standby. If anything goes south, I'll need assistance ASAP."

"We've got your back," Jonah said. "Just say the word and we'll be there. Well, Declan will be there for you. I'd come, but I think I'd be better at manning the computers, trackers and other technical support. But if you need me there, I'll come."

"No worries. Sometimes it's easier to get in and out with fewer people."

"Okay," Jonah said. "I'll keep you up to date."

"Don't forget to send me Pruett's lake cabin address."

"On it," Jonah said. "Out here."

Mack sped to Riley's apartment, barely slowing for the light signals. He couldn't get there fast enough. All the while, he wondered what had spooked her and why she'd felt the need to go after her brother on her own. Had making love to her scared her so badly she wanted to get away from him? If that was the case, he'd keep his hands to himself until they found Toby. After he'd made love to Riley, not touching her would be difficult. He wanted to hold her in his arms and take all her pain and worry away. And he wanted to make love to her again and again. The woman was sensual, sexy and amazing in bed.

Why the hell had she run?

Chapter Eleven

The drive to Riley's apartment passed in a blur. When she arrived, she dug in her purse for the key and let herself in. Focused on what she had to do next, she hurried across the threshold of the front door. A sound behind her made her pause. Footsteps?

She started to turn but was shoved from behind so hard she stumbled into the apartment, lost her balance and fell hard to her knees. She hadn't expected to be attacked, but she should have reacted faster. Her father would have been disappointed in her response.

The door slammed behind her and a sharp-toed shoe slammed into Riley's ribs.

She grunted and rolled to her side, looking up at the woman who'd just kicked the crap out of her. She knew the woman, but not in the context of her apartment.

"Tracy?" Riley clutched at her throbbing rib. "What the hell?"

"You're the one who started all this mess. You're the one who got Mr. Moretti killed and me fired. If you hadn't meddled, I'd still be working at Quest, and Steve wouldn't have dumped me."

Tracy cocked her leg and shot out another kick.

This time Riley was ready for it. Twisting to the right, she avoided the sharp-toed shoe, snagged the woman's ankle and pulled hard.

Tracy screeched and threw her hands in the air, searching for purchase, finding none. She crashed to the floor, landing hard on her back. She lay for a moment, stunned.

Riley rolled over and straddled the woman, pinning her wrists to either side of her head. "First of all, Moretti got himself killed by dealing with the wrong people. He was selling proprietary secrets to a foreign country. I didn't make him do that. I just helped the FBI to discover who was dealing dirty."

"So he sold some secrets. They'd have gotten them anyway. Computers can be hacked. Nothing is secret anymore." Tracy bucked beneath Riley, but she couldn't go anywhere.

"As for getting you fired, that was HR," Riley reminded her. "With Moretti gone, they had no use for a secretary to an empty position."

"I needed that job. I have a mortgage and bills to pay. Do you know how hard it is to find a job that pays as well?" Tracy jerked at her arms. "Let go of me. This is all your fault."

"And what do you mean by Steve dumped you? Steve Pruett? I didn't even know he dated."

"He did," Tracy practically spat out. "Me! Until a few days ago. Then he called and said he was done. Dropped my clothes and toothbrush off on my front porch and hasn't returned my calls since." Tears welled in her eyes. "He's done. And it's all your fault." She bucked again. "I hate you, Riley Lansing. You're poison!"

Riley couldn't help feeling sorry for the woman. But her hardship wasn't Riley's fault so much as Tracy's bad luck with her boss and poor choice of a boyfriend.

"Do you know where Steve's lake house is?" Riley asked.

She snorted. "Yes, of course. We spent weekends there before he dumped me. But what's it to you?"

"Tell me where his cabin is, and I'll see if I can get you back on at Quest."

"Why should I tell you where Steve's lake cabin is? Isn't it enough he dumped me? Now you're making a play for the man?" Trace shook her head. "No way."

"Fine, I'll just call the police and report you for assault. If you have a criminal record, you'll never find a job."

The woman sagged beneath her and stopped struggling. "Oh, what's the use anyway? I've lost Steve. I don't have a job, and I'm going to lose my house. If I go to jail, at least I'll have a roof over my head and three meals a day." Tears leaked from her eyes. "Go ahead, call the police."

Frustrated beyond patience, Riley bit back a curse. "I'd rather you tell me where Steve's lake cabin is."

"Why do you want to know?"

"He has something of mine that I want back."

"Find him yourself," Tracy said. "I owe you nothing."

For a long moment, Riley stared down at the woman

with tears dripping down the sides of her face. "I'm sorry this all happened to you, but it's important that I find Steve. Please, tell me where I can find his cabin."

Tracy sighed. "Let me up, and I'll tell you."

Riley frowned. "You're not going to try anything, are you?"

"What could I try? You're clearly better at fighting and pinning someone than I am." Tracy didn't pull at her wrists or move beneath Riley.

Shifting slowly, Riley released Tracy's wrists, one by one. Then she swung her leg off the woman and pushed herself to her feet.

Tracy lay for a moment on her back.

Riley reached out a hand to her.

The woman grabbed her hand and let her pull her to her feet. "I'll tell you where Steve's cabin is if you don't turn me over to the police." Tracy gave her an address.

Riley repeated it to her, committing it to memory. Then she opened the door and held it for Tracy. "You should go now. And just so you know, I'm sorry you lost your job."

Tracy bent to retrieve a small backpack from the floor by the door and turned in the doorframe. "Moretti was an idiot. He had a good thing going at Quest. He shouldn't have gotten involved in selling secrets."

"No, he shouldn't have," Riley agreed.

"And I shouldn't have turned a blind eye to his activities." She dug in the backpack as if unearthing keys. "But you know—" Tracy pulled a small handgun out and aimed it at Riley "—you shouldn't have set him up."

Riley stared at the gun, her pulse quickening, her thoughts racing through several scenarios. "Do you even know how to use that thing?"

Tracy stared down at the gun in her hand. "There's not much to it. You point and shoot." She raised her arm, leveling the weapon at Riley's chest. "If I'm going to jail, it might as well be for a damned good reason."

Riley could see when the woman's finger tightened on the trigger. She dived to the side in a flying somersault and rolled to her feet.

The gun went off, hitting the wall behind where Riley had been standing the moment before.

Tracy swung the gun toward Riley's new location. Before she could pull the trigger again, a man stepped up behind her and grabbed her around the waist, clamping her arms downward against her sides.

The gun went off, the bullet hitting the floor beside Tracy's foot. "Let go of me!" she screamed.

"Not until you drop the gun," Mack's deep, resonant voice said.

Riley's heart swelled in her chest as she rose to face Tracy and Mack. She grabbed the gun from Tracy's hand, dropped the magazine from the handle and expelled the round in the chamber. When she was done, she stared over Tracy's shoulder at Mack. "Thanks."

Mack gave Riley a slight chin lift. "Call the police."

Riley shook her head. "We don't have time. She gave me the address to Steve's lake cabin. I'm going now." Riley swiped her car keys off the table in the hallway and stepped past Mack holding Tracy.

Mack's hand shot out and he grabbed Riley's arm.

He repositioned his other arm to clamp Tracy in his grip. "You're not going on your own."

"I don't need anyone's help." She lifted her chin, her lips pressing together. "This is my problem. I'll take care of it."

"You can't go there alone. If Steve's desperate, he could do anything."

She squared her shoulders. "I'm willing to take that risk."

"Even if it means Toby will be hurt?" Mack pinned her with his gaze.

For a long moment, Riley stared into his blue eyes, and then her shoulders sagged, just a little. "No."

Mack glanced down at the woman in his grip. "We can't leave her. She might give Steve a heads-up."

Riley twisted her lips. "I'm not staying to babysit her. If there's a chance we can find Toby, I want to be there. The kid has to be beside himself and scared."

"My phone is in my back pocket." Mack tilted his head to the side. "Get it. Call Declan. Tell him what's going on and ask him to send a backup to hold this woman until we can get to Pruett's lake cabin."

"He won't be there," Tracy said.

"Why do you say that?" Riley asked.

"It's being renovated," she said. "He hasn't been visiting the cabin for the past few weeks."

"Would he go anywhere else?"

Tracy shrugged. "Where else would he go? His parents live in Ohio, and he doesn't have any close friends or siblings in the area."

Riley met Mack's gaze. "We have to check. It's the only other place I can think of."

Mack nodded. "We will."

Tracy's eyes narrowed. "What's Steve got that you want? Is he stealing secrets like Mr. Moretti? If so, he can rot in hell with Moretti."

"I don't know if he was stealing secrets, but he took something I care a great deal about." Riley hesitated telling Tracy that Pruett might have taken her little brother. Not many people knew she had a brother. And from the way Tracy was acting, she didn't know what Steve was up to. If Steve had dumped her several days before, he might not have wanted her to know about the kidnapping he would undertake. If, in fact, he was the kidnapper who'd taken Toby.

Tracy squirmed in Mack's grasp. "You can't hold me forever."

"Oh, we won't," Mack said. "As soon as help arrives, we'll be gone."

Riley placed the call to Declan. While she waited, Riley keyed the address into her cell phone and brought up the directions to get to Pruett's lake cabin. Thirty minutes away. She tapped her foot, counting the seconds until help arrived, freeing her and Mack to go after Pruett.

Within ten excruciating minutes, Declan arrived at her apartment with Mustang.

"We'll take her from here." Declan and Mustang each took an arm and led Tracy into Riley's apartment. "Let us know what you find."

"Will do," Mack called out.

Riley was already through the door. She ran toward her car and slipped in behind the steering wheel.

Mack quickly caught up and dropped into the passenger seat, folding his long legs into the car.

She didn't wait for him to close the door before she pulled out of the parking lot and onto the street. Then she pressed her foot to the accelerator, racing down the dark street toward the edge of the city and out into the countryside.

For the first five minutes, silence reigned inside the confines of the vehicle.

Riley was fine with that. She didn't have much to say to Mack.

"Why did you leave Charlie's place without letting us know?"

Riley stiffened, but she forced a shrug. "I needed to move on and find my brother. Why does it matter?"

"I thought we were doing this together. What made you change your mind?"

"It doesn't matter."

"To me, it does." He turned in his seat and faced her.

Riley kept her attention on the road, but she could see him clearly in her peripheral vision and the light from the dash. His brow furrowed, and his lips were drawn into a line.

"Why?"

"Maybe I read you wrong, but I thought we had something special going."

Her chest tightened. "Or not. What's special without trust?"

His frown deepened. "What are you talking about?"

"A partnership can only work if the two people trust each other."

"What have I done to lose your trust?" he asked.

"My trusting you isn't the issue."

"I don't know what you're talking about."

"It doesn't matter."

"Yes. It. Does." He touched her arm lightly.

Even as lightly as he touched her, it made her flinch and swerve.

Mack pulled back his arm and sat back in his seat, his lips pressed together. "We can talk about this after we get to the cabin."

A heavy weight settled in Riley's belly. "Or maybe we don't need to talk about anything. We really don't have anything to talk about, anyway."

Mack tilted his head, frowning. "Have I done something to make you mad?"

Riley focused on the road ahead. "No."

"Yeah, I can see that." He sighed. "You can tell me what's wrong, or I can continue asking questions until I hit on the right issue. Either way, I'm a patient man."

When she didn't answer, he nodded. "Okay. Was it something to do with the way we made love?"

She shot a quick glance his way. "No, of course not."

He nodded. "Good to know. Was it something I said?"

Riley's jaw tightened. "I'm not playing games with you, Mack."

"So it was something I said." He touched a finger to his chin. "I can't remember specifically what I said, but I'm sure I put my foot in my mouth on more than one occasion."

"Oh, for Pete's sake," Riley exclaimed. "Partners are supposed to trust each other."

"Yes…and?"

"And you don't trust me." There, she'd said it. "And why should you? I'm Russian. As far as anyone is concerned, I should be deported, sent back to my mother country, banned from ever returning to the United States." Her chest squeezed so hard she could barely breathe. "Only I don't know Russia. I grew up here. I can barely speak the language." She hit the steering wheel with the palm of her hand. "Damn it, I love this country. It's my home. I'd do anything to protect her."

"Pull into the gas station at the next exit." Mack pointed to the exit sign indicating a gas station.

"No." Riley sniffed, a tear finding its way down her cheek. "We have to get to the lake cabin before something horrible happens to my brother. Trust me or not, I'm going to find my brother. And if we have to leave the country, we'll leave together. As a family."

"Riley, pull over." This time he spoke in a much more commanding tone.

She gripped the steering wheel harder as they approached the exit, refusing to slow her trajectory. "I won't let them hurt my brother."

"We won't get to your brother if you don't pull off and put fuel in the tank," he pointed out. "Pull off."

A quick glance at the gas gauge brought Riley out of her pity party. She yanked the steering wheel at the last moment and sent the car onto the exit ramp and into the service station. When she rolled to a stop at a pump, she sat for a moment, her entire body shaking. A chuckle started low in her belly and rose up her throat in hysterical laughter, which quickly turned to a sob. "See? I make a lousy spy."

Mack got out of the vehicle, came around the side, jammed his credit card into the machine, activated the pump and stuck it into the tank. Then he yanked open her door and held out his hand.

Riley looked up at him through a wash of tears. "You don't trust me."

He didn't wait for her to put her hand in his; instead, he pried her fingers off the steering wheel, dragged her out of the vehicle and into his arms. "You are one stubborn, hardheaded woman, you know that?"

She remained stiff in his embrace, her hands resting on his chest, though she didn't push him away. "Why are you helping me?"

"Because Charlie asked me to and—"

"And she trusts me." Riley laughed, without humor. "Though why she would trust me, I don't know. I tried to kill her."

"No on both counts." With one hand around her, Mack reached out with the other and tucked a strand of her hair back behind her ear. "I was helping you, at first, because Charlie asked me to. Now, because I care. And quit putting words into my mouth. I don't know where you get the idea that I don't trust you."

She didn't want to admit she'd eavesdropped on his conversation. Riley looked over his shoulder. "I can tell."

"Then you don't know me." He pressed a kiss to her forehead. "I wouldn't make love with a woman I don't trust." He brushed his lips across the tip of her nose.

Riley lifted her chin, a shiver of awareness rippling through her veins. "Lots of spies make love to people they don't trust to get information out of them."

"Is that why you made love with me?" He pulled back, a frown pulling at his brow.

She shifted her gaze to his, unable to look away. "No," Riley whispered.

Mack gripped her shoulders. "Why did you make love with me?"

Her lips trembled, and she hated herself for showing her vulnerability. "Why does it matter?"

"Because you matter to me. A lot." He let go of her shoulders and cupped her cheeks between his palms. "For some crazy reason, I like you. I want to get to know you better. And I'd want to help you even if Charlie wasn't in the picture."

She frowned up at him, her heart swelling. "You would?"

"Yes." His lips tipped upward. "And I trust you."

"Even though I'm a Russian spy?"

A smile spread across his face. "Maybe even more so because you're a lousy Russian spy."

Her frown deepened. "I'm not lousy. I just didn't want to kill Charlie after all she'd done for me."

"My point exactly." He pulled her close and pressed his lips to hers in a brief, hard kiss. "I trust you, and I want to make love to you again. But most of all, I like you and want to get to know you better."

The pump clicked off, signaling the end of their brief break.

"We need to get moving," Mack said, almost as if he regretted having to let go of her.

Riley nodded.

"Want me to drive from here?" he asked.

Yeah, she might be giving up control, and that might appear weak, but her hands shook and she couldn't seem to catch her breath when Mack held her so closely. "Yes, please."

He walked her around to the other side of the car, held the door for her and helped her into her seat. Then he hurried to replace the pump handle and screw the gas cap on. A few moments later, they were on the road again.

Riley stared at the pavement in front of them, her heart and emotions in a turmoil. She felt warm all over at Mack's words. Then she chilled with her next thought. How could a former marine care for a Russian spy?

And as the miles ticked away, she prayed they'd find Toby and free him from his captor. Anything beyond that goal could wait to be resolved. Toby came first.

Chapter Twelve

Mack switched off the lights as they neared the location of the lake cabin. Half a mile away, he pulled the car to a stop and shut off the engine. He checked the weapon he wore beneath his jacket and opened the door to get out.

"Why are we stopping?" Riley got out of the car and stood beside Mack.

"We'll go the rest of the way on foot. That way, Pruett won't know we're there before we get to the door. If he has the boy, he won't have time to hide him." He shot a glance her way in the light from the stars overhead. "Ready?"

Riley nodded.

They followed the road, checking numbers on the mailboxes as they went until they neared Pruett's. From the road, they couldn't see anything but a dim light in the woods, along a rutted gravel road that led in.

Abandoning the road, Riley and Mack entered the woods, moving in the deep shadows of the tree canopy, with limited patches of starlight to guide them as they walked parallel to the gravel road. Soon the cabin appeared in a clearing, a single light shining through a window.

When Riley started forward, Mack held out a hand to stop her. "Let me go first." Pruett might be an engineer and a desk jockey, but he also might understand booby traps and how to set them.

Easing forward, Mack checked for trip wires and security cameras. When he found none, he waved Riley forward.

The cabin stood on piers, the windows a little higher than eye level unless one was to climb up on the porch. Since the porch would expose them too much, Mack ruled that out.

"You'll have to look," Mack whispered. He bent his long body, squatting low. "Climb on my shoulders."

Riley gave him a hesitant look. "Are you sure?"

He nodded and jerked his thumb toward his back. "Hop on. You'll be able to see into the window. Be careful no one sees you."

Riley slipped her legs over his shoulders and rested her hands on his head.

Mack straightened and, holding on to her thighs, shifted sideways toward the window.

"Stop," Riley said softly, her fingers curling into his hair.

He liked the warmth of her legs around his neck and the way her fingers feathered through his hair. But they were there to find Toby. "See anything?" Mack said, his voice barely above a whisper.

"Not yet." She leaned a little to her left. "Wait. I see someone lying on the couch."

"Pruett?"

"I can't tell," Riley said.

"What's he doing?"

"I can't tell," she said. "He's not moving."

"Not moving asleep?" Mack asked. "Or not moving dead?"

"Uh…" She leaned a little farther to the left. "I don't know."

Mack didn't like that he couldn't see in, but Riley couldn't lift him up. "Any sign of Toby?"

Her body seemed to sag. "No."

"Hold on, we're moving around to another window." Mack walked with Riley on his shoulders around to another window at the back of the cabin. The ground sloped toward the lake, making the window even higher from their level. "Can you see inside?"

"This is a bedroom." Riley leaned forward, pressing her hands on top of his head. "It's dark in the room. I can't see much, but I don't think Toby's in there."

"Moving." Mack moved to the next window.

"Another bedroom. I can't see Toby," she said, her voice flat, disappointed.

The next window proved to be the kitchen and again, no Toby.

Riley tugged at his hair. "Let me down."

Mack bent to a squat.

Riley dropped to the ground. "I'm going in."

"What if he's armed?" Mack asked.

"You're armed. You can shoot him."

Mack shook his head. "I'd be trespassing on his property. He'd have every right to shoot me first."

"Then we'll ask him to let us in. No guns necessary. We'll be stranded on the road because our car broke down."

"And he'll believe his coworker just happened to be in the neighborhood?"

"If Steve's got Toby, I'll shoot him myself. We won't need an excuse." Riley turned toward the porch. "Stay here. It might get sticky."

"I'm coming."

"Suit yourself." Riley marched up the steps and knocked on the door.

Mack followed, just as determined to find Toby as Riley, and even more determined to keep her from getting herself killed.

Mack tugged Riley to the side of the door. If Pruett had a gun and started shooting, he'd aim for the door and the person standing on the other side. The wall gave a little bit of cover. Not much, but at least out of the direct line of fire.

The sound of feet hitting the floor came to them, and then footsteps leading toward the back of the house.

"He's heading for the back door," Riley said. She leaped off the porch and raced around to the back of the house.

Mack struggled to keep up, afraid Pruett would be desperate and try to hurt Riley.

Riley had just reached the back porch when Mack ran around the corner.

A man burst through the rear entry, flinging the door open so hard it hit the wall.

Before he could reach Riley, she ran up the steps and planted herself in front of the man.

"Hello, Steve," Riley said, her tone even, dangerous.

"Riley," Pruett said. "What are you doing here?"

"I thought you might be able to help me."

Pruett tried to go around her, but Riley stepped in his path. "Going somewhere?"

"I think I left the stove on at my house in the city," he said.

"Yeah?" Riley snorted. "Well, I can tell you that you didn't."

"But I did. I need to get there and turn it off before the house catches fire."

"The stove isn't on, and the house isn't going to catch fire." Riley stepped closer to Pruett. "But maybe we should check inside your cabin and see if the stove is on here." She stepped closer to Pruett.

Mack climbed the porch steps. "Right. Perhaps you need to show us your stove."

Pruett's eyes widened when Mack stepped up behind Riley. He backed up, and his brow furrowed. "My stove isn't on here. I'm going to have to ask you to leave."

Riley shook her head and advanced on the man. "We're not leaving until we're certain your stove is off."

Pruett edged toward the door. "You're not invited into my cabin."

Riley's eyes narrowed. "I think we are."

"I'll call the p-police," Pruett stuttered, not sounding at all convincing.

"Go ahead." Riley walked up to the man and poked a finger at his chest. "Call the police."

The man's gaze shifted from Riley to Mack and back to Riley. He dived for the door and slammed it closed.

Mack reached the door before the man could lock it. He twisted the knob and applied a muscled shoulder to the paneled wood.

The door slammed open, shoving Pruett backward. He staggered until his back hit a wall. "You're t-trespassing," he said. "You can't come in."

"Yes. We can." Mack barged in and towered over the engineer. "Unless you think you can make me leave."

RILEY ALMOST LAUGHED at the way Pruett cowered under Mack's glare.

"Why don't you want to let us in, Steve?" She walked past Pruett into the kitchen. Everything had a place in the neat little kitchen, and everything was in its place. "Do you have something to hide?" She pushed the stainless steel toaster from one position to another, leaving a fingerprint on the steel, and moved on.

Steve squeezed around Mack and hurried after Riley. "No. No. I have nothing to hide." He moved the toaster back to its original position and used a paper towel to wipe the print off.

"Nothing at all?" Riley opened a cabinet door where glasses were lined up neatly, and pulled out a tumbler. She walked to the refrigerator and took out a bottle of orange juice, sluiced it into the cup, spilling a couple of drops on the countertop. "You don't mind if I help myself to a drink, do you?"

Pruett stared at the drops of juice on the countertop. "No. Help yourself and then leave."

"Why are you in such a hurry to see us leave? I'd think it would be lonely out here all by yourself." Riley drank the juice and set the glass on the counter. "Are you by yourself, Steve?" She moved toward the hallway leading to the bedrooms, searching for any doors she couldn't see from outside the house. Could the man be hiding Toby in a closet?

"Of c-course I'm alone." Steve lifted the glass, placed it in the sink and wiped the counter with a paper towel.

"All alone?" Riley said as she headed down the hallway to the two bedrooms. Her heart sped as she neared the first one and flipped the light switch. A dull yellow light illuminated the room. A dark walnut bed stood against one wall, covered in a neat, solid gray comforter and white pillows.

Riley checked beneath the bed and in the closet, searching for any sign of Toby or of a hidden door. The closet contained exactly five hangers with jeans on two, two button-down white shirts and a winter coat zipped from hem to neck.

Abandoning the room, Riley hurried to the next room where a white iron bed was pushed against the wall and covered in a blue-and-white quilt, trimmed in red. Pillows were stacked neatly against the headboard, and a small lamp stood on a nightstand beside the bed. Riley checked in the closet, starting to get worried they wouldn't find anything and tired of playing games with Pruett, when all she wanted was her brother.

The closet was empty, except for a box fan. When she bent to look beneath the bed, a small swath of fabric caught her eye near the wall by the headboard. She reached beneath the box spring and snagged a garment and pulled it out into the open. Her heart sank into the pit of her belly and then rose to choke the air out of her throat. She held a small hoodie in her fist, her hand shaking as she stared at the dinosaur on the front left side.

She turned with the garment in her hand, her gaze shooting to Pruett. "Where did you get this?" she demanded.

Pruett's eyes widened, and he dived for the front living area.

Mack was faster, catching the man by the back of his collar before he could get through the front door. Holding him easily by his shirt, Mack walked Pruett back to stand in front of Riley. "Answer her," he commanded.

Pruett's face paled. "I don't know."

"Wrong answer," Riley said. "Try again."

"It must have been there since I bought the house," the engineer said.

Riley shook her head and glared at the man. "Where's Toby?" She took a step toward Pruett and got in his face. Her lips peeled back in a vicious sneer. "Where's my brother?"

Pruett held up his hands "I don't know what you're talking about. I didn't even know you had a brother."

Riley shoved the jacket into the man's face. "Don't lie to me. This is Toby's jacket. Where is he?" Her hand and her voice shook with her rage.

Mack grabbed Pruett's arm and yanked it up behind his back, pushing it high between his shoulder blades. "Are you going to tell us where the boy is, or am I going to have to hurt you?"

Riley wanted to be the one to inflict pain on her coworker. "Just tell us where he is and we'll leave you alone."

Pruett's face screwed up in pain. "Ow, ow. You're going to break my arm." He danced up on his toes, trying to relieve the pressure on his arm.

"That's not all I'm going to break." Mack pushed the arm up higher.

"Okay. Okay. I'll tell you what I know," the man cried.

Mack backed off on the pressure but didn't release the wrist he held behind Pruett's back.

Riley crossed her arms over her chest, her heart pounding, her attention on the man standing in front of her. Finally, she'd find Toby.

Pruett looked at the jacket and glared. "Damned kid did nothing but cry."

Riley reached out and slapped Pruett's face. "Bastard! He was probably frightened out of his mind. Where is my brother?"

"I gave him to that woman."

"What woman?" By this time, Riley was so frustrated she could have shaken Pruett until his teeth rattled. "Where is she?"

"At her home in the Arlington slums with her own brats. I should never have gotten involved in this. She said it would be easy money. All I had to do was take the kid. I didn't know I'd be babysitting the brat."

Grinding her back teeth, Riley fought to keep from

pounding her fist into Pruett's face. "What woman? Does she have a name?"

"Bridgett, the night cleaning woman."

Riley's head jerked up. "Bridgett? She had you take Toby?"

"She paid the loan shark to get him off my back. In return, all I had to do was get the kid and deliver him to her. She didn't tell me I'd have to hold him overnight. I don't even like kids."

"Where does Bridgett live?" Riley asked, her tone tight, her fists tighter.

He rattled off the address and jerked his head toward Mack. "Now call off your Neanderthal."

"I ought to let him break every bone in your body for kidnapping a little boy. You had no right to take him."

"Good grief." Pruett sneered. "It's not like I hurt him or anything. I slipped through his window, picked him up while he was sleeping and left. It wasn't until he woke up that he started screaming."

Riley slammed her fist into Pruett's gut, her anger making her see red. "I hope you rot in hell." She strode past Mack and Pruett, rubbing her bruised knuckles. "Come on, Mack."

"What do you want me to do with him?" he asked.

"Bring him. We can't have him warning Bridgett."

"We can drop him off with one of the guys," Mack suggested.

"Yeah," Riley agreed. "And once we find Toby, we'll file charges and have him hauled off to jail."

"She swore she wouldn't hurt the boy," Pruett said. "I wouldn't have taken him otherwise."

"Shut up," Riley said without looking back at the man. "There's no excuse for stealing a child from his home. None."

"Why did she want him?" Mack asked.

"She said she was worried, and she was going to take him to a better place to live. I needed the money—she offered to pay off my debt. How was I to know he was related to Ms. Lansing?"

Riley didn't slow as she pushed through the front door and out onto the porch. She couldn't believe the man could be so callous about abducting a little boy. "It doesn't matter who he was related to. You had no right to take him." She dropped down off the porch and turned to Mack. "I'll get the car."

He nodded. "The keys are in the ignition."

Riley jogged away, taking the road instead of cutting through the woods. Her heart hurt for Toby. The child had to be so confused and scared. She ran all the way back to her car, dived into the driver's seat and pulled up to the house.

"Pruett and I will ride in the back seat, if you don't mind driving," Mack said. "I called Declan. He's sending Gus to meet us at an exit close to where we're going. He'll take care of Pruett until we can find Toby." Mack shoved Pruett into the back seat and slipped in beside him. "Make any stupid moves, and I'll make sure you regret it."

Pruett shook his head, rubbing his arm. "I'm done with all this. Find the kid so I can get on with my life."

"Declan's getting quite the collection going," Riley muttered. "Does he have sufficient staff?" She met Mack's gaze in the mirror.

Mack's jaw tightened. "He'll have to."

Riley pulled away from the house, bumping along the gravel to the main road. As soon the tires hit pavement, she laid her foot to the accelerator and raced back to Arlington.

Within thirty minutes, she'd dropped Pruett with Gus, Mack had moved up to the passenger seat, and they'd driven to within a couple blocks of Bridgett's house. As before, they parked two blocks away and walked the rest of the way to the address.

The building was a small cottage on a street full of similar small houses with peeling paint, sagging eaves and broken bicycles scattered across the small yards. Its windows had been blacked out, and no movement could be detected from within.

Riley and Mack circled the house, searching for any sign of occupancy. Finally, Riley shrugged, walked up to the front door and knocked.

A child's cry sounded from inside.

Riley gripped the door handle, twisted the knob and pushed as hard as she could. The door was locked. She pulled her file from her back pocket and fit it in the keyhole. Her hands shaking, she worked to unlock the door, not knowing whether the child who'd cried had been Toby or one of the janitor's. It didn't matter. If there was even a small chance it was Toby, she had to get to him before anyone hurt him.

The lock clicked and the knob turned.

"Stay low." Mack pushed past her, entering the residence, his handgun drawn.

Riley ducked down, hurried through the door and hugged the shadows. The lights had been turned off, but a dull glow came from a night-light close to the floor.

They entered a living area strewn with ragged blankets on the couches, battered toys littering the floor and dirty dishes lying on boxes used as end tables.

Nothing moved, and there was no sign of the people who'd created the mess.

Mack eased down a hallway, passing the entrance to a small, dirty kitchen with sippy cups, plastic plates with half-eaten dinners, and dirty pans scattered across the counter, as if someone had interrupted a family's meal.

A door clicked shut in another room in the small house. The sound of a sob came from down the hallway.

Riley started in that direction, but Mack quickly passed her and reach the next doorway before she could.

Mack eased open the door to a small bedroom.

A gasp and a whimper made Riley peek over Mack's shoulder.

Crowded in the corner, huddled close to the floor,

were the janitorial aide, Bridgett, three small children and Toby.

"Toby!" Riley cried out, and pushed past Mack.

Her brother glanced up at her, his eyes wide, dark circles smudged beneath them. "Riley?" Tears slipped down his cheeks as he staggered to his feet and raced into her arms.

Riley scooped him up and hugged him close to her chest.

Mack stood over her, his gun pointed at the woman still huddled on the floor with the three small children.

"Please, don't hurt us," she said, tears welling in her eyes. "I didn't want to do it. But they made me." Her bottom lip trembled and her body shook with a silent sob.

"Do what? And who made you do it?" Mack asked.

"A woman and two men." Bridgett clutched her children closer. "They said they'd turn me in for stealing supplies from Quest."

"Why didn't you tell someone?" Mack asked. "Surely they would've understood."

"I was afraid. I didn't want to go to jail. Even if I didn't go to jail, they'd take my children away. My babies would have no one." She buried her face in the dark hair of a pretty toddler who wore pink pajamas and had a smear of cheese across her cheek. "They would split my children up and send them to foster homes. My children would not know their siblings. I wouldn't be there to protect them."

Riley held Toby, listening to Bridgett's story. She

didn't care. She had her brother in her embrace, and that was all that mattered.

Toby's little arms wrapped around her neck in a stranglehold. After a long, hard hug, Riley pushed him to arm's length and studied him from head to toe. She brushed a lock of his hair away from his forehead and gave him a watery smile. "Are you okay?"

He nodded and flung his arms around her neck again, holding tightly as if he would never let go.

Riley laughed, the sound catching on a sob. When she turned to look up at Mack, a shadow fell over the doorway. Her heart leaped into her throat. As she opened her mouth to scream, a hand swung out with a dark stick and hit Mack in the back of the head.

Mack staggered and dropped to his knees.

A large man in dark clothing and a dark ski mask stepped through the door and hit Mack in the head again.

Riley pushed Toby behind her and jumped to her feet. Before the man with a stick could hit Mack again, she kicked the man's wrist, knocking the stick loose, sending it flying across the room.

As she cocked her leg to kick again, another figure entered the room also wearing dark clothes and a ski mask.

This man caught her around the waist and clamped a meaty hand over her mouth. She fought, elbowing him in the gut and stomping his instep, but the hand over her mouth also held a cloth with sweet-smelling perfume.

Within seconds, the fight leached out of Riley. Her

muscles refused to cooperate, and she went limp in the man's arms. Darkness consumed her. Her last sight was of Mack, lying motionless against the floor.

Chapter Thirteen

Mack fought the darkness, pushing through a gray haze to get to Riley. Every time he thought he'd make it, he slipped back into the abyss. Someone threatened Riley. She was in trouble. He couldn't just lie there and let her be taken or harmed.

Again, he pushed through the thick gray cloud and blinked open his eyes. Gloom still surrounded him.

The murmur of voices let him know the dimness wasn't from unconsciousness, but the lack of light in the room where he lay with his face on a hard surface.

"Mama, is the man dead?" a child's voice asked.

"I don't know," a woman's voice responded.

Then a soft hand brushed across his brow and reached down to touch the base of his throat. "He's still alive," she said. "Get my cell phone."

The patter of bare little feet sounded on the floor, passing by Mack's head. He could see the shadow of a very small child inching past him to the open doorway.

Mack shifted his hands beneath himself and pushed his body up to a sitting position. His vision blurred, and he nearly threw up.

"Mister, you should lie down until I can call an ambulance. You could have a brain or spine injury. Movement could make it worse."

He turned his head to see the woman named Bridgett kneeling beside him. The movement made his head swim and his vision fade. Forcing himself to stay awake and alert, he moved his head more slowly, taking in the room, the bed, two very small children and the sound of another moving about the house.

"Where's Riley?" he asked, his voice gravelly, his tongue feeling like he'd swallowed a wad of cotton. He frowned. "And Toby. Where's the boy?"

Bridgett's forehead wrinkled and her eyes filled. "They took Miss Lansing and the boy."

"Where?"

"I don't know." She wrung her hands.

"Why didn't you try to stop them?" As soon as he said the words, he knew they were stupid and spoken in anger. Not anger at Bridgett, but at himself for not anticipating the attack or hearing their approach.

"They told me if I interfered, they'd kill me." Bridgett held open her arms as the oldest of her daughters ran back into the room carrying a cell phone.

Bridgett wrapped the child in the curve of one arm while she took the cell phone in the other hand. "I'm calling for an ambulance and the police."

"Don't do it for me. I'll be gone before they get here." He bent forward, dragged his feet beneath himself and stood. As soon as he was upright, he swayed and staggered a few steps. He braced his hand against the wall and waited for the dizziness to pass.

"Sir, you should sit until the EMTs arrive," Bridgett said. "You could have a concussion."

"I can't sit. The more time that passes, the farther away they will get with Riley and Toby." He pulled his own cell phone out of his pocket and hit the number for Declan.

Declan answered after the first ring. "Mack, where are you?"

Mack touched the back of his head and winced. "I'm at the house of the woman who performs janitorial services at Quest. She had Riley's brother. We were attacked, and now they have Riley and Toby. Get Jonah on that GPS tracker and find Riley. Did Pruett have anything else to say? Was his only contact Bridgett with the cleaning service?"

"He confessed to making the call to Riley so that she could hear her brother's voice. But he swears he only ever had contact with Bridgett."

"And do you believe him?" Mack asked.

"He sounded legit." Declan chuckled. "And Gus might have scared him a little."

Mack's lips curled slightly as he imagined Gus getting in the overwrought engineer's face. Then his jaw tightened. "We need the names of the people who forced Bridgett and Pruett to do what they did. More than that, I need directions to where they've taken Riley and the kid."

"Working on that," Declan said. "Jonah's on it. As soon as he's got her in his sights, we'll feed you the information. He's also been busy going through all the people Riley has had immediate contact with. We're not getting much of anything."

"What about the nanny?" Mack asked.

"We searched on her name and traced her back to where she lived next door to Riley's home when she was growing up. Margaret Weems moved in at the same time as the Lansings. We didn't find any other information on her previous residence. It was a dead end."

Too many dead ends.

"I'm heading for the car. As soon as you get a bead on Riley, call." He ended the call and glanced at Bridgett. "Are you going to be all right?"

She gathered her children around her and nodded. "I didn't want to do it, but I'm going to my mother's house in Raleigh tonight. I don't feel safe here."

"Good. In the meantime, lock your doors."

Bridgett shook her head. "That didn't do much good for me. You were able to get in."

"True. Take what you need and leave as soon as possible." He headed for the door.

Bridgett reached out and touched his arm. "Are you going to tell the management at Quest I took some of their supplies?"

"I'm not," he said.

Bridgett drew in a deep breath. "I'll purchase the toilet paper I took and return it. I can't afford to lose my job over three rolls of toilet paper. I just couldn't afford to buy any, what with the cost of child care taking most of my paycheck."

Mack felt for the woman but couldn't afford to stick

around, not with Riley in danger. He dug in his pocket and pulled out a business card and a wad of cash. He pressed them into her hand. "Take the money, get the kids to a hotel room and call this number in a couple days. Mrs. Halverson might be able to help you."

Bridgett pushed the money back at him. "I can't take your money. I shouldn't have taken the supplies. I'm responsible for my actions and my children. I'll do what's right."

Mack curled her fingers around the money and card. "We all need a little help sometimes. Keep it."

He didn't give her the opportunity to hand it back a second time. Mack left her house and ran the two blocks to Riley's vehicle. Once he was inside and had switched on the engine, his cell phone rang.

"We have her on the tracking program," Declan said. "You're on speaker with Jonah."

"Give me the directions," Mack said as he whipped the car out onto the road.

"Head into downtown DC."

WATER SPLASHED ONTO her face brought Riley to consciousness. She snorted some up her nose and coughed. When she tried to raise her hands to push the wet hair out of her face, she couldn't move her arms.

She looked down at where her wrists were ducttaped to the arms of a utilitarian metal office chair. For a moment, her brain couldn't grasp what was happening. Her gaze shot around the room, taking in the concrete block walls of what appeared to be a basement lit by a single dull yellow light hanging by a cord from the ceiling.

Riley's pulse skittered in her veins, and her gut knotted. She pulled at the tape binding her wrists to the chair.

"You didn't think you could lie to us and get away with it, did you?" a deep male voice said from behind her.

A man circled her. He wore dark pants, a dark shirt and a fedora pulled low over the bridge of his nose. The minimal lighting cast a deep shadow over his face.

Riley couldn't tell who he was, nor did she recognize his voice. She could sense the danger in the way he walked and tapped a metal rod against the palm of his hand.

He hit a switch on the metal rod and touched it to her bare skin.

A jolt of electricity blasted through her.

Riley screamed, the pain so blinding it nearly made her pass out. She dragged in a breath, fighting to remain calm. "Where is my brother?"

The man tapped the wand against his palm again. "You will never see your brother again."

"Like hell I won't." Riley jerked against her bindings. She planted her feet against the floor and tried to rise, chair and all.

A strong hand clamped down on her shoulder, forcing her to see sit down.

"Charlotte Halverson lives." The man paced in front of her. "Your job was to kill her. Because you did not fulfill your duties, your brother is lost to you forever."

Riley sat silently, anger burning deep inside. She refused to believe she would never see Toby again. If it were the last thing she ever did, she'd find her brother and kill the people who stole him from her.

"Do you know what we do with agents who are not loyal to the mother country?" He smiled, his lips parting in a feral grin. "Some would think that we would kill the agent." The man snorted. "That would be too easy. We do not waste years of training without first attempting to re-assimilate the protégé back into the fold."

He paced several steps in front of her, turned and paced back the way he had come, all the while tapping the rod against his palm.

Riley tried to memorize the contours of the man's face and commit them to her memory for when she would track him down and kill him. But after a few minutes of watching him pace, she shifted to the rod in his hand, knowing what pain it could inflict.

The man in black stopped in front of her and barked out, "Who do you work for?"

Riley bit down hard on her tongue to keep from answering.

The wand shot out and bit into her arm, sending a shock of electricity through her body.

Riley clamped her jaw tight, refusing to even whimper, though the pain was excruciating.

His eyes narrowing, the man in the fedora leaned closer, his fetid breath making Riley gag. "You will learn the proper response to that question." He raised the wand again.

Riley dug her feet into the concrete floor, jerked forward and rammed her head into the man's chest, knocking him backward several feet.

The fedora remained in place even though the man staggered, tripped and fell, landing hard on his backside.

Again, a hand clamped on her shoulder, shoving her back in her seat and the chair legs back to the floor.

She landed with a jolt that rattled her teeth.

Once the man on the floor rose, he hit her again with the electric prod.

Electricity shot through her entire body.

He held the prod against her arm so long the pain caused her system to shut down. Darkness became her friend.

MINUTES, MAYBE HOURS later, Riley awoke to someone tugging at the tape on her wrists.

When she opened her eyes, Riley stared into the eyes of Margaret Weems, her nanny.

"You won't have much time," the woman said.

"Margaret?" Riley blinked and stared around the room. "Why…how did you find me?"

"I can't explain now," she said. "Toby is in a room down the hall. You have to leave now, before they come back."

"Before who comes back?" Riley shook her head. Then the images she'd thought were just a nightmare came back to her. "You need to get out of here. Go," she insisted. "If they catch you, they'll torture you."

"You think I don't know that?" She cut away at the

tape on Riley's right wrist, freeing her hand from the chair. Then she rounded to the other side and slipped the blade of a knife beneath the other band of duct tape and ripped through it as well.

Riley rose from the chair and peeled the rest of the tape from her wrists, taking a layer of skin with it.

"You have to hurry," Margaret urged. "They will be back soon."

"I'm not leaving without you." Riley hooked the woman's arm and half dragged her toward the door.

Margaret set her feet into the concrete and yanked her arm free of Riley's hold. "Go without me. I will only slow down you and Toby."

"But they will kill you."

"My job here is done." Margaret stepped backward. "It is time for you to make your own decisions about who you are and what you believe in."

Riley shook her head, her eyes narrowing. "What do you mean?"

"I was there when you were born. I worked alongside your parents when you got your training." She lifted her chin. "I knew what they had planned for you, yet I still didn't stop it from happening. It was my job to protect you and your brother until such a time when they would call you to duty."

"What are you talking about?" Riley stared at the woman as if for the first time. She'd known Margaret all her life. The woman was like the grandmother she never had. Riley trusted her with her life, and more importantly, Toby's life.

Margaret's gaze shot toward the door. "You need to leave now."

"You need to come with me," Riley said.

"No," she said, "my job is done. They will hunt me down for releasing you." She shook her head, the lines around her eyes and mouth seeming so much deeper. "I don't have the strength to run."

Riley's chest squeezed tightly. "I don't know what you've done, or what role you played in kidnapping my brother. But I won't let them hurt you."

Margaret held up her hand with a small pill pinched between her fingers. "They won't hurt me," she said with a smile, and slipped the pill beneath her tongue.

Riley leaped toward the woman, but she was too late.

Margaret dropped to her knees and slumped to the floor. She coughed twice, and foam bubbled from her mouth.

"Holy hell, Margaret." Riley knelt beside her. "Spit it out."

Margaret shook her head and raised her hand. "Take my ring."

"No, Margaret, you wear it." Riley held the woman's hand and stared down into her eyes.

Margaret coughed again. "Take the ring. It has meaning. Find it, and you will know what to do." Her last words faded into silence, and all tension left her body.

Riley pressed her fingers to the base of Margaret's throat, searching for a pulse. There was none. Her nanny, and her old friend, was dead.

As she released Margaret's hand, she felt the cool metal of the ring Margaret had wanted her to take. She recognized it as one Margaret had always worn on her right hand. It was made of yellow gold, white gold and rose gold bands twisted together. The ring had seemed very important to Margaret. What she meant about finding the meaning of the ring made no sense to Riley. She didn't have time to work through the riddle. Instead, she slipped it from Margaret's finger and pushed it into the pocket of her jeans.

The sound of footsteps alerted her to people moving in the hallway outside the door.

Riley dived behind the door as it opened.

A large man dressed in black, wearing a black ski mask, stepped into the room and nearly tripped over Margaret's body. As he bent toward the woman on the floor, Riley balled both fists together and hit the man in the side of the head as hard as she could.

The big man fell over on his side.

Before he could rise, Riley kicked him in the face, breaking his nose.

The man yelled, his eyes teared, and he grabbed his face and hunched over.

Riley dived past him into the hallway. She didn't know which door hid Toby, but she vowed to find him and free him before these monsters tortured him as well.

Chapter Fourteen

"You should be within a block of the building where she's being held," Jonah's voice said from the speaker on Mack's cell phone.

"Mack?" a female voice came across. "This is Grace."

He recognized Grace's voice. "Where's Declan?" Mack asked.

"He's on his way," Grace said. "He has Gus, Mustang and Snow with him."

"What's his ETA?" Mack asked as he pulled Riley's car over to the side of the road.

"They should be right behind you," Jonah answered. "I have them up on the GPS as well." Jonah gave him the address of the building in which he'd find Riley.

Committing the name and numbers to memory, Mack turned to see headlights heading his way. His grabbed his cell phone, switched it to silent and waited for the other members of his team to climb out of Declan's truck.

Declan hurried toward him, carrying a handgun in one hand and a heavy flashlight in the other.

"Who's guarding Charlie?" Mack asked.

"Seems since the cat was out of the bag, she'd be safer at her own house," Declan said. "Cole and Mustang sneaked her out of the hospital on a gurney and into the back of a laundry truck. They got her back to her house and its state-of-the-art security system. Cole and Jonah are with her. We thought you might need a little help here."

Mack nodded. "I'm guessing there were at least two guys who jumped us. There might be more where we're heading." His fists clenched. "Those two guys should never have surprised me like that."

"Don't beat yourself up," Declan said. "The main focus now is finding Riley and getting her and her brother back."

"Agreed. Let's do this." Mack took the lead, determined to find Riley and end the threat to her and her brother.

Declan, Mustang, Snow and Gus fell in behind him. Their training as Force Recon marines kicked in and they moved from shadow to shadow, closing in on what appeared to be an abandoned building that might have been a small factory or machine shop.

When they came within spitting distance, Mack held up his fist.

The team stopped in place. Declan moved up in line with Mack.

"See the broken window near the right corner of the rear of the building?" Mack pointed. The window was high enough off the ground that they wouldn't be able to just look inside.

Declan nodded. "I'll give you a boost so you can make a quick assessment."

Mustang and Gus split off and circled to the other side of the building. Snow provided cover should someone discover Mack and Declan while they were exposed, attempting to get a look inside.

Mack checked left and then right before he ran for the building. Declan ran with him. As soon as they reached the wall below the broken window, Declan bent over. Mack stepped up on his back and pulled himself up to the window.

Inside the structure was old machinery covered in dust and dirt. The place looked like it hadn't been occupied for at least ten, maybe fifteen years. What was unusual was that in a far corner there was a dull light over a doorway. Mack would have assumed all electricity had long since been shut off.

Mack dropped back to the ground.

"See anyone?" Declan asked.

"No."

Moments later, Gus and Mustang returned from their reconnaissance of the rest of the outside of the building.

"There are three entrances," Mustang said. "One is on the front of the building. It's a huge double door that has been boarded up. There's a side door that was probably used for employee entrance and a loading dock at the rear."

"Which entrance do you suggest?" Mack asked.

"The rear dock," Gus reported.

"Did you see any guards posted?"

Gus shook his head. "Not one."

"That doesn't make me feel confident," Mack said. "They could be lying in wait in the shadows. We'll have to be careful breaching the building."

The men set off, following the shadowy exterior of the neighboring building until they reached the back corner of the old manufacturing business.

Then, one by one, they ran across to the loading dock.

Mack found a door near the truck loading area. The door wasn't locked, nor was it dusty like the rest of the interior appeared. He twisted the knob slowly and eased the door open.

Inside and to the left was a chair with a guard seated in it, his head tipped back, resting against the wall. The man was half asleep, if not completely out. And he had a military-grade rifle lying across his lap.

Mack eased up to him, grabbed the rifle and hit him in the head with the butt of his own weapon.

The man slumped over and fell to the floor.

Declan pulled zip ties out of his back pocket, then secured the guard's wrists and ankles and slapped a piece of duct tape over his mouth.

"Where'd you get the tape?" Mack asked.

Declan chuckled softly. "I always bring a little bit in my pocket. It can fix anything."

They checked the immediate vicinity for more guards but didn't find any. Declan waved the other two men into the building and they spread out, searching the main floor for offices or rooms in which they might have hidden Riley and Toby.

They came up empty as they worked their way past

large rusting machinery to the other end of the building and the door with the light glowing over it.

Mack reached the door first and stepped through, holding his pistol in front of him. The door was a stairwell leading downward into a basement. The dirty yellow light was barely bright enough to illuminate the stairs. Mack tiptoed downward into the bowels of the building. Near the bottom of the staircase were two guards standing on either side of a broad hallway.

They didn't see Mack coming because they were looking down the hallway.

Footsteps sounded on the filthy concrete floors.

Mack's attention turned to what the two men were staring at.

A figure ran into one of the rooms off the hallway.

The men spoke to each other in Russian. One of them left his post and ran after the figure.

Mack slipped up behind the other man and grabbed him around the throat in a headlock. He squeezed hard, cutting off the man's air. He held him tightly in a stranglehold.

The man was large but unable to break free of Mack's grip. Soon, he went limp from lack of oxygen. Once again, Declan pulled out the zip ties and secured the man's wrists and ankles. Then he pressed duct tape over his mouth and dragged him into an empty room to the man's left. Already, the guy had regained consciousness and was fighting mad, making grunting noises in an attempt to capture the attention of other members of his group in the building.

Mack didn't wait for Declan and the others. He figured they didn't have much time before others discovered they were there. They had to find Riley and Toby soon.

The sound of a struggle drew Mack's attention. The figure that had disappeared into the room down the hallway had been smaller, not bulky like the guards. The thought that it might be Riley had him running down the hallway.

Another door burst open in front of him and three burly men dressed in black barreled through. A shout went out from the lead man.

Mack didn't have time to do more than react. He ducked low and plowed into the first guy, hitting him square in the gut, sending him flying backward into one of the others. The two men fell in a heap on the floor and scrambled to untangle themselves.

The third man stepped aside, letting his comrades crash without taking him down with them. He threw a meaty fist toward Mack.

Mack twisted sideways.

The fist missed his face and rammed into his shoulder, jerking him around.

Mack staggered backward, righted himself and went after the man.

A gun appeared in the man's hand.

Adrenaline firing through his veins, Mack didn't slow. He sent a side kick into his wrist. The gun went off before it flew from the man's hand and hit the floor, skittering out of reach.

The bullet hit the wall beside Mack.

He didn't care. As long as he could keep moving, he would.

Sounds of struggles and a muffled scream came from the doorway down the hall. Riley needed him. He was certain. One man in the way wouldn't keep Mack from reaching her.

He swung his fist, catching the man in the chin, sending him slamming back against the wall behind him.

Gunfire went off behind him, but Mack couldn't shift his attention from the man in front of him. Cocking his leg, he shot a powerful kick into the man's thigh.

The distinct sound of a bone snapping echoed off the concrete block walls. Mack's opponent dropped to the floor.

Declan was there with zip ties to keep the man immobile.

Together they secured the other two men and all their weapons.

With the acrid scent of gunpowder still stinging Mack's nostrils, he jogged toward the doorway where the guard had followed the slim figure inside.

Grunts and thumps sounded from within.

"Leave my brother alone," Riley's voice sounded.

His heart racing, Mack pushed through the door to find Riley in the clutches of one man, while another held Toby around the waist like a quarterback carrying a football.

The boy kicked and fought as hard as his little body could. "Let go of my sister!" he yelled.

Mack started for Riley but stopped short when he noticed the gun in her captor's hand. The gun was pressed to Riley's temple.

"Don't worry about me," Riley said. "Help Toby."

"Move and I put a bullet through her head," said her captor, a large man with shaggy black hair and a rugged, pockmarked face. "And when she's dead, I'll kill the kid."

Riley stiffened, her fade hardening into a mask. She looked to Mack. Her eyes narrowed slightly and she gave the briefest of nods. Then she jabbed her elbow into the man's ribs and ducked out of his grip. The gun went off.

Mack's heart stopped for a moment.

But the bullet hit the wall instead of Riley's head. She broke free of her captor's grip, rounded behind him and kicked at the back of his legs. His knees buckled and he fell to the floor. Riley grabbed his wrist, the one holding the gun, and twisted it up behind his back. He held on as long as he could, until the gun fell from his grip and clattered to the floor.

A shout rose from the man holding Toby, and he dropped the boy to the floor. He shook his hand, where a bright red bite mark appeared.

Toby scrambled on all fours toward Mack.

The man who'd been holding him dived toward the kid, snagged his ankle and yanked him back.

Mack launched himself across the room and drove his fist into the man's face.

The thug released his hold on Toby and brought his fists up to defend himself against Mack's furious onslaught.

As he fought Toby's captor, he could see Riley in his peripheral vision. She'd jumped on the back of the man who'd threatened to kill her and her brother and held his arm tightly up between his shoulder blades.

Declan pushed through the door, scooped the boy up into his arms and handed him off to Mustang, who'd arrived behind him.

Mack threw a punch to his guy's gut.

The man doubled over as Mack brought up his knee, jamming it into his face. Then he grabbed the man's collar at the back of his neck and sent him flying behind Mack into Declan.

Declan sent the man facedown on the floor and planted a knee in his back.

Mack swung around, kicked the gun out of Riley's prisoner's reach and smiled down at her. "You make it hard for a man to save you."

She nodded. "I don't need a man to save me, but it's nice to know you could."

Declan cinched his guy's wrists with zip ties and handed a couple extras to Mack. He and Riley secured her prisoner and left him lying on the floor.

Mack helped Riley to her feet and into his arms.

Gus and Snow appeared in the doorway.

"The rest of the building is clear," Gus said.

"We found a body in another room. An older woman. No sign of struggle, but possibly poisoned. She had foam in her mouth."

Riley laid her head against Mack's chest. "The woman was Margaret Weems. My nanny."

"Your nanny?" Declan asked, his brow furrowed.

Riley nodded. "She was my handler." She shook her head. "I never knew. I thought she was the kind older woman who always lived next door to my parents. She was my surrogate grandmother. And when my parents died in that car wreck, it was natural for me to hire her as Toby's nanny."

Mack's chest tightened at the sorrow in Riley's face. "Who poisoned her?"

"She did it herself." Riley twisted a ring on her finger that hadn't been there before. "She helped me to escape. I think she was tired and wanted to go out on her own terms." She lifted her chin toward the men tied up on the floor. "They would have killed her anyway."

Mack brushed a strand of her hair back behind her ear. "Are you okay? Did they hurt you?"

Riley rubbed her hand over her arm. "I'm okay."

He could tell she wasn't, but he refused to argue. Not when they might still be in danger. "Let's call the police and get them to clean up this mess."

"Better yet, let's call the FBI," Riley said.

"Are you sure?" Mack asked. "We could get you as far away from this as possible before we let them in on what's going on."

Riley shook her head. "No. I'm ready to face them. I've lived with this hanging over my head for so long, I need to deal with it, no matter the consequences."

Mustang entered the room, carrying Toby.

Riley smiled at the child and held open her arms. "Toby, sweetie. Everything is going to be all right."

The boy fell into her arms and buried his face against her neck. "I was scared."

"I know. So was I. But you were so brave." She kissed the top of his head. "Would you like to come live with me in the city?"

He lifted his head and stared into her face. "Yes, please." Toby kissed her cheek and wrapped his arms around her neck.

Mack's heart swelled at the love between the brother and sister. Riley would do anything for the kid. Even lay down her life for him.

She looked at him over Toby's head.

Mack held his arms open.

Riley stepped into them, still holding Toby. Mack wrapped them in his embrace and held them, praying he could do this for a lot longer. Maybe the rest of his life.

Declan stepped out of the building to get good cell phone reception to place a call to Charlie, who made the call to her contact in the FBI. Within twenty minutes, several unmarked vehicles arrived to process the scene in the abandoned factory.

Mack waited in fear of the FBI taking Riley prisoner and escorting her to an undisclosed location where they would interrogate her.

But they didn't. They thanked her for being an upstanding American citizen and doing the right thing, despite the odds stacked against her. She'd still have to answer questions, but she wasn't going to jail or a detention facility to be interrogated.

Two hours after the incident, Mack sat with Riley on a concrete step outside the old factory, with Toby asleep in his lap.

"What's going to happen from here?" he asked.

Riley shrugged. "I don't even know whether or not I'll be allowed to work at Quest anymore."

"Seems to me you're one of the most patriotic people in this country, despite what your parents and handler had in mind for you."

"You see it that way, but I doubt Quest will. They will learn that I was a trained Russian spy. They won't look beyond those words."

"My mother always told me, 'Don't borrow trouble.'" He slipped an arm around her shoulders. "You worked with the FBI to find out who was stealing secrets from Quest. Surely Quest will take that into account and let you stay on."

"I hope so. I'm Toby's only support. I need my job." She leaned into the curve of his arm. "What's going to happen to us? Now that I have Toby back, you'll move on to another assignment for Charlie."

"I'd like to see you still." Mack glanced down at the sleeping boy on his lap. "If you and Toby will have me around."

Riley wrapped her arm around Mack's waist. "I'd be sad if you didn't come around. I've been so busy being a provider and part-time parent to Toby, I forgot what it was like to be just me."

"I'd love to have the chance to learn who you are

and be a part of Toby's life. I think my brother would have liked him. He's a fighter, this kid."

"Thank you for not giving up on us," Riley said. She leaned up in his arms and brushed her lips across his. "I think I could get used to having you around."

Mack's heart warmed. Surrounded by Riley and Toby, he'd never felt more complete. Since his own brother's death, he'd gone through life trying to prove to himself and the memory of Aiden that he was worthy of the life he'd been granted and that had been stolen from a little boy.

He didn't have to chase after that proof anymore. But he vowed to be a part of Riley's and Toby's lives. And he would do his best to make sure they had the long, healthy lives they deserved.

Epilogue

Riley sat on the arm of the chair beside Mack in Charlie's living room. The team of Force Recon marines sat in a circle of sofas and chairs with Charlie at the head of the group.

Toby was in the kitchen with Charlie's chef, making cookies for all of them, happily chattering away to a master chef like he was his best buddy.

Riley rested her hand on Mack's shoulder. A week had passed since Margaret's death and the subsequent arrests of Steve Pruett, Tracy Gibson and the six men who'd been involved in Riley and Toby's abduction.

"I've worked with my contact in the FBI to clear Riley of all suspicion."

"Did you mention she'd been sent to assassinate you?"

"I did," Charlie said. "I also told them she didn't go through with it and never would. Riley is a true-blue American, despite her training as a Russian sleeper spy."

"And they bought it?" Riley asked.

Charlie nodded. "My dear husband wasn't the only

one who had tight connections with the FBI. I have my own contacts, and they assured me you would have no trouble obtaining clearances and continuing your work in the Special Projects division at Quest."

Riley smiled. "Thank you, Mrs. Halverson. I was worried about how I'd provide for myself and my brother if I lost my job."

"Rest assured," Charlie said, "I also had a talk with one of the members of the board of directors at Quest. Though Steve Pruett, Tracy Gibson and Bridgett Paulson were arrested, I understand Ms. Paulson is out on bail to be with her children."

"Who offered to bail her out?" Mack asked. "I got the impression she didn't know anyone who could afford that kind of money."

Charlie shrugged. "I don't keep up with all the ins and outs of every investigation. I'm sure someone came up with the money. The poor woman was conscripted into the service of the Russians under duress. Like most women, she would do anything to protect her children, even set out electronic surveillance devices in her place of employment and pass on the orders and the packet of money to Steve Pruett to kidnap a child. She didn't know what was in that packet until Pruett dumped the boy in her lap."

"I'm surprised they let her out, and that they didn't take her children away from her," Riley said.

"I'm betting someone of influence had a lot to do with Ms. Paulson's bail being set low. She'll probably get off on her part in the kidnapping and the bugging of your office."

Charlie sighed. "She did, however, lose her job. But I have it on good authority she has an even better position that doesn't require her to work at night. She was able to place her children in a reputable day care and she'll be home with them every night."

"Again, I can't imagine who made that happen." Declan shook his head, his lips quirking upward.

Grace stood behind where he sat, her hand on his shoulder. "Charlie, you're too kind."

Again, Charlie shrugged. "What good is money if you can't help out other people less fortunate?"

"I'm glad Bridgett and her children won't suffer because of what happened. She was merely a pawn in a larger game." Absently, Riley twisted the ring on her finger. "I'm just sorry Margaret decided she'd had enough and took her own life." She stared down at the ring on her right hand. "She left me this ring with the strangest request."

Charlie's eyes narrowed. "What ring?"

Riley slipped the ring from her finger, crossed the room and held it out to the widow. "Her last wish was for me to look for the meaning of this ring and I'd know what to do." She shook her head. "I did a Google search on the ring and found the symbol to be a pattern called a trinity knot. The inscription inside the ring is in Russian."

"Can you read it?" Mack asked.

Riley snorted. "My parents were Russian, but in their effort to Americanize me, they refused to speak Russian in our house. I can't even read a word of Russian." She turned to Charlie to take the ring.

The older woman's face was pale, her eyes rounded, and the hand holding the ring shook. "I've seen this before. I know this ring."

Riley frowned. "Did you know Margaret?"

Charlie shook her head. "No. But I knew my husband. Or at least I thought I did." She took the ring and left the room, hurrying to another part of the house.

Riley frowned, her gaze following the widow until she disappeared down a hallway leading toward the master bedroom.

Mack stood and slipped an arm around her waist. "What do you make of her response?"

"I don't know what to make of it."

"Do you suppose Mr. Halverson knew Margaret?" Riley's roommate, Grace, asked.

Riley shrugged. "Apparently, there's a lot I didn't know about the woman I regarded as my surrogate grandmother. I thought she was just a nice old lady. Not a Russian sleeper spy handler. I wish she hadn't taken her life. I have a million questions I would have liked to ask her." She gave her roommate a sad smile. "I considered her a member of my family. She probably knew my parents even better than I did."

"She obviously cared about you and Toby, or she wouldn't have set you free in that basement," Mack noted.

"True. Now I'll never know the true extent of the underground spy movement."

"Perhaps the ring is a key to what more can be found," Grace suggested. "One of our classmates in college studied Russian. I think she went on to be a professor at one of the colleges here in the DC area. We could see if she can translate the inscription."

Riley nodded, wondering if Charlie would return the ring to her. The woman had been gone for several minutes with no sign of returning.

"What did you find out about the men in the factory basement?" Mack asked Declan.

"Charlie's contact in the FBI ran a background check and facial recognition software on them. They were Russians here on expired visas. They traced them back to connections with the Russian spy network. They were known for some pretty heinous torture treatments against the motherland enemies."

Riley shivered, her body remembering the shock of the electric cattle prod. She was very fortunate the marines had found her sooner rather than later. Though Margaret had helped her to escape, she wasn't so sure she'd have made it out alive if Mack and his team hadn't arrived when they did.

She leaned into the strength of his body, thankful he'd been Charlie's bodyguard at that gala. Riley truly believed fate had brought them together. And if at all possible, she hoped they could stay together for a very long time, getting to know each other better. Her body warmed at the thought of getting to know Mack's body better, knowing it would be a challenge with Toby living with her. But she was up for the challenge and couldn't imagine a life without her little brother.

Mack had been to her apartment several times since the incident in the old factory basement. Toby had taken to him immediately. Apparently, the boy had needed a strong male role model in his life.

Riley couldn't think of anyone who better fit that mold.

Moments later, Charlie reappeared with another ring. This one was bolder and broader. A more masculine version of the one Margaret had given Riley.

It had the trinity knot symbol on top and the same inscription inside, всегда и навсегда.

Jonah stepped forward. "We could enter the phrase in an online translator," he suggested.

Everyone in the living room followed him to the computer lab Mr. Halverson had constructed prior to his death.

Jonah sat at his keyboard, booted the computer and waited. When the monitor blinked to life, he quickly selected a translation application, switched the keyboard to Russian and keyed the letters of the inscription.

A second later, they had their answer.

Always and forever.

Riley shook her head. "I still don't know what it means. And I don't know what I'm supposed to do with it."

"I'll ask our classmate to research the rings and the inscription," Grace said. "Maybe she will come up with something more specific." She tapped her chin, and her brow lowered. "Come to think of it… I swear I saw something in one of the files I looked in when I was in your old boss's office at Quest. There was a file marked 'Trinity' in the cabinet in his office. I didn't think much of it then, but perhaps it has something to do with the ring, since it has the trinity knot on it."

Riley stared at her friend, her thoughts going beyond Grace's pretty face. "It's all too coincidental."

"I don't believe in coincidence," Mack said.

"I'd like to know what they all have to do with each other," Riley said. "I can visit Emily Monday morning when the university is open and I might find her in her office."

"You've had enough excitement for a lifetime. Why not let one of the others check into the rings?" Charlie suggested. "No one will be watching them or expecting them to go on the hunt for ring meanings."

Riley wanted to follow through on everything to do with the rings, Margaret's assignment and anything else tied to her connection with the Russian trinity knot rings.

"Toby needs you. If you start digging into the rings and their meaning, you might put him at risk again."

Charlie nodded. "Mack will be with you and the child until we're certain you aren't going to be taken again to be retrained and brainwashed. I'd feel better if you didn't go after the rings and their meanings."

"Me, too," Mack said.

Riley's mouth pressed into a thin line. "But it's my life. It's the reason all of this happened in the first place."

As if on cue, Toby entered the room with a tray almost as big as he was, piled high with several different kinds of cookies. He was followed by the chef, who carried another tray with a large pitcher of lemonade and glasses filled with ice.

Riley took one look at the little boy's beaming face and knew she couldn't drag him into the fray again. Toby deserved a normal life where he wasn't being kidnapped or tortured by people who would use him as a spy in their own selfish or political machinations.

"Okay," Riley said quietly. "I'll leave it up to you to assign someone else to research the rings." She handed the rings back to Charlie and bent to Toby. "What have you got here?"

"Cookies," Toby said, a smile spreading across his face as he attempted to set the tray on a coffee table, nearly dumping the cookies on the floor.

Riley grabbed the tray on one side and Mack grabbed the other, steadying it until it rested solidly on the table.

"And Chef Saulnier has lemonade for everyone." He looked up at Riley. "May I have a cookie and lemonade with the big people?"

Riley smiled down at him. "Of course you may." She handed him a napkin. "Choose the one you want."

He reached for a large chocolate chip cookie and placed it on his napkin. "These are the best." He glanced at the chef. "No offense."

"None taken," the chef said, and backed out of the room, leaving them to enjoy the lemonade and cookies.

The men waited for Grace, Riley and Charlie to make their selections before they made their own.

Charlie held her cookie in her hand, her gaze slipping across each of the marines in her living room.

Riley could almost imagine the wheels turning in the older woman's mind. Finally, Charlie's gaze landed on one of the other men. "Mustang, how's the house hunting?"

He shrugged. "I'm still looking. I have a lease on an apartment that doesn't run out for another three months, so I have plenty of time to make a decision." He gave the widow a twisted smile. "Why do you ask?"

"I'm thinking, if you're not too busy house hunting, you might like to make a visit to this Russian expert."

He nodded. "I can do that. When would you like me to do this?"

"As soon as possible." Charlie crossed the room to him and laid the two rings in his palm as if placing the weight of the world in his hands. "I get the feeling these rings might give me a clue as to who murdered my husband."

Mustang closed his fingers around the rings. "I'll get right on it."

"Let me get a picture of those." Jonah pulled out his cell phone and snapped a photo of the rings in Mustang's palm. "I'll run a photo recognition on the rings as well."

"If you don't mind," Riley said, "I think it's about time to get Toby back home. He has a busy day ahead of him. He starts a new school tomorrow and I want him to be rested."

Mustang slipped the rings into his pocket and gave Mack a bear hug, clapping a hand against his back. "Glad we wrapped up this little party without losing any of us."

"Thank you all for your efforts in keeping me, Riley and Toby alive," Charlie said. "I couldn't have done it without Declan's Defenders. The marines don't know what they're missing, but I'm glad I found you. We might yet learn what happened to make someone want to kill my husband."

"We'll do the best we can. In the meantime, I wouldn't consider you out of danger," Declan said. "A kidnapping attempt and an order to poison you aren't leaving me feeling all warm and fuzzy."

Charlie drew in a deep breath and let it out slowly. "Thank goodness I have you all to look after me and others who come along. And thank you, Declan and Grace, for agreeing to move onto the estate until we resolve these issues."

Riley frowned. "You're moving out of the apartment?"

Grace nodded. "We haven't had time to talk, but yes. Since I'll be working closely with Charlie, she thought it would be best if I lived closer. And Declan will need easy access to the computer room and Jonah if he's going to lead the others in their work with Declan's Defenders."

"I'll miss you," Riley said.

"Yeah, but it will work out better, since you have Toby living with you now. You'll need that extra bedroom for him." Grace hugged Riley. "I'll move my things over the next week. Toby needs a room all his own."

Riley helped Toby clean up his cookie crumbles

and wipe the chocolate off his face. Already, his eyes drooped, and he was ready to go home.

Mack lifted him in his arms, and the boy laid his cheek on the marine's shoulder.

Riley's heart swelled. The man would make a good father. Losing his own little brother at a young age had made him more aware of children and their needs.

Not only would he make a good father, he'd make a good husband. Not that she was thinking that far ahead. They'd only just met a week before. But she felt as if she'd known him much longer.

The man was honest, caring and protective. He'd be there for the ones he loved and give them what they needed.

Love.

Her pulse quickened as she contemplated the future. A future that included Mack and Toby.

"I can call a taxi to take us home. You don't have to drop us off," Riley offered, knowing she'd rather have Mack take them home. And when they got there, she'd ask him to come in for a drink and maybe more...

"I brought you here. I'll take you home." Mack frowned. "You're not trying to get rid of me, are you?"

She slipped her arm through the crook of his elbow. "On the contrary, I want to make sure you aren't getting tired of me and my ready-made family."

Mack patted Toby's back, a smile slipping across his face. "I kind of like this ready-made family. If you don't mind, I'd like to stick around. You know. Ask you on a date. With Toby, of course. We hardly got to know each other during all the excitement."

"I feel like I know you already." Riley leaned her cheek against his arm.

"I hope that's a good thing," he said.

"Only the best." She squeezed his arm and let go as they reached his truck and he opened the back door.

Mack settled Toby in the back seat and buckled him in. The boy's eyes never opened. He was down for the count, for the night.

Mack opened Riley's door.

She stepped into the opening without climbing up. Instead, she turned to face him.

He leaned in, closing the distance between them, and brushed his lips across hers. "I've wanted to do that all evening."

Riley wrapped her arms around his neck and stood on her toes to press her lips to his. "And I've wanted you to do that for the past four hours."

He settled his hands on her hips and pulled her close. "Does it matter that we haven't been on a first date?"

She shook her head. "Not in the least. I told you… I feel like I know you."

"You don't even know my favorite sports team or color or where I grew up."

She shook her head. "None of that matters. I know what's here." She pressed her hand to his chest. "You have a big heart, capable of a lot of love. That's all I need to know for now." She gripped his cheeks between her palms and angled his head down to hers and kissed him with all her heart and soul.

He held her against him, deepening the kiss until

his tongue slipped past her teeth to caress hers in a long, sensual glide.

When at last they came up for air, Mack pressed his forehead against hers. "Always and forever," he murmured.

She leaned back and looked up into his eyes. "Why do you say that?"

"I think I could fall in love with you…always and forever."

Her heart felt as if it would burst. "Don't you think it's too soon to say that?"

He shook his head. "I know what's in my heart now. I'm not going to change my mind. But if you need more time to come to the same conclusion, I'll give it to you. I'm in this for the long haul."

"Good, because I can't think of anyone I'd rather spend my life getting to know." Riley looked up into the man's eyes, her own reflection shining back at her. "Always and forever."

* * * * *

SMOKIES
SPECIAL AGENT

LENA DIAZ

Thank you Allison Lyons and Nalini Akolekar.
As always, thank you Connie Mann and Jan Jackson
for your friendship and support in this crazy business.

Chapter One

Frozen ground crunched behind her. Remi Jordan whirled around. The trail was empty. She whipped back the other way. Nothing except shadows met her searching gaze. The woods had gone as silent as a tomb. Even the icy wind had quit blowing, as if the entire mountain was holding its breath, waiting to see what would happen next.

Waiting to see if *she* would be next?

Remi drew a slow, deep breath, the chilly air prickling her lungs. Sound could carry for miles up here, or not at all, and seemed to bounce all over the place. Figuring out the direction it came from was nearly impossible. Someone was definitely stalking her. But figuring out where they were, and how far away, was beginning to feel like an impossibility.

Stepping to the side of the path, she listened intently and pretended to study the two-by-six white blaze painted on the bark of a spruce tree. Similar patches of paint in varying colors served as guideposts all up and down the Appalachian Trail. She'd seen dozens of them since she'd begun her daily AT hikes on the Tennessee side of the Great Smoky Mountains National Park.

She shoved both her hands into her jacket pockets. If the person following her was close enough to see her, he probably thought she looked vulnerable, oblivious to danger. But she was far from helpless. Her right hand caressed the butt of a loaded SIG Sauer 9 mm hidden in her pocket.

The gun had been a gift from her father on her eighteenth birthday, the butt of the weapon engraved with her name. He'd been critically ill for months and knew he wouldn't make it to her nineteenth. It was his fervent hope that the pistol would do what he no longer could— protect her, keep his remaining daughter safe.

Her throat tightened. If her father knew what she was doing, he'd feel hurt, betrayed. He'd berate her for taking unnecessary risks with her safety. But how could she sit and do nothing? Ten years ago she'd done nothing. Then her twin sister had disappeared and was never seen again. That one, horrible mistake haunted her every single day. Having another woman's death on her bruised and battered conscience was more than she could bear.

As if a switch had been flipped, the wind picked up again. The crisp pine-scented air was heavy with the promise of snow as it whipped the long blond strands of her hair back from her face. Evergreen branches clacked together, their needles brushing against bark with an unsettling *shuh-shuh* sound. And somewhere overhead a bird twittered, as if everything was right with the world. As if nature itself denied the evil that had once taken place here, evil that was again poised to strike, to destroy another family, unless Remi could find a way to stop it.

Could she have imagined footfalls echoing her own? Could she be wrong in thinking that someone had been trying to match his steps to hers, to disguise his pursuit? She considered the idea, then discarded it. Her faults were many, but *imagining* things wasn't one of them. There was no other reasonable explanation for the sounds she'd been hearing since starting out on this trail at sunup.

I'm close this time, Becca. So close. I can feel it.

She could almost see her stargazing, unicorn-loving twin sister rolling her eyes in reply. It was her signature trademark, especially when the two of them were together. When they were kids, it had made Remi furious. Now, she wished with all her heart that she could see her sister roll her eyes at her just one more time.

I miss you so much, Becca. So. Much.

Once again, she started down the well-worn path. It wasn't long before another sound sent a fresh rush of goose bumps across her skin. This time, she didn't stop. Instead, she scanned the woods from beneath her lashes, trying not to be too obvious as she searched the shadows surrounding her.

What had she heard? The whisper of fabric against a tree? A rattle of loose rocks across a part of the path sheltered by the tree canopy, where there wasn't much snow to reveal anyone's passage? Or was it simply a raccoon skittering through the underbrush searching for its next meal?

This feeling of unease outdoors was foreign to Remi. Normally, she was more at home outside than inside. She especially loved mountains—or at least, the mountains back home in Colorado. These lush, evergreen-choked Smokies were as different from her dramatic soaring Rockies as a black bear was from a polar bear. Both were beautiful and special in completely different ways. But this unfamiliar wilderness seemed to be closing in on her, thickening the air with a sense of menace and filling her with dread.

Was this how Allison Downs had felt when she'd hiked

through the Shenandoah National Park and was never seen again?

Or Melanie Shepherd in the Dry Tortugas?

Or even her own sister, when their high school senior class trip had gone so horribly wrong?

"Stop being a spoilsport, Remi. That waterfall is supposed to be gorgeous by moonlight and I'm tired of being stuck here in this stupid tent. No one else's parents make them go to bed at ten o'clock. It's embarrassing." Becca tried to push through the tent flap, but Remi blocked her way.

"It's too dangerous," Remi told her. *"Daddy said it's the wrong time of year to go up that trail. The water level is too high and the rocks are slippery with ice. Besides, since when do you care about nature, other than those stupid constellations you love to look at?"* She studied her sister. *"You're meeting someone, aren't you? Some boy."*

Becca rolled her eyes. *"You're just jealous because no one asked you to party."*

"I knew it. Who? Billy Hendricks?"

Another eye roll. *"Oh, please. Billy's like a lapdog, panting at my heels. What's the challenge in that? I've hooked a much bigger fish than silly Billy."* She laughed and tried to move past Remi. But Remi grabbed the sleeve of her sister's jacket and held on.

"Becca, stop. You're going to ruin this whole trip. If Daddy finds out that you're sneaking out, especially to meet a guy, he'll take us back home early."

Her sister's mouth tightened. *"If anyone is ruining this stupid trip, it's Dad, not me. At least the other chaperones have the sense to leave their kids alone. No one else's parents are in a tent right next to theirs. He's smothering us."*

"He loves us. He wants to keep us safe."

"From what? Last time I looked, cancer wasn't lurking in the woods."

Remi drew in a sharp breath. "That's low, Becca. And completely unfair."

Remorse flashed in Becca's light brown eyes, which were a mirror of her own. For a moment, Remi thought her sister was going to give in, maybe even apologize for using their mother's recent death from breast cancer as a barb in an argument. But Becca suddenly shoved her backward, forcing her to let go of the jacket.

Becca's hands tightened into fists at her sides, a clear warning for Remi not to try to stop her again. "There are fifty kids out here in this stupid campground and ten chaperones. Ten! We can't even skin a knee without stumbling over some anxious parent with a first aid kit. You'd think we were still in elementary school instead of planning which colleges to go to in the fall."

"Becca—"

"This is your fault. Our entire trip has been a disaster, all because you told Dad the school needed another chaperone. You know how overprotective he is. You should have kept your mouth shut. And you're going to keep it shut this time or I'll make you regret it. You owe me this. Leave me alone. Let me have some fun." She flung open the tent flap and disappeared into the night.

Remi swallowed hard at the memory of her sister's long, wavy dark hair rippling out behind her. That was the last time she'd ever seen her.

A little farther down the trail, the trees and brush on her right thinned out and then disappeared altogether. A fifty-foot break revealed endless miles of dense, forest-covered peaks and the occasional bald where disease or insects had killed large swaths of trees and undergrowth.

Charred earth and blackened trunks spoke of wildfires that had ravaged this area in recent years. And through it all, little white puffs of mist rose toward the sky like ancient smoke signals, adding to the blue-white haze that gave this section of the Appalachians their name.

She stopped, mesmerized. Not by the scenery. But by thoughts of her sister so long ago. A lifetime ago. Had Becca made it to this section of the AT the night she disappeared? Was this the spot her killer had chosen for his attack? Had she looked out over this beautiful vista underneath a bright full moon, completely unaware of the danger that crept up on her from behind?

If Remi was the killer, this was where she'd make her move. It was remote, isolated and empty. She hadn't passed anyone since leaving the trail shelter this morning, miles from here. It was too cold to attract many hikers at this time of year. The crowds of northbound thru-hikers, or NOBOs, with dreams of completing the two-thousand-mile trek in one year from Georgia to Maine wouldn't clog the trail until spring. The lack of NOBOs to contend with was one of the reasons the ill-fated senior class trip had been planned for midwinter instead of closer to graduation.

Remi could easily imagine Becca standing here, memorizing the way moonlight spilled its light across the peaks and valleys, so she could tell her tree-hugging twin all about it when she returned to the tent. Or looking up at the stars, so much easier to see on the mountain, away from what Becca called the "light pollution" in the city. More likely, she could have been standing here waiting for whatever boy she'd gone off to meet. The identity of her secret admirer had never been discovered. It could have been Billy Hendricks, even though she'd denied it. Or the golden boy of their senior class, Garrett Weber, except that he already had a girlfriend at the time. Whoever it was, none of the boys at camp would admit to meeting her in the woods. Why would they? They would have made themselves suspects in her disappearance.

Remi studied the gap, a chill skittering up her spine. This was definitely a perfect place for a trap, an ambush. The steep drop would have blocked her sister's escape to the west. Thick trees and brush to the east would make it difficult to get very far before being caught. If someone was behind her, she'd have to shove past them to run up or down the trail.

What happened to you, Becca?

Scuffling noises sounded behind her.

She whirled around, yanking her gun out of her pocket and bringing it up in one swift motion.

Chapter Two

A hulking, dark-haired man dressed in green camouflage stared at her from twenty feet away, his face a mask of menace and hatred. He suddenly shoved his hand into his pocket.

"Freeze!" she yelled.

Ignoring her order, he tugged at something dark and metallic in his pocket that seemed to be caught in the fabric. *A gun!*

"No!" another man's voice yelled from off to her left somewhere.

Camo-guy yanked the gun free.

Remi squeezed the trigger. *Bam! Bam!*

Camo-guy's eyes widened in disbelief and he dropped like a rock. Remi jerked toward her left to face the next threat. A second man barreled into her, slamming them both to the ground, crushing her right shoulder. Agony knifed through her. She gritted her teeth and tried to push him away.

He rolled off her.

Fighting through the blinding pain, she flopped onto her back and tried to force her right arm to cooperate so she could point her gun at him. Except he wasn't there. And she didn't have her gun.

The sound of someone running had her turning her

head to see her attacker drop to his knees beside the man she'd shot. He moaned and writhed on the ground, clutching his side.

She frantically looked around for her pistol. There, a few feet away. Her SIG was under a bush, where it must have landed when she was knocked down. Clutching her hurt arm against her chest, she scrambled forward on her knees. Awkwardly leaning in, she thrust her left hand beneath the branches, fingers scrabbling against the dirt.

"Oh, no, you don't," a deep voice snarled behind her. Her attacker was back.

She dived for the gun.

He grabbed her right ankle and yanked backward.

She cried out in frustration and kicked her legs. One of them slammed against his thigh. It was like hitting a solid rock. The impact had her clenching her teeth.

He swore. Maybe she'd managed to hurt him, too.

She kicked again, this time knocking his hand off her ankle.

She lunged forward, desperately reaching for her SIG Sauer.

Strong fingers clamped around both her calves like vice grips. He jerked her backward, so hard and fast that her jacket and shirt bunched up beneath her. Dirt and rocks scraped her belly, tracing a fiery burn across her skin.

Twisting around, she brought up her knee toward his groin as she swung a left hook at him.

He dived sideways, avoiding her knee, but not her fist. The blow caught him hard on his temple, making him grunt. But it didn't slow him down. He threw himself on top of her, pinning her to the ground.

She bucked her hips, trying to throw him off while she struggled to coil her left hand into a fist for round two.

Good grief, he was strong, a powerhouse of muscles that made her Pilates workouts seem like a pathetic waste of time. She could probably outrun him. Running was one of the few things where she excelled. But she had to get him off her first. She drew back her fist again.

He flipped her onto her stomach.

Hot lava boiled across the nerve endings in her battered shoulder. Bile rose in her throat. She could feel him fumbling for something, his hips moving alarmingly against her bottom as he turned to the side. Was he going to rape her?

"Let me go." She struggled harder, pushing through the pain.

He reared up and jerked her arms back. Agony seared her shoulder. She cried out. Dark spots swam in her vision.

The feel of cold steel against her wrists had her stiffening. He was trying to handcuff her! She twisted and snaked against the ground, desperately trying to keep him from getting the cuffs into position. Her shoulder felt as if it was being shredded with a hot poker, but she couldn't let up. If he got those cuffs fastened, she was as good as dead. Her vision clouded. She was close to passing out from the pain.

"Fight, Remi. You can do this!" Her sister's voice echoed in her mind.

The ratcheting sound of the cuffs locking into place sounded behind her. He shoved his hands into her jacket pockets, took her cell phone. Then he ran his hands quickly up and down her body. She cursed at him and tried to arch away.

"Stay there. Don't move." The command from her

captor sounded more like an angry growl than an order. His weight lifted off her and once again he was gone.

She collapsed against the ground, the fight draining out of her. There was nothing else she could do. She squeezed her eyes shut. *I'm so sorry, Daddy. Please forgive me, Becca.* A whimper clogged her throat. *Becca.* Her sometimes sweet, always impetuous, infuriating twin. Maybe it was fitting that they'd both die in the same place, together as always, cradle to grave.

Remi lay unmoving. What was her assailant doing now? Without him weighing her down and her struggling against him, the agony in her shoulder became bearable. The black fog dissipated and the fuzziness in her head evaporated.

A low murmur had her turning her head. The man who'd cuffed her was on his knees again beside his partner in crime, saying something to him. His neon orange backpack strained across his broad shoulders, the color contrasting sharply with his black pants and black shirt. The wounded man writhed on the ground, his teeth bared like a rabid animal caught in a trap.

"Idiot! Stop wasting time. Get up while he's distracted. Run!"

Her sister's voice was so loud inside Remi's head that she half expected to see her forever-seventeen features twisted with fury.

I'm so sorry, Becca. It's all my fault. Everything is my fault.

Pent-up grief swept through her like a tsunami, obliterating everything in its path. It drowned her in a sea of sorrow that was just as fresh now as when she was a teenager. Losing both her mother and her sister the same year had nearly destroyed her. The death of her father a little over a year later *had* destroyed her, or at least, the person she used to be. She'd had to remake herself into someone new just to survive. A harder, tougher Remi Jordan. Or so she'd thought. Yet here she lay, helpless, about to die. *You're right, Becca. I'm an idiot.*

"Stop feeling sorry for yourself, Remi. Get your lazy butt up and run! Now! You owe me!"

You owe me. Her sister was right. She had to at least try. Remi tried to jerk upright, then gasped at the white-hot pain that shot through her shoulder. She shuddered and braced her forehead against the cold ground, gulping in short breaths of arctic air.

"Get up!" Becca yelled again.

Remi drew a ragged breath and awkwardly wiggled her body. Without the use of her hands to push herself up, it took a ridiculous amount of time to make it to a sitting position. But at least with her hands cuffed behind her back, the pressure on her shoulder was making it go blessedly numb. Maybe she could do this, after all.

She braced herself to try to stand, and risked a quick glance at the two men. The one who'd cuffed her had his backpack on the ground beside him and had taken out a first aid kit. With one hand pressing gauze bandages against the injured man's side, he sat back and reached his other hand toward his waist.

Remi stiffened, expecting him to pull out a gun, maybe even hers. Instead, he lifted the edge of his jacket to reveal a thick black belt.

A *utility* belt.

With various leather holders clipped to it, like the kind that held handcuffs.

And a two-way radio.

A horrible suspicion swept through her, freezing her in place.

He grabbed the radio and pressed one of the buttons on the side. As if he sensed her watching him, his gaze flew to hers. The radio crackled and he spoke into the transmitter.

"This is Special Agent Duncan McKenzie. I located the woman the witness at the shelter reported seeing with a gun. But not before she shot a hiker. I need a medical crew up here, ASAP."

The blood drained from Remi's face, leaving her cold and shaking. Her gaze flew to the man she'd shot. He was pale and still on the forest floor, his eyes closed. And beside him, hanging out of his pocket, was the gun he'd pulled on her.

Except it wasn't a gun.

It was a cell phone.

Dear God. What had she done?

Chapter Three

Hunching in his jacket against the bitter wind, Duncan paused behind the unfamiliar SUV in the gravel lot by the office trailer. The vehicle's plain exterior and dark color would typically help it blend in and avoid being noticed. Not here. Surrounded by white vehicles with green stripes down their sides and the brown National Park Service arrowhead shield on their doors, the SUV stuck out like a white-tailed deer in a herd of elk.

The license plate was federal government issue, but not the kind used by the NPS. All Duncan knew for sure was that whatever alphabet agency was here, they hadn't simply dropped by on their way someplace else. Nestled deep inside the Great Smoky Mountains National Park, this satellite office was miles from the nearest town, Gatlinburg. The steep, winding access road was a challenge during the summer, nearly impossible during the winter without a four-wheel drive. Which meant their visitor was here on purpose. Something big must be going on, and Duncan aimed to find out what that was.

He jogged up the salted concrete steps at the end of the long trailer to the only door, a solid steel monstrosity designed to keep out the occasional curious black bear. The deep scratches in the prison-gray paint proved just how solid, and necessary, that precaution was. Even the huge metal storage shed at the end of the lot was reinforced with heavy steel bars. Working in the wilderness was dangerous in more ways than one. He pulled open the door and stepped inside.

Seventies-era dark wood paneling sucked up most of the light, in spite of wide windows set high up on the longest opposing walls. Four desks were tucked end to end beneath those windows, leaving a center aisle of worn rust-colored shag carpet. His boss, Yeong Lee, faced him from behind another, larger desk at the end of the aisle. Across from him, occupying the two metal folding chairs reserved for visitors, were a large black man in a charcoal-gray suit and a petite Caucasian woman with long blond hair cascading down her back.

As Duncan hung his jacket and gloves on hooks beside the door, he exchanged greetings with the only other people inside, Rangers Nick Grady and Oliver McAlister. Skinny freckle-faced Grady was a green-around-the-gills new recruit, while white-haired McAlister, with his gravelly smoker's voice and stout frame, was a permanent fixture in the park. Dubbed Pup and Pops, the two were sitting together to the right of the door at McAlister's desk. As usual, Pops was mentoring Grady about something on the computer screen.

Duncan paused beside McAlister. "Thanks for helping me out this morning. Did the prisoner give you any trouble?"

He shook his head. "No trouble at all and no thanks needed. If you hadn't been here at 0-dark-thirty and taken the call for us, we'd have been the ones assigned to head up there, anyway. What's the story on the hiker? Did he make it?"

"He got lucky. The bullet passed through the fleshy part of his side. Lost a lot of blood and they've got him on IV antibiotics to stave off infection. But he's expected to make a full recovery." He motioned toward the couple across from Lee. "Which agency decided to pay us a visit? Any idea why they're here?"

McAlister exchanged a surprised look with Grady, his bushy eyebrows climbing like albino caterpillars to his hairline. "You don't recognize the woman from this morning?"

Duncan frowned and studied her as best he could from across the room. The long blond hair did remind him of the shooter's hair. But since McAlister had taken her into custody, that wasn't possible. Was it? She lifted her left hand, motioning in the air as she spoke to Lee. She also gave Duncan his first clear view of a royal blue shirt-sleeve and the cream-colored jacket folded over the arm of her chair. He sucked in a sharp breath, his hands fisting at his sides. It was her. The combination of blond hair, blue shirt and off-white jacket couldn't be a coincidence.

If he'd been a second slower this morning, he'd either be sporting some seriously bruised ribs thanks to his Kevlar vest, or he'd have had his head blown off, depending on the aim of the woman sitting in that chair.

"Why isn't she locked up?" Without waiting for McAlister's reply, he strode up the aisle to Lee's desk and turned to face the woman once again. Except, this time, she wasn't pointing a gun at him.

The white sling cradling her right arm forestalled the angry words he'd been about to say. Instead, suspicion heavy in his tone, he demanded, "What happened to you?" She wouldn't be the first suspect to fake an injury to delay being booked into jail.

Her dark brows rose. "You did."

"Is that supposed to be funny? Because I find it incredibly offensive."

She held her left hand in front of her in a placating gesture. "I'm just stating facts. When you slammed me to the ground, you dislocated my shoulder." She shrugged, then winced and clasped her left hand over her right shoulder as if she was in pain.

He wasn't buying her act. And he sure as certain wasn't letting her version of events go unchallenged. "I think what you meant to say was that I tackled you to keep from being shot, after you'd just shot an unarmed man and then turned your pistol on me."

A red flush crept up her neck. "I thought the hiker had a gun. And you attacked me. I was protecting myself."

"The only one attacking anyone up there was you." He tapped the lump on his temple where she'd punched him, which he knew already had a visible bruise.

Her jaw tightened, but she didn't respond.

He waved toward the back right corner of the trailer. "Why isn't she locked up in the holding cell? Or on her way to jail courtesy of Gatlinburg PD? She could have killed Kurt Vale."

"Could have?" Her eyes widened. "Then…he's alive?"

The hopeful tone of her voice sounded false to him. "The time for concern would have been *before* you pulled the trigger and shot an innocent man. But if you're asking whether you managed to kill him, the answer is no. I just left him at the hospital after the doctor stitched him up."

"I'm glad he's okay."

Ignoring her, he turned to his boss. "What's going on here?"

Lee addressed the man silently observing them from the other side of the desk. "FBI Supervisory Special Agent Leon Johnson, meet Special Agent Duncan McKenzie, criminal investigator with the National Park Service."

Johnson held his hand out without bothering to pry

his generous frame out of the ridiculously small folding chair beneath him.

Duncan leaned across the desk and shook the agent's hand, but his attention once again turned to the woman. Four hours ago she'd shot a hiker. Now she was parked beside an FBI agent. Why? Since he regularly studied the FBI's ten most-wanted-fugitives list, he knew she wasn't on it. But she must have done something pretty dang bad to warrant the FBI showing up, especially this soon after the shooting. So why wasn't she handcuffed? Or in the cell while the agent spoke to his boss?

"I'm a little lost." Duncan glanced back and forth between Lee and Johnson. "Since our shooting suspect is sitting beside an FBI agent, I assume there's something else going on that involves her, besides what happened this morning. Can someone catch me up here?"

"What's going on," Johnson said, "is that your shooting suspect is one of our agents. She was off duty, supposed to be on vacation, not running around shooting people."

Duncan stared at him in shock. The woman from this morning's shooting was a Fed? A fellow law-enforcement officer? He hadn't gotten to speak to her after the shooting. He didn't even know her name. He'd been too busy trying to keep Kurt Vale from bleeding out. As soon as McAlister and Grady had arrived to take her into custody, he hadn't given her another thought. Instead, he'd helped the medics get Vale down the mountain to the waiting ambulance.

"You're FBI?" He couldn't quite wrap his head around that.

She stood and held out her left hand, since her right one was in the sling. "Special Agent Remi Jordan."

He eyed her hand like he would a poisonous snake.

She took the hint and sat back down.

Johnson laboriously rose to his feet and tugged his suit jacket into place. "Special Agent Jordan has waived her right to an attorney and has declined my offer to stay here with her. She has assured me that she's prepared to fully cooperate with your investigation. Isn't that right?"

She gave him a curt nod, but didn't meet his gaze.

"I've already taken her badge," Johnson said. "And your crime scene unit logged her gun as evidence. She's now on administrative leave, pending the results of your investigation. If either of you gentlemen need anything further from my office, let me know." He tapped a white business card sitting on the desk. "Now, if you'll excuse me, I need to get back to Knoxville." He grabbed his coat from a peg behind Lee's desk and then shrugged into it as he headed toward the door.

Duncan watched the man leave, distaste burning like acid in his throat. For the first time since the shooting earlier today, he felt a tug of sympathy for the woman sitting on the other side of the desk. No matter what she'd told Johnson, the man was her boss. It was his duty to look out for her. He should have insisted that she get a lawyer, or brought one with him. Lee sure would have. He'd fight like a rabid bobcat to defend every member of his team. Justice would be served, of course. But he'd do everything he could to ensure that his officers' rights were protected.

Lee pushed back his chair and stood. "Special Agent Jordan, with you getting that shoulder patched up and your boss asking us to wait until he got here to talk, we haven't had much of a chance to discuss the details of the shooting. Special Agent McKenzie will take your statement. In the meantime, my stomach is eating a hole through my spine. I'll head down the mountain and get us all some lunch. Any dietary restrictions or preferences I should know about?"

Her expression turned wary as she obviously debated whether or not to trust him. From the way her own boss had just acted, Duncan couldn't blame her.

"That's very nice of you," she told Lee. "Thank you. And no, no restrictions. Whatever you get is fine and much appreciated."

"All right. I'll be back in an hour, give or take." He grabbed his gloves and heavy jacket hanging on the wall behind his chair and motioned toward Pup and Pops. "Grady, you're my pack mule this trip," he called out. "You can chauffer me into town while I check my email on my phone."

From the grin on the kid's eager face, he must have thought he'd won the lottery. He jumped up so fast that he almost overturned his chair.

Pops shook his head, but a smile played around his lips as he turned to his computer monitor. Grady started peppering Lee with questions about procedures and re-ports before Lee could even close the door behind them. The pained expression on his face when he glanced back had Duncan wondering if his boss already regretted his decision to take his newest employee with him into town.

Duncan motioned toward the back wall. His anger had given way to grudging curiosity now that he knew his suspect was in law enforcement. With a federal agent in-volved, he could understand why Lee had chosen not to turn her over to the local police. Instead, the NPS would handle it as an interagency courtesy—at least for now. It was up to Duncan to get the answers to the questions that had been rolling around in his head from the moment he'd taken a hiker's call early this morning.

"Special Agent Jordan, if you'll take a seat in the other room, I need to grab my laptop to take notes."

She stood and waved toward the reinforced-glass and steel door on the far right. "In there?"

He followed her gesture. "Ah, no. That's the holding cell. In spite of what I may have said earlier about locking you up, in the eight years that I've worked here, we've never once used that room for its intended purpose. It's stuffed with boxes of office supplies and old case files." He motioned toward the door on the far left. "I meant the conference room. I'm sure you were shown where the restroom was earlier." He motioned toward the middle door. "If you need—"

"No, thank you." She moved stiffly past him and marched into the conference room like a prisoner heading to death row.

Chapter Four

When Special Agent Remi Jordan passed Duncan, he was struck by how petite she was. The top of her head barely reached his chin. In blue jeans and a simple blue blouse, without a jacket to provide bulk, she probably didn't tip a hundred pounds on a scale. Her right arm being trussed up in a sling only emphasized her vulnerability. Seeing her this way, with this morning's drama stripped away, and no gun, Duncan realized she appeared utterly defenseless. And he had the inexplicable urge to offer his protection, to reassure her that everything was going to be all right.

That would be foolish and wrong on so many levels, especially because it would probably be a lie.

As a trained officer, she should have used deadly force as a last resort. Instead, she'd used it as her first response. She'd shot an unarmed man while off duty, on vacation, according to her boss, with no provocation that Duncan had seen. She could be looking at charges of attempted murder, attempted manslaughter or, the very least, assault. If by some miracle she avoided charges and didn't go to prison, she'd likely still lose her job with the FBI. And she'd almost certainly face financial ruin in the civil courts. With another law-enforcement officer as a witness, Vale could ride that gravy train all the way to the bank.

Duncan stood in the doorway, watching her consider the four padded wooden chairs, the square vinyl-topped table that was more appropriate for playing cards than for a conference or an interview. But like everything else in this trailer, the table and chairs met the main requirement—they were small enough to fit the tiny space.

She apparently decided not to bother with a chair. Instead, she moved to the lone window at the other end of the room. Facing away from him, she stared through the glass at the snow, which was falling again.

"Special Agent Jordan?"

She glanced over her shoulder. "Remi, please. Calling me Special Agent every time you ask me a question is going to get really old, really fast, for both of us."

"Remi. Unusual name. Is that short for something?"

"Remilyn, after my grandmother. But my mom's the only person who ever called me that."

"Called? Then she's—"

"She passed away when I was seventeen. Breast cancer."

The slight wobble in her voice told him that she'd loved her mother, and that her death—he was guessing eight or nine years ago—still hurt.

He counted his blessings that both his parents were still alive and doing well. He couldn't imagine not being able to drop by their cabin, share a beer with his father or ask his mother's advice.

"My condolences," he said, and meant it.

She gave him a crisp nod. "Thank you."

He waved toward the sling. "While I wouldn't have changed the actions I took this morning, I do regret that you got hurt. What did the doctor say about your shoulder?"

She hesitated, the wary expression she'd given Lee firmly back in place. "The EMT rotated it into the socket. It's fine."

He waited, but when she didn't elaborate, he asked, "You were taken to the hospital, right? You were seen by a doctor?"

"All a doctor would have done was tell me to schedule an appointment with a physical therapist. I had the EMT treat me in the back of the ambulance, and told him I didn't want to go to the hospital."

She didn't *want* to go? She shouldn't have been given a choice. She was under arrest, her well-being the responsibility of the National Park Service while in their custody. McAlister and Grady should have *made* her go to the hospital, with them as her armed escorts.

"What did the EMT give you for pain?" He didn't want her to suffer. But equally important, he didn't want a defense attorney down the road having her statement tossed out on the basis that she was heavily medicated, which affected her mental state and her ability to understand her rights.

"I haven't had a chance to take anything," she said. "My purse is locked in the trunk of my car at the trailhead. I don't have any pills with me here."

"I've got some ibuprofen in my desk if you want."

She frowned as if puzzled by his offer. Had she expected him to chain her to a chair and allow her only bread and water?

"I'd appreciate that. The shoulder does ache a bit."

"If you prefer to go to the hospital for an MRI—which I strongly recommend—and to get a prescription for the pain—"

"Over-the-counter pills will be fine."

Visions of future defense attorneys were still dancing

in his head. She really should go to the hospital. But it was her shoulder, after all. Not a head injury. And she'd been given medical treatment by the EMT. It was probably safe to take her statement.

"I'll be right back."

"Special Agent McKenzie?"

"If I'm calling you Remi then you have to call me Duncan." He added a smile that he was far from feeling. But keeping things friendly would make the interview go much more smoothly. Orders from her boss to cooperate would go only so far if she had something to hide about why she was in the mountains with a gun. He'd start out playing good cop and see how things went.

She gestured toward the side of his head. "Duncan. I really am sorry about everything that happened. I hope that doesn't hurt too much."

It took him a second to realize she was talking about punching him. His grin was genuine this time. "You've got a wicked left hook."

Her answering smile seemed reluctant, but also genuine. "I'm right-handed. You got lucky."

He laughed. "So I did. No worries. We'll talk everything out and then decide where to go from there. Okay?"

She blew out a shuddering breath, her face relaxing with relief. "Sounds good."

When he reached his desk, he pulled his laptop from the bottom drawer just as his cell phone buzzed. He took it out of his pocket and checked the screen. It was Lee. A quick glance toward the open door of the conference room confirmed that Remi was still standing at the window, looking out. Duncan plopped his laptop on the desk and sat down to take the call.

"Hey, boss. Did you shove Grady into a snowbank yet to shut him up?" he teased.

"Have you started interviewing Special Agent Jordan yet?"

The terseness of Lee's tone immediately had Duncan on alert. "About to. Why?"

"Johnson had his assistant send me an email. I forwarded it to you. It makes for some interesting reading. Skim it before you talk to her."

"Why?"

"Humor me." The line clicked.

Duncan sighed and flipped open the laptop. There were fifteen unread emails since just this morning. Most had to do with the case he was in the process of closing, a string of vehicle break-ins and vandalism he'd been working for the past four months. The small band of local teens behind the crimes was in jail. Now it was just a matter of paperwork and testimony once the trials were underway—assuming they even went to trial.

None of the kids had criminal records. And knowing his friend Clay Perry, the district attorney, Duncan figured he'd likely plead them out. Clay was a father of five and had a seemingly endless supply of patience and empathy for kids—whether they deserved it or not.

Their parents would pay hefty fines and the little hoodlums would soon be back on the streets. And Duncan would have to arrest them all over again a few months down the road when they started up again, or turned to other types of crimes. It was an endless cycle, one that he and Clay often debated over cold beers, sizzling steaks and friendly poker games.

Not seeing anything particularly urgent in the subject lines of the emails, he clicked on the one from his boss. The message was brief, simply telling Duncan to read the attachment.

It took half a minute for the memory-hogging document to load on his screen. When it did, he frowned. Why would Remi's boss feel it was necessary to send this? And why would Lee want Duncan to read it prior to the interview? How could this possibly be relevant to the shooting?

He let out a long breath and dutifully clicked through several pages, quickly scanning the headings of each section. He began to wonder whether he'd missed the punch line to an inside joke. Then, five pages in, he quit scanning. He leaned closer to the monitor and read every single word. Then he went back to the beginning and read it all again.

Chapter Five

Remi's fingers tightened against the windowsill as she watched the snow falling even harder outside the conference room window. She was trying to find her center, calm her nerves in anticipation of the upcoming inquisition. But so far it wasn't working. She'd interviewed suspects dozens of times over the years. But she'd never once been on the other side of the table. And she wasn't looking forward to the experience. Especially since she couldn't even explain to herself what had happened this morning.

She was sick at the thought that she could have shot an unarmed man. But every time she replayed the confrontation in her mind, the memories ticked through like the frames of a movie, replaying exactly the same way that she remembered, never changing.

Scuffling sounded behind her.

She turned, gun in hand, finger on the frame, not the trigger.

A man in camouflage, a look of such menace on his face that she had zero doubt he was the one who'd been stalking her. Or was he just angry that she was pointing a gun at him?

She told him to freeze.

He pulled a gun out of his pocket. It had gotten caught

on the fabric of his jacket. But he still pulled it out. She could picture it, clearly. He couldn't have been more than twenty feet away. It was a Glock 19, 9 mm, a weapon she'd seen many times during her career.

She'd moved her finger to the trigger, because she had to. Shoot or be shot. Kill or be killed. She'd fired, in self-defense, only one shot, because there was another threat, off to her left.

Duncan. Knowing he was there had likely distracted her just enough to save Vale's life. Normally, she was an excellent marksman.

He'd tackled her, knocking her pistol loose.

A few minutes later, the man she'd shot lay on the ground, a cell phone hanging out of his pocket. The phone was black. So was the gun. But the first was a rectangle, the last a pistol. Nothing alike. She could never mistake the two.

Could she?

Her knuckles grew white against the wooden sill. Could she have been so distracted by thoughts of her sister, by the same grief and anger that had plagued her for years, that she'd seen something that wasn't there? Had she wanted so badly to believe that the man in front of her was the one responsible for the disappearances, that her mind had played tricks on her?

Five years. She'd been in law enforcement for five years. She was far from being an expert, still new in many ways. But she found it hard to believe that after all that time she could screw up this badly. The man, this Kurt Vale guy, had to have had a gun. But if he did, then where was the gun now?

"Hello? Remi? Anybody home?"

She blinked, bringing the room, and Duncan, into focus. She instinctively scrambled back several steps to put more distance between her and this rather tall, intimidating man in front of her.

His eyes widened and he, too, stepped back, giving her more space. "I didn't mean to startle you." His jaw tightened and his dark blue eyes looked down toward her side.

She followed his gaze and realized her left hand was balled into a fist and half-raised, as if she was going to slug him again. Her face flushed hot and she forced her fingers to uncurl. "Sorry. You…surprised me."

"Like Kurt Vale surprised you up on the ridge? Right before you shot him?"

Her face grew hotter. "He had a gun."

"The only gun I saw was in your hand."

"That's because you saw my gun first and assumed that I was the threat. You probably never looked at him after that. If you hadn't attacked me, you'd have noticed that he was pulling out a weapon, too. A Glock 19, 9 mm."

He spread his hands in a conciliatory gesture. "I'd like to believe you. I really would. But it's hard to support your story when only one gun was found—yours. A crime scene unit processed the scene. The evidence they collected where Vale was lying included bloody gauze and a broken cell phone. That's it."

"Broken?"

"From the fall. The phone fell out of his pocket. Hit some rocks on the ground beside him, which shattered the screen."

"Why did it fall out, unless he was pulling something else out of his pocket and knocked it loose?"

His brows arched. "Like his hands? To hold them up and show you he was unarmed?"

She pressed her lips together.

He sighed. "Let's take it step by step." He motioned toward the table, which had a laptop sitting on it. Across from that were a bottle of water and a container of over-the-counter pain pills. Both were open, their caps lying on the table. "I imagine that shoulder's hurting quite a bit. Why don't you get some pain meds on board, before we officially start?"

"He had a gun," she insisted.

"I'm sure you thought that he did."

There was no judgment in his tone, no condemnation. Instead, he sounded surprisingly empathetic. Which of course meant that he was good at his job, good at defusing her anger, making her feel less defensive. Not because he cared about her or felt solidarity with a fellow law-enforcement officer, but because he wanted her in an agreeable mood so she'd answer his questions. She wanted to be angry at him for using interview tricks and techniques on her. Instead, she couldn't help but admire him for it. If she was in his position, she'd do the exact same thing.

She stepped around him and sat in the chair with its back to the door. She figured she'd hear the door if someone opened it. And more important, she didn't want to turn her back on Duncan, who was still standing by the window where she'd left him, watching her as if he was trying to figure her out. Fine. She'd just watch him right back.

Taking her time with the pills, she studied him from beneath her lashes. He was a handsome man, no denying that. He wasn't much older than her, maybe thirty or so. His tanned face was a study in angles and hard edges a camera would love, made even more interesting by the combination of nearly jet-black hair and midnight-blue eyes. But it was his height—about six foot three—and those broad shoulders and toned, muscular body that made her hyperaware of her own small stature. If he was just a man, and she was just a woman, she'd have probably been excited and intrigued by his size and strength. But as a federal agent with her freedom and her career on the line, he intimidated her, which made her resentful.

Two long strides later, he was sitting across from her, pulling his laptop toward him. His gaze settled on her with an intensity that was unnerving. "Are you sure you don't want me to take you to the hospital?"

"I'm fine," she assured him. But from the skeptical look on his face, she didn't think he believed her.

"Everything in here is recorded." He waved toward the camera anchored near the ceiling on the wall to her left. "For your protection and mine."

"I saw the camera as soon as I walked in. I assume someone is also watching us through the one-way glass in the top of the door behind me."

"They could if they wanted. But I think Pops is more interested in finishing his reports so he can leave on time today."

"Pops?"

"The only ranger in the office right now, the older guy, Oliver McAlister. We call him Pops because he's been here longer than anyone else and treats us all like his kids."

He smiled again, making her wonder if he was trying to put her at ease or whether he was one of those people who always seemed happy. Those kind of people got on her nerves and made her fingers itch for her gun. Not having its familiar weight on her hip made her feel naked and vulnerable, a feeling she didn't like one bit.

"Please state your name and address for the video."

"Remilyn Jordan." She listed her street address. "Greenwood Village, Colorado."

"Colorado? I thought you lived in Tennessee and worked out of the Knoxville field office."

She shook her head. "I work in Denver. Johnson came over from the nearest field office, the one in Knoxville. But he's not my regular boss. He's my pseudoboss while I'm here under investigation."

"Got it. Greenwood Village, Colorado. Can't say I've ever heard of it."

"Outside of Denver, about an hour from Boulder, give or take."

"I bet it's beautiful there. Great mountain views of the Rockies."

"It's beautiful," she conceded.

"But you decided to come here on vacation, to another mountain range."

"Is that a question?"

He smiled again. "Before we go any further, I need to remind you about your rights."

"We can skip that part. *Pops* Mirandized me on the way down the mountain."

"I figured he had. But I still have to tell you your rights on camera. Like I said, for your protection and mine."

Not seeing the point in arguing, she suffered through his recitation of the Miranda warning.

"Do you understand each of these rights as I've explained them to you?" he asked.

She nodded.

"You have to say it," he reminded her.

"Yes." She sighed. "Yes, I understand my rights. Yes, I'm willing to speak to you without a lawyer. Can we just talk this out and get it over with?"

The plastic water bottle crackled between her hands. She hadn't even realized that she'd picked it up. She set it down.

"I can't imagine you driving all the way here from Colorado. Did you fly in? Then rent a car while you're in town?"

"Actually, no. I drove. As you're well aware, I brought a weapon with me. Driving was easier than going through the headaches that declaring my weapon would require on a plane."

"Especially since you're here off duty, on vacation."

"Exactly."

He opened his laptop, typed for a moment. "Where are you staying?"

"A motel a few streets back from the main drag in Gatlinburg." She told him the name.

"You've been in town how long?"

"A couple of days."

"And what have you been doing every day while you've been here?"

She hesitated. How much should she reveal? Cooperating was her best chance at trying to avoid any charges. But would her purpose in being here help her, or hurt her?

"Do you need me to repeat the question?" he asked.

"I've been hiking trails in the Great Smoky Mountains National Park, mainly the Appalachian Trail."

"Every day?"

"Every day."

"Why?"

She blinked. "The same reason anyone hikes, I suppose. To see nature, the beautiful scenery. To get away from the pressures of my job. The Smokies aren't at all like the mountains back home. I wanted to see something different."

"It's February. The temperatures are hovering in the twenties at night, forties and fifties during the day. And that's in town. Up here at these elevations, it gets even colder. Not to mention the ice and snow. Want to try again? Why are you hiking in freezing temps in the middle of winter?"

"I'm not the only hiker up here at this time of year. I've seen several."

"There are some, yes. Not many. What I'm interested in is why *you're* here at one of the worst times of year to be outside in the park."

She stared at him, her left hand beneath the table now, her fingers curling against her palm. "I like solitude. I like to be alone. And I don't mind the cold."

His silence told her he wasn't buying her answer. He waited, probably hoping she'd feel compelled to fill the silence, divulge something she didn't want to share. But she knew interview techniques. She wasn't saying anything unless she was answering a specific question.

"Why did you shoot Kurt Vale?"

She sucked in a breath, thrown off-kilter by the abrupt change in the conversation. But rather than rush to defend herself, which could have led to her spilling all sorts of things, she took a moment to regain her composure. When she was sure she was in control, she said, "I was standing at a gap in the trees, admiring the scenery. I'd heard someone following me earlier, so when I heard a noise behind me, I naturally whirled around and drew my gun. To defend myself."

"What did Vale do?"

"He drew his gun, a Glock."

"He didn't have a gun. I saw him standing twenty feet away from you. And I saw you, holding your SIG Sauer, pointing it at an unarmed man."

"That's not what happened. You saw him, then me. And as soon as you realized I had my gun out, you no longer looked at him. At that point, you deemed that I was the threat, and you charged at me. You didn't look back at Vale and see that he'd pulled out a gun and was about to shoot me. I yelled at him to freeze. He didn't. I had no choice but to fire my weapon."

He leaned forward, crossing his forearms on top of the table. "Here's the thing, Remi. The only way that story holds water is if we found a gun at the scene, this Glock you say he had. But the only gun we found was your SIG Sauer, the one that I saw you aim at Kurt Vale, the one I saw you fire."

She shook her head. "You're wrong. If your crime scene techs didn't find Vale's gun, they missed it. They should go back and look harder. It has to be there."

"After I knocked you to the ground to keep you from shooting an unarmed man a second time, I rendered first aid to the victim. He was shot in the side and was losing a lot of blood. He was in no condition to run off somewhere and hide his alleged gun, then run back and lie down, all in the span of the few seconds it took me to knock you down and then go to him. The only items he had with him were his wallet, his car keys and his cell phone. I contend that the cell phone is what you saw in his hand, not a pistol."

"You're wrong."

He held his hands up. "I want to believe you. I want to be wrong. Convince me."

She tapped her fingers against her leg. "I agree that Vale didn't have the opportunity to go hide his gun somewhere. After I shot him, and he fell to the ground, it must have come loose. The momentum of his fall could have knocked the gun into the woods. That's exactly what happened when you knocked me down. My pistol flew into the bushes."

"True. It did. But only a few yards away. And I ran at

you, trying to reach you before you pulled the trigger. I'm a big guy. The force of me hitting you and falling to the ground with you is more force than if Vale simply dropped where he stood after being injured. Don't you agree?"

Reluctantly, she nodded. "Agreed."

"And yet your gun only flew about six feet away. Wouldn't you expect Vale's gun, if he had one, to have gone only a few feet, given that set of parameters? Therefore easily found by either me or the crime scene tech team later?"

She didn't answer. What could she say?

"After taking your gun, I was with Vale the rest of the time. I was there with the medical team. I escorted them down the mountain to the waiting ambulance. At no time did I ever see a gun."

He waited. Again she said nothing.

"This might be a good time to tell the truth," he said.

She was starting to regret apologizing for punching him.

"I *am* telling the truth."

He sat back in his chair. "So the gun just, what, walked away on its own?"

"Maybe Vale threw it."

"Sure. Okay. When he was lying on the ground bleeding out?"

"At any time when he was on the ground when you were on top of me. He could have tossed it away."

"The crime scene techs would have found it."

"Not if they didn't know to look for it. You never spoke to me after the shooting. You didn't ask me why I shot Vale. You didn't know he had a gun, so you wouldn't have told the techs to look for one."

"Valid point. Rangers McAlister and Grady took you

into custody before I went down the mountain with the medical team. Did you mention at any time to either of them that you thought Vale had a gun?"

Once again, he found the hole in her argument. She clenched her jaw in frustration. Of course she'd told them that Vale had a gun. She didn't want someone to think that she'd just arbitrarily shot an unarmed man.

"I'll take that as a yes," he continued. "I'll be sure to verify that with the rangers. But I imagine it will be in McAlister's report. He's the one who would have sent the crime scene guys up there, too. And I'm sure he would have told them to perform a thorough search for a second gun. Again, I'll happily verify that when I read their reports. Just to be extra certain, I'll ask them, too. But we both know what they'll say. They looked for a gun. They didn't find one. Again, this would be a really good time to come clean, to dig yourself out of the hole you're getting into."

She shook her head.

"Let's start again with why you're here."

"I told you. I'm hiking."

"In the winter."

"In the winter," she snapped.

His brows rose. "Okay. So you like the cold. You like treacherous, slippery trails with snow and ice. Not my thing. But I can see the appeal for some people. The mountains are definitely beautiful with their snowcaps."

He was going somewhere with this. She decided not to help him by rising to the bait. She sat back and waited.

"So you're out hiking, enjoying the frigid weather. You heard someone else on the trail, behind you, so you—a trained FBI agent—whirled around and shot him. Do I have that right?"

"I told him to freeze. He didn't."

"Right. Left that part out. You heard someone behind you, whirled around, yelled for him to freeze, then you pulled the trigger."

"After he pulled a gun out of his pocket, yes."

"Because you thought he was walking on the same trail as you? You assumed he was following you?"

"Yes. No." She shook her head in frustration. "It's more complicated than that."

He rested his forearms on the table again. "I'm all ears."

She really, really wanted to punch him. "He wasn't simply following me. He was *stalking* me through the woods, for quite some time. At least half an hour."

His brows rose. "Stalking you?"

"Hunting me. Matching me stride for stride. When I took a step, he'd take a step, echoing me so that it was difficult to be sure if someone else was out there, following me."

"Following you."

"Would you quit repeating everything I say?"

He held up his hands in a placating gesture. "How long have you known Kurt Vale?"

"Known him? I've never met him."

"But he's been stalking you. I think you used the word *hunting*."

"Yes. Exactly. He was hunting me. That's how it seemed. I could hear footsteps—"

"Echoing yours."

"You're being condescending."

"My apologies."

He wasn't sincere and they both knew it. He was tripping her up, making what had happened seem…trivial. She tried again to explain. "I was scared, okay? I believed he was after me."

"Why would he be after you if he didn't know you?"

"Because…" She hesitated. Would he believe her if she told him? Things weren't going so well. If she was on a jury listening in on this conversation right now, she'd lock herself up and throw away the key. Duncan certainly didn't believe her. That was obvious. He wasn't likely to believe her *wild theories*, either, as her boss in Denver called them. Instead of telling Duncan her latest theory, her reason for being here, she tried again to stick to the facts of what had happened. What she needed to do was make him understand her fear, that she'd felt threatened. She would never shoot someone otherwise. She wasn't a cold-blooded murderer.

"You're a man," she said. "An intimidating one, size-wise, especially to a woman who is half your height, like me."

He smiled. "Half might be stretching it."

He was back to playing good cop, trying to charm and disarm her with those smiles of his. She cleared her throat. "My point is that even though I'm trained in self-defense, I know my physical limitations. I had a gun with me for protection—"

"You expected that you might end up in a confrontation and need your weapon?"

She'd not only expected it. She'd hoped for it. But telling him that would seal her fate.

"Hope for the best, prepare for the worst. I took my gun with me just in case. This morning, when I was walking the trail, I heard sounds—"

"Sounds?"

"Rocks pinging against other rocks, like someone's feet had accidentally kicked them. A coat or jacket brushing against a tree."

"The sounds any hiker might make while heading down a trail."

"No, no, you don't understand."

"I want to." He leaned forward, his dark blue eyes watching her with an intensity that was unnerving. "Make me understand, Remi. Tell me the truth."

She could practically hear Jack Nicholson yelling, "You can't handle the truth," his famous line from *A Few Good Men*. Hysterical laughter bubbled up in her throat. She forced it down, drew several long, deep breaths.

"The sounds I heard weren't loud or obvious. They were…stealthy. Like someone was trying to be quiet. It was difficult to pinpoint the direction. But someone was definitely following me. Not hiking, like I was. They were actually specifically following me. I'm absolutely one hundred percent certain." This time she was the one to lean forward, her gaze clashing with his. "I tested my theory. Every once in a while I'd stop, with my foot in the air instead of taking my next step. I heard him, a thump in the distance, as if he was walking in sync with me, using my footsteps to hide the sound of his. But when I stopped suddenly, in midstride, he couldn't. That's when I knew for sure. Do you understand?"

He didn't say anything. He didn't have to. The skeptical look on his face said it all.

They watched each other for a full minute before he leaned back again. "Let's see if I have this right. You were scared."

"Yes."

"Someone was following you."

"Yes."

"You were convinced they were stalking you."

"Yes."

"That they intended you harm."

"Definitely."

"How long were they following you?"

"At least half an hour."

"At what point did you call the police, knowing some-one was following you, stalking you, someone you felt wanted to do you harm? When did you call?" He looked down at his keyboard, as if ready to record the time.

She stared at him, feeling the trap closing around her. She hadn't even seen it coming.

He looked up, feigning surprise. "What time did you call the police during this half hour that you felt your life was in danger?"

Her left hand went reflexively to her cell phone, which McAlister had returned to her and which was now in her jeans pocket. "I didn't call anyone."

"You didn't?"

"No. I didn't."

"Really? Why not?"

"Cell phone service?" she blurted out. "No signal?"

"Are those questions or statements?"

She pursed her lips.

"Are you stating, on the record and on camera, that you tried to call, but couldn't get a signal?"

Her mouth went dry. She'd made a guess about lack of cell phone service and didn't have a clue whether or not she could have gotten a call through. But she would bet that *he* did. He probably knew where every cell tower was in these mountains, where you could get a signal and where you couldn't. Technically, she hadn't outright lied yet. She hadn't specifically said that she'd looked at her phone and saw no bars. But if she told him she'd tried to call, she'd be crossing that line. She'd be lying to a fed-eral officer in the course of an investigation, a crime that alone could send her to prison and destroy her career, if it wasn't destroyed already.

"No." Her voice came out as a dry croak. She cleared her throat, then reached for the bottle of water and took a long swallow.

He waited until she'd finished and set the bottle down. "No, you didn't have a signal, or no, you didn't attempt to call for help?"

Good grief. He was like a fox after a rabbit.

"I'm a law-enforcement officer," she said. "I had a gun for protection, if I needed it. Although I was afraid, and worried that someone was after me, I felt confident in my ability to protect myself."

"Did you call the police?"

"No. I did not."

He smiled. "That wasn't so hard, was it? You told the truth. Cell coverage is spotty and unreliable throughout the park. That's why we carry radios. But there's a cell tower not far from here that provides excellent signal strength. You would have easily gotten a call out if you'd tried."

She pressed her left hand to her stomach. It felt like a kaleidoscope of butterflies was fluttering around inside her. Or a swarm. Or whatever a gazillion butterflies was called.

His smile faded. "Of course that brings us back to the original question of why you didn't try to call anyone. Using your own logic, if you were thinking like a law-enforcement officer, using your training, you would know to call for backup. Standard operating procedure when you're in danger. Why didn't you call?"

She didn't answer.

"You truly believed that Mr. Vale was coming after you?"

"Yes," she whispered.

"Then why, when you could have called for backup, did you choose to risk your life and face him all alone?"

Because I wanted to catch the bastard myself.

She pressed her lips together to keep from blurting out those very words.

Silence filled the room. He stretched his long legs out in front of him and let out a deep sigh.

"I was the first one at the office this morning," he said. "I was the only one here when Zack Towers called to report that he'd shared one of the shelters on the Appalachian Trail last night with another hiker. When you left, you must have put your hand in your pocket to check your gun. He saw the outline of the pistol and called it in. No guns are allowed in any national park unless you're one of the rangers or investigators working for the National Park Service. That rules you out."

Her shoulder was beginning to throb from sitting in one position so long. She rubbed it to ease the ache. "There was a hiker with me in the shelter last night. I don't remember him being named Zack, though. I thought his name was Sunny."

Duncan nodded. "Sunny's his trail name. He's one of our regulars around here, shows up every year around this time, one of the few who likes to hike the AT during the winter. He's a section hiker."

"Section hiker?"

"Since you're out here hiking the Appalachian Trail, I assumed you would have studied up on the lingo." He let his words hang in the air between them.

Wearying of his game, she said, "I'm only doing day hikes. Normally, I stay in the motel each night and come back in the morning. I don't know all the terminology because, obviously, I'm not one of those people who can miraculously afford to dedicate nearly a year of their lives to become a two-thousand-miler. That is what they call people who hike from Georgia to Maine in one season, right? NOBOs are the northbound hikers. SOBOs are the southbound ones?"

He nodded. "Sounds like you studied a little bit about the AT before coming here. I wonder why you'd do that? Maybe because you wanted to make sure there wouldn't be a lot of hiker traffic around to see whatever it is that you're actually doing here?"

"Or maybe I learned way more than I ever wanted to know about this cursed place when I was here on a stupid senior trip back in high school," she snapped.

His look of surprise had her closing her own eyes and cursing to herself. She was getting too stirred up, too frustrated. And as a result, she'd just told him something way too close to her true purpose in being here.

The sound of him typing had her opening her eyes.

He typed a moment longer, then looked at her over the top of the screen. "What's your natural hair color?"

She blinked. "Excuse me?"

"Your eyebrows are dark. You're a brunette, right?"

"And this matters why?"

He turned the laptop around so she could see the screen. There, in living color, smiling and looking carefree, was her sister in the picture her father had given to the police when Becca went missing. It was the picture from the flyer they'd circulated by the hundreds in Gatlinburg after she disappeared. It was the same picture he'd put on the website he'd created to try to generate leads that would help him find his daughter. But they never did.

Becca.

Her throat tight, she whispered, "Why are you doing this? What do you want from me?"

Something flashed in his eyes. Sorrow? Regret? Empathy? Whatever it was, it didn't bother him enough to close the laptop, or minimize the picture of her sister. Instead, his gaze searched hers.

"What I want is what I've wanted all along—the truth. I want you to admit that you came here because your boss, and the Behavioral Analysis Unit, refused to believe your theories about serial killers. I think that you dyed your hair blond to make yourself fit the criteria for whatever serial killer you're currently theorizing about. And I think you very nearly killed Kurt Vale because you mistakenly thought that he was that killer." He tapped the screen, drawing her attention to her sister's picture again. "So, tell me, Remi. What's the current theory? What killer are you after? If I hadn't stopped you, would you have murdered Vale because you believe he killed your sister?"

She swore a string of obscenities at him and shoved herself up from her chair. She threw a few more insults out into the universe for good measure, then stalked out of the room.

Chapter Six

Duncan plopped his legs on top of his desk and grabbed a red apple out of his snack drawer. "Shouldn't Lee and Grady be back with lunch by now?" he complained around a mouthful of the sweet, juicy apple. "I'm starving."

McAlister stood beside Duncan's desk, looking out the front window. "What do you think she's doing?" He motioned toward Remi as she stalked back and forth in the gravel parking lot, golden hair bouncing around her shoulders, cell phone glued to her ear.

Duncan shrugged. "As red as her face is, she's probably yelling at Supervisory Special Agent Johnson for emailing a copy of her personnel file to us. Or she's freezing. Or both. When she calms down she'll realize she left her jacket in here."

"Maybe I should take it to her." In four steps, McAlister had the puffy white coat in his hand, ready to play the chivalrous knight to their fuming guest.

"Don't," Duncan said. "She has more incentive to come back inside on her own if she's shivering."

McAlister dropped the jacket on top of Duncan's outstretched legs and braced his hand on the wall beside the window. "You don't seem worried that she'll take off."

"Where's she gonna go?" He frowned at a large bruise

on the apple and turned it, looking for a better spot. "She doesn't have her car up here. She's injured. No backpack of supplies. No jacket. I'll bet you dinner that she won't last five more minutes outside." He took another bite.

"I think you just bought me dinner."

Duncan glanced up. Remi wasn't on the phone any-more. She was running, fast, across the gravel, heading away from the trailer. She was already halfway to the road. "Ah, hell."

McAlister started laughing.

Duncan tossed the rest of the apple in the trash and grabbed Remi's coat.

"I'm thinking a big medium-rare steak will do the trick," McAlister called after him as he ran for the door. "One of those delicious fill-it mig-non numbers at The Peddler Steakhouse. Or maybe a New York strip."

"Rain check," Duncan yelled, grabbing his jacket and gloves before barreling outside. He cleared the concrete steps in one leap and landed with a bone-jarring crunch on the gravel.

Remi was nowhere to be seen.

The door opened behind him and McAlister leaned out. "Looks like she's headed to town. She turned left at the road."

"Thanks, Pops!" Duncan sprinted after her, yanking on his gloves and jacket as he went.

Five minutes later he was back at his Jeep, cursing as he hopped inside and tossed Remi's coat on the seat be-side him. How a woman a hair over five feet tall could outrun his long stride was beyond him. He would have caught up to her eventually, but closing the gap between them had been taking far too long.

He peeled out of the parking lot, adding a few new

gravel dents to the metal storage shed that housed their ATVs and snowplow attachments.

It didn't take long to catch up to her in the Jeep. She was running on the shoulder of the road at a ground-eating pace. As he slowed alongside her, he rolled down the passenger window.

"Need a lift, pretty lady?" he drawled.

The tightening of her mouth was the only sign that she'd heard him. She stared straight ahead, her hair whipping behind her. Something about her stride seemed off. It dawned on him that it was because of her hurt shoulder. She was using her left hand to hold the sling, probably so it wouldn't bounce against her chest as she ran. Judging by the lines of pain bracketing the side of her mouth, it wasn't working very well.

The cold made her cheeks ruddy. But the rest of her face, and her arms, were even paler than before. Apparently, he'd goaded her enough that she was willing to cause herself pain rather than answer more of his questions.

Someone give him an award. He was officially the biggest jerk on the planet.

"I'm sorry," he called to her through the open window, careful to keep the Jeep a safe distance away in case he hit a patch of ice. "Did you hear me?"

"I heard you," she bit out.

"And?"

Her jaw tightened. "What are you apologizing for?"

"For doing my job?"

"Wrong answer." She still wouldn't look at him.

"And for using personal information in an unintentionally mean way to try to break you down so you'd tell me the truth."

"Unintentional? Seriously?"

"I wasn't trying to *hurt* you, Remi. I was using the tools I had to make you answer my questions. I realize now I might have gone too far. And I really am sorry about that."

She glanced at him, looking more surprised than angry now.

"To be fair," he added, "I was doing it for your own good."

Her look turned incredulous. "For my own good? Using the tragedy of my sister's disappearance to *break* me was for my own good?" *Crunch, crunch, crunch.* Her boots kept rhythm in the snow on the road's shoulder.

"I ran track and field at the University of Tennessee," he said. "I'll bet you could beat half the guys on my team. How fast can you do a mile if you go all out?"

"First, UT, the Big Orange, really? Second, let's skip the small talk. I'm not your friend, Duncan McKenzie."

"You could be. If you wanted. And what's wrong with UT?"

"Buffaloes beat fruit any day of the week."

"University of Colorado?"

She nodded.

"At UT, we're known as humanitarians, you know, the Tennessee Vols, or volunteers. Orange is our color. Not our fruit."

"Whatever. You've got a dog as your mascot. A big, powerful buffalo trumps that."

"Smokey's a bluetick coonhound. I bet he'd nip at the heels of Ralphie the Buffalo and send him running for cover."

She rolled her eyes.

Neither of them spoke as they rounded a curve. When they were on a straightaway again, he said, "I do want to help you—even if you are a CU Buff." When she didn't respond to his teasing, he added, "I don't want to put a fellow law-enforcement officer in jail—as long as you can give me a plausible explanation behind the shooting. You definitely aren't telling me the whole story. And I suspect what you aren't telling me has to do with your sister. Am I right?"

Crunch, crunch, crunch.

"Okay. I could be wrong about that," he allowed. "I'm still open to an explanation that will make sense of what happened. There has to be more to the story. You don't strike me as a cold-blooded killer or even the reckless-endangerment type."

"Gee, thanks for that resounding vote of confidence."

"Give me some leeway here. We didn't exactly meet under the best of circumstances. If you were in my position, wouldn't you be suspicious? At least to start off?"

Thump, crunch, thump. There wasn't much snow in this section of the road. They slowly turned another curve, then straightened out.

"I guess so," she relented.

"All right. Let's work with that. I'm an investigator, like you. Just doing my job. Clay and I are buds, but I need facts to back up my recommendations about possible charges."

"Clay?"

"Clay Perry, the district attorney. He's a Vols grad, too."

"Oh goody."

He grinned, then sobered. "It's in your best interest to talk to me, Remi. You need to tell me all of it, the whole truth, or I won't be able to keep you out of jail."

When she didn't say anything, he added, "Be honest. You're more angry at your boss than at me. He's the one who shared your personnel file with Johnson, who shared it with my boss, who shared it with me. I'm just the little guppy in the big pond here."

She stumbled, then straightened. "He shared my personnel file with you?"

Well, dang. Maybe he shouldn't have mentioned that little piece of information. "I thought you figured that out. Wasn't he the one you were shouting at on the phone?"

"Yes. But I just thought he *told* you about my background, my family tragedy. I didn't know he shared… everything."

"I guess the possum's out of the sack now. My bad. I shouldn't have told you that."

"Possum? Never mind. Must be a Tennessee thing."

"Actually, I think it's a McKenzie thing."

Her lips twitched, then thinned.

"I saw that. Made you smile."

"It happens. Don't take it personally."

"You wound me deeply, bonny lass." He used his best Irish accent. But instead of laughing, she turned her head and looked straight at him with a somber expression. The bleakness in her eyes sent a pang straight to his heart.

"You hurt me," she accused.

"I know." He cleared his throat. "I know, and I'm sorry. I really am."

"But you'd do it all over again?"

He started to tell her no, but then thought about it and shook his head. "Honestly, I probably would."

She said something beneath her breath that no doubt would have burned his ears if he'd caught the words.

"If I did have the chance for a do-over," he said, "I'd lock the conference room door so you couldn't run off. And I'd feel awful later for doing it. That's how I feel right now. Like a big fat donkey with long ears and a furry butt."

A choked sound escaped her. She cleared her throat and kept running.

"Come on, Remi. Even your goose bumps are getting goose bumps." He held up her jacket. "It's warm and toasty in the Jeep."

Her gaze shot longingly to the jacket. She slowed to a jog.

He slowed the Jeep.

She stopped.

He swore as he drove past her, then stopped and backed up.

She rested her left arm on the door. "I'm not going back in that interrogation room without a lawyer."

He groaned. "My boss will be thrilled. But I suppose I earned that. If you won't talk to me, though, I'll have to lock you up. You're still under arrest, still in my custody. And with nothing to give the DA, that's where you'll remain."

Her brow furrowed. "You're not playing fair."

"You're the one threatening me with a lawyer." He shivered dramatically.

Her lips twitched again, then she gave in to the impulse and smiled. "I like you, Duncan McKenzie. You're handsome and funny when you aren't being a bully."

He grinned. "Am I blushing? 'Cause I feel like I'm blushing."

"Shut up." She fumbled with the door handle.

"Hold on. You can't climb up in this thing with that shoulder." He jumped down and had just reached the passenger door when she hopped up inside.

She arched a brow. "Look, Pa. I did it all by myself."

"Are you always this stubborn?" He stood in the V of the open door, grabbed the seat belt before she could and gently pulled it over her shoulder.

As he clicked the buckle into place, she said, "I don't like to feel helpless."

He lifted his head, still half inside the truck with his hand on the seat belt, dangerously close to her hip. Her eyes widened. But he didn't pull away. Instead, he met her gaze, all teasing gone.

"I'm so sorry about your sister," he said. "I've got three brothers and am blessed to still have both of my parents around. Losing one of them—even my black sheep baby brother, who causes more pain than joy in our family—would, well, it would probably destroy me. The fact that you've survived, and built your life around seeking justice for others in spite of your pain, is humbling and amazing. I'm honestly, truly sorry for your loss and that I hurt you."

Her eyes seemed overbright, as if she was fighting back tears. "Thank you," she whispered.

"Remi?"

She sniffed. "Yes?"

"Sometimes you have to take a leap of faith in life. I think this may be your time to take that leap."

Her brow wrinkled. "What do you mean?"

"I like you. And not just because you're gorgeous."

Her eyes looked like big moons as she blinked at him.

"I want to help you," he said. "Because you seem like a good, decent person. You've been dealt some tough cards that aren't your fault. As a result, you got yourself in an untenable situation. But you have to trust me and help me to help you."

"Are you trying to talk me out of getting a lawyer?"

He chuckled. "No. But that would be a nice boon. I admit it."

"Then what are you asking?"

He sighed and backed away to a safer distance. She

was way too beautiful, and tempting, up close. Something he'd been able to mostly ignore before now. But somewhere in the past few minutes they'd crossed the line from interrogator and suspect to...something else. He needed to be careful in how he proceeded, at least until he figured out the dynamics going on between them.

Resting his arm on the roof above the door opening, he said, "I'm saying that a burden is easier to bear if you share it. From what I read in your file, and knowing that both your real boss and your pseudoboss threw you under the bus by sharing your personnel file with us, I can imagine that you've felt isolated at work for a long time. And since you haven't asked to be allowed to call a boyfriend or even a friend all day, I'm guessing you're alone in your private life, too."

She stiffened. "That's none of your business. And you're veering back into being-a-jerk territory again."

"Maybe so. I guess I'm rusty at being a friend. Being a workaholic, I don't have a girlfriend at the moment, either, in case you're wondering." He winked. "Between the job and family, I don't get out much these days."

"I can't tell if you're trying to explain your behavior or whether you're hitting on me."

He winced. "Did I really sound that smarmy?"

She nodded.

"My bad." He held up his hands in a placating gesture. "I admit, you're beautiful and funny when you aren't punching me. But I really am offering an olive branch here."

She rolled her eyes, then seemed to reluctantly grin. "Am I blushing? 'Cause I feel like I'm blushing."

He chuckled. "Did we just make a truce?"

She grew serious. "No."

He sighed with disappointment. "Ah, well. I figured it might be too much to ask. It's too soon. I'll try again later."

She laughed. "You're impossible. I think we just became friends. That's way better than a truce."

"Friends. Sounds good." He shut the door and hurried to the driver's side. After getting in and buckling his seat belt, he said, "Friendship or not, I still have a job to do. I have to take you back until the matter of charges, or no charges, is settled."

He turned the Jeep around and headed up the mountain. "Do you have a specific lawyer in mind?"

"Never needed one before. I don't exactly have one on speed dial."

"Speaking off the record, as a friend, I can make a few calls. My dad's known as Mighty McKenzie, a retired federal judge who has the reputation of a bulldog when it comes to getting justice. Mom's a former prosecutor and can hold her own against anyone, too. Between the both of them, I'm sure they know someone to recommend."

"Duncan?"

"Hmm?"

"It looks like there's a road up ahead on the left. Could you pull in there, please?"

He looked where she was pointing. "That's an old birdwatching trail, not really a road anymore. The underbrush grew up too thick around it and we don't maintain it. Plus, it leads to an abandoned farmhouse that's ready to slide off the edge of a cliff. It's off-limits."

"I didn't say drive down the whole length of the road. Just pull in a little out of the way and park. I'm pretty sure this four-wheel drive Jeep can handle it, aren't you?"

He looked at her in question.

"I'm asking as a friend," she said. "Take a leap of faith for me."

He grinned and gave her his best *Back to the Future* Doc Brown impression. "Road, who needs roads?"

Her lips twitched, telling him she'd gotten his vague paraphrased classic movie reference. Which definitely had him liking her more. Maybe he'd test her *Guardians of the Galaxy* knowledge sometime.

"All right," he said. "Hold on. This *leap* is going to jar your shoulder."

"I ran all the way here. A few more bumps aren't going to make much of a difference."

He slowed and then turned onto the narrow trail. As predicted, the Jeep bounced around, even though he was being as careful as possible. Branches scraped the roof, then the sides. His boss was going to love how he was treating government property. A new paint job might be in the Jeep's immediate future. But he was more worried about how the bouncing might impact Remi. He winced after hitting a particularly rough spot, and looked at her.

"That's far enough." Her voice was raw, her posture stiff as she held on to her hurt arm. "Stop so we can talk."

He put the Jeep in Park and turned to face her. "Okay. I leaped. What do you want to talk about?"

"I don't want a lawyer."

"O…kay."

"What you said back there, in the conference room, right before I stormed out, is very close to the truth."

He frowned. He'd said a lot of things. "Which part?"

"You read my whole personnel file?"

"Every word." Twice.

"Then you know that I joined the FBI with the intention of becoming a member of the Behavioral Analysis Unit one day, although that hasn't happened yet. I wanted to learn how to profile and capture the worst types of killers out there, serial killers."

"Because you think your sister was…taken…by a serial killer?"

"Not exactly. I don't have any evidence that points to that. But I figured if I studied with the best and brightest investigative minds out there, it would eventually help me in my personal quest to discover who took my sister. And if I could put away some really terrible monsters along the way, it was a win-win."

"But that's not what happened."

"No," she said. "It isn't. To be fair to my boss, he's right that my sister's disappearance is an obsession for me. It influences, informs, every decision I make, and it has cast a shadow over my entire career. I've read my sister's case file dozens of times, social-media stalked Billy Hendricks and Garrett Weber—the two most likely suspects. But nothing ever came of it, no new information, nothing to point to the guilt of either of them. So I've poured my energies into other crimes, other victims, other suspects. I've come up with some pretty crazy theories over the years, thinking I've tracked down patterns that indicate killers are operating in a specific area. And I've brought those theories to my boss and the BAU. They listened to me the first few times I went to them. They even dug around, looked into my claims. But I was new, made a lot of mistakes and my theories were disproved."

"Every time?"

"Every time."

The pain in her voice had him reaching for her hand without even thinking about it. Her eyes widening was what made him look down and realize that he'd laced their fingers together. Even with his gloves on, it felt so right that he didn't let go. Neither did she.

"Go on," he said, surprised at how good it felt to hold

her hand. "You were saying that your theories were always wrong."

"Yes." Her voice sounded hoarse. She coughed. "I, ah, came up with a new theory about six months ago that I've been working on. But this one I haven't told anyone about. I wanted to be sure first. I've cried wolf too many times in the past. No one takes me seriously. So I decided to do something about it on my own, to try to get some kind of proof before going to the BAU again."

"Am I right in thinking that dyeing your hair was part of that search for proof?"

"I bleached it because the man I'm after abducts and presumably kills women who have straight blond hair and are in their midtwenties. I'm twenty-seven and figured that sacrificing my brown locks to match his preferred-victim characteristics was a small price to pay to get this man off the streets. Or out of the woods, I suppose. I believe he's targeting women in national parks, like this one. I've examined hundreds of missing persons cases to arrive at my theory."

"So you thought it was a good idea to come here and offer yourself as bait."

She winced and tugged her hand free from his. He belatedly realized he'd been squeezing too tightly.

"Sorry," he said. "I'm having a hard time wrapping my mind around the fact that you would put yourself in harm's way like that. With no backup. If I hadn't been there, if Vale had been the killer and he'd managed to sneak up on you without you hearing him, things could have gone very differently this morning."

"What makes you so sure that he isn't the killer? You haven't even heard my theory."

"Well, for one thing, he didn't have a gun."

She narrowed her eyes in warning.

"Okay, okay," he said. "Maybe his gun, knives, rope, duct tape and the rest of his serial killer torture implements were hidden away in a go-bag that he didn't have on him at the time. Maybe he keeps his go-bag in his car, like I keep mine in my Jeep, minus the torture implements, of course. Go ahead. I'm all ears. What's the theory?"

"If you're going to make fun of me, I won't bother. I can get that kind of treatment from my boss any day of the week."

"Ouch. All right. I'll be good. Go on. Tell me about your research."

She hesitated, as if weighing whether or not to trust him. Then she let out a long breath. "I need a piece of paper."

"How very old-fashioned of you." He popped the glove box open and dug around inside. "Fresh out of paper. How about a napkin?"

"That'll work."

He set a napkin on the seat between them and closed the glove box.

"Pen?" She held her hand out expectantly.

"Oh, right." He rummaged around in a pile of change in a cup holder and extracted a pen. "Here you go. It might be a bit sticky. I spilled some coffee in there this morning and haven't had a chance to clean it."

She grimaced and turned the pen, apparently to a less sticky spot. Then she drew a series of dots on the napkin, seven in all, and connected them with lines. She held it up to him. "What does that look like?"

He tilted his head, studying the drawing. "Is this one of those sexual harassment things? It kinda seems inappropriate, unless this is a friends thing instead of agent-to-agent stuff."

Her eyes widened. "What?" She turned the napkin toward her. "No. I don't even…no. It's a unicorn. Don't you see it?" She flipped it around again.

He stared at the dots and lines and gave up. "I'm guessing you didn't win any art awards in school."

She dropped the napkin to her lap. "I'm being serious."

"So am I. That doesn't look like a unicorn."

She plopped the napkin on the seat between them. "The Big Dipper doesn't look like an actual dipper, either. Not really. You have to use your imagination. In your case, maybe you should borrow some of mine, since you apparently don't have one."

"This is us being friends again, right? Insulting each other? It's fun. I don't know why I don't have more friends."

"I do," she grumbled.

He grinned.

She tapped the drawing. "The horse—"

"Unicorn."

"The *unicorn* is facing to the right. It's in profile. That's why there are only two legs. This is the horn." She ran a fingernail between two of the dots. "These are the withers—the shoulders, basically." She pointed to the other lines and named the various parts. "It's a constellation. It's called Monoceros now. When it was first discovered, the full name was Monoceros Unicornis."

"If you say so. What does that have to do with women going missing?"

"Each star represents a specific geographical location where a woman disappeared. When I superimpose the constellation over a map of the southeast section of the United States, the points line up."

The Jeep shook. They both looked up. Leaves fluttered on the bushes by the trail. Farther down, tree branches swayed up and down in the wind, like a crowd doing the wave at a football game. The sky was darkening overhead. But it was far too early for the sun to be going down.

"The weather guys have been warning about a storm all week. Looks like it's finally starting to roll in," he said. "I reckon we've got a couple hours of clear skies left. But up here the temps will start dropping long before that. We should head back to base."

She let out a sigh. "All right. Maybe Pops has an archaic pad of paper I can use. It'll work better than a napkin."

He smiled. "Knowing Pops, I imagine he does. The man keeps printouts of every case our team has ever worked on. He's responsible for half the stuff we have in storage."

He put the Jeep in Reverse, since there wasn't any room to turn around. He'd just backed onto the road when his phone buzzed. After checking his mirrors to make sure that no one was heading up the road behind them, Duncan looked at the screen. It was his boss. He'd likely passed right by them while they were parked on the trail. He and Pup were probably at the trailer, wondering where he was, and where Remi was. He should have called Pops and let him know that he'd found her, safe and sound.

He answered the call. "Hey, Lee. I've got Remi with me and—"

His boss interrupted him, and made a startling announcement. Duncan's gaze flew to Remi, his stomach dropping as if he'd just gone downhill on a steep roller coaster. "All right," he said when Lee finished. "We're on our way." He ended the call and punched the gas, sending the Jeep racing up the road.

"Duncan? What's wrong? What's going on?"

"You said you've been looking at cases where women went missing in national parks, plural. But you chose this particular park when you tried to bait the killer. Why?"

"That's what I was showing you earlier. It's all about the constellation and how it lines up with the various locations."

"Explain it to me."

"We just missed our turn. The trailer was back there."

"I'm taking you up the mountain, back to the gap where we were this morning."

"I don't understand. I thought it was dangerous. A storm is blowing in."

"That was Lee on the phone. He just got a call about a missing hiker, in the same area you were in this morning. The hiker's a woman in her midtwenties with long blond hair." He glanced at her horrified expression and immediately regretted his lack of finesse with his announcement.

"She hasn't been gone long," he said, trying to reassure her. "People do get lost up here a lot. It doesn't mean anything nefarious is going on. But the coincidence is too strong to ignore. If there's even a chance that her disappearance is connected to your theory, then I need to know everything you can tell me about your research. Right now."

Chapter Seven

Remi awkwardly reached her left arm across her lap and grabbed the armrest as Duncan's Jeep careened around a curve. If it weren't for her seat belt she'd be pinging around the interior like a pinball. As it was, her right shoulder kept bumping the door enough to have her biting the inside of her cheek and tasting blood.

Another turn and he had to slam his brakes to keep from ramming into the back of a long-bed pickup truck with a pair of ATVs bouncing around in the back.

"Pops never did learn how to drive over the speed limit," he complained, riding so close to the truck in front of them that Remi wanted to scream.

"How did you know a woman would go missing here? How did you know it would happen today?" he asked.

"I didn't."

He shot her an aggravated look. "I thought we were being honest with each other. A woman's life could be on the line."

"Don't you think I know that? I'm not lying." She definitely preferred the grinning, playful Duncan over this serious, all-business side.

He slammed the brakes again, narrowly missing Pops's bumper as the man maneuvered around a dip in the road. She grabbed the handle above the door window to keep from being thrown around. "Good grief, would you slow down before you get us killed?"

Surprisingly, he did. Not by much, but enough so that her insides no longer felt like they were rattling against her ribs.

"Your latest theory," he urged again, his voice laced with impatience. "The woman who disappeared is Sheryl Foster. She's got a husband and two small children. If you know anything that might help us find her, I need to hear it."

Her heart sank. "I wish… I don't…" She clutched the handle above her harder. "I wish I could help. But I'm not a criminal profiler. And I haven't run across anything yet that gives me a clue about the identity of whoever is behind these abductions. Offering myself as a potential victim was my big plan to draw him out. I've got nothing else."

"There are seven dots on that map. Different parks, right?"

"Different parks."

"Why did you come to this one? Why didn't you choose one of the others?"

"Because he'd already hit the other parks. This was the last one to make the constellation complete."

"The seventh dot?"

"Yes."

He seemed to consider that a moment. "What about the timing? How did you know he'd strike today?"

"I believed he'd strike this month, not today specifically. The unicorn constellation is only visible during February. The stars are very faint. You'd have to know something about astronomy to even know to look for it, and of course have a good telescope."

"You're an astronomy expert?"

"Not really. But I know more than the average person, by osmosis. My twin sister, Becca, she was totally into it. Had tons of books on the subject, telescopes. Every school project from elementary school on was about planets and stars and wormholes. Half her clothes either had a picture of a star on them or some kind of scientific fact about the stars." She waved her hand as if waving away her words. "My point is, we were really close, and shared a bedroom most of our lives. Whether I wanted to or not, I ended up learning about this stuff."

"Five minutes." He jerked the wheel to keep them from bouncing into a ditch.

Remi's pulse slammed in her throat. She half expected them to slide off the road at the next curve and barrel into a tree. She swallowed and kept her gaze on Duncan rather than the rocks and trees rushing past them in a blur. Pops was definitely going over the speed limit now. Probably because he was terrified that the tailgater behind him was going to ram his truck.

"Thoughts of Becca are never far from my mind. She disappeared here, in this park, over a decade ago. So when I began working for the FBI and started my own research on the side, I focused on murders and disappearances in the Smokies. It spiraled out from there."

"You think this guy is the same one who abducted your twin?"

"No, actually, I don't. The victimology is all wrong. She was much younger than the other women. And she had shoulder-length curly brown hair, like me. At least, when I'm not in bait mode and styling or dyeing my hair accordingly."

His gaze shot to hers again. "Please tell me you haven't done this before, changed your looks and paraded yourself in some remote area, purposely offering yourself up as bait for a killer."

She chewed her bottom lip.

He swore.

She drew a bracing breath. "Like I said, because of Becca, I tend to focus on missing persons cases in national parks. I'm hoping one day I'll stumble onto something that will help me solve her disappearance. But in the meantime, I started noticing disappearances of young blond Caucasian women, always the same time of year, in February. I plotted them out on a map. That's when I saw the pattern."

He still seemed to be upset over her baiting killers. His jaw was clenched so tight the skin had gone white. Remi sensed that his anger wasn't directed *at* her, it was on her behalf. He was concerned about her safety. She couldn't fault him for that. And couldn't deny that it felt good that one person in this world actually cared, even if only because he was a decent guy and would care about anyone putting themselves in harm's way. She could pretend it was because she was special to him, an actual friend. It felt too good not to try to hold on to that feeling, at least for a little while.

His deep voice broke into her thoughts. "The pattern you saw, it was the unicorn in the stars?"

She nodded, but since he wasn't looking at her she added, "Yes. There were six points, only one left to make the pattern complete. Six data points isn't much to pin a theory on, especially when the constellation in question isn't one that most people have ever heard of. I mean, what are the odds of some serial killer out there being a star nut like my sister and even knowing about Monoceros? The only reason I knew about it was because Becca loved unicorns and had a picture of Monoceros on our bedroom wall. But I couldn't shake the coincidence that the constellation is only viewable in February, and all of these women went missing in February. I figured if my theory was right, he would definitely strike here this month. So I took vacation, and took a chance."

Her throat felt tight as she admitted, "I should have told you all of this as soon as I was arrested. Instead, I sat there trying to protect myself and hoping you'd let me go so I could go back on the ridge. If I'd told you, maybe you could have—"

"What? Evacuated half a million acres? Warned all blond women to stay away from the Smoky Mountains for the entire month of February?"

"When you put it that way, it does sound ludicrous."

"A few years ago," he said, "we had out-of-control wildfires raging through this area. We blocked off roads and issued warnings on TV, radio, handed out flyers, you name it. People still went into the mountains." He glanced at her. "Trust me, Remi. This isn't something for you to feel guilty about. The only person who owns that guilt is the man who abducted Mrs. Foster—if she was even abducted. She may just be lost. And if she is, we'll find her. All right?"

She nodded and forced a smile. His words did make her feel better. But they didn't completely erase her guilt and unease. All she could do was hope and pray that the missing woman really was lost, and that the rangers would find her quickly, before the storm made them put their search on hold.

Duncan wrestled the Jeep over another bumpy section of road. "Back to your theory. Did the seven stars exactly correspond to the national park locations?"

"You mean was everything to scale, right? Like a

million miles between stars equals one hundred miles between abduction sites?"

"Something like that."

"Not at all. I admit I played loosey-goosey when drawing the lines on my map to correspond to the constellation. It was an approximation, not exact science. Which was yet another reason I didn't feel comfortable going to the BAU just yet."

"Then I'm still not following how you decided the killer would strike here. There are four hundred eighteen national park sites in this country. Dozens of them could work with that map you drew."

"True, but those four hundred eighteen sites include monuments, battlefields, forts and half-a-dozen other subcategories. While only sixty include National Park in their name, and are what most people think of when they envision a national park—namely that it's a huge area of land set aside for conservation and recreation. Most, but not all, include mountains, too, and rivers, streams, waterfalls, or in the case of Florida, beaches. All of the women disappeared in one of those sixty official national parks. And only one of those sixty locations could complete that constellation pattern. This one, the Great Smoky Mountains National Park. It was either here, or my theory would be disproven. Honestly, I expected it *would* be disproven. I don't exactly have a great batting average where theories are concerned."

"It may still not pan out."

She nodded, but she had a feeling that he didn't believe that any more than she did. Her gut was telling her that she'd finally stumbled onto a theory that matched reality, and that Sheryl Foster was in a world of trouble right now.

He was silent for a moment, as if he was weighing everything she'd said. If he was her boss, he'd throw her a few eye rolls right about now. Then he'd give her the usual *stick to the work you're paid to do* lecture. Her rote reply, that she was doing this research on her own time, never gained her any brownie points. If anything, she lost them, because he'd prefer that, if she wanted to go above and beyond, she'd do it on the active cases sitting on her desk rather than her "obsession."

"You did your homework," Duncan said.

No judgment. No knocking her down, accusing her of going off on wild tangents. He simply chose to believe her. She could almost hear Alanis Morissette crooning the lyrics to her hit song "Ironic," lamenting things like getting a death row pardon a minute too late. Wouldn't that be something? To finally find someone who not only listened to her, but was willing to take a chance on her being right, but the circle was closed? The seventh data point was already on the map. The killer had taken his last victim, and they were too late to stop him. Could life really be that cruel?

Stupid question.

The Jeep bounced even worse as he turned off the road onto a part of the mountain that flattened into a plateau. Dozens of other vehicles were already there. Several groups of people were heading into the trees, either on foot or doubled up on ATVs.

She held on tight to the handle, wincing when her shoulder hit the door. When the Jeep finally stopped, she eased her death grip and gingerly lowered her arm.

They were high up on the same mountain she'd been on this morning. It seemed so remote, isolated, until she noticed the cell tower on the right side of the field. Ahead of them, McAlister already had his tailgate down and was hooking up a ramp to unload the ATVs. Special Agent Lee and Ranger Grady were standing beside McAlister.

They must have heard about the missing woman and headed straight to the site without stopping at the trailer.

"Wait here." Duncan kept the engine running and hopped out to talk to his coworkers. A few moments later, he got back into the Jeep. He set a small white bag on the seat between them and then leaned across her to open the glove box. The utility belt she'd seen him wearing this morning—had that really been only this morning?—was in the compartment. He pulled it out.

"Is your cell phone charged?" he asked.

"Yes. Why?"

He motioned toward the passenger window. "There's the cell tower I mentioned earlier. If you need to make a call, you'll be able to get through. Add my cell phone number to your favorites." He rattled off the number while she keyed it in.

"Stay in the Jeep with the heater on. There's plenty of fuel, so that shouldn't be a problem. Plus..." He tapped the bag between them. "There's a sub, chips and a bottle of water in there that the boss got you for lunch. There are more bottles of water in the back and more snacks if you're still hungry. There's even a blanket behind the seat if you're not warm enough. I keep a go-bag in my Jeep at all times, with all the essentials, in case I end up stranded in a snowbank."

"And your orange backpack."

He smiled. "And my orange backpack, yes. That's a slimmed down version of my go-bag. Something all of us get in the habit of taking if we think there's any possibility that we might be out on the trails for more than an hour or so."

"Why are you offering me a sub and a blanket? I thought I was going with you."

He shook his head. "No way. You're suspended and

facing potential criminal charges. I can't have you at a crime scene. But no one's at the trailer right now, either. So for the moment, you're stuck here. I'm sorry about that. But I need you to wait here. Plus, there's something else to consider." He pulled his phone out and scrolled through the text messages. "Lee texted me this when I was talking to him a few minutes ago." He tapped the screen and turned it around. "This is the missing woman."

Remi pressed her hand to her throat. The resemblance was uncanny. "She looks like…me."

"Exactly." He shoved the phone back into his pocket. "Her family's up there with the search and rescue team. I don't want them seeing you and getting hopeful, even for a few seconds, before their brains catch up to their emotions and they clearly see the height difference. Sheryl Foster is half a foot taller than you. Then again, most people probably are."

His smile was a ghost of his former smiles, and she realized he was trying to lighten things up, to make her feel better. He really was a good man.

"I understand," she said. "I'll wait here."

"Thanks." He tightened his hand around the utility belt. "I'm going to assess the scene, but I should be back within the hour. I won't be part of the search and rescue team. We've got people far better trained than me for that. My boss will work with SAR on that end. My job is to coordinate the investigation, get the other investigators already on the scene to conduct the necessary interviews, get the lines of communication set up between the crime scene techs and—"

"Wait, crime scene techs? I thought she was just missing at this point." As if *just missing* wasn't bad enough. "Is there reason to believe something bad already happened?"

"The techs will help us examine her last known location. It's the base of operations, where the search begins. They'll look for evidence to help the SAR team. Once I make sure everything's in place and everyone knows their respective duties, I'll drive us back to the trailer and organize an investigative team on that end. Like I said, I won't be gone long. We've got all hands on deck for this, lots of investigators and rangers being called in. We do this a dozen times a year, like clockwork, every time someone gets lost. We all know the routine. Ninety-nine times out of a hundred, we find missing people in a handful of hours and bring them back home, safe and sound."

Again, he smiled. Again, she wasn't buying it. He was just as worried as she was. But she played along and smiled back.

He left her in the Jeep and hurried toward McAlister, who was waving impatiently for him to hurry up. Lee and Grady must have driven off on one of the ATVs that McAlister had unloaded, because they were nowhere to be seen and one of the ATVs was gone. As soon as Duncan hopped on behind McAlister, the ATV took off across the field, then disappeared into the forest.

Remi leaned forward and peered up at the ominous storm clouds gathering overhead as Duncan's parting words ran through her mind.

Ninety-nine times out of a hundred, we find missing people in a handful of hours and bring them back home, safe and sound.

She didn't have to ask him what happened in that hundredth case. She already knew.

DUNCAN STOOD ON the ridge, a flurry of activity happening behind him as crime scene techs hurried to make casts of footprints before the storm could destroy the evidence.

But it was what Duncan had just found that had chills going up his spine.

He knelt beside the outline of two shoes. They were small, he'd guess a woman's size seven boot, with a distinctive pattern on the sole—the same pattern he'd noticed on the bottom of Remi's boots when he'd left her handcuffed on the ground so he could tend Vale's injuries. She'd stood here, looking out through the gap, before Vale and he had come upon her from different directions.

And so had someone else.

Just a few feet behind her, off to the left behind some bushes, were the impressions of another pair of boots, a man's boots. They were about the same size as Duncan's, which told him the man who'd made them was probably over six feet tall. They were pointed toward the ridge, the toe of one print mashed heavily into the dirt, as if he'd squatted down, the way someone would do if he was trying to hide.

If a man had come up here wanting to enjoy the view, he wouldn't duck down behind these bushes and view the gap through the branches. He'd walk out in the open and stand on the ridge, like Remi had done.

The footprints had then turned in a semicircle, as if he'd been here when Remi walked down from the ridge, and watched her. Which meant he was likely here during the shooting. He'd hidden in these bushes and seen the whole thing. Which also meant something else.

Remi was likely right when she'd said someone was echoing her footsteps, sneaking up on her in the woods.

But it wasn't Vale, and it wasn't Duncan. There'd been another man out here shortly after dawn.

And he'd been hunting Remi Jordan.

Duncan straightened and motioned to one of the techs

who was processing other footprints down by the trail where Sheryl Foster had disappeared.

"Sir?" the tech asked.

Duncan pointed at the prints by the bush. "Cast these, too, when you get a chance. And send a picture to the SAR team so they can be on the lookout for those prints."

The tech nodded and took out his camera to snap some pictures.

Careful to keep to the side so he didn't step on any evidence, Duncan followed the prints down the slope. They ended a few feet from the AT, behind another group of bushes. And on the other side, within reaching distance, was a set of yellow evidence tags.

They marked the last known footprints made by the missing woman.

Chapter Eight

Long after the sun had set, Remi leaned against the back wall of the National Park Service trailer, desperate for just one moment where she wasn't being pushed or shoved or in danger of being trampled.

The chaos of ringing phones, fingers tapping on computer keyboards and people yelling to each other gave the appearance of progress, that something was being done that would eventually result in them finding the missing woman and returning her to her family.

But Remi knew appearances could be deceiving.

The same type of activity had consumed the campsite ten years ago after the sun had come up and Remi woke to an empty tent. She'd immediately told her father about Becca going to meet a boy the night before. The rangers were there within minutes. Eight hours had passed from the last time she'd seen her sister to when the search parties headed out to look for her. No trace of Becca was ever found. Only *two* hours had passed from the time Foster went missing and SAR began their search. Yet no sign had been found of the missing mother of two.

"We're leaving."

She turned, surprised to see Duncan beside her, wearing his jacket and gloves. Her coat was clutched in his right hand. In his left was a thick brown satchel stuffed so full of papers and folders that he'd never get it closed. He held her jacket out.

She hesitated, then carefully eased her right hand out of the sling to put her jacket on. He helped her, making the process much less painful than when she'd put it on by herself in the Jeep, while waiting for him to return from the crime scene.

A few moments later, they were heading down the mountain with the Jeep's heater on full blast and the headlights reflecting off the light blanket of snow covering the road.

"Did we leave because of the storm? It doesn't seem nearly as bad as I thought it would be."

He slowed for one of the many dangerous curves on this steep, narrow stretch of road. Snow flurries swam in the headlights like swarms of moths under a lamppost. "The storm is only going to get worse. The winds in the mountains can whip up to hurricane strength at the higher altitudes. Sleet and snow make the going slippery. Visibility will approach zero in a few hours up there." His voice was tight, clipped.

Remi's heart sank. "They've called off the search, haven't they?"

"SAR has taken shelter inside a cave to wait out the worst of the storm. My boss is telling everyone at the trailer to bug out. That trailer is a satellite office, not typically used as a command post for an investigation this big. It made sense to be there today since it's so close to Foster's last known location. But the base of operations will likely switch to one of the larger, permanent structures at a lower elevation, probably the offices in the Sugarlands Visitor Center."

"But not tonight?"

"Not tonight. There will still be people working the

case around the clock. But they'll work from home until this storm blows over."

Remi could well imagine the grief and despair, maybe even anger, when the Foster family was informed that the search was being suspended. Her family had been lucky. The search had gone on for a full week before being called off. But even then, her father had been devastated and furious. He'd yelled and begged the park service to keep looking. In the end, he'd gone home a broken man. The day he'd died, he'd been clutching a picture of Becca to his chest, tears rolling down his cheeks. It broke Remi's heart every time she thought about it.

"How long is the storm supposed to last?"

"Two to three days."

She inhaled sharply. "Two to three days? But… Sheryl Foster—"

"Has a backpack of supplies. This isn't her first time camping up here. Hopefully, she'll hunker down in a cave, or the hollow of a dead tree, and keep warm. SAR will be out looking for her as soon as possible."

She wanted to argue, to yell at him and everyone else that they needed to get back out there and find her. But he was right. They'd be risking more lives if they did.

A few minutes later, at the base of the mountain, he pulled into a parking lot that was empty except for one lone, dark blue car. Hers. But it wasn't blue anymore. It was pristine white, blanketed with snow. He pulled up beside it.

"Even if you had full use of both of your arms, I wouldn't let you drive in these conditions," he said. "There's too much ice and snow and you don't have a four-wheel drive. I'll take you to get your car when the weather clears up. But I figured you might need your purse. You mentioned it was in the trunk." He held out his hand. "Give me the keys and I'll get it for you."

As she handed him her keys, she asked, "Then you're taking me to my motel?"

"Where else would I take you?"

"Technically, I'm still under arrest. I was worried I might be spending the night in the Gatlinburg jail."

"Yeah, well. I'm a big softy. Plus, by leaving your car here, you'll be stranded. There won't be any taxis or Ubers out in this weather. I think I'm safe leaving my prisoner at Motel 6 tonight."

"It's not a Motel 6."

"Close enough."

She arched a brow. "Federal agent salary. I couldn't afford the Hilton."

He grinned. "I'm with you on that. But I would have sprung for a Holiday Inn."

He popped the door open, but she stopped him with a hand on his arm. He looked at her in question.

"Thank you, Duncan. You've been kinder to me than I deserve. I really appreciate it."

He glanced down at her hand. His Adam's apple bobbed in his throat, and for once, he seemed to be at a loss for words. Finally, he nodded and got out.

A few minutes later, with her purse sitting between them, they were back on the road heading toward Gatlinburg.

"I feel bad that you're going out of your way to take me home," she said. "I hope you don't get stuck out in the storm."

"This Jeep's like a mountain goat. And I've got chains for the tires if I need them. Besides, I don't live all that far from your motel. My cabin's in the foothills a few miles from there. Thanks for the concern, though. It's nice to have someone worry about me besides my mom."

She groaned. "Mom? You're comparing me to your mom?"

"Trust me." His voice sounded husky. "That's definitely not how I think of you."

Her mouth went dry. She should have come back with a sassy reply. But intelligent thought seemed to have deserted her.

"Have you lived in Gatlinburg very long?" Good grief, she was making small talk as if they were on a blind date.

"Been here my whole life. I grew up in a cabin at the top of one of these mountains. My parents still live there. My brothers and I—"

"How many did you say you had?"

"There are four of us."

"Four boys? Your poor mom."

He grinned. "She'd love you for commiserating with her like that. She blames us for every gray hair on her head." His smile faded. "My brothers Adam and Colin still live in the area, while my youngest sibling, Ian, lives…" He shrugged. "Only God knows where. He's about due to pop in again. This is the longest he's gone without any word."

"I hope he's okay."

"Ian's more than capable of taking care of himself. He's definitely not nice or sweet like your sister, Becca. He's the black sheep of the family, the rebel who has caused more than his share of tears and angst." He shrugged. "In spite of all that, he's family and we love him. I'm sure he'll be home soon."

Unlike her sister, who would *never* come home.

He grimaced and glanced at her, regret heavy in his expression, obviously wishing he could take back his words.

She rushed to cut off the apology that she knew was coming. "What makes you think my sister was nice or sweet?"

His eyes widened. "I just…assumed. You're identical twins and you're, ah, well…"

She took mercy on him and gave him a reassuring smile. "*Nice* and *sweet* are two words my sister would never apply to me. And I assure you, that's the last way that anyone would describe Becca. She was never the sugar and spice and everything nice sort of girl. She was more the snakes and snails and puppy dog tails variety, probably a lot closer to your rebel brother. She was impulsive, argumentative and a completely disruptive member of our household. My dad used to say that if he was the drinking type, she'd have made him an alcoholic."

"I can tell by your voice that you loved every hair-pulling, aggravating thing about her."

"I did. I do. I miss her every day."

She shoved back the strands of hair that kept escaping the ponytail she'd fashioned while at the trailer. But her hair wouldn't stay put. She gave up and pulled the holder out, letting her hair fall past her shoulders.

She caught him glancing at her, his throat working as he looked at the long strands. Heat seemed to radiate between them, thickening the air.

They rode in silence as they entered town. But as he turned down the main street, he said, "Seems odd to me that a group of kids from Colorado would come all the way to Tennessee for their senior trip. Especially since you left one mountain range for another."

She shrugged. "It was a compromise. A lot of us wanted to stay in the mountains near home for the trip. Others, like me, wanted to go somewhere we'd never been."

He seemed to consider that, then nodded. "Makes

sense when you put it that way." His smile faded. "Earlier you mentioned two potential suspects in your sister's disappearance. Weber and Hendricks? Whatever came of that?"

"Not much. Becca left our tent willingly, to meet a guy. But she didn't say who he was. Since she didn't have a boyfriend at the time, it could have been any of the guys at our camp. It was a high school senior class trip. There were a couple dozen senior guys, easily. And we weren't the only campers. There were several other tents a ways off from ours, other men. But the two guys you mentioned were in our class, and seemed the most likely to me to have been involved."

She clasped her left hand into a fist on the seat beside her. "Garrett Weber was the most popular and devastatingly cute guy in class. Becca had a terrible crush on him. Billy Hendricks was just as *un*popular as Garrett was popular. He had a crush on Becca. And, to be honest, she played on his feelings, using him as a tagalong if she didn't have anyone else to go with. But it never went as far as he wanted it to go. She was never serious about him."

"What about Garrett? Was he serious about her?"

"Not that I know of. He had a girlfriend at the time. I can't imagine him or Becca ignoring that and running off to meet each other. But she had it for him bad. If he'd shown any real interest, she'd have had a hard time resisting. Between the two, Garrett seems like the one she'd run off to see. But Billy is the one I could picture holding a grudge and wanting to harm her. And yet Billy had an alibi. Garrett didn't. Not one he could prove, anyway. He was in his tent, alone."

"But the police didn't think he did it?"

"Not really. There just wasn't anything in his background to suggest violent tendencies. No motive. And no physical evidence to support that he might have left his tent—no grass or mud on his shoes from trouncing around in the wilderness, no wet or dirty clothes. The whole investigation stalled pretty fast." She shook her head. "It's been hard, really hard. Which is why I want to do everything that I can to help another family avoid missing their loved one the same way."

When he pulled the Jeep up to her motel and parked in front of her door, neither of them moved. She wasn't sure what he was thinking. But a melancholy had fallen over her. She felt like she was about to say goodbye to a good friend, even though they barely knew each other. And she didn't know what to expect in the coming days, whether she'd end up in jail or free, whether she'd end up without a job or helping with the investigation. The only thing she was sure of was that she didn't want to be alone with her memories of Becca and fears for the missing woman. But she didn't know how to tell him that, or even what she'd be asking if she did.

"I guess I'd better go." She reached for her purse.

His hand was suddenly on her shoulder. "Wait."

The seriousness in his tone had her searching his gaze. "Is something wrong? I mean, something *else*?"

"I've been debating this since I left the office. But you deserve the chance to look it over, even though I don't think it will help."

"Look what over?"

He rummaged through the satchel of papers on the floor that he'd brought with him when they left the trailer. He pulled out a manila folder that was several inches thick, and set it on top of her purse.

The folder had darkened with age. It was curling at the edges. Coffee stains colored one corner.

"What's this?"

"Pops wanted me to give it to you. He's been working in the park since before I was born. He documents everything that goes on in the office in thick manila folders. They aren't official in any way. But a lot of times, he puts copies from the official files in there. And he adds his own personal notes, impressions, things you wouldn't list in a report."

He cleared his throat, looking uncomfortable. "I don't know whether you noticed, but the cell in the office trailer is filled with boxes. Aside from office supplies, the rest of them belong to Pops. He went through them earlier and took out that folder. It's a cold case, the disappearance of Becca Jordan."

Remi stared at the folder beside her. "I've read her file. One of the first things I did when I began working violent crimes for the FBI was to request a copy of it from NPS's national headquarters, the Washington Support Office. WASO's file didn't have any record of a Ranger McAlister as having worked on her case."

"They wouldn't, because he's not a criminal investigator. The law-enforcement variety of rangers are park police and everything that goes with that in a wilderness location—including helping search parties and rescuing people who need help on the trails. Not to mention dealing with fugitives on the run, the rare hostage situation. They pretty much do everything—except the actual investigations."

"That's your job."

"That's my job," he agreed. "Or in major cases, like today, we called in more investigators from the Atlanta regional office and a few park sites closer in to help out. My point is, it's not Pops's responsibility to work cases. But he's old-school, keeps notes on everything, anyway.

And he can't stand to see a case go unsolved. There have been many disappearances in the Smokies over the years. Most people are found. But, as you well know, some of those cases go cold. Unless someone calls in a tip or new evidence turns up, there's no reason to look into those cases again. So sometimes Pops, on his own time—"

"Reviews the cold cases, tries to solve them."

"Just like someone else I know." He smiled. "Like I said, he's not a trained investigator. I don't think he's ever solved any crimes. And I don't know that his notes will help—especially since his observations are mostly secondhand. He would have helped with the search, of course. But not the investigation, the interviews. Still, maybe something he wrote will help you gain a new perspective. Doubtful, but maybe. It was important to him that I give you the folder."

She swallowed. "Please thank him for me. That was very thoughtful."

"Don't get your hopes up, okay? The odds of you finding out what happened to her after all these years is slim to none. And the odds of you finding her…"

"Alive?"

He nodded. "The odds are pretty much zero. You know that, right?" His voice was soft, almost tender.

"I work in violent crimes. I know the statistics far better than most."

He helped her out of the car and into her room. Then he hesitated just outside the opening. "There's something else you need to know." His gloved fingers curled around the door frame. "When you said you thought someone was echoing your footsteps, stalking you up on the mountain this morning—or yesterday morning now—you were right. I found footprints that told the story. When you stood on the ridge looking through the gap in the trees, a man was watching you from the bushes, and it wasn't Kurt Vale. If Vale and I hadn't come upon you when we did, he might have abducted or killed you. So if you look at the shooting with those facts in mind, it's a blessing what happened with Vale. It probably saved your life."

Chapter Nine

Duncan balanced the tray of disposable coffee cups and bag of food in one hand as he rapped on Remi's door the next morning. The wind made a moaning sound as it blew around the eaves, the storm still raging, though not as hard as last night.

When no one answered, he knocked again, louder this time. He glanced around the motel parking lot behind him. The main drag through town was just a couple streets over. Remi's motel didn't have a restaurant. Had she headed up the street on her own in search of breakfast? Snow covered everything as far as the eye could see. Even though it wasn't snowing right now, it would be again in the coming hours. He couldn't imagine her wanting to venture out in weather like this with a hurt arm. One wrong step and she could lose her balance and wrench her shoulder.

The sound of the lock being clicked had him turning back around, to see a delightfully disheveled special agent blinking at him from the barely open door.

"I'll never forgive you for waking me at the crack of dawn. What time is it?" Her tone was far from welcoming. In fact, it sounded downright hostile.

He grinned. "Medusa's got nothing on your hair this morning."

She made a halfhearted attempt at finger-combing the yellow bushy halo around her head. If anything, she made it worse. She grumbled beneath her breath and pulled the door open the rest of the way.

He promptly forgot how to breathe.

She was wearing thin gray sweatpants and a gray Colorado Buffaloes sweatshirt. The sling wasn't over her shoulder yet, so she was clasping her hurt arm against her belly. What she probably didn't realize was that it pulled her shirt tight against her, revealing the sumptuous curves of her breasts. She wasn't wearing a bra. And she was cold.

He swallowed, twice. With Herculean effort, he forced his gaze up to eye level. Another swallow, and he rasped, "I come bearing gifts." He coughed to clear his throat, and held up the drink holder and food bag. Good grief, she was beautiful like this. All soft and sleepy and grumpy.

She shivered as if just noticing how cold it was outside. Then she grabbed one of the cups of coffee with her good hand, held it to her nose and inhaled deeply. "You're forgiven." She headed toward a door on the far end of the room. "I need five minutes."

He had a brief glimpse of white subway tiles before the door closed behind her.

He blew out a ragged breath and stepped inside. From the first moment he'd looked into Remi's soft brown eyes and seen the delicate curve of her face, there'd been no question that she was beautiful. It was one of those things he'd ticked off on a laundry list of attributes, as he would when observing any suspect—Caucasian, approximately five feet two inches tall, golden-brown eyes, long straight blond hair, mid to late twenties, attractive. It was enough for a description if he had to put out an alert to be on the lookout for her. But now he knew the rest of her matched the beauty of her face.

Those thin sweats had outlined every mouthwatering curve.

He'd half convinced himself last night, after getting home, that the sizzling attraction he'd started feeling toward her ever since they'd declared their friendship was a product of his natural empathy for the situation that she was in. He couldn't help but want to help in any way he could. But he'd expected that after a good night's sleep, the next time they were together he'd be able to think of her as just a peer, a fellow law-enforcement officer. And he'd be able to get back to the business of investigating Vale's shooting, while his team focused on the Foster disappearance. But as soon as she'd opened that door, he was lost. He really had it bad for Remi Jordan.

Conflict of interest much?

He shook his head and looked around for somewhere to set the food. The room was clean, and surprisingly modern, with a wood-look porcelain tile floor that was so popular these days. Obviously, the motel had gone through some recent renovations. But the reno hadn't done anything about its dimensions. It was just big enough for a queen-size bed, a dresser across from it, and a small round table by the lone window, with two wooden chairs. Since the table was covered in papers, and the dresser was covered with even more, he set the bag on one of the chairs and took the other chair for himself.

He idly sipped from his coffee as he scanned the pages on the table. He'd assumed they would be from the cold case folder he'd given her last night. But then he saw a picture of a constellation, and realized he was looking at her research. Seven white dots that represented stars were connected by lines. To him, it didn't look like a horse at all, let alone one with a horn in the middle of its forehead. He supposed she was right that he didn't have a good enough imagination. But it was the words written by each dot that held his interest.

The rear hoof was labeled Dry Tortugas National Park, Florida, Melanie Shepherd. What he supposed was the rear end of the horse was labeled Hot Springs National Park, Arkansas, Amanda Powell. In neat succession, every single data point had a location and name associated with it, along with a date.

Congaree National Park, South Carolina, Jacqueline Stuart.

Mammoth Cave National Park, Kentucky, Mindy Brooks.

Cuyahoga Valley National Park, Ohio, Rose Walling.

Shenandoah National Park, Virginia, Allison Downs.

And then, written in fresh ink, the newest entry: Great Smoky Mountains National Park, Tennessee, Sheryl Foster.

"Thanks for the coffee."

He glanced up to see her walking toward him, holding the cup in her left hand. She was still wearing those distracting clingy sweats, but she'd most definitely put on a bra. And she was wearing the sling again. Plus she'd brushed out her halo of blond hair. It was slightly damp, as if she'd wet it down. But it wasn't straight like yesterday. It rippled in waves, some of it forming curls that bounced on her shoulders.

He longed to plunge his hands into her hair and see if the curls were as soft as they looked. It took a good deal of control to try to keep his expression clear so that his completely inappropriate fascination with her didn't show. He really needed to get a grip.

"Curly," he said, stating the obvious.

"Natural curl, a total pain. It takes me a good hour to flat-iron it straight to head out on the trail."

"To offer yourself as bait." He still couldn't believe she'd put herself at risk that way.

She shrugged, then winced and set her coffee on top of a stack of papers so she could rub her hurt shoulder. She looked around, then grabbed a bottle of ibuprofen off the table by the bed.

He leaned over and took it, opened the cap, then handed it back to her. "Why not just perm it straight if your plan was to walk the AT all February until you caught the killer's attention?"

After drinking down three pills, she lowered her cup. "I considered it. But having already bleached it blond, if I permed it my hair would probably all fall out. Not an attractive look for me."

As much as he loved her hair, he didn't think it would make her any less attractive if she was bald. She was sexy, period. Not just because of her curvy figure, either. She was smart, dedicated and had a wicked sense of humor.

And...he really needed to get back to business and stop thinking about her that way.

He motioned toward the tabletop with its pile of pictures and papers. "How long did you say you'd been accumulating this research?"

"Six months, give or take."

"And before that? Another case of disappearances?"

She nodded.

"What color did you dye your hair for that one?"

"Red."

He swore. "Do you realize how lucky you are that you haven't been killed already?"

She grabbed the bag off the chair and sat down. "Do I smell bacon?"

"You're trying to distract me."

"Yes, I am. Do I smell bacon?"

He reluctantly smiled and let the subject drop. "Bacon, egg and cheese croissants. They're both for you. I ate mine on the way here. They should still be warm. I made them right before I drove down."

Her eyes widened and she peeked inside the bag. "These are homemade?"

He chuckled at the surprise on her face. "*Homemade* is too strong a word. I already had the croissants from a local bakery. I just threw some eggs and bacon in grease, slapped some cheese on top and voilà. Breakfast sandwiches. The coffee's from my K-Cup machine. I just tossed it into a couple of disposable cups." He took a sip of his coffee and pulled another sheet of paper toward him.

"Oh, my gosh." Her words came out muffled around a bite of sandwich. She set the sandwich down and put her hand in front of her mouth. "Heavenly."

He grinned. "If you like my thrown-together breakfast sandwiches that much, you'd die for my mac-n-cheese. Straight out of the box, powdered cheese. Mmm, mmm, good."

"Amateur. My frozen pancakes top your boxed mac-n-cheese any day." She took another bite of sandwich.

"You might win that one. I make great pancakes, from scratch."

She blinked. "From scratch? Now you're being cruel."

"Be really nice to me and I might make you some one day." He thumped his finger on the paper in front of him. "You've done a *lot* of research on these missing women. Did your boss let you do any of it on the clock or did you have to do all of this on your own, in addition to your normal caseload?"

She took a quick sip of coffee to wash down her food, then wiped her mouth with a napkin. "All on my own time. My boss doesn't like me doing any of this."

"You interviewed the families?"

"No. That was where I drew the line. This is my project on the side, with no official backing. I couldn't bear to get anyone's hopes up by introducing myself as FBI years after the initial disappearances. The families would have thought I had new leads, that maybe they'd finally get the answers they've hungered for. I didn't want to give anyone false hope."

"That's very insightful of you, and kind. I honestly don't think I would have thought of it in those terms. But I can see that you're right."

Her mouth tightened. "I have the *bonus* of knowing what it's like to be on both sides."

"Then these interviews are from the *original* investigations?"

"That's right. I visited each park, spoke to the detectives who worked each disappearance, sweet-talked copies of their files from them. They were surprisingly forthcoming. I didn't run into one single person who was worried about a Fed butting her nose into their business without being invited. Then again, I guess you could say my status as the family member of a missing woman gave me added credibility. I admit I played the empathy card to get what I wanted." She waved toward the hundreds of pages spread out in front of them. "Not that it did me much good. I haven't come up with one viable suspect."

She took another bite of her croissant while he scanned page after page of interviews, timelines, victim descriptions, witness statements—not that anyone had really witnessed much of anything. Mostly it was people talking about when they saw the person in the days leading up to her disappearance.

When she'd finished her sandwich, she rolled the bag closed with the second croissant still inside and set it on the floor. "What about your team? Have you spoken to them this morning? Did they piece together anything new?"

"Hard to say. Everything we're doing is just background, time lines, things that will eventually help us prove a case in court, if it comes to that. But nothing so far has generated a true lead that will help us find her. Our investigators canvassed miles of the AT yesterday, talked to everyone they came across before we were forced to pull out. My team checked the logbooks in the shelters—"

"Logbooks?"

"I forgot you're a newbie at trail life."

"Newbie might be stretching my knowledge level."

"There are shelters throughout the Appalachian Trail, like the one you stayed at the night before the shooting." He paused. "Why did you stay overnight that particular evening?"

"Stupidity. Wasn't paying enough attention and got surprised when the sun started going down. I belatedly realized I was way too far from my car to make it back before dark. I knew I'd get lost and I didn't want to die of hypothermia. I'd studied the maps enough to know where the nearest shelter was, and headed there."

"I don't remember you having a backpack," he said. "And I don't remember the complainant who saw your gun describing you as having any supplies with you."

"Yes, well. I wanted to have my hands and arms completely free and be ready to react. You were going to tell me about logbooks, I think?"

Her eyes pleaded with him to let the subject of her unpreparedness drop. He was still in shock, and amazed that she hadn't died of exposure without the right supplies. But she obviously felt embarrassed over the whole thing and he didn't see the point in making her feel worse.

He cleared his throat. "Logbooks. Okay. Many of the shelters have them. It can be anything from a spiral notebook to a leather-bound journal. It's like an old-fashioned guest register at a bed-and-breakfast. People leave their names—usually trail names rather than their legal names—along with dates and maybe a few sentences or paragraphs about their experiences on the AT. Or advice for others at the shelter, maybe warning them about some kind of hazard on the trail, or letting them know a water source has dried up in a certain area."

"Sounds like something that would definitely help with an investigation. Maybe we should—"

"Already done. Examining the logbooks at nearby shelters was one of the first things we did. We have pictures online in the case file of relevant pages in the logs. It will take a while to track down the different people who wrote in those logs. And, of course, not everyone signs the logbooks. You didn't."

"I was too busy keeping an eye on the other hiker in the shelter, that Zack Towers guy, and watching the woods around me. I barely slept a wink that night. Didn't even occur to me to explore the shelter for something like what you just described. I didn't see anything like that sitting out anywhere."

"The one at your shelter was stored in a plastic bag to keep it dry, and placed in a wooden box under the sleeping platform."

"Looks like I have a lot to learn about trail life."

"Only if you intend to hike the Appalachian again."

"Whatever it takes."

Her chin was set in a stubborn line. She was willing to do anything, risk anything, to catch the person responsible for the women's disappearances.

"Funny how I hiked several days without anyone else noticing my gun in my pocket," she said. "Just how well do you know this Zack Towers guy? Maybe he's the one I heard following me. Maybe he called you hoping you'd take my gun away, leaving me without a weapon to defend myself."

He laughed, then sobered. "You're serious? You've pegged Sunny as a serial killer?"

"Why not? He looks harmless, but he's a big guy, capable of overpowering most women easily enough."

"Big as in tall, sure. But he's scrawny. The guy doesn't weigh much more than you. He's got hiker's legs, I'll give him that. But I can't see him coming out the winner in a physical confrontation. He'd more likely turn tail and run."

"You said yourself he's a regular, that he comes up here every year about this time."

He held up his hands in surrender. "Maybe you're right. You never know about people. Everyone has their secrets. But let's start with some background, for my benefit. Walk me through more of your research. Give me the short version of what you've compiled."

"The short version is that I really don't have much. I mean, I have a lot of useless details about each of the victims. I can tell you what they were wearing when they disappeared, who was the last known person to have seen them, why they were in each particular park, even what they ate before they disappeared. But other than their physical attributes and the national park angle, and my constellation theory, nothing I have is helpful. None of them had anyone in their lives who would have wanted to harm them. It seems completely random, a stranger abduction, the absolute hardest kind of abduction to solve."

"I haven't seen any lists of who drove in and out of these parks on the days of the disappearances."

"There's only one." She spread the pages out even more, apparently seeing some kind of organization to the clutter that escaped him. "Here it is." She handed him a small stack that was stapled together. "That's from the most recent disappearance. Well, the one before ours here. Allison Downs, Shenandoah National Park. That particular facility has video of everyone coming and going at the park entrance. Since it's digital and only takes up space on a computer hard drive, they have video going back for years. They let me sit in their security office and create my own paper log of all the vehicles and people coming and going in the few days before and after Allison disappeared."

"You compiled this by hand? There have to be hundreds of listings here."

"Three hundred fifty-seven. And yes, I stared at video for a full week while writing all of that information down. It was a lot of work."

"Impressive. You have license plates on a lot of these, descriptions of the occupants."

"It would be impressive if any of it had led me to Allison Downs. But it didn't. And none of the other parks had any records going that far back. Those disappearances had been years before. So I have nothing to compare my list against."

"We keep video indefinitely."

She straightened. "You have video?"

"I do. It's accessible online in the file-sharing area of our investigation wiki. We've started making lists. I've got someone working on it right now, actually. But it's a painstaking task, as you well know." He pulled the Shenandoah list toward him. "But now that we have something to compare it to, maybe—"

"—we'll see the same vehicle at both parks."

He nodded. "If we get lucky, yes. And if the bad guy drove into the park. He could have ridden in on motorcycle, through the woods, and not even come by the cameras. It's a huge park."

Her shoulders slumped with disappointment. "I'm getting nowhere on this. I could use some help, a fresh set of eyes. What are your plans today?"

"Well, originally, I wanted to come check on you, make sure you had everything you need until the storm blows over—feed you breakfast. Then I was going back up to my cabin to work on the Sheryl Foster investigation." He cleared his throat. "Plus, I need to follow up on the shooting investigation. I want to check on Vale in the hospital, ask him some more questions."

She stiffened at the mention of Vale. "Make sure you ask him where he tossed the gun."

"I will."

She blinked. "You will?"

He nodded. "When it's okay to go back up the mountain, I'll have someone conduct a broader search of the area with a metal detector."

"Thank you."

"You're welcome. Of course, you know whoever took Foster can't be Vale, right? Even if he did have a gun? Vale is in the hospital. He has an airtight alibi."

"Are you sure about that? Maybe he left the hospital against doctor's orders and—"

"I called this morning. At the time of Foster's disappearance he was with a doctor."

"Nothing's ever easy, is it?"

"It can be less difficult if you team up with someone and help each other. Do you want to work together?"

She straightened. "Don't tease me. That would be cruel."

He chuckled. "I need to keep an eye on you anyway, at least until I get with the DA on your case. I can't think of a better way than to take you up to my cabin. I'll let you view the video and whatever lists my team has already put together. You can compare them with your Shenandoah list and see if anything shakes out. Meanwhile, I'll look into some other angles and see if I can't expedite the investigation into Vale's shooting. I'm sure you'd like to get that resolved, one way or the other."

Chapter Ten

Remi sat at the big yellow pine table in the cabin's rustic eat-in kitchen, her laptop in front of her. Duncan had created a temporary login for her and had her hooked to the wiki site his team used for their investigations. And she'd been viewing videos of the park's entrances for hours, freeing up one of his investigators to work on another aspect of the case while she worked on the list. But it was taking forever, and the video was grainy, a lower quality feed than what she'd had in Shenandoah. She was getting a headache from squinting at the freeze frames of the license plates.

When they broke for lunch, she walked around the main room of the cabin, stretching her cramped muscles as she admired the exquisite floor-to-ceiling stacked stone fireplace with a roaring fire popping and snapping inside it. The view out the picture windows was lovely, but everything was white. She imagined it would be breathtaking in the summer, or the fall with the changing leaves stretching up and down the mountaintops far into the distance. Cabins like this, with views like this, didn't come with a federal agent's salary. He either had another source of income, or he was crooked. Even though she hadn't known him long, she had zero doubt that his money came honestly.

Hours later, back at the table poring over reports and videos and lists, she was feeling like a pretzel again. The longer she sat, the more her shoulder ached.

"Looks like you could use some more Vitamin I." Duncan shoved his phone into his pocket and entered the kitchen from the vaulted great room, where he'd gone to make some calls.

"Vitamin I? That's what you call ibuprofen?"

"The drug of choice for all trail hikers. And FBI agents who've been hunched over their computers for most of the day." He grabbed a bottle of pills from a cabinet and set it opened in front of her, along with a bottle of water for her and one for himself. "Just how bad is your shoulder? I'm sure I could make it to the hospital in my Jeep and get you seen by a doctor."

"In this weather?" She motioned toward the large windows flanking the fireplace in the other room. It wasn't snowing at the moment, but trees still swayed in the wind.

"It's not as bad as it was when we drove up here this morning. I think the storm will blow over earlier than predicted."

"Well, my shoulder isn't an emergency. A few Vitamin I's and I'll be as good as new." She swallowed a couple pills.

"Are you this much of a slob at home?" he teased, and started straightening the papers on the table.

She slapped his hand away. "Stop that. I have a system. If you move stuff I won't be able to find anything."

"A system, huh? Prove it. If I want the research on the Hot Springs disappearance, where should I look?"

"Right over here." She tapped a jumble of pages about a foot to his left.

"Lucky guess. Cuyahoga Valley?"

"Here." She tapped another stack.

He arched a brow. "Mammoth Cave National Park."

She pointed to a stack to his right.

He picked up the first page, scanned it, then set it back down. "Okay. You have a system."

"It's not easy being smarter than everyone else. But I bear my burden the best that I can."

He rolled his eyes. The gesture reminded her so much of Becca that her throat went tight.

"Remi?" He touched her hand. "You okay?"

"I'm fine. Just…thinking." She blinked and stared at her computer. But she couldn't quite bring it into focus. She sighed and sat back. "I can't look at these grainy videos anymore, not right now, anyway. You guys need better cameras."

"That's what happens when a bureaucrat in DC sets the budget."

"You were in the other room on the phone quite a while. Find out anything new?" she asked.

"Actually, I was about to surprise you with some good news."

"They found Sheryl Foster? She's okay?"

He winced. "No. Sorry. Didn't mean to give you false hope. It's still a bit too rough out there for the SAR team to resume their search."

Disappointment was bitter in her throat. "What's the good news then?"

"My district attorney friend, like us, is working from home, waiting out the storm. I spoke to him about your case and he agrees with my recommendations. No charges will be filed against you. As of this moment, you're free to go. Or once I can get you back to your car."

She pressed her hand to her chest, some of the tension and pain in her shoulder seeming to magically ease at his words. "I didn't know how worried and stressed out I was about that until now. It's like a boulder has been lifted off me. But I thought you still needed to go interview Vale in the hospital before your final recommendations."

"I did. Over the phone earlier, in the other room. He didn't have anything new to offer to help with the investigation. But he also said he wasn't interested in pressing charges. That's not his decision, of course. But he added that he wouldn't sue you in civil court. He feels guilty for scaring you. He feels partly to blame and said he couldn't in good conscience try to benefit financially when his own actions contributed to what happened. He thinks of it as an unfortunate accident. Period."

She sat there, stunned at the sudden turn of events. "That's certainly unexpected, especially in today's society, where everyone sues everyone over any little thing."

"You don't sound very happy."

"I am. I guess. I just…" She shook her head, thinking back to that moment on the ridge.

Scuffling sounded behind her.

She turned.

A man in camouflage faced her from twenty feet away.

She told him to freeze.

He pulled a gun out of his pocket.

Or had he?

"Remi?"

"I just… I just keep picturing him pulling that Glock out of his pocket. How could he not be our guy?"

He rested his forearms on the table. "You've taken people's statements many times, right?"

"Of course. Dozens of times."

"Have you ever taken eyewitness statements from two people who saw the same thing, and their statements were polar opposites? But you believed both people were absolutely one hundred percent certain about what they'd seen?"

She started to cross her arms, before remembering her sling. Instead, she fisted her left hand on the table. "Every investigator I know has. But that doesn't change what I saw."

"Doesn't it? You need that cell phone to be a gun."

"So I'm imagining a gun that was never there."

"I think so, yes."

She wanted to shake her head. But he could be right. She knew it was possible. People often convinced themselves they'd seen something, because they wanted so hard to believe it. Was that what she was doing now? Convincing herself she'd seen a gun because the alternative was too hard to accept—that she really had shot an unarmed man?

"Just think about it, Remi. Maybe once some time passes, you'll see it differently."

"Maybe," she grudgingly allowed, hating that he might be right.

"As for your job, you're not out of the woods there. I have no idea what your employer is going to decide about your future career with them."

"The bureau was a means to an end from day one, anyway," she said. "My goal all along was to join the BAU. But after this latest episode, I have no illusions about that. Maybe I'll go into the private sector and become a private investigator. I'd have a lot more freedom to pursue the cases that I'm most interested in."

"If you ever want any PI tips, let me know. My future sister-in-law used to work for one and could teach you a thing or two."

"Future sister-in-law? You have a wedding coming up in the family?"

"We do. Jody Ingram is marrying my oldest brother, Adam. They met during a case last summer. His leg was severely injured in an accident in the mountains. As soon as he's recovered enough, they'll set a date. It'll be the first wedding for us McKenzie brothers. Unless Ian got married without telling us. Honestly, I wouldn't put it past him." He waved toward the stacks of paper. "You wanted a break from the computer. Let's talk it out, throw around any ideas either of us has. I updated my boss and this morning's shift of investigators about your theory."

She groaned. "Great. Now they'll all think I belong in a straitjacket."

"Does it really matter? Personally, I'm willing to consider anything if it will help us find a missing woman, or keep others from suffering the same fate. As far as your theory, one part is nagging at me. I know there are a lot of blond women out there, because so many dye their hair. But how many have long straight hair? And of those, how many go hiking in the parks? It seems far-fetched that he's always lucky enough to find a victim to match his favorite victim criteria."

"I don't agree. It's not like he's targeting a specific day in February. He has the entire month to look through the park, watch people, wait until the perfect woman comes along. Then he snatches her." She waved toward the computer screen, which was dark now because it had timed out. "Trust me. I've seen plenty of women who fit his profile while looking through the videos both for Shenandoah and the Smokies."

He tilted his head, considering. "How many is plenty?"

"I haven't really been counting. But just in viewing the past week from your park, I'd guess that I've seen five or six. Extrapolate that to an entire month and he has twenty to twenty-four potential victims to choose from.

The problem now is that, if he took Foster, his pattern is complete. There's no reason for him to stick around. We'll probably never catch him."

"I'm not ready to concede defeat just yet. Let's follow this through. What do we know, or think we know? He has a type, he waits days, weeks, until someone of that type comes along, then he abducts her. What we don't know is what he does after he takes her. If he waits a full year between victims, what's he doing the other three hundred sixty-four days of the year? This guy is cold and calculating, a psychopath. Abducting these women is an addiction for him. He lives for this. Can he really wait an entire year between abductions?"

"Good point. But I looked for other similar abductions. I don't see how I could have missed any, if that's what you're thinking."

"What if he has more than one victim type?"

She stared at him. "I don't... I don't understand. Are you thinking that, say, every six months he abducts someone? Maybe he's working on another constellation with different victim criteria? Like brunettes, or redheads?"

He spread his hands out to his sides. "Just exploring possibilities. Trying to figure this guy out. One victim a year doesn't seem like enough to me. I'm picturing him like a tiger in a cage, pacing around, getting anxious while he watches the calendar. Most serial killers I've heard of kill more frequently, or in clusters. And they don't always stick to a specific type. Ted Bundy preferred college-aged women with long brown hair parted in the middle. But he confessed to a biographer that his first kill was a man. And one of the early victims that he's suspected of killing was only eight years old. When the need to kill is driving one of these psychopaths, they strike out at victims of opportunity who may or may not fit their ideal preferences. I just think we should look at other disappearances and see if there are more that we might be able to attribute to this same guy. The more data we have, the more likely we'll find mistakes he's made along the way, mistakes that may help us track him down."

"The BTK killer, Dennis Rader, killed ten people. But he went years between kills, one time as many as eight years," she countered, not quite ready to give up the theory she'd worked on for so long.

"He's more an exception than a rule, though, isn't he?" He was equally unwilling to drop his line of inquiry.

"I guess so," she said grudgingly. "Most of them do kill more often. All right. We can do it your way, take another look. But I'm worried we'll spend all our time off on a wild-goose chase."

"Then let's limit our search, and the amount of time we spend on this."

She nodded, still not convinced. "How about geography? If we search the whole country, we could spend weeks, months, going over missing persons cases."

"Not if we limit them to national parks, the sixty main sites. We can even limit it just to the seven sites you already identified, stick with your original theory, just expand on it. For one thing, let's not restrict the time frame. Maybe you found the key abductions in February that form the constellation. But he reinforces that pattern during another season, maybe during the summer."

She punched a key to wake up her computer, and was about to type a URL, then slumped back against her seat. "I'm on administrative leave. I can't get into any of the national databases I normally access."

"We're both Feds. I've probably got access to many of the sites you use. I've looked into plenty of missing persons cases over the years." He rounded the table and pulled a chair up beside her. After logging on to one of the main missing persons law-enforcement databases, he turned the computer back to her. "You do the honors."

They took turns searching various databases, expanding their criteria to include homicides as well as disappearances in national parks, operating on the theory that if there were more victims from this same man, some of the bodies could have been found. There were a surprising number to dig through when homicides were included. They had to weed through suicides, for one. Sadly, aside from falls and drownings as the leading causes of death in the nation's park system, suicide was right up there. Apparently, people found solace in walking into the wilderness and ending their lives up close and personal with nature.

After a quick break for a dinner of grilled cheese sandwiches and tomato soup, they were back at their own computers, considering each case, taking copious notes. Once they felt they had all the cases that could possibly be relevant, they split them up and began eliminating them one by one.

Finally, Remi sat back, staring at the three cases she couldn't rule out. A sick feeling began to settle in her gut as she checked the locations and dates. She felt Duncan's gaze on her and looked up. From the other side of the table, he peered at her over his laptop.

"Verdict?" he asked.

"I have three that I can't rule out."

"Me, too. Read off what you have."

She swallowed, then read the locations. "Dry Tortugas, Cuyahoga Valley and Mammoth Cave."

His eyes widened. "Hot Springs, Congaree, Shenandoah."

She fisted her left hand on top of the table. "You were right. How could I not have seen this pattern before? He's abducting two women every year in the same locations. First a blonde, then a brunette. Maybe more if we missed something else."

"It's not your fault. It's tunnel vision," he said. "As soon as you found the original pattern, you were naturally blind to a new pattern. And we can use this to find him. Even if he took Foster, he's not finished. He's not going anywhere."

"Do you have the exact dates that each of your three victims went missing? I need the date for each one."

"Give me a second. That's buried in my notes." As he located the data, he read it aloud to her. When he finished the last one, he stared at her intently. "I'm not liking the sound of this."

She finished filling in the matrix she'd created for the six new victims, then nodded. "It's right there in front of us. Every time he abducts a blonde victim, he abducts a brunette—"

"Two days later," they both said at the same time.

"If Foster was his first victim, then he's already out there looking for the next one," she said. "He's going to abduct her tomorrow."

"I'll call my boss, have him officially invite the FBI into the investigation. We'll get the teams working on the evidence from the other cases we've found. There's physical evidence in some of these additional cases, forensic evidence on the three whose bodies were recovered. We'll get him, Remi. We'll get this bastard and lock him up."

"But will we get him in time?"

The anguish in his gaze reflected her own. They had less than twenty-four hours to fit all the pieces together, to try to stop a killer from taking another victim. And what about Sheryl Foster? Were they already too late for her? Was she shivering in the snow somewhere, staving off a sadistic man and wondering if anyone was ever going to come save her?

She glanced past his shoulder to check the weather, and blinked in surprise. "Duncan. The storm."

He turned around in his chair.

The pine trees outside the windows weren't swaying in the wind. Everything was quiet.

"It's over. The blizzard has moved on," he said. "Search and rescue can get out there and find Foster." He shoved his chair back from the table. As he stood, he said, "I'll check in with Lee, get a status on SAR, bring everyone up to speed on what we've discovered." As soon as he pulled his phone out of his pocket, it buzzed. He checked the screen, then answered the call.

"Hey, boss. I was just about to…"

Remi watched his face go pale as he listened to whatever Lee was telling him. He listened for several minutes, saying only the occasional "okay." Finally, he said, "All right. We're at my cabin. We'll head there now."

She watched him slowly round the table to where she was sitting. She pushed herself to standing and looked up into his misery-filled eyes.

"What is it?" she asked. "Did they…did they find Sheryl Foster's body?"

"No." His voice sounded strained. "SAR headed back out over an hour ago. They're still looking for her."

"Then why do you look like someone kicked your dog?" She sucked in a breath. "Did he already abduct the second victim, take her early? Another woman is missing?"

He shook his head. "No one else has been abducted that we know of. But the SAR team did find someone. Remi, they found a skeleton."

Chapter Eleven

Duncan walked beside Remi, holding her left hand to help her keep her balance as they stepped over rocks and crunched across fresh snow behind a SAR team leader. Duncan would have preferred not to bring her out here at all. But his boss had insisted. With her hurt shoulder and her arm in a sling, she wasn't as steady as she needed to be, especially going downhill through the woods on steep grades without a true trail to follow. But he knew there wouldn't have been any point in him trying to stop her once his boss told her about SAR's discovery. So here he was, with Lee and a team of rangers and investigators keeping a respectful distance behind them. He hated that he'd forever be linked in her mind with the second worst day of her life, right up there with the worst day—when her twin sister went missing.

Then again, he hated to think of her going through this without having someone with her who cared about her. And he definitely did, more than he would have thought possible in such a short time. Not that it would matter after this. She'd never be able to look at him again without remembering the scene he was taking her to. And that, as they said, would be all she wrote. She'd go back to Colorado, leaving him and her bad memories behind.

In her shoes, he'd probably feel the same way. But it still sucked no matter how he looked at it.

"It's not her. The skeleton isn't Becca," she whispered beside him.

He didn't bother replying. She'd been repeating those two sentences to herself every few minutes since the moment he'd told her about the discovery of human remains. They'd been found about a mile west of the gap where Remi had stood so recently, and yet so very long ago, in terms of everything that had happened since then.

Up ahead, the underbrush and trees gave way to a clearing surrounded by woods on two sides, rocks on the other sides. The crime scene techs had rigged a twenty-by-twenty temporary cover over it, orange waterproof fabric attached to four metal poles driven into the ground. And beneath the orange cover, in the very middle, lay a white sheet.

They stopped a few feet from that sheet. One of the techs squatted down, his gloved hand resting on the corner of the fabric as he waited for Duncan's signal.

"You don't have to do this," Duncan whispered. "We can wait for DNA results and—"

"I want to. I need to know. DNA would take too long."

"They'll have to confirm with DNA, anyway. This is pointless. Lee shouldn't have demanded that you come down here. And you don't have to do anything he tells you to do. Let me take you back up the mountain and wait for the medical examiner to do his job."

She tilted her head back, her gaze finally meeting his. "You're a good man, Duncan. You don't know how much it means to me that you care, that you want to protect me. But I need to do this. I need to know. And I need you to understand. Okay?" She tightened her grip on his hand. "Okay?"

"I'm going to have to turn in my man card after this. I'm supposed to be comforting you, not the other way around."

She smiled. "Your man card is safe. You've been comforting me this whole time."

He pulled her to him, not caring who watched or what they thought, and carefully hugged her, mindful of her hurt shoulder. She rested her cheek against his chest and drew a shaky breath. Then she stepped away and tugged her hand from his.

"Let's get this over with." She straightened her back and turned with him to face the crime scene.

He signaled the tech, who pulled the sheet away, revealing a body bag. Duncan had been surprised to see the sheet when they'd approached, thinking the team was compromising the scene by allowing the cotton fibers to potentially mix in with the skeleton and surrounding dirt. But now he understood. They'd already excavated the site, collected the evidence. The remains were in the zipped bag waiting to be transported up the mountain. All that needed to be done now was to see whether Remi could identify the artifacts with the skeletal remains, provide a tentative identification to speed things along. The crime scene guys were trying to soften the blow, be respectful of Remi's feelings.

The same tech leaned down and, this time without waiting for a signal, unzipped the top of the bag and pulled it down halfway. The corpse was exposed from the middle of its rib cage to the top of its skull—a skull that still had wisps of long, dark, curly brown hair, enough to clearly show the woman had been a brunette.

He heard Remi's sharp intake of breath as she no doubt saw what he saw—the gray concert T-shirt with a picture of country music singer Toby Keith, along with a list of concert dates from a decade earlier—the same shirt listed in the missing posters that were in Becca Jordan's file. A fine gold necklace with a star-shaped medallion hanging on the end was draped around her neck and tangled up in what was left of her hair. The necklace looked just like the one from the case file pictures.

They'd finally found Becca Jordan.

Remi crouched down and leaned toward the skeleton. She started to reach toward it, but the tech stopped her.

"Miss, I'm sorry. We don't want to risk cross contamination. You can't touch her."

"Give me a glove."

"Miss—"

"Give her a glove." Duncan crouched beside her, lightly gripping the back of her jacket to keep her steady.

The technician grabbed a latex glove from a black bag a short distance away and held it out toward Remi.

Duncan took it. "Let me."

Remi nodded and held out her hand. He rolled it on and tugged it down to cover her left wrist. Then he moved back and held on to her jacket again.

With her hand covered, she drew a deep breath, then reached down and grasped the skeleton's jaw.

The tech gasped in surprise and started forward. But Duncan gave him a warning look so he wouldn't interfere. Lee could yell at him later. As far as he was concerned, this was the risk his boss accepted when he'd insisted that Remi come down here.

She was careful, obviously mindful of not wanting to compromise any evidence. But she gently pushed the jaw down, revealing a set of perfect white teeth that had probably cost Becca's father a fortune in orthodontics.

"All the way, please," Remi said. "The zipper. I need you to unzip it all the way."

"I'm sorry, ma'am, but I don't think—"

"Do it," Duncan ordered.

The tech looked past him and Duncan turned to see what he was looking at. Lee stood about ten feet away with the SAR team. Duncan stared at him, daring him to tell Remi no. But his boss didn't hesitate.

"Go ahead."

Duncan turned back to the tech. "You heard him."

Shaking his head the whole time, the man carefully unzipped the bag all the way. He peeled it back, obviously worried about losing any potential trace evidence that might still be with the remains, even this many years later.

Remi leaned down close to the body again, slightly off balance with her hurt arm, but trusting Duncan to keep her secure. He held on tight to her jacket as she gently turned the right wrist, then moved the skeleton's left femur. She closed her eyes, said a brief prayer that Duncan doubted the others could hear, then held her hand out to Duncan.

"You can take it off now."

He peeled off the latex glove and gave it to the crime scene tech, then helped her stand.

"Are you okay?" He searched her eyes, surprised that there weren't any tears. She was holding up far better than he'd expected under these circumstances.

"I don't know." Her voice held a mixture of sadness and relief. She seemed bewildered, not sure what to do next.

"Come on. Let me get you out of here." He took her hand and led her to his boss.

Lee had a somber look on his face as he awkwardly patted Remi's good shoulder. "I'm sorry for your loss,

Miss Jordan. I assure you we'll handle your sister's remains with the utmost respect."

"That's very kind of you, Special Agent Lee." She motioned toward the body bag lying beneath the orange cover. "But that's not my sister."

Chapter Twelve

Remi glanced at the others sitting around the table in the NPS trailer. Since the storm had passed and the recent crime scene was so much closer to the NPS satellite office than to the offices in the Sugarlands Visitor Center, Lee had opened up the trailer again for business. Everyone who was anyone was crammed inside.

Someone had brought in a much larger table for the meeting. It sat in the middle of the trailer, since it wouldn't have fit in the conference room. Remi didn't have a clue how they'd managed to get the thing through the door. Maybe the legs came off. She wasn't sure. Didn't care. What mattered right now was that she once again had the attention of the BAU. And this time, they weren't ignoring her or shooting down her theories. They were actually listening from the other end of the conference call while Special Agent Lee and her embarrassed pseudoboss out of Knoxville sat beside each other surrounded by rangers and NPS investigators, explaining what had happened.

"I'm not following." The voice of Chris Jensen, the lead BAU guy on the call, sounded through the phone's speaker. "How does she know the remains don't belong to her sister? She said at the beginning of the call that the corpse was wearing her sister's shirt and necklace."

Beside her, Duncan gave Remi an encouraging nod.

She leaned toward the phone positioned in the middle of the table. "*She* is sitting right here and can speak for herself. My sister, Becca, was a junk food addict. She had five cavities by the time she was eight years old. She was also stubborn and refused to wear her retainer after my dad paid a fortune for braces. Her teeth had already started going crooked again her sophomore year, which was the source of many heated arguments between her and my parents. The skeleton the SAR team found had perfectly straight teeth. And no fillings."

There was the brief sound of someone murmuring to someone else on the other end of the phone.

"More importantly, Becca was fearless and rebellious, a dangerous combination. When she was fifteen, she took a joyride on a neighbor's dirt bike into the foothills of the Rocky Mountains. She had a horrible wreck, broke her right wrist and her left leg. She had a long metal pin surgically placed in her femur. It was never removed. The skeleton showed no signs of any breaks in the leg or wrist. And no metal pin."

"That metal pin could have fallen out over the past decade. Maybe a wild animal carried it off."

The ME was sitting across from her and motioned to let her know he would answer. "I'm Dr. Hennington, the medical examiner. There were no signs of previous breaks or any marks on the skeleton that would indicate use of medical devices such as pins. I've also reviewed the reports in Miss Rebecca Jordan's file that list her medical history. That skeleton isn't Rebecca Jordan."

"Then how did her shirt and jewelry end up on the skeleton?" Jensen asked.

Duncan took a turn at answering the questions. "This is Special Agent Duncan McKenzie. I believe the man who abducted Sheryl Foster is the same man who abducted Rebecca Jordan ten years ago."

"Hold on," Jensen said. "That's a big leap."

"Not at all. It makes perfect sense," Duncan said. "Footprint evidence proves the same man who abducted Sheryl Foster was stalking Special Agent Jordan. I find it impossible to believe that killer would later stage a corpse with the clothing and jewelry of Special Agent Jordan's missing sister and there not be a link. We've got one killer in the park, gentlemen. And he's taunting Special Agent Jordan, letting her know that he's the one who killed her sister."

"All right," Jensen said.

Remi exchanged a shocked look with Duncan. "All right what?"

"I concede the two cases are likely linked. We'll pull the file on Rebecca Jordan and get a team to reexamine that while we work the current case. Any suspects from the old case you can share off the top of your head?"

Remi swallowed against her tight throat. The BAU was actually going to look into her sister's case again. She couldn't believe it. "Yes. There were two boys at the camp. One has an alibi, the other didn't. But I think you should take a fresh look at both of them—Billy Hendricks and Garrett Weber. And you might want to look into a section hiker who was out here the other night, Zack Towers. I'd like to know whether you can rule him out in Mrs. Foster's disappearance."

Duncan's mouth tightened. He obviously didn't agree with her assessment about the hiker he knew as Sunny. But he'd said his team would take a fresh look at him. Whether they had or not, having the BAU take a look, too, couldn't hurt.

"We'll get right on it," Jensen said.

The room devolved into noisy conjecture as everyone tried to talk over everyone else. Remi sat back. She'd done her part. She and Duncan had opened the meeting with an explanation of her original theory, along with the modifications Duncan had offered about the additional six cases. Everyone had listened intently to her and Duncan when they'd explained their findings. She was being taken seriously, finally. At least by the rangers and NPS investigators. And it felt good.

Except that other than this phone call, she was precluded from aiding in the investigation.

Her official boss in Colorado had refused to reinstate her. The only reason that he hadn't reprimanded her for "brainstorming" the case with Duncan—her boss's word, not hers—was that with the addition of the six new cases occurring exactly two days after the original six, at the same parks, it was no longer a question of whether her theory was right or not. There was no way to explain all those cases as a coincidence or unrelated events. Still, she wasn't allowed to help.

"Want to get out of here?" Duncan whispered next to her ear.

"More than you could possibly know," she whispered back.

He grasped her elbow, and used his body to shield her as he hustled both of them outside. Once they were in his Jeep again, heading down the now familiar road, she said, "I suppose that now that the DA isn't pressing charges, you're released from babysitting duty. You can drop me off at my car and head back to the outpost. I know you'd rather be there helping with the case."

"Not happening. Everything changed the moment we saw that skeleton with your sister's shirt and necklace. The killer did that to get your attention. He's daring you to go after him. And that's exactly what you're not going to do. It's too dangerous. Lee agrees with me. You and I are going to grab your belongings from your motel room. Then you're staying with me at my cabin. Think of me as your official bodyguard. I'm keeping you out of the park until this killer is caught."

She frowned at him. "I know I've been ridiculously emotional and borderline incompetent since I got here, but I can still—"

"Who said that?"

She blinked. "What?"

"You've been understandably emotional about your sister, and this case, with everything that's happened. And because of your stellar investigative work, we now have a good chance at catching this guy and stopping him. As far as I'm concerned, you deserve a commendation, not condemnation. If it weren't for you, no one would even know that we've got a serial killer stalking our parks. Now that we know, we can save lives and put this guy away. The only incompetents around here are your boss, the BAU guys who refused to listen to you and anyone else dumb enough to doubt your brilliant theories."

She stared at him, stunned by his impassioned defense of her. "Thank you, Duncan. You can't imagine how good it feels to finally have someone who believes in me."

He held his right hand out, palm up.

She hesitated, then put her hand in his.

He squeezed it. "You're very welcome."

When he let her go, her body was humming with pleasure from that one simple touch.

"By the way," he said, "I got something for you while we were organizing that conference call." He unzipped his jacket halfway and reached into an inside pocket. When he pulled out his hand, he was holding a familiar-looking hip holster, with a very familiar SIG Sauer 9 mm pistol inside it.

Her hand shook as she took it from him. "My pistol. I was afraid I'd never get it back."

"It's not loaded. But I've got ammo at my cabin. I noticed it was engraved with your name, figured it was probably special in some way. Even though your jerk boss didn't reinstate you yet, I didn't see any reason to hold on to your personal property. As far as I'm concerned, whatever happened with Vale was an accident. And there's no reason you shouldn't have your gun back."

"This means so much to me. It was a gift from my father, on my eighteenth birthday."

"I think I got socks for my eighteenth birthday. And herpes, from Genevieve Landry."

She laughed. "I know it seems odd for a father to give his daughter a gun. But after losing Becca, he was terrified of something happening to me. He was very ill, cancer. Just like my mom, except a different kind. He knew he wouldn't be around much longer. So he did the only thing he could do."

"He gave you his protection, even beyond the grave. I think that's a wonderful gift."

She smoothed her fingers over the engraving. "I miss him. And Mom. And my sister."

"I miss Genevieve Landry."

She rolled her eyes. "You totally made that up."

"You're right." He grinned. "I didn't get socks for my eighteenth birthday."

She shoved him good-naturedly, then ran her fingers across the pistol once more. A tear dropped onto her hand. She gasped in dismay and set the gun in the console between them so she could wipe her eyes. "Sorry. I swear I'm not a crier. This place, everything that's happened here. You. I just… It's all…"

His hand settled on top of hers again. "It's okay to cry, Remi. You've been through a lot. You don't always have to be tough, especially not in front of me."

She sniffed and wiped her eyes again.

"I'm not wearing a sling on my shoulder," he said, "in case you haven't noticed. Which means I can easily withstand the pressure of a beautiful woman leaning against me." He waggled his brows and gave her one of those sexy grins that seemed to make the temperature in the Jeep go up ten degrees.

She laughed and scooted as close to him as she could with the console between them. Then she laid her head on his shoulder. It fit perfectly, like he'd been made for her.

"I'd put my arm around you if it weren't for the road conditions. I need both hands on the wheel. You'll have to use that excellent imagination of yours and pretend."

She smiled and closed her eyes. "I'm imagining it right now. You're an excellent hugger."

"The best. Any time you need a hug, I'm your guy."

"You're a good man, Duncan McKenzie. I'm really going to miss you when I go back home."

"And here I thought you'd be glad to get rid of me."

"Not a chance."

At the motel, it didn't take long for her to throw her clothes into a suitcase and check out. The place had been clean, the bed comfortable. But she was more than happy to say goodbye and head up to Duncan's cabin. It would be nice to have someone around for a change. For the first time in years she felt hopeful, like things were coming together.

Regardless of what happened with her job, she'd finally connected the dots for real and had teams of people working on finding justice for over a dozen women. If that was her legacy at the FBI, she'd take it. And gladly move on with a smile to a new job.

She closed her eyes and settled against Duncan's shoulder as he started up the road toward his cabin. It was dark outside now. The inside of the Jeep was toasty warm. And even though he was in no way soft, she loved pillowing her head against him. He was exactly what she needed right now, in so many ways. And she self-ishly took what he offered, even if it was just a shoulder to lean on.

Warm. She was so pleasantly, wonderfully warm. And comfortable, so comfy. She snuggled into the pillow and pulled the blanket up higher over her shoulder.

Wait.

Pillow?

Blanket?

She opened her eyes, then gasped and sat straight up. This definitely wasn't Duncan's Jeep. And she hadn't been snuggling against his shoulder, at least, not a mo-ment earlier. She was on a bed, cocooned under the covers. The lights were off in the room, but a door was cracked open to another room and a light was on in it. A bathroom. She could see the shiny glass tiles in the shower, the brown marble vanity. She recognized that bathroom. The first time she'd been in Duncan's cabin he'd given her a tour. She was in his master bedroom.

In his bed.

Her pulse, which was still thumping pretty fast from her surprise at waking up somewhere unknown, sped up even more. Just the thought of being in his bed sent a jolt of longing straight through her. But where was Duncan?

As she glanced around, she saw a note lying on the nightstand next to the bed. The moon was full and lit the room with a soft glow. But it wasn't bright enough for her to read the note. She remembered her phone was in her pocket earlier. Sure enough, it was still there. She pulled it out and used the light to read what Duncan had written.

You pretty much passed out on the way here. I figured you needed the sleep, so I didn't wake you. See you in the morning. D.

He'd left a bottle of ibuprofen on the nightstand, too, along with a bottle of water.

She smiled and set the note down. He was a wonderful man, in so many ways. She glanced at the moon and stars visible through the trees in the large picture window at the far end of the bedroom. It was definitely still nighttime; she just couldn't tell how late. A quick check of her phone told her it was a little after ten. Good grief, she'd slept for hours. But Duncan had been right. She'd needed it. She felt refreshed, relaxed, good for the first time in, well, days. Even her shoulder wasn't nearly as painful as it had been. Maybe in another week or so it would feel as good as new and she wouldn't have to go through therapy at all.

Therapy. She remembered Duncan had a hot tub on his back deck, with an incredible view of his sloping backyard, the thick woods, and miles and miles of mountaintops. It really was a beautiful place. At night, with the moon and stars out, and twinkling lights of other cabins perched throughout the mountains, she bet it was breathtaking. And that hot tub could probably do wonders for her shoulder.

She glanced at her suitcase sitting on the floor by the dresser. Nothing in there would work as a bathing suit, and she certainly hadn't packed one for a winter trip. Of course, if she'd thought she'd end up in a cabin with a hot tub on the deck, she would have. Then again, who needed a bathing suit if they had their birthday suit.

Would Duncan mind? She didn't see a strip of light under the closed bedroom door. He must be in the other bedroom, asleep. If she was quiet and didn't wake him, no harm done. Mind made up, she headed into the attached bathroom for a quick shower. Then, with a big, fluffy white towel wrapped around her body, she shoved her feet into her house slippers and padded across the carpet to the door in the bedroom that led to the deck, which ran along the entire back of the house.

She'd left her sling on the bed, had taken some pain pills and figured if she could just get into a comfortable position in the tub, she could let the jets and the hot water work their magic. She stepped outside, shivering when the chilly air hit her. She carefully closed the door, trying not to make any sounds that might wake Duncan. Then she turned around and hurried toward the tub, about twenty feet away.

The lid was up and the jets were on. She hesitated. Had Duncan used the tub earlier and forgot to turn it off? Or did people leave them on during the winter to keep the water hot? She had no idea, never having had a hot tub. The only time she'd ever used them were at hotels, by the pool. And those were always on.

She flicked her fingers through the water. It was exquisitely warm. Perfect. She couldn't wait to get in. She dropped her towel, carefully stepped over the side so she wouldn't lose her balance with only one good arm and slowly sank into the water. She moaned in delight. It felt even better than she'd imagined it would. She scooted to the back side of the tub where it was shaped into seats beneath the water, and turned around.

Duncan stood ten feet away, staring at her, eyes wide with surprise. He was barefoot, wearing nothing but a towel slung low on his hips. He had one hand on the sliding glass door, which was half-open, and carried a six-pack of bottled beer in his other hand.

She gasped and ducked lower in the water, crossing her arms over her breasts, wincing at the tug on her right shoulder when she did so. "I'm so sorry," she said. "I didn't realize you were coming out here. I thought you were asleep and hoped you wouldn't mind."

His mouth quirked in a half smile that did all kinds of crazy things to her belly. "I don't mind at all." His Adam's apple bobbed in his throat as his gaze dipped to her arms. Then he looked out over the mountains as he swallowed again. When he looked at her once more, there was no mistaking the impact seeing her naked, even if only from behind, had had on him. The towel did little to hide his aroused state.

She felt her cheeks flush and forced herself to look up, to meet his gaze, as well.

He winced. "Sorry about that. It's kind of automatic every time I see you. Curse of a lecherous mind, I suppose."

"Every time you see me? Really?"

He let out a shuddering breath and dropped his hand from the door. "Oh. Yeah. Every. Time. Can't honestly say that I'm sorry I stepped out when I did. That's a sight I'll probably treasure until my dying day." He chuckled. "But I'll leave you to it. I imagine that hot water will really help that shoulder feel better. I'll see you in the morning."

"Wait."

He'd started to turn away, but stopped and looked over his shoulder at her, his eyebrows arched as he waited.

Struggling with words, she finally waved toward the six-pack in his hand. "Aren't you going to offer me a beer?"

He looked down as if just remembering he was carrying something. He smiled ruefully. "You gonna come get it or do you want me to bring it to you?"

She flushed. "Well, I'm certainly not going to come get it. I don't have a bathing suit on."

"Yeah." His voice was husky. "I noticed." Without waiting, he slowly moved forward with the grace of a panther, his eyes never leaving hers. He stopped right beside where she was sitting and squatted down. He pulled a bottle out as he gazed into her eyes, and twisted off the cap. "Here you go." He held it out to her.

If he looked down he'd see everything. But he stared at her eyes, and didn't move, didn't look away. He just waited, as if daring her to move her arms.

Keeping her right arm crossed over her breasts, she reached for the beer. Their hands touched, and a jolt of yearning shot straight through her. He seemed to feel it, too, because his gaze heated and fell to her lips.

"Th-thank you," she whispered, taking the beer.

His gaze rose to hers again. "Anytime." He let go of the bottle, watched her pull it to her lips and take a drink. His Adam's apple bobbed again.

She saw the tension around his mouth, his eyes, and she made a decision right then and there. She dropped her right hand.

He blinked, but kept his gaze glued firmly on her face. She saw a bead of sweat break out on his forehead in spite of the chilly air.

She took another drink of beer, then stretched her left arm out, set the beer on the railing and rested her arm on the edge of the tub. She was open to his gaze, her breasts just inches below the water. And she didn't move to cover them.

"Remi…" His voice was thick, deep. "Is there anything you want to ask me?" The bead of sweat rolled down the side of his face. His nostrils flared, like a stallion scenting a mare.

"Yes, actually." She had to clear her throat to continue. "About your eighteenth birthday—"

"I was kidding about Genevieve Landry. She graduated high school a year before I did and never gave me the time of day." He grinned. "Or anything else."

"Then what are you waiting for?" She scooted over in the hot tub seat to give him room.

He dropped his towel and vaulted over the side. She had an all too brief glimpse of muscled thighs and… everything before he plopped into the water beside her. Squealing and laughing, she turned away from the tidal wave that splashed over her, drenching her.

He was laughing, too, and then he was pulling her onto his lap, settling her thighs over the tops of his, feathering his hands around her waist.

She froze, water frothing just below her breasts. Her hands were on both his shoulders, the pain in her right shoulder barely even registering. Nothing was going to distract her from the amazing feel of a naked Duncan McKenzie beneath her thighs, her bottom, his hard erection pressing against her belly as his suddenly serious dark eyes stared intently into hers from less than a foot away.

There weren't any lights on, but there was enough moonlight that she could see the outlines of the cords standing out in his neck, the taut muscles of his chest rigid, like the rest of him, as if he was stunned to have her there and was trying to hold back. She decided to make it easy for him. Because she had no intention of holding back now that she finally had him exactly where she wanted him. Well, maybe not exactly, but close enough. For now.

She leaned forward, closer, unable to hide a feminine smile of triumph when his gaze dropped to her breasts. But just as she was about to claim his mouth with hers, he lifted his powerful thighs, angling her up, and then sucked one of her nipples into his hot mouth.

She gasped at the fiery sensations streaking straight to her core and dug her fingers into his shoulders. He didn't seem to notice. If anything, he seemed even more turned on, the thick length of him jerking against her beneath the water as he sucked and stroked and kissed her breast. Then he did the same to her other breast, and she almost climaxed right then. Good grief, he was good at this. So good. But even if he wasn't, she would have enjoyed anything he wanted to do to her, with her, because this was Duncan.

As he kissed and caressed and licked his way across the undersides of her breasts, she knew she was finally where she most wanted to be. The fact that she could never live in the place where her family had been torn apart, and knowing he'd never want to leave because his own family was here, told her this was the only time they'd ever be together. There was no future for them. And that nearly broke her heart. These feelings she had were so new that she probably shouldn't trust them. But they were so strong, stronger than any bond she'd ever felt with anyone else, that she knew they were solid, real, and that it would likely destroy her the day she had to tell him goodbye.

He drew back and lowered her, mindful of her right arm, gently moving it in the water to keep it resting on his shoulder so he wouldn't jar her. He frowned when he framed her face in his hands.

"Regrets already?" he asked. "If you want to stop, I will. Say the word."

The look on his face told her he probably thought he'd die if she made him stop. But just knowing that he would stop had all the good feelings coming back. He was a smart, sexy, considerate, incredible man. She was at least half in love with him, somehow, in such a short time. But there was no denying how she felt. And if this night was all she had, she wasn't going to waste it.

"No regrets." She pressed a soft kiss against his mouth, then whispered in his ear, "I'm on the pill, to regulate my body. But the result is the same. It's safe."

He gently pulled her back. "No Genevieve Landrys in your past, either?"

She laughed. "No Landrys in my past."

He grinned again and his eyes went to half-mast. "This is going to be so good." He gently moved forward, pushing her deeper into the water.

"What are you doing?" She clutched his shoulders as he turned with her and sat her back on the seat.

He carefully placed her right hand on what amounted to an armrest on the molded seat beneath the water.

"Loving you." He winked, then disappeared beneath the water.

His mouth fastened on her and she would have bolted out of the tub if he hadn't been holding her thighs. She shuddered and arched against him, her eyes squeezing shut as he did wicked things with his mouth and tongue. She forced her eyes open, wanting to see him. The sight of him there, just below the surface, kissing her so thoroughly, was the most erotic thing she'd ever seen in her life.

She whimpered and couldn't be still, arching and moving against him. He sucked her, hard, enough to make her swear and rise up off the seat from the sheer pleasure that spiraled through her. Then he burst from the water, dragging in huge gulps of air. Droplets cascaded off his golden chest. His eyes were so dark they were almost black as he once again sucked her nipple into his mouth.

"Duncan," she breathed, then moved her hand beneath the water, searching for him. He shifted his hips and guided her, until the long, thick length of him was in her grip. He shuddered against her and moved his hips again, thrusting through her fingers. She wanted him so much she was trembling, wanted to feel him inside her. She wanted him in her mouth, to kiss him as he'd done her.

"Duncan…" She couldn't say more. Her entire body was drawn like a tight spring, ready to come undone.

He moved his mouth to her neck, his hips still gently thrusting as she ran her hand over and around him, squeezing and stroking him beneath the water. Then he took her earlobe in his mouth and she gasped, her palm automatically tightening around him. He jerked in her grip and then pulled back, positioned himself at her entrance. He looked deep into her eyes and grasped her hips. Then he raised up, his chin at the top of her head as he pushed the tip of himself into her.

She whimpered again and fastened her mouth on his neck. He whispered erotic love words in her ear, then braced his hands on the hot tub on either side of her, still pushing slowly, carefully into her, as if he was worried about hurting her. She didn't want slow and careful. She wanted hard and fast. She wanted all of him. And she wanted it now.

Her shoulder was forgotten. She put both her hands on his shoulders and raised her legs, the movement pulling him in deeper. His whole body shuddered, and then, as if a rope had broken and his restraint was gone, he moved hard and deep into her, filling her, over and over, the water splashing and slapping between them. Tears of pleasure and joy flowed down her face, but she didn't care. This was Duncan, inside her, loving her, and she wanted to treasure every movement, every ounce of heat, every plane and angle of his body as he shared it with her.

She grasped his hips, then gripped his hard, tight bottom, pulling him to her, pushing her own hips against him. They rode each other hard, each giving and taking, sharing their bodies, their hearts, their souls until the world around them disappeared. Until everything centered on the building pressure between them.

She climaxed first, her body bowing up, her knees coming out of the water as her body milked his. He came moments later, his shaft tightening so hard inside her that she climaxed again before the ripples of her first one had subsided. Then he slowly, ever so slowly, lowered himself back into the water. He collapsed on the bench beside her and pulled her on top of him, his hands going around her waist.

They were both breathing hard, their ragged breaths frosting in the chilly air. But she was anything but cold. As boneless and limp as she felt after their acrobatics, she imagined that she might have slid under the water and drowned if he hadn't draped her body over his and held on to her. But she would have died happy.

She rested her cheek against his chest, his right hand gently gliding up and down her spine, her thighs cradling his. Where he'd been hard and thick against her before, now he was soft and warm, his sated length pressed against her beneath the water. It felt…right, being held in his arms like this, as if he cherished her as they came down to earth together.

Gradually, the world around them seemed to come into focus again. Some kind of night bird made a deep throaty sound from the woods. A soft breeze, nothing like the violent storm of yesterday, rustled the leaves on the trees. The water bubbled and frothed around them.

"I could lie like this forever," she murmured against his chest. "I need a Duncan pillow."

He chuckled and swept her wet hair back from her face. "I'm happy to be your pillow anytime." He moved his left hand up to her right shoulder and gently massaged it. "How's the shoulder?"

She winced and pulled back. "On fire. I was able to ignore it earlier. But all this…" Her face flushed hot again. "All this *activity* has it aching, in spite of the hot water and the ibuprofen I took."

Guilt flashed across his face. "I shouldn't have—"

"Oh, yes you should have. Trust me. The pain is worth it."

He grinned. Then he kissed her, thoroughly, and once again his body began to harden against hers below the water. When he pulled back, she could see desire tightening his features, darkening his eyes.

"You're kidding," she said. "I feel like a limp noodle here. And you're already, ah…"

"You're adorable when you blush," he said. "But we need to get you out of this water before you turn into a prune. And we need to immobilize that shoulder. Let's get you back inside and to bed."

"Only if you're coming to bed with me."

He waggled his brows. "Invitation definitely accepted." He turned her in the water with her good side against him, one hand supporting her thighs, the other around her waist. "I'm going to lift you out. Brace your hurt arm."

"I can get out on my own. You don't have to pick me up."

He started to lift her.

She grabbed her hurt arm and pulled it against her chest as he rose out of the tub like a Titan rising out of the sea. Water cascaded off both of them as he effortlessly stepped over the side with her cradled against him. With no concern for the trail of water they were leaving in their wake, he carried her into his bedroom.

Chapter Thirteen

Remi shoved her plate of pancakes away and sat back in her chair. "Enough. You're like a drug dealer, pushing all this food on me. I won't be able to roll out the door if I eat all of this. I thought you were Irish?"

He blinked, in the process of clearing both their plates from the kitchen table. "I am. Or at least my grandparents are, on both sides of the family. What's that got to do with you not eating enough?"

She rolled her eyes. "From the mounds of bacon, potatoes, eggs and pancakes you've been throwing at me this morning I'd have thought you were Italian. Don't they have traditions of seven-course meals or something like that?"

That sexy grin of his made another appearance, sending her pulse into overdrive. "Throwing food at you, huh? A food fight could get very interesting."

"I'm being serious."

"So am I." He waggled his brows.

She couldn't help it; she laughed. "You're incorrigible. I have a hard time believing you're not the black sheep of the family who caused all the trouble growing up."

"I never said I didn't cause any trouble." He winked and carried the dishes to the sink.

Remi sighed, then cleared her throat in case he'd heard

her. The man didn't need any encouragement to distract him once again from work. If he thought she was getting all lovesick over him he'd cart her off to the bedroom, again, and they'd spend another hour wrapped in each other's arms. Not that she didn't want to. Good grief, the man was incredible and she loved being with him. But the time for sleep—and extracurricular activities—was long over. The sun was up. It was a new day. And they had a killer to catch before someone else died.

"You look like you're trying to solve the world's problems."

She pulled over one of the stacks of research folders that they'd moved out of the way for breakfast. "We'll work on the world's issues next. First, we need to see if there's something else we've missed on this case, something that might help Lee and the others find Sheryl Foster and the man who took her."

His heavy sigh was more of his teasing. She knew that. Because he was already reaching for his own set of folders. And she knew that he was just as dedicated to the case as she was, if not more. He was the one who'd practically pushed her out of bed this morning, saying they had a long day ahead of them and needed to get to it. That day included them doing everything they could remotely, from the cabin—since Lee still didn't want her near the park—to try to piece clues together and help in any way they could.

It was close to midday when they both sat like zombies, tired from lack of sleep and frustrated from having come up with no new leads.

"I don't get it," he said, shoving a pile of folders away from him.

"What don't you get?"

He waved his hand as if to encompass all the paperwork on the table. "The logistics. How he's abducting these women and making them disappear so completely, so quickly. How does he escape the net, and then manage to stage a skeleton from a previous kill all under SAR's noses?"

"Maybe he has a car waiting somewhere obscure and has his route mapped out. He grabs the woman, holds her at gunpoint and makes her double-time it to his car. Then he ties her up in his trunk and is miles away before SAR is even looking for her."

"We're talking midwinter. There's lots of snow on the ground. If you're really careful you can mostly stick to rocky soil or step under heavy tree canopies so you don't leave as many prints. But you have to leave some. And how do you get your victim to walk as carefully as you? Seems like we'd have to see more footprints."

She shrugged, then winced and rubbed her shoulder. "Could he drug his victims? Knock them out and carry them?"

"If he went a very short distance, sure. But even someone small like you carried over someone's shoulder is going to make hiking through icy rough terrain a lot more dangerous and strenuous. And his footprints would be heavier. It would be a lot tougher to hide the path he took." He shook his head. "There has to be another explanation for how he's getting his victims out of the immediate area without leaving a trace."

She nodded, remembering the crunch of frozen ground when Vale had been behind her. "He doesn't march them out of the area. Then, what? Could he, I don't know, drug his victim, toss her on his shoulder, then rappel off one of the cliffs and get away? That could explain the lack of footprints. But I have no idea if it's even feasible."

Duncan stared at her so long she glanced down to see

if she was having a wardrobe malfunction or something. Nope. Her T-shirt was in place, the sling over it with her arm nestled inside.

"You might be onto something," he finally said, as if he'd been thinking it through. Then he nodded, "Yes, that could work."

"Rappelling?"

"No. At least, not in Foster's case. Her family wasn't that far away. Even if the killer had his equipment set up and ready to go, the buckles and harnesses are noisy. Suppose he wrapped them in cloth to mute the sound, the whole process of going over the side, feeding the rope, pushing off the mountain with your boots—it's a lot of work and it's not quiet. He'd be doing it with a body strapped over his shoulder or across his back. Again, not easy, and definitely not silent. Her family would have heard him."

"Okay, but you said I was onto something."

"And you might be. What's one of the first rules of training when you're clearing a room?"

"Look everywhere. Side to side, down and up."

"Exactly," he said. "There's another dimension on a big mountain to consider, one we haven't thought about before. We haven't looked down, *inside* the mountain."

"Inside? What do you mean? Like, caves? Caverns?"

"They're all over the Smokies. None up on that part of the trail where Foster's footprints stopped. But what if there are caves beneath it? And some way to get to them quickly and easily?"

She slowly nodded. "I never would have thought of that. But it makes sense."

He pulled his phone out. "I'll call Lee and have him send some searchers out to the last known location of Sheryl Foster and see if they can find a hiding place underneath. They might have to rappel down that cliff themselves to get the lay of the land. From there, maybe they can figure out whatever device or trick our bad guy is using." He punched in his boss's number.

Chapter Fourteen

Shortly after lunch, Lee called back. The look on Duncan's face as he listened to his boss was a mixture of excitement and wariness. Frustrated at not being able to hear what was going on, Remi cupped her ear.

Duncan smiled. "Hang on, Lee. I'm going to put you on speaker so Remi can listen, too." He pressed a button, then set his cell phone in the middle of the table. "Go ahead. You said you found something."

"A trapdoor, up on the ridge, right in the bushes where you saw his footprints. One of the bushes was part of it. There was a foot of dirt on top of the door and the bush was growing on it. After the team hiked down the mountain and came up from below, they saw an opening, a cave below the ridge. So they had someone aboveground looking for a way in while they climbed up. Long story short, the trapdoor is pretty sophisticated. It's heavy and operates on a hydraulic system. Once activated, it pops up about two feet high. Roll something into the opening and slide in after it, and down you go. It's just big enough to hide a body and give him room to, well, do whatever serial killer bastards do when they abduct someone."

Remi clutched her left hand in a fist, her breath coming out in shallow bursts as she waited for the rest. No matter how much she tried not to think of her sister, she couldn't simply pretend that Becca wasn't a part of this. Had she been in that cave? What had the man who'd taken her done to her?

Duncan kept his gaze glued on her as if trying to lend her his own strength.

"We're sending in an electronics expert to examine the door and how it operates. But the prevailing theory is that it can be opened or closed by a cell phone."

"The guy planned this for a long time," Duncan said. "What did you find inside the cave?"

"We found Sheryl Foster. The medical examiner thinks she was dead within the first hour after she disappeared. She was already dead before we started looking for her."

Remi's heart lurched in her chest. She fought back the burn of tears and kept her composure. But she sent up a silent prayer for Sheryl Foster's family.

"There was evidence that another body may have been in the cave at one time," Lee continued.

Remi tensed.

"The ME thinks it was the skeleton we found yesterday, based on a visual of the soil samples from both locations. Obviously lab testing will be required to confirm the theory."

Remi drew a ragged breath.

"We're notifying teams in the other parks to look for caves and trapdoors in the vicinity of where victims may have been last seen, in case he uses this same MO in those locations."

After the call ended, Remi told Duncan she needed to be alone and went into the bedroom. She sat on the bed, hugging a pillow to her chest as she tried to center herself again. She wanted to find Becca, put her to rest once and for all. And being pulled back and forth these past few days, thinking her sister had been found—twice now—then realizing she hadn't been, had her in emotional turmoil. She wasn't sure how much more of this she could take.

She reached for her cell phone, thinking to pull up some pictures of Becca, to remind herself of the good times they'd had so very long ago, to buoy her spirit. But her phone wasn't plugged in and charging beside the bed. Because, of course, this wasn't her motel room or even her room back home. Duncan had carried her in here last night. It hadn't occurred to her this morning to get her charger out of her luggage or her phone out of her purse and charge it. By now, the battery was likely dead.

Drawing a deep, bracing breath, she straightened and thought about Duncan instead. He was like a rock in a storm. Nothing seemed to faze him. And right now he was in another room in the cabin, working on the case that she should be working on. She could do this. She had to do this, now, before the killer went after someone else, the brunette to finish his two-victim routine. Sitting around feeling sorry for herself and missing her sister wasn't helping anyone. She tossed the pillow aside and went looking for Duncan.

She found him in the family room, with a roaring fire blazing in the fireplace flanked by two enormous picture windows overlooking the mountains. He was pacing back and forth, talking on his cell phone at the other end of the room. There were papers in his hand that he kept referring to as he spoke, but she couldn't make out his words. More papers were spread out on the floor around the couch, and on the coffee table. He was getting just as messy as her.

She sat on the couch and he looked back, smiling as he signaled that he'd be off the phone soon. Once he ended the call, he crossed to the couch, his look of concern turning to surprise as he sat on the coffee table facing her. "You're okay?"

"I'm good. Just needed a few minutes. I'd really hoped to find Mrs. Foster alive."

He grimaced. "Me, too."

She waved toward the papers scattered around. "Bring me up to speed. Let's catch this lowlife."

He leaned toward her and gently cupped her face. "You're an amazing woman, Remi Jordan."

He gave her a quick kiss, then moved back before she could even respond. She longed to follow him, climb onto his lap, curl around him like a cat and never let him go. That shocked her, forcing her to keep her hands off him like nothing else would have. How far gone was she that she could even think about wanting, needing this man, with everything else going on right now? If she wasn't careful, she'd fall in love with him. And that was a dead-end road to nowhere.

"That was Jensen on the phone. He's convinced that Becca was the killer's first victim. That changes everything."

She grew still, stunned. She'd studied profiling and serial killers enough over the years in her quest to join the BAU to understand the significance. "First kills are often someone the killer knows."

"We need to look at the people Becca knew," they both said at the same time.

"Talk to me about your sister. Tell me everything."

"Everything will take too long."

"Focus on the last year, her senior year in high school. You already mentioned Hendricks and Weber, and the BAU is looking into them. Tell me more. Who were her friends. Did she have any enemies. Just say everything you can think of—thoughts, impressions. Don't worry about facts. Do a brain dump about everyone she came into contact with on a regular basis, even if they weren't in her immediate circle of friends. It could be someone who watched her, resented her because she wouldn't date them. No clue is too small." He pulled his computer onto his lap and typed as she spoke.

It was slow going at first, dredging up memories buried for ten years. But she closed her eyes, at Duncan's insistence, and tried to put herself back in high school and remember. Everything. Duncan coached her to think about the smells, the sweaty locker room from gym class, or pizza in the cafeteria, whatever it took to help her get back to that place in her mind. And just like the smell of irises, daffodils, pansies and pink roses in her mother's garden back home always made her feel like her parents were with her once again, those high school smells had her walking the halls in her mind, and seeing her sister's beautiful youthful face.

The words flowed. The memories she'd forgotten were unbottled and came spilling out. She was laughing and crying as she gave him everything she had, until she was spent. Where he'd always been so kind and gentle with her in recent days, Duncan reverted back to his all-business persona, pushing her harder, demanding answers, names, making her dig deeper when she thought she couldn't remember. And it worked. She remembered far more than she ever thought she would. And then, finally, he relented and got her a bottle of water. Then he sat in front of her and began reciting back the highlights he felt were most relevant, and the list of people—all potential suspects—that he'd drawn up.

"That's positively frightening to think there were that

many guys in her life who might have wanted to harm her," she said.

"I'm sure most of them would never have wanted to hurt her. But each one of them was significant in some way, or might have had a reason to feel rejected. We have to examine them all. Based on the footprints I found up on the ridge, our guy is probably six feet tall or more. Do you remember any guys that tall at the time of the senior trip? Granted, guys can still grow after high school. But does anyone come to mind from back then to give us someone to focus on?"

"I can only think of a few, maybe five or six."

"Are Hendricks and Weber two of them? Those are the names that you keep bringing up."

"They're the main ones I remember, ones my sister knew. And yes, both were six feet or close to it."

"Earlier you said Hendricks, this Billy guy, had an alibi."

"He was with another girl in the camp that night, Felicia Reynolds."

"Are you sure? Did you ask the girl?"

"Well, no. But the police did. It was in their reports."

"Tell me about Weber. You said he was popular."

"Everyone had a crush on him, including me. But he had a girlfriend. And as far as I know he'd never two-timed anyone before. But even if he would, my sister wouldn't. Becca was all about girl power, a dyed-in-the-wool feminist in the making. She would have never poached another girl's guy." She shook her head. "There's no one else I can think of that she'd have gone off with. But she was super outgoing, and in that guy-crazy phase of life. I suppose it's possible that someone else on the trip caught her eye. I've looked into everyone at the camp over the years and didn't get anywhere. I don't think this is helping."

"Well, I'm new to this case, so bear with me." He grabbed the cold case file that Pops had compiled. After flipping through it halfway, he pulled out a sheet of paper and handed it to her. "That's the list of all the kids on the trip. Even though you've seen a list like that before, take a fresh look. If you were Becca, who might you have gone off to see?"

She sighed and looked at the list. "Got a pen?"

He pulled one of the drawers in the coffee table open and handed her a pen.

She crossed off the ones that she knew her sister didn't like at all. Crossed off two who'd had girlfriends. "That leaves three, including Billy. But I know the police, and the Park Service investigators at the time, looked into all of these. I don't think we're onto anything new."

"Maybe, maybe not." He thumbed through the file. "There aren't any pictures in here. I don't suppose you happened to bring your school yearbook with you."

"Totally slipped my mind. Usually I pack it." She rolled her eyes.

His fingers flew over the keyboard. A moment later he scooted closer beside her with her high school's website on the screen. She was excited at first, but both of them realized quickly this was a dead end. There wasn't an archive section or old yearbooks on the site, just the current school year photos.

Next, he did a web search on Billy's name. But it was a fairly common name and too much came up to be useful. Something she'd learned herself over the years.

"What about one of those ancestry, family tree websites?" he asked. "Maybe someone has a public family tree with him listed and has photos and other facts about him, or the other two, that might help us."

"I never thought of that," she admitted. "Are you a member of one of those sites?"

"Nope. Maybe I don't have to be to perform a search." He pulled up several, and all of them required membership. He pulled out his wallet and used a credit card to join the most popular site. "Remind me to cancel my membership later. This stuff is expensive."

She smiled and together they explored the site, searching all three names. But nothing useful turned up. Billy wasn't on any of the trees they found. And what they found of the others didn't really provide anything pertinent to ruling them in or out as suspects.

"Let's go low tech for a minute." He set the laptop aside. "Tell me about Billy, specifically, since he's the one you first thought of as a suspect. You said she teased him?"

Her face heated. She felt as if she was being disloyal to her sister. But this was important, so she continued. "Becca was a bit…wild. She liked to have fun. Billy was good-looking but kind of a nerd. So when we were in school, she pretty much snubbed him. Everyone knew he liked her. But she didn't give him the time of day. But outside of school, sometimes, well, she led him on, let him take her on dates or to the movies. But it was never anything serious. He just wasn't, well, cool enough for her to be seen with by her friends."

"Ouch. I can see that damaging a young guy's fragile ego." He held up his hands. "Not that I'm saying your sister was bad for doing that. She was just acting the way teenagers often do. But if Billy is the sociopath type, that could be a potential trigger. I think we need to focus on him to at least try to rule him out." He tapped his knee, looking thoughtful. "We need to look into his alibi. We need to talk to Felicia Reynolds."

Thanks to the FBI, they had Felicia Reynolds, now Felicia Swanson, on the phone in ten minutes. Duncan's face was grim when he ended the call.

"She lied. Billy wasn't with her all night. He was only with her from midnight on. Your sister left your tent around ten."

Remi pressed her hand to her chest. "Why would she lie about that? My sister was missing."

"She didn't believe that Billy was the kind of guy who would hurt anyone. And she liked him. So she didn't think she was hurting anyone by lying. She felt she was doing good, by keeping the investigation focused on people who might have had something to do with Becca's disappearance. She swears even now that she knows Billy would never have hurt Becca."

Remi fisted her hands beside her. "I can't believe she could be that stupid. What's a killer look like, anyway? Ted Bundy was good-looking, wore a suit, went to college. No one would have ever pegged him as a killer, but he was a monster who brutally murdered dozens of women."

"Let's focus here. Billy may not be our guy. Are there any pictures of the senior trip that you can access on my laptop? I'd like to see this Billy, plus the other guys who were there."

She started to shake her head, then stopped. "Wait. Becca's website. My dad, after Becca disappeared, set up a website trying to spread the word about her disappearance and get people to search for her. I look at it about once a year, when the web-hosting bill comes due. I always think about canceling the service, letting the site go. But then I wonder how my dad would feel, and I pay the bill. Keep the website active another year. There are lots of pictures of her friends, from school, probably from the trip, too. Dad put everything he could think of online and encouraged people to post comments and clues, whatever they thought might help." She told him the URL.

He brought up the site and she pointed out the various people in her and Becca's life from back then. He was paging through several shots taken at school when he stopped and backed up to a previous photo. "Is this you and your sister?"

She leaned in and smiled. "Yep. That was during our junior year. Becca went blond for several months. I'd forgotten about that."

He stared at her. "But you stayed a brunette. Twins— one blonde and one brunette."

Her smiled faded. "One blonde. One brunette." They exchanged a long look.

He turned back to the screen and pointed just past Becca's shoulder. "Who is that?"

She blinked. "That's Billy. And he…he looks…angry."

"Furious is more like it. Do you have any idea why?"

She shook her head. "Knowing Becca, it could be anything. Like I said, she strung him along, but ignored him at school. Let's say he was mad enough to…kill her. Where would the constellation stuff come into play? He wasn't all that smart. He certainly wasn't into astronomy. He was more the remedial science kind of guy who barely managed to pass each year."

"Did he know your sister was into astronomy?"

"Everyone did. But he couldn't have known about the unicorn constellation, unless he was in our bedroom and saw it taped to the wall. And that, I can promise you, never happened. She might have been a tease with Billy.

But she would never have brought him home without me knowing, certainly not into the bedroom we shared."

"Was your house a yellow two-story?"

"Yes, but why—"

He clicked the home page tab, then zoomed in on a collage of pictures she'd seen hundreds of times over the years and had gotten so used to that she never really *saw* them anymore. The first one was her family, all four of them standing in the front yard of their home, her mama's beautiful flower garden behind them and the two-story yellow house behind that.

The second was of Becca standing in front of the wall of the bedroom the two of them had shared, with her pride and joy behind her—the picture of the unicorn constellation.

Remi's hand shook as she ran a finger over her sister's outline, then the unicorn behind her. "He knew, about the stars."

Duncan set the laptop aside. "What color was Becca's hair during the senior trip?"

"Brown. Which is one reason why I never connected her disappearance with the missing blonde women. But then, if it is Billy, that kind of makes sense, doesn't it? If he had some sick fantasy, an obsession, with Becca, maybe in his mind he's killing her over and over again. He kills blondes to kill her when she was a blonde, and brunettes for when she was a brunette. Psychopaths don't exactly follow the kind of logic we use. In their minds, that might make sense."

"We need to find Billy Hendricks."

Something bright flashed in Remi's eyes. She blinked and instinctively moved to the side, then gasped at the red dot of light on her left shoulder.

"Get down!" Duncan grabbed her arm and yanked her with him to the floor.

Boom! Glass exploded behind them, raining down onto the hardwood floor like pennies bouncing off a metal roof. Feathers floated through the air like snow.

Duncan twisted against her. He heaved the massive wooden coffee table onto its side and pulled her with him behind it.

She risked a quick glance over her shoulder and saw the bullet hole in the middle of the couch cushion where the feathers must have come from. She looked back the other way, toward the windows, but Duncan and the coffee table blocked her view. The table was solid, thick wood. But could it block a shot from a rifle? She had no idea. They needed to move to a safer location, especially if whoever had fired at them was still out there.

"Duncan, someone's—"

"Shooting at us. I know. They're up high, probably in one of the trees behind the deck."

Boom! Boom! Duncan swore and shoved her against the floor. Feathers floated around them. More glass rained down, tinkling as it landed on the hard surfaces around the room.

"He's at our two o'clock," Duncan said. "And he's got a scope with a laser sight. If I hadn't seen that red dot on your arm, he'd have hit you. We need to get out of here." He looked left and right as if weighing the distances between various pieces of furniture, while keeping both of them out of the line of fire by staying below the top edge of the table he'd upended.

"My gun is in the bedroom," Remi said.

"So is mine." He sounded disgusted with himself. He looked around, then grabbed a handful of glass shards from the floor. He tossed them past the left edge of the coffee table.

Boom! A hard thunk shook the table and little pieces of wood puffed up from the edge.

"That's some hard wood," Remi said. "Remind me to kiss whoever made your table."

He gave her a lopsided grin. "It's mahogany. I'm sure Dad will enjoy that kiss. At least until Mom slaps him."

She laughed and shook her head. "I can't believe you have me laughing when someone is trying to kill us and my shoulder feels like it's been twisted out of its socket all over again."

"Ah, man. Did I do that?" He started to reach for it.

She pushed his hand away. "You saved my life. Don't you dare apologize for wrenching my stupid shoulder."

"I really need to force you to see a doctor now."

"If we survive this, you won't have to force me. Forget Vitamin I. I want the hard stuff."

He snorted and looked around again. "All right. Here's what we're going to do. We need to keep this table between us and the shooter. I'm going to scoot it about a foot to the left. We have to scoot with it. I just need a couple of feet and then I can make a run for the fireplace."

"What do I do?"

"Your job is to stay here and not get shot. I've got a hunting rifle hanging over the mantel and a box of shells underneath it. I'm going to grab that and circle around and take this guy out."

"If you lay some cover fire I can get to the bedroom and grab my gun."

He leaned toward her, forcing her back against the couch. "A pistol doesn't have a chance against a rifle with a scope and laser sight. You stay right here and wait for me. Promise me."

"Oh, good grief, Duncan. I'm an FBI agent, not a helpless civilian. I can get my gun and circle around from the other side. We can flank him and catch him."

Boom! Boom! Boom! Thunk, thunk, thunk. Pieces of sawdust filled the air as the battered coffee table gave up little bits of itself.

He arched a brow at her.

"O…kay. I think I'll just lie right here until you get back."

"Good idea. I'll move the coffee table on three. Draw your legs up."

She drew her legs up.

"One, two, three." He heaved the heavy piece of furniture toward the left, scooting his body behind it as he did.

She scooted along with him, and was glad that when he'd yanked her off the couch he'd managed to pull her down onto her good side. Otherwise, she probably wouldn't have been able to move at all. She wished she could stop and check her shoulder. But every minute they lay here they were putting their lives at risk. The last few shots had sounded like they'd gone a good distance into the thick mahogany. She had no idea whether the next shot might crack the thing in two, leaving them without any cover.

"On three." He counted down. They moved in sync again, then one more time. They'd gone almost three feet. But was it enough to be out of the line of fire? He looked around for something to throw.

"Here." Remi handed him an ink pen. "It was in my shirt pocket."

"Thanks." He tossed it past the left side of the table. Nothing.

He looked back at her. "Either we're out of his line of sight now or—"

"He wants us to think we are."

"Only one way to find out." He scrambled forward in a half crouch, half run, then dived past the table.

Boom! Boom! The floor splintered inches from his right foot. He swore and rolled toward the fireplace, then scooted back against the wall of stone that formed the floor-to-ceiling chimney and hearth.

Remi cursed even more than he had, blasting the shooter for his mean trick in making Duncan think he might be safe.

"I'm okay," he called out. "You can quit cursing."

She cursed some more, just to be ornery and leaned toward the couch to get a better view of him.

Keeping his back to the wall, careful to stay away from the still unbroken window on the left, he inched closer to the center of the fireplace. Then he jumped up on the hearth and grabbed the gun from over the mantel, along with the box of ammo in the decorative wood box beneath it. After loading the rifle, he jumped down, apparently considering his next move.

She considered his options, too. If she was in his position, there was probably only one thing to do. Make a run for it. The only question was which direction—left or right? The shooter had obviously seen him sprint from behind the coffee table. The stacked-stone chimney above the roofline made it clear that he had to be by the fireplace. Had the shooter moved to another vantage point where he'd have an angle at the other window? The shooter had to be in a tree. Moving to another tree would require that he climb down, then up the next one. That would take time. Duncan must have come to the same conclusion, because his hand tightened around the rifle and he looked toward her. His brows drew down.

"Remi. You need to back up farther behind the table. And stay here. You promised."

"Technically, I didn't *promise* anything."

"Remi—"

"Just hurry and get him, okay? I don't even have my cell phone to call for backup. The battery's dead."

"Yeah, well, don't beat yourself up. Mine's charged, but it's sitting on the kitchen table, where it's doing us absolutely no good."

She swore again.

He grinned. "I'll be back in time for dinner, honey." He shoved some extra shells in his pocket.

"You'd better be. Stay safe, Duncan. I can't… I don't…"

His expression softened. "Tell me all about it when I get back." He gripped his rifle in his right hand and took off for the front door.

A rifle cracked behind him. Glass shattered. He threw the dead bolt and lunged out the door.

REMI DUCKED, COVERING her head and drawing her legs up to her chest as more rifle fire seemed to explode around her. She'd heard the sound of Duncan diving to the ground outside while the shooter fired shots through the window on the other side of the fireplace. But the angle was all wrong. Slivers of wood kicked up from the log walls on the other side of the room, well above the floor. The shooter must have been climbing down the tree, or maybe he'd moved to another one while Duncan was getting his gun.

Either way, he hadn't been high enough to get a bead on Duncan when he'd run for the door. Which was good and bad. Good because he'd missed Duncan. Bad because he was lower to the ground now and had to know

Duncan was coming after him. Bad guy with a gun was likely on the ground now, too, and positioning himself for an ambush.

She couldn't just lie there and hope Duncan had thought about the same thing. She needed to get her gun and back him up. With her right hand out of commission, even if she'd had the benefit of a long gun, she'd have zero accuracy. But accuracy wasn't what he needed from her. He needed a distraction, a diversion.

Using the same trick that Duncan had, she grabbed some shards of wood and glass off the floor and tossed them in the air. Nothing. She tried again. Still nothing. Hoping that meant the shooter wasn't looking through his scope at her position and waiting for her to appear, she pushed herself to her feet. The pain from her right shoulder was blinding. Black spots swam in front of her eyes. She drew deep breaths, forcing oxygen into her lungs. Her vision cleared. She was going to have to tie her arm tightly into place so she could stand the pain without passing out. For now, though, she settled for clasping her right arm with her left.

If the gunman had been watching, he'd have had a perfectly clear shot at her. No way could she squirm and drop and roll like Duncan had. But no bullets came flying through the window. She drew a ragged breath and ran for the kitchen. She made it through the archway and swiped Duncan's cell phone off the table, biting her lip at the pain in her shoulder when she let her bad arm go. Then she ran into the back hall.

She'd just made it to the bedroom when she dropped to her knees. The phone fell from her hand and she grasped her hurt shoulder. Hot tears were streaming down her cheeks. The pain was worse than before. If she survived this day she'd probably end up having surgery, and be lucky if she ever regained full use of the thing. That thought had her burning mad and up on her feet again. The psychopath outside had taken everything from her, including possibly the use of her right arm. No way was he going to take Duncan, too.

She grabbed the phone, but the home screen was locked. Without Duncan's pass code she couldn't call for backup.

Boom! Bam!

Two different guns fired outside. If she was going to help him, she needed to get out there. Now!

She put her sling on and brutally tightened it to immobilize her arm against her chest. Then she shoved Duncan's phone in her pocket and grabbed her pistol out of the nightstand drawer. Loading a magazine was awkward but she managed to balance it between the bed and her thigh and jam the gun down on top of it, locking it in place.

She ran for the back door. She didn't even stop to look for either man. She flew past the hot tub and bolted down the stairs to the backyard. Then she stopped, aiming her pistol toward the trees as she used the deck stairs for cover. Nothing. Where was the gunman? Where was Duncan?

Whack. Smack. Crack.

She didn't know what those sounds were, but she took off running toward them, assuming they had to have come from at least one of the men. She rounded a copse of pines and slid to a halt on some dried up pine needles.

Duncan stood ten feet away, his chest heaving from exertion. And at his feet, his neck twisted at an impossible angle, lay the gunman, his sightless eyes staring up at the canopy of tree branches overhead.

She ran to Duncan, barreling into him and wrapping

her good arm around his waist. He grunted from the impact, then steadied himself and put his arms around her.

"It's okay," he whispered against the top of her head. "It's okay. It's over."

She squeezed him, hard, then pulled back, wincing at the tug of pain in her right shoulder. "You're okay? He didn't shoot you, did he?"

"I'm okay. He ran out of ammo and charged me. I could have shot him. But he just looked so…young. I tried to give him a chance. But he pulled a knife. I didn't have a choice." He frowned down at her. "I told you to wait in the cabin."

"Yeah, well. I've never been good at following orders. And I wasn't going to lie there waiting to be rescued when someone was trying to kill you."

He looked at the pistol still in her left hand, pointing at the ground, and his face paled. "Aren't you right-handed?"

She shoved the gun in her pocket. "I figured I could create a diversion, if nothing else."

He scrubbed his face and shook his head. "Thank goodness it didn't come to that."

She grinned, feeling lighthearted in knowing that the ordeal was finally over. "I was going to call for backup. But I didn't know your code to unlock your phone." She handed it to him and he slid it into his pocket, looking too drained to make a call just yet. She understood the feeling. Everything had happened so fast, too fast. The world felt off-kilter, just plain…off. They both needed to catch their breath.

Still smiling, she finally looked down to see whether she knew the shooter. She stopped smiling. An older, harder-looking Billy Hendricks lay on his back, his rifle a few feet away, where it must have landed when he'd realized he was out of ammo. All these years she thought she was searching for a stranger, when the man who'd killed her sister was someone she'd known.

Duncan put an arm around her waist, as careful as ever not to jar her shoulder. "Don't look at him. Don't let him hurt you anymore. It's over."

She forced her gaze away. "I know. It just feels…surreal. Strange. All these years I thought Billy was just one of us, someone who knew Becca. He even posted on her page, the website my dad put up, saying he was praying for us." She shivered, and it had nothing to do with the chilly air and the fact that she wasn't wearing her jacket. "And all along, he was the one who'd taken her from us."

"It's freezing out here. Why don't you head up to the house and warm up in front of the fire?" he said. "I'll be up in a few minutes, right after I call this in and get the crime scene guys on their way. Then I'm taking you to the hospital. No arguing this time."

"Don't worry. I won't argue. I want some really good drugs and I don't know any dealers around here." She grinned, and then headed toward the house.

DUNCAN WAITED UNTIL she was out of sight before sliding down to the ground and resting his back against a pine tree. Feeling unbelievably weary, he pulled out his cell phone, and placed the call to his boss. He turned on the speaker function and set the phone on a nearby rock. Then he yanked off one of his socks and held it against his lower left side, putting pressure on the laceration that Billy had made before Duncan was able to disarm him.

Chapter Fifteen

"Enough with the fifty questions," Duncan said over the phone. "I'm freezing out here. When will the crime scene techs arrive? I can't stand guard duty all afternoon and night, keeping wild animals off the perp." He frowned at the blood-soaked sock and tossed it to the ground. He tugged his other sock off and pressed that to his side. He was glad that Remi had listened to him, for once, and went to the house to warm up. But, also knowing her, he was mildly surprised she hadn't thought to come back with a jacket for him. Then again, she hadn't realized he planned on waiting out here for the techs this long.

"They should be there in a few more minutes."

"Good." He pulled the sock away and swore.

"Duncan. What's wrong?"

"Nothing a few stitches won't cure. The perp stuck me with his knife before I got him in a headlock. The stupid wound won't quit bleeding."

His boss swore enough for both of them. "Why didn't you tell me you were wounded? Hold on."

Duncan closed his eyes and pressed the bloody sock against his side as he listened to his boss order one of the others to get an ambulance to his house.

"They're ten minutes out. How bad is it?"

"Apparently worse than I thought. I'm getting woozy."

"That may be the only thing that saves you from my wrath. Blood loss might excuse your poor judgment."

Duncan figured the fact that he was slowly freezing to death could also help explain why his brain wasn't firing on all pistons. He should have told his boss right away that he needed a medic. But Lee had fired off so many questions he'd been too busy answering them to realize how badly he was bleeding. The stupid thing wouldn't stop no matter how hard he pressed.

"Did the suspect have any ID on him?" Lee asked. "And if you haven't already checked, don't do it now. Just be still and keep pressure on the wound."

"I don't have to check. I recognize him from pictures I saw while Remi and I were researching the case earlier. It's Billy Hendricks, from Colorado originally. He went to high school with Remi and her sister."

"Billy Hendricks? Are you sure?"

Duncan glanced at the dead man's face, the same face he'd seen standing behind Remi and Becca in the hallway of their school, looking like he wanted to murder Becca. And then, later, he had. "It's Hendricks. I'm sure. He had an alibi for Becca's murder, said he was with another girl, Felicia Reynolds, that night. But she admitted today that she lied to cover for him."

"Did she tell you why?"

"Something about believing he was too nice to do something like that, so she wanted to protect him. She was sweet on him at the time."

"Maybe she doesn't know the whole truth then and really just thought she was helping him out. In reality, she was just giving him a cover to use with the chaperones."

Duncan frowned. "What are you talking about?"

"The BAU has been looking, and I mean looking hard, into the backgrounds of all the men who were on that senior class trip, including Billy Hendricks. The night that Becca Jordan disappeared, Hendricks was an hour away using a fake ID to drink and gamble at Harrah's Cherokee Casino."

"Harrah's. Are you sure? That never came up in any of the reports, not even Pops's informal file he kept on the investigation."

"You can blame the almighty tourism dollar and politics for that little jewel. The FBI had a separate report they didn't include in the file that they shared with our office back then. Apparently, when they interviewed Hendricks he confessed to sneaking into the casino. Video confirmed he was there and couldn't have abducted Miss Jordan. But having an underage kid get past their security could have jeopardized their liquor license and caused them embarrassment on top of that. The mayor of Gatlinburg at the time stepped in with the FBI and convinced them to keep the casino jaunt a secret. The FBI knew Hendricks wasn't their guy, so they really didn't care if the casino and mayor wanted to keep things quiet and not damage the casino's reputation or endanger its liquor license. Bottom line, there's just no way that Billy Hendricks abducted Becca Jordan."

Duncan frowned. "That doesn't make sense. If Billy didn't kill Becca, then why would he come here and try to kill Remi? It made sense in a psychopathic kind of way that if he killed one twin and saw the other one later, he'd want to kill her, too."

"I don't know. It's too bad that he has an ironclad alibi for Becca's disappearance, because he *doesn't* have an alibi for Sheryl Foster's. Not that we've been able to find, at least. He's a long-haul trucker and had a delivery in this area the night before she was abducted. He doesn't have another haul scheduled for several days. The FBI obtained video from a local gas station that showed his rig driving through town and out toward the park the night before Foster disappeared. They haven't found that rig on any other video since then. That leads me to believe he'd holed up somewhere nearby, and was doing his best to stay out of sight. My guess is we'll find his rig, which is just the cab since he delivered the trailer he was hauling, somewhere close to your cabin, maybe parked at one of the rentals that tend to be vacant this time of year."

Duncan was having a hard time wrapping his mind around what he was hearing about Billy. The guy didn't abduct Becca. But he could have abducted Foster. And he'd tried to kill Remi. Why would he do that unless he was involved in her sister's disappearance somehow? If Billy had been Becca's killer, then it made a sick kind of sense that he'd wanted to kill the other twin, too. It even seemed reasonable that he'd come here because he was worried that Remi was onto him and would figure out he'd murdered her sister. But since he wasn't the killer, why attack Remi? There was no motivation for him to be here. It couldn't be a random coincidence.

One blonde. One brunette.

Two different types of victims.

Billy had an alibi for one victim, but not the other.

Duncan's blood ran cold in his veins. His hand tightened on the phone.

"Lee, you said the FBI is looking into the alibis of the men who participated in that senior trip. What about alibis for the other abductions and killings at other parks? What did they find out about Hendricks?"

"Give me a minute."

Duncan heard the sound of papers shuffling.

"Okay, got it. Lots of stuff to check out, but so far Hendricks has alibis for a handful of the cases and doesn't have any verifiable alibi for the others."

"Which ones does he not have alibis for? What do those victims have in common?" He waited. "Lee?"

"Blond. The ones we can't verify his alibi for are the blonde victims."

"And he alibis out for the brunettes?"

"So far, it's looking that way."

Billy didn't kill Becca.

But he could have killed Foster.

Two different victims.

One blonde. One brunette.

Duncan's gaze shot toward the cabin. "Two killers. Why didn't I see it? One prefers blondes, the other brunettes. Billy had a partner. He kills the blondes. His partner takes the brunettes." He was about to hang up on his boss to call Remi and warn her. Then he remembered that her cell phone battery was dead.

He swore and shoved himself to his feet, then fell against the tree. He swore again, wobbled back to standing, then swiped the cell phone from where it had fallen and took off through the trees.

"Remi!" he yelled as soon as he cleared the tree line. The shattered windows on the back of the house were like gaping maws mocking him with the silence behind them. "Remi!"

"What's going on?" Lee demanded.

"Two killers," he repeated, between gasping breaths as he jogged up the steep incline. "Someone's working with Billy. Someone he's known a long time, maybe even since high school. They're tag-teaming. Billy kills the blondes. His partner kills the brunettes."

"But if Billy killed Foster, didn't he already get his

blonde? Why go after Remi? She's blond. What about that whole constellation thing?"

"She's a natural brunette. She dyed her hair for this case. Billy knew Becca and Remi. He knew she wasn't a true blonde. And so would his partner. If Billy was on the ridge staking out Foster when he saw Remi, he might have gotten confused, thinking he was seeing Becca again, except as a blonde." He reached the bottom of the stairs and fell to his knees. He was dizzy. Had to draw a deep breath. Forced his feet back under him and bounded up the stairs.

"Why take Foster at all then? Why not just take Remi as his blonde victim?"

"Because Vale and then I showed up and messed up his game. Billy took Foster as a substitute. We already know they go off script, kill others, based on what you found in the cave. Remi was too tempting to pass up. She was the one who got away. That's why Billy came here. Or maybe he was worried his partner would go after Remi because she's a natural brunette, and he wanted to beat him to it, because she was Becca's twin. Maybe he felt territorial. Who knows how these sick minds work?"

"It all makes sense in a macabre way. Where is she?"

Duncan tried to throw open the sliding glass door. It was locked. He ran to the right and leaped through the opening where one of the picture windows had been. "Remi! Remi!" He sprinted through the kitchen to the back hall, into his bedroom.

"Duncan, report. Where is Special Agent Jordan?"

He rushed to the other bedroom, checked both bathrooms, vaulted down the stairs to the basement level. Nothing, nothing, nothing. He hurried back upstairs and burst out the front door. He didn't stop until he was standing in the middle of the road, looking all around as he turned in a circle.

"Where is she?" his boss asked again.

"Gone." Duncan forced the word past his tight throat. "Remi's gone."

Chapter Sixteen

Remi kicked at the taillight from inside the trunk once again, twice, then collapsed back in exhaustion. She knew all the tricks for getting out of a locked trunk, like pulling the emergency release.

There wasn't one.

Or breaking the back seat so she could get out that way.

There was a piece of steel at the back of the trunk, no way to even reach the seat.

Or shatter the taillight and stick something through the hole, like her foot or her hand, so passersby would see it and call the police.

Whoever had knocked her out and abducted her from Duncan's house had put a wire mesh cover over the lights, making it impossible for her to break them no matter how hard she tried.

The only good thing was that whatever her captor had used to drug her had the side effect of numbing her shoulder. Otherwise, bumping around in the trunk would likely have had her writhing with pain.

How long had she been riding around in this trunk? Since she'd been unconscious for part of the journey, she couldn't be sure. Ten minutes? Thirty? An hour? Whoever had abducted her had to know the cabin belonged to a federal officer. The Jeep parked out front with its NPS shield was a huge giveaway. Was the driver meandering around town to make sure no one was following him? Had he stopped somewhere and hid out for a bit, while she was still asleep, making sure there wasn't any traffic before he pulled out again? All those questions were running through her mind without any answers, and one overriding thought kept repeating itself.

I'm going to die.

Duncan's face swam in her mind's eye. Duncan. At least he was safe. She didn't have to worry about him being in the middle of this, whatever this was. What an unexpected, wonderful bright spot in her life to have met him. She just hoped he wouldn't blame himself for whatever happened to her. It wasn't his fault. It was this jerk's fault who'd captured her.

I'm going to die.

Probably, yes. Most likely. But she wouldn't go easily. She might be small, and injured, but she still had her wits, plus fingernails and, luckily, shoes on her feet, so she could scratch and kick him. And she could run. Miles and miles. All she needed was the element of surprise, and she'd take off like a deer with a pack of wolves on its tail.

And if he caught her? Well, then she'd just have to figure out how to kill him, without getting herself killed. Because she hadn't spent her entire adult life locking animals like him up only to die at the hands of one. Somehow, she'd figure a way out of this.

The car slowed, then turned right and started up an incline. The road was curvy, tilting her from side to side, but she braced herself to keep from falling over. A few minutes later, the car slowed again, then braked hard and turned right, throwing her against the side of the trunk.

She sucked in a sharp breath at the resulting burn in her shoulder muscles. The drugs were starting to wear off.

She tilted her body in the other direction, taking the pressure off her shoulder. The car started bouncing up and down and side to side. Something scraped the roof with a metallic scratching sound. Something else scraped along the left side. She gritted her teeth against the fiery pain in her shoulder, not to mention every other joint in her bruised and battered body. A little while later, a loud rushing sound filled the air. A waterfall. Not a large one, but there was no mistaking that sound.

They were back in the mountains.

DUNCAN LIFTED HIS head from the examining room table to look at Lee. "Did the guys find any trace of—"

Thunk. The doctor shoved his head back down. Again.

"Hey," Duncan complained, glaring at him. "Would you stop doing that?"

"I'm trying to keep you from bleeding to death. Hold still so I can finish closing the wound."

The doctor jabbed the needle into his skin. Duncan automatically jerked from the motion, but thankfully, his side had been numbed. He narrowed his eyes at the doctor, figuring he'd done that on purpose.

"Just be still," Lee said, drawing closer to the table. "You're in no shape to join any search parties, anyway. The best way for you to help Special Agent Jordan is to use that brain of yours to help us figure out who has her and where he's taken her."

Duncan glared at the doctor again. "I'm perfectly fine. They're loading me up with IV fluids. I just need Dr. Jekyll here to finish his stitches. Sometime today would be nice."

The man shook his head and kept sewing.

Lee leaned over Duncan. "That's a nasty cut. Looks like a shark took a bite out of your side. You're really lucky you didn't bleed out before the ambulance got there."

The doctor snipped the thread and paused with his needle in the air. "Yes, he is. Extremely lucky. But next time, ask for another doctor." He tossed his garbage in the medical waste container and stalked out without another word.

Duncan grimaced as Lee helped him sit up. "Guess I owe him an apology. But he was so slow. He knew I'm in the middle of a case and needed to get out of here fast." He reached for his shirt at the foot of the table, then grimaced again, seeing the blood all over it.

Lee snatched it and tossed it in the trash. "You can't put that back on. Civilians would see all that blood and call 911, thinking an ax murderer was on the loose. I'll get one of the guys to bring you a shirt from one of their go-bags."

Duncan gave him a droll look. "Really? Whose shirt's gonna fit me?"

Lee frowned. "What did your mama feed you and your brothers growing up? Whole hogs?"

Duncan rolled his eyes and hopped down from the table. He looked around, then grabbed a hospital gown and yanked it on. "This will do for now. Maybe you can get a couple of the guys to drive my Jeep here. I've got a go-bag with extra clothes inside."

"Will do."

"Which room is Vale in?" Duncan asked, as he strode into the hallway. "I only spoke to him on the phone before. I want to talk to him again, show him Billy's picture, see if he remembers anything else that might help us figure out a description of whoever has Remi, if nothing else."

"Vale's not here," Lee said. "I thought the same thing as you when I got here. I had one of the other guys go ask him if I could interview him. But he's gone."

Duncan stopped and turned. "What do you mean, gone? He nearly bled out a couple of days ago."

"So did you, less than an hour ago. And yet here you are, all stitched up and running around."

"I was slashed, not stabbed. Vale was shot. Big difference. No way should he have been released yet." He headed to the information desk, flashed his badge, and a few moments later had the information he needed. He headed back toward Lee and passed him on his way down the hall. "Tell me everything you know about Vale," he called over his shoulder.

Lee rushed to catch up to him. "Okay, but where are you going in such an all-fired hurry."

"I know the guy who runs security here. I've worked with him many times on other cases."

"Again, why?"

Duncan paused outside the security office. "Because Vale left the hospital against medical advice. And he'd told me over the phone he had no interest in bringing charges against Remi, or suing, even though he probably could have gotten a lot of money if he had. Could be nothing, but could be something."

"What, you're thinking Vale is our other guy, Billy's partner?"

"Maybe. Maybe not. But I know one thing. Vale had plenty of time to leave the hospital and get to my place and grab Remi. And I also know that Remi was convinced he had a gun up on that ridge."

"But we never found one."

"Doesn't mean he didn't have one. He could have thrown it when I was handcuffing Remi, just like she said."

"You're reaching."

He whirled around. "I'm desperate. And I've learned a lot about Remi. She's smart, and honest. If she says he had a gun, that's good enough for me. I just want to do one thing. Find out if he had any visitors while he was here, and if so, whether Billy was one of them."

Twenty minutes later, a grainy image from a hallway camera came up in the security office, showing a familiar man walking to Vale's hospital room.

"Billy," Duncan and Lee said at the same time.

"And he brought a bag. Clothes, maybe? For Vale?" Lee wondered.

"Just this morning," Duncan added. "I bet he came to tell Vale he was going after Remi. But Vale wanted her for himself. So after Billy left, Vale decided to go after him, maybe to stop him, or maybe just to claim Remi as his next victim."

As they watched the recording being fast-forwarded, Lee got a call. He quickly took it, then hung up, looking pale.

Duncan's mouth went dry. He couldn't even bring himself to ask. He just waited.

"It's not Remi," Lee rushed to assure him. "That was Pops. He was with a crew I sent back to the ridge, looking for any fresh signs that someone might have gone that way again. He found a gun, about forty feet into the woods from where you performed first aid on Vale."

"What kind of gun?" Duncan demanded.

"Glock 19, 9 mm."

Duncan swore. "I never should have doubted her. If I'd listened, really listened, I could have—"

"What? Arrested the guy she shot? The victim? Her story didn't hold water at the time. Hindsight is twenty-twenty. You can't blame yourself. Besides, we don't know for sure that Vale is involved. He may have had a gun like her, for protection, and didn't want to get in trouble so he tossed it."

"You believe that?"

"I believe the facts. And those are pretty slim pickings right now."

"Here you go," Duncan's friend said. "He's coming out of the room, ten minutes after he went in."

Duncan and Lee stared at the screen. Billy stepped out of Vale's room, no longer carrying the bag. And beside him, fully dressed, was Vale. They both walked down the hall and got into the elevator.

"Son of a—" Lee began.

"Vale's our guy," Duncan said. "We need to get a BOLO out right away on him. And we need to figure out what he's driving, what he does for a living, how he got here and where he may be holed up. And we need to find out all of that yesterday."

THE SUDDEN CESSATION of movement bothered Remi more than all the bouncing that had made her shoulder throb with pain. Her captor had stopped the car. Which meant they were wherever he planned to take her, and that he was about to get on with it, do whatever he planned to do to her.

She twisted around, positioning her feet toward the rear bumper. He'd taken away her sling and zip-tied her hands together, in front of her. And he hadn't bound her legs. So she had at least those two things going for her. If she could surprise him when he opened the trunk, she could kick out at him, throw him off balance and then throw herself out of the car. Then she could take off running.

The car shook. A door slammed. Shoes crunched against the ground as he rounded the vehicle, coming toward the back.

She scooted closer to the bumper side, lifted her knees higher.

Click. The trunk sprang up. Something dark loomed in front of her.

She kicked with all her strength. Her legs hit the dark shape, but it was like hitting nothing. Her body jerked forward with her momentum and she tumbled out of the trunk onto whatever she'd kicked. A tarp! He'd waved a tarp in front of her and she'd charged like a raging bull. He'd tricked her.

Laughter had her jerking around. A man stood over her, the sun behind him so she couldn't see his face. And he was too far away for her to kick him, even if she could. Her legs were tangled up in the heavy tarp. She desperately shuffled her feet, trying to get free.

"Your sister tried the same thing when I opened the trunk to get her out."

Remi froze and stared up at him. Becca? He was the one who'd taken Becca?

"She kicked me good. Hit me square in the jaw." He chuckled again. "But I've taken far worse than what she dished out. Still, I figured you might think like her, try that same trick. I was ready this time." He crouched down, the sun no longer obscuring his features, or the big serrated hunting knife in his right hand.

Remi sucked in a breath as recognition dawned.

"That's right." He grinned. "Kurt Vale, pleased to meet ya. But we met once before, didn't we? Up on that ridge. If it wasn't for my gun getting caught in my pocket,

I'd have popped one off before you did." He tapped his side and winced. "And I wouldn't be sporting a bullet hole now. Then again, I'd have had to kill that stupid cop who showed up, and then the whole police force, local and Feds, would have rained down on me. I guess you did me a favor, in hindsight. Everyone thinks I'm the victim here." He laughed again. "What a trip, huh?"

"What did you do to my sister?" she demanded, eyeing the knife in his hand.

"Nothing she didn't want me to do. Not at first, anyway." He winked.

Remi's stomach clenched.

"Don't worry." He slid the knife into a leather holder strapped to his thigh. "I'm about to do you a favor right back. I'm about to answer all your questions, by showing you exactly what I did to your sister, in intimate detail. I figure it's only fair, don't you? You've been searching for her all these years. I think it's time you finally found her."

He waved toward the trees around them. "This is where I brought her that night, in the trunk of my car. Easy peasy, because she snuck out of camp to meet me, following the instructions in my note to keep to the hard rocky parts of the trail so she wouldn't leave any footprints for a nosy chaperone to follow."

"You're lying." Remi very slowly moved her legs, trying to slide them out from the tarp so she could make a break for it. "She didn't even know you. She wouldn't have gone to meet with you."

"True. She didn't know me, even though I'd seen her from afar. I was a friend of Billy's, a year younger. You didn't realize that, did you? He was tired of Becca snubbing him and asked me to join him on the senior trip to teach her a lesson. So that's what I did, followed the buses up here and set up camp out in the woods. Billy gave her that note. I waited. And out came beautiful Becca, right into my arms."

"Liar." Remi's right foot was free. She pulled the fabric toward her with her left hand, slowly, and sought to keep him distracted as she tried to free her left foot. "She wouldn't have gone to meet Billy, either."

He cocked his head. "Well, now. Who said anything about her meeting Billy? That Garrett fellow was who she was sweet on, Garrett Weber. Popular guy in school. Total wuss. Lived down the street from me. But the girls liked him well enough. When Becca read that note saying he'd dumped his girlfriend because he wanted her instead, she couldn't get out of camp fast enough."

Oh, Becca. Grief shot through Remi, but she tamped it down. Her left foot slid free. *Now.*

She yanked the tarp up and threw it over his head.

He let out a guttural yell, cursing at her as he grabbed at the cloth.

She scrambled to her feet and bolted for the woods.

Chapter Seventeen

Duncan tucked his shirt into his jeans, glad to ditch the hospital gown now that a couple of his peers had driven his Jeep to the NPS trailer and brought him his go-bag. He thanked them, then leaned over the enormous table in the middle of the office, a black Sharpie in his hand as he looked at the map of the Great Smoky Mountains National Park and surrounding area.

"Patterson, you said you searched grid eighteen?"

Patterson, one of the rangers on loan from Atlanta, gave him a thumbs-up from the other side of the room where he was getting coffee.

Duncan circled the grid, wrote Patterson's name and placed a black checkmark beside it.

"Pops, where did your team search?" he called out.

"You don't have to yell. I'm right beside you, son."

"Oh, sorry." Duncan scrubbed his face. It had been an hour since he'd left the hospital, two since Remi had been taken. Where was she?

"We searched here." Pops pointed to the map. "And here. Just finished that one. What area do you want me to try next?"

Lee had been talking to some other investigators and searchers, and came over to stand beside Pops. "I've got crews in five grids in the park right now." He took Duncan's pen and circled those. "Gatlinburg PD has road-blocks in and out of town. We've got roadblocks on every major route in and out of the area."

Duncan shook his head. "It's taking too long. We'd need thousands to search the whole park. And we all know we can't block every potential access point. The area's just too big." He tossed his pen down. "Has the BAU told you anything useful about Vale yet?"

Lee shrugged. "Just what we learned thirty minutes ago on the last status call. That he's a long-haul trucker, like his buddy Hendricks was. Different companies, but similar routes. Vale grew up in Colorado, went to the same high school. Got in trouble a lot, spent time in de-tention, which is where we figure he first met Billy."

"They must have been friends back during the senior trip, ten years ago," Duncan said. "Vale either followed the class up here, planning on mischief, or was here be-fore they arrived. Either way, he and Billy likely planned the attack on Becca. That whole casino visit was prob-ably to give Billy an alibi. Meanwhile no one even real-ized Vale was around."

Pops thumped the map. "Unless you come up with a better plan, I'm going to take my men over by the Sugar-lands Visitor Center and see if we can find anyone who saw Vale in the likely time frame if he did come back to the park with Special Agent Jordan."

"Oh, he came back, all right," Duncan said. "This is a game for him. It started with her sister here in the park. He toyed with Remi with that skeleton. He's going to finish it here, too."

Pops grasped his shoulder in a tight squeeze. "We'll find her. Black Charger, right? The car that's registered to Vale?"

"Colorado plates." He rattled off the number, which

he already knew by heart. "Don't forget to ask about Hendricks's rig. It's a white Freightliner with Colorado plates, too. We didn't find it near my cabin. Vale may have taken the rig instead of his car."

"You got it." Pops grabbed his coat and headed out the door with a handful of rangers.

Lee marked the visitor's center on the map, along with Pops's name.

Duncan looked around. There were a dozen people on the phones, on computers, looking at maps, and dozens more out in the field. But no one had scared up even one report of a black Charger or white semitruck cab near his cabin or near the park today. So how had Vale gotten away from his house with Remi, without a single neighbor on that long road remembering either of those vehicles?

"What's going on in that head of yours?" Lee said.

"Vale. Obviously he drove Remi out of the area and then likely drove her up here, to the park somewhere. But no one near my cabin saw a semitruck or a Charger. I don't exactly live in a subdivision with a neighborhood watch group. But there are plenty of cabins nearby and that's a fairly busy main road to that particular area. Someone at a gas station at the bottom of the mountain, or a restaurant, or a store, had to have seen something. You pulled all closed-circuit surveillance video in the area?"

"I pulled everything within a five mile radius. There wasn't one single semi up on that mountain in the time frame that we need. There were two black Chargers, both with local plates. Both were ruled out. Gatlinburg PD tracked down the owners."

Duncan dropped his head, his hands braced against the table. "Think, think, think. What am I missing? He couldn't have physically hauled her through the woods.

Our team would have found evidence of that. And there's just nowhere to go up there. He had to drive out. She was tied up either in the back seat or in the trunk. But he had to have her in a vehicle. All that video footage, did the police look for Vale, specifically, as the driver? I think we can narrow it down to a car, something with a trunk or back seat where no one would see Remi."

"They're not amateurs. I'm sure they looked at every vehicle that passed any business with a camera with a view of the street. And before you ask, no, there's no point of entry up on that mountain where you live that isn't covered by a camera. The police were thorough, looking at every driver of every car and truck that came through. It's like the two of them just disappeared, or flew out in a helicopter or something." He snorted, without amusement.

Duncan frowned, Lee's words running through his head. "How's the neighborhood canvassing going?"

"Every house, RV, shed, hell, even hot tubs within a few miles of your place have been searched. She's not up there, Duncan."

He closed his eyes, his arms still braced on the table. Vale and Remi had come down from the mountain. There was only one road he could have used. Cameras would show every vehicle going up or down. So how could Vale drive right past them and the police not realize it was him?

He jerked his head up. "A police car. Vale's got a police car, or an NPS vehicle. Something official that the police wouldn't look twice at when they were scanning the video. Tell them to look again, but this time look for something official, not a civilian vehicle."

Lee already had his phone out. While he spoke to Gatlinburg PD, Duncan studied the map of the area closest to his house. He was making a huge assumption that Vale would risk coming back into the park. But he also knew about killers' signatures, and how important it was to a serial killer to complete his ritual. Which meant Vale had to bring Remi here. But where, in over a quarter of a million acres, would he take her? Again, logically, it seemed like he'd take her back to the ridge where Foster had been taken. But that place had been searched twice today already. So where was he?

He put X's by the roads that led up the mountain near the ridge, where Becca had disappeared all those years ago. There were four roads to that area, not counting the one that passed in front of the NPS trailer, which wasn't a road civilians used.

Duncan grew still, looking at the map. A road to the area near the senior class campsite, that few people traveled, would be extremely tempting to someone like Vale. In fact, it would be perfect.

Lee ended his call, his face grim. "You were right. A police car headed down the mountain within five minutes of you calling me from your cabin to report that Hendricks had been killed. And the officer who uses that car can't be reached. They're sending patrol to his house now."

"Where's his house?" Duncan asked, even though he was fairly certain he already knew the answer.

"Same mountain as you. About a mile away."

"Put a BOLO out—"

"Gatlinburg PD's already got that handled. They'll contact businesses with cameras along the main road leading from where they saw that police car and track its movements, figure out where it went." He rattled off the car number. "I'll get all my guys searching for that police cruiser. We'll check our own video around the park entrances, see if it came up one of the main roads."

Duncan strode toward the door.

"Where are you going?"

"To search the road out front. It's the most likely place he would have gone." Duncan grabbed his coat and gloves off the pegs on the wall.

"Duncan, stop," Lee called after him. "You're in no condition to—"

He let the door close on his boss's words and took off in a run toward his Jeep.

HE WAS HERDING HER, like a border collie forcing a lost lamb back to the other sheep, and she couldn't do a dang thing about it. There was simply nowhere else to go. His crashing footfalls pounded after her in the brush, that irritating laughter floating to her in the breeze. He was making no attempt to hide where he was and didn't have to. She'd made the mistake of following the trail where the road ended, thinking it would be easier to run full out that way and escape. But the killer knew these woods better than her. He knew the path ran along some cliffs, with steep drops onto sharp rocks below. As soon as she'd reached the cliffs, she'd jerked around to head back, to try to thread her way through the woods somewhere else. And he'd been right there, grinning at her, holding that impossibly long, jagged-edged knife that looked like a close cousin to a machete.

She'd shivered, bile rising in her throat. She didn't want to die. And she really didn't want to get hacked to death.

"This is exactly what Becca did," he'd said, laughing again. "She ran down the path, just like you. You're making this too easy!"

She'd taken off running, with him loping after her.

Help me, Becca. Where did you go? Where should I not go?

She glanced around, desperate for a break in the trees, somewhere to hide. But the rock face of the mountain loomed on her right, the steep drop-off to her left.

Maybe where the trail curved up ahead there would be somewhere to hide, a way to ambush him. It was her only hope right now. Clasping her hurt arm against her chest, she put on a fresh burst of speed.

DUNCAN SWORE AND turned the Jeep around at the field with the cell tower. He'd gone down the mountain first, to the parking lot where he'd once taken Remi to get her purse out of her car. The lot was empty. He'd driven around the perimeter, just in case Vale had pulled the stolen police car just inside the tree line. But there was nowhere for him to go. The trees were too thick in this section. Even an ATV couldn't get through here. He'd headed back up the mountain, all the way to the top, to the field where he'd once parked in order to see where Sheryl Foster had been abducted. Again, nothing.

He headed back down for another sweep of the road, going slowly as he thought through everything. He'd just passed the opening to the gravel parking lot and the NPS trailer when the radio in his glove box squawked. He grabbed it and clicked to respond.

"Duncan here."

"It's Lee. Where are you?"

"Just east of the NPS trailer entrance. Why?"

"A camera at the trailhead at the bottom of our access road picked up the stolen police car heading up there about half an hour ago. They're still scanning through additional video, but so far, they haven't seen it come out. Duncan, he's on our road somewhere. Has to be."

He slammed his brakes. He'd just passed the bird-watching trail where he'd parked to talk to Remi. If Vale had come up this way, maybe he'd turned down that same trail. It was worth a look.

He shifted into Reverse and zipped back to the entrance. Sure enough, fresh tire tracks dug into the damp grass where snow had been earlier, but had since melted. And the grass just past that was flattened from a recent passing.

"He's on the old bird-watching trail, two miles west of NPS. I'm going in."

"Wait, I don't even know what that is. What are you talking about?"

"It used to be a road, years ago. Then it was used as a trail, but it was deemed too dangerous and closed after that. Ask Pops. He's the one who showed it to me when he was teaching me the area. Two miles down the mountain, then head south."

Lee yelled at some of the rangers to grab their coats. "Stay put. We're coming to you."

"No time." He tossed the radio onto the seat beside him and slammed the accelerator.

REMI STOPPED AND bent over at the waist, panting, desperately trying to pull oxygen into her starved lungs. The distance she'd run wasn't great. But it had been over harsh terrain. Adrenaline was pumping through her body, and she'd been running at full speed rather than the slower pace of a cross-country runner. Her side ached. Her thighs were burning. Her arm was screaming at her. Constant pain and fear combined to steal her stamina and threatened to leave her lying on the ground, quivering like a beached jellyfish.

"Oh, *Reeemiiii*… I'm coming for you, darling."

The sickening sound of Vale's taunting had her jerking upright. The man wasn't human. He never seemed to stop to rest. He just kept coming.

The sound of steel scraping against the rock wall of the mountain that trapped her in on one side had her whimpering.

"I hear you, Remi! I hear you!"

She'd never hated anyone so much in her life. She drew a ragged breath and started running again. She'd just rounded the latest curve in the dangerously narrowing trail when it opened into a wide clearing. There were trees to her right, and a gray, weathered structure directly in front of her. She hesitated, not sure what to do. Try for the trees? Hope the rocky face of the mountain didn't continue around to the right and block her in again? Or head into the structure and hope she could find something to use to defend herself?

What did you do, Becca? Help me make the right decision.

Shoes skittered on rocks. He was coming up fast, just past the last curve in the trail.

What would Becca have done?

Remi made her decision, and heaved herself forward.

DUNCAN SLAMMED THE brakes and wrestled the steering wheel, bringing the Jeep to a teeth-grinding halt just inches from the police car. Vale had turned it sideways at the end of this section of trail, where it widened into a clearing before continuing again on the other side through the trees. He'd probably done it on purpose, either hoping to make a quick turnaround and getaway when he came back to the car, or blocking anyone who might come after him.

Duncan grabbed his radio and jumped out of the Jeep, aiming his gun at the police car as he ran to check inside. "Lee, come in. It's Duncan."

"We just found the trail. We're coming up."

"You're about ten minutes behind me. I found the police car." He rounded to the open trunk and wasn't surprised to find it empty. He frowned and leaned in close, then picked up a long blond hair from the carpet. Remi. He glanced around.

"The officer was killed," Lee announced. "Gatlinburg PD found him in a ditch, tossed like garbage. I've got three guys with me. I'll call for more now that we know we're on the right path. Wait there."

Duncan bent down, studying the footprints, figuring out what had happened based on the marks in the dirt. Then he took off running toward where the path continued beyond the clearing. "Can't wait. It looks like he had Remi in the trunk. She must have tried something. Maybe she hit him when he opened it. She has a mean left hook. He threw a tarp on her, probably intended to roll her up in it and carry her somewhere. But she got away, ran into the woods on the far side. I know this trail, Lee. It's a one-way ticket to the cliffs. No way out except to turn around. If I wait, she's as good as dead."

"Understood. Just don't get yourself killed, all right? I don't want to face those brothers of yours if you do."

He leaped over a fallen log, wincing at the feel of something tearing on his left side, probably his stitches.

Hang on, Remi. I'm coming. Just hang on.

He pounded through the woods, not even trying to be quiet. It didn't matter. In fact, he hoped Vale heard him. After all, he had a gun, and Remi didn't. Duncan knew where this trail ended, certain death with no safe hiding places if a murderer was chasing you. And Vale had a head start. Was he even now hurting Remi, using her in whatever sick fashion he'd used all the women he and Hendricks had abducted and killed over the years? Duncan had to do something, anything, to give her a fighting chance. He had to distract him, get Vale to go after him instead of Remi. And there was only one way to be absolutely certain the man heard him.

He raised his gun toward the sky and squeezed the trigger.

REMI JERKED AT the sound of a gunshot. So did Vale. He skidded to a halt in front of the dilapidated building, knife raised as he glanced over his shoulder.

Remi had been certain her sister would have rushed inside. So instead, she'd hurried around the right corner of the outside of the building, feeling terribly exposed. But she'd found a large rock, about six inches across, and she'd picked it up. She planned on bashing Vale's skull in when he went inside, searching for her. But as she carefully peered around the building at him, instead of going inside, now he stood in indecision.

Bam!

Another shot.

Vale grunted and turned around. He shoved his knife in its holder and reached down to his other ankle. He pulled out a Glock 19, just like the one he'd had at the ridge, and disappeared back down the path.

Remi stood frozen in shock. Vale had a gun all this time, could have mowed her down with a hail of bullets. But he'd wanted to stalk her instead, enjoy her fear. And now he was going after whoever had fired those shots.

The pain in her shoulder was suddenly too intense to

ignore. She dropped the rock, her chest heaving as she leaned against the wall, holding her arm and trying to catch her breath. Whoever had fired those shots had given her some extra time, time to form a better plan if Vale came back. And she wasn't going to waste it.

She ran into the building to see if there was something she could use. It wasn't large, maybe twenty by twenty. It had been a barn or small house at one time, probably twice its current size. But the elements had taken their toll, shearing off the back half of the building and sweeping it down the cliff to the rocks below. Why someone had built the structure so close to the edge was beyond her. Then again, maybe a piece of the mountain had broken off over the years, making a once safe building now a perilously dangerous one. If someone ran straight through to the back, they'd fall out into space, then plummet to their death below.

Was that what happened to you, Becca? She prayed it wasn't, prayed that her sister hadn't suffered such unspeakable terror, knowing the whole time she was falling that she was going to die.

Bam!

Another shot sounded from outside, much closer than before.

"Vale!" a voice called out. "Come and get me, you sick fool!"

Duncan! That was Duncan's voice. What was he doing? Making himself a target to save her?

No. She couldn't lose him, not like this, not sacrificing himself for her. She had to help him. Somehow. She whirled around and ran back through the building. Then she skidded in the dirt and turned. What had she seen? Something had flashed at her as she'd run past. Was it something she could use to help him? She rushed back in and looked to her right, toward an old fireplace. There was something white, something… She rushed forward, then fell to her knees. Amid the ashes of a fire from long ago, lying over a wrought-iron grate, was what she'd been searching for for a decade.

Becca.

Her bones were covered with soot. Her once beautiful hair, what was left of it, lay in curly piles around her skull. And sticking out of her left femur was a lethal-looking steel pin, like a spike sticking out of the side of a club. It was the pin that had caught Remi's attention, somehow catching a ray of sunlight through one of the cracks in the ruined ceiling overhead.

Tears cascaded down onto her hand as she reached into the grate.

DUNCAN WOBBLED ON his feet, shaking his head to try to make both Vales turn back into one.

Vale chuckled. "Seeing stars, are ya now?" He circled in front of Duncan, his knife clutched menacingly in his right hand. "Me, I've never been one for astronomy or astrology or whatever it's called. But Billy, well, he was obsessed. All because of that stupid girl he wanted and could never have, Becca." He shook his head and gestured toward Duncan's side. "I don't know why I'm even bothering to toy with you. As much blood as you're losing, you're gonna pass out any minute now. No fun. Too easy."

"Give me back my gun if you think this is too easy."

Vale flashed a bright white smile. "If I'd wanted a gunfight I wouldn't have tossed both our guns after sneaking up on you. Still, yeah, I admit I might have been hasty. That's two guns you've cost me. And I aim to collect."

He suddenly charged at Duncan, knife raised.

Duncan leaped to the side and swept his foot around in a circle.

Vale went sprawling to the ground and did a face plant against an oak tree.

Duncan ran toward him to grab the knife, then jerked back just in time to avoid being stabbed as Vale jabbed it toward him.

Vale swore viciously and climbed laboriously to his feet, then wiped his mouth, glaring when his hand came away wet with blood. "You're gonna pay for that."

"Where's Remi?" Duncan asked, trying to buy time as they circled each other. All the while, he kept glancing around, looking for a stick, a big rock, anything he could use to give him an advantage. On any given day, he could have beat Vale, no problem. But he'd lost too much blood and was struggling just to keep from passing out. "Where is she?"

"Let's just say she's with her sister." He laughed again.

Duncan's heart sank. No, he couldn't believe this man. He was lying. Duncan had to believe that Remi was okay. Anything else was unthinkable.

They continued to circle. Vale lunged forward. Duncan leaped out of the way, the blade so close he could feel the cold air rushing around it as Vale swung it in a deadly arc.

"Put the knife down, Vale. It's not too late to try to cut a deal. Remi for your life. I could talk to the district attorney, get him to take the death penalty off the table if you give up and tell me where Remi is."

"Give up? I'm not the one bleeding to death here. And I'm the one with the knife. Have you lost your mind?"

"Did you think I came here alone?"

Vale's eyes widened. He looked at the trees around

Duncan as if searching for others hiding behind him. "You're bluffing."

"Nope." Duncan pulled his radio out and hit the button. "Lee, how far out are you?"

Vale had started forward, but stopped when Lee answered. "A couple of minutes. We heard shots but you weren't answering."

"Had the volume down so it wouldn't distract me in our little fight here. Those were warning shots, from me to Vale. I don't have my gun anymore and he's got a knife. Come in hot. Shoot first. Ask questions later." He glared at Vale. "Kill the bastard." He tossed the radio to the ground.

Vale narrowed his eyes. "You just signed your death warrant." He let out a guttural yell and charged like a bull.

Duncan waited until Vale was almost on him before diving to the ground and whirling around with both hands clenched together, swinging his fists toward Vale's head. He hit him hard, throwing him sideways.

The knife skittered out of Vale's hands.

Duncan made a grab for it, but Vale got it first and slashed up and around, slicing Duncan's arm.

He swore and stumbled back, a fresh wave of dizziness making him stagger.

Vale stumbled, too, struggling to maintain his balance.

Duncan quickly backed up, then slammed against a tree behind him.

Vale grinned, victory in his eyes.

"Duncan! Catch!"

Duncan whipped his head around at the sound of Remi's voice. He automatically reached up for what she'd thrown, some kind of club. He caught it and whirled around, swinging it at Vale's head as his assailant swung his arm down toward Duncan's chest.

The club caught Vale in the temple. The knife glanced off Duncan's chest and flew harmlessly through the air. Vale's eyes rolled up and he fell to the ground, unmoving.

Duncan stood unsteady on his feet, his hands fisted as he waited for Vale to get up. He didn't. The side of his head where Duncan had hit him was soaked with blood. The club he'd used appeared to somehow be connected to his head. Something metallic was sticking out, some kind of long pin.

"Duncan, are you okay? Duncan?"

The sound of Remi's footsteps had him turning just in time to catch her in his arms. He clasped her to him, breathing in her scent, his face buried in her hair.

"Remi. Thank God. Remi."

"You're bleeding." She pushed out of his arms, her eyes wide with fear as she looked at his side. "He stabbed you."

"No. Billy did."

She blinked. "Billy?"

He pulled her against him again. "I'm fine. Don't worry about me. Now that I know you're safe, I'm fine. Thank God you're okay."

She put her arms around him, hugging him back.

The sound of running feet had both of them turning. Lee and four rangers burst from the cover of trees, guns raised.

"Hold up," Duncan called out. "We're okay. Vale is down."

As the men rushed around them, checking on Vale, Duncan slowly lowered himself to the ground. But he didn't release Remi. He held on to her, unable to let her go.

"Duncan, your side. We need to bandage it. And, oh no, your arm. It's bleeding, too!" She pressed her hand against his chest, her eyes filled with anguish and concern.

He feathered his fingers through her hair, unable to stop smiling. "You're okay. Please tell me you're okay."

She smiled. "I'm okay."

"Duncan," Lee called out. "Where the heck did you get this bone? The thing has a long pin in it."

"Bone?" He looked toward Vale and the rangers, then back at Remi. "What exactly did you toss to me when I was fighting Vale?"

"A miracle. From Becca to me to you. She saved us, Duncan. Becca saved us both."

Chapter Eighteen

The sun was just coming up, casting a warm glow over Remi's beloved Rockies in the distance. She clutched a spray of early spring flowers in her hand as she stared out over the rows of headstones that seemed to stretch to the horizon. In the past, her trips to this cemetery had always made her sad, knowing that Becca's small stone beside their mother's and father's was simply a place-holder, that Becca was still missing and might never be laid to rest with her family.

But she had been found.

And she'd been laid to rest almost a month earlier. As Remi walked the path between graves toward where Becca's new marker had been set, the tears in her eyes weren't tears of grief as they'd been in the past. Instead, they were tears of gratitude. Becca was finally at rest, beside her loving parents, who would watch over her for all eternity.

Although Remi would never know exactly what happened to her sister, it no longer mattered like it once had. Because it was over. Finally. For all of them. For the first time in her adult life she felt…free. She could move on, begin anew, have a fresh start without the constant questions casting a dark pall over her life. The drive to search for answers and bring her sister home was over.

So why wasn't she happy?

She knew why. Duncan. She missed him, more than she'd ever expected. They'd been thrust together for such a short time, in a powder keg of stress and danger, and a white-hot attraction that had been so consuming, so… impossible, given the situation, that she hadn't trusted it. As soon as Becca had been found, and after Remi's shoulder was seen to and she knew Duncan was going to recover from his wounds, she'd taken her sister home for a private ceremony and laid her to rest in this cemetery between her parents. And she'd gone on with her life. Or tried to. But moving on was proving to be much more difficult than she'd anticipated.

Duncan.

He'd called her several times after she'd left him at the hospital. But she was too much of a coward to talk to him. She didn't know what to say. Instead, she'd simply texted him that she was okay and left it at that.

How could she start a new life, with or without him, move forward, when she didn't know where she wanted to go, what she wanted to do? At least before, she'd had a goal—find Becca. Now? She was like a ship lost at sea, not knowing where to turn.

Her boss had been willing to keep her on at work. But in retrospect, all his criticisms over the years had been spot-on. She'd taken the job with the FBI only because of Becca. And without the need to search for her anymore, what satisfaction she'd once had there had fizzled. She just didn't have that drive she'd once had. She wanted, needed, something else. She just didn't quite know what that might be.

Thankfully, her father's foresight in having a generous life-insurance policy all those years ago, and her subsequent investment of that money, gave her the cushion she needed while making that decision. She'd resigned her position at the FBI. And now she needed to figure out what to do next.

Shaking her head at her jumbled thoughts, she carefully adjusted the bouquet in her hands. The arrangement of irises, daffodils, pansies and pink roses had been culled from her mother's garden, yet another remnant of the past that Remi hadn't been able to let go of all these years. She'd never even moved out of her parents' house. Now the space felt oddly stifling, like she no longer belonged there. She'd put it up for sale last week. It felt… weird, putting it on the market. But it also felt right. She was going to turn twenty-eight in a few weeks. And it was as if she'd just graduated high school and was trying to figure out what she wanted to be when she grew up.

She really hoped she figured it out before it was time to retire.

Stepping past the last row of headstones before her family's, she stopped, and stared. There were three rectangular gray marble tombstones, each with a marble vase attached to the base. And each vase had fresh flowers in it, red roses. The last time that Remi had been here was after the private memorial service that had consisted of the preacher, herself and a handful of Becca's old high school friends who were still in the area. She hadn't come back because she'd waited for the ground to settle, knowing the headstone couldn't be placed until then.

So who had left the fresh roses?

Kneeling on the ground, she winced, then caught herself with her left hand on her mother's tombstone. The right shoulder was getting much better with therapy. She didn't even wear the sling anymore. But it still reminded her on occasion that the injury was there, with a fresh rush of pain that zapped her like a jolt of electricity. She rubbed her shoulder, then picked up the flowers she'd brought and arranged them around the roses.

After finishing with the vases on both her parents' graves, she moved to the last one, Becca's. That's when she saw the piece of paper folded up and perched between two of the roses. She carefully pulled it out and unfolded it. Her hands shook as she recognized the handwriting. It was the same as what she'd seen on another note, sitting on a nightstand, on a cold February night, a lifetime ago.

Remi, I hope that with Easter coming up in a few days, the time of fresh starts and new beginnings, that you, too, are able to get that fresh start that you wanted. It is my fervent wish that you be at peace and that you're happy. But no matter what, you'll never be alone. I'm there with you, in thought, in spirit. Always. All my love, Duncan.

A drop of moisture plopped onto the paper, making the ink bleed. She glanced up at the sky, expecting to see rain clouds. But it wasn't raining. She was crying. She wiped her eyes, let out a shaky breath and looked down at the note.

"All my love, Duncan."

"All my love."

"Love." Was that an Irish salutation or did it mean that he actually loved her?

"Idiot! Stop wasting time."

She snapped her head up and looked around.

"Get your lazy butt up."

She jerked her head toward the tombstone, and blinked. "Becca? Is that you?"

"Get up!"

She climbed awkwardly to her feet, bracing herself

with her left hand, favoring her right shoulder. The voice had been so loud, so…real. Just like when she'd been in the Smokies, lying hurt on the ground, and she'd heard her sister's irritated voice in her ear, telling her to run. She looked around, relieved when she didn't see anyone else close enough to realize she was hearing voices. Then she licked her dry lips. "Becca? Is…is that you? Are you trying to tell me something?"

The wind picked up suddenly, rattling the note in her hand. She looked at it, sad to see that she'd obviously had more than one tear fall on the paper. Her tears had pretty much obliterated the ink. All she could read now was "my love, Duncan."

A gust blew against her, pushing her back several feet, and snatched the note from her hands. She grabbed at it, but it swirled just out of her reach, bouncing across the grass in the direction of the parking lot.

She hesitated, looked at her parents' tombstones, at Becca's.

"Run!"

Remi smiled, fresh tears dripping down her cheeks. "Subtlety never was your strong suit, was it, sis?" She wiped her eyes and looked at the three pieces of stone. And she knew this wasn't where they were. Her family would always be in her heart. She would carry them with her wherever she went. They would never be alone.

And neither would she.

The wind tugged at her hair again. She smiled. "I love you, Mom, Dad. I love you, too, Becca."

A warm gentle breeze, nothing like the raging wind from earlier, picked up the long tendrils of her curly dark hair and settled them softly around her shoulders.

She let out a ragged breath. "Thank you, Becca." She took off running toward her car.

DUNCAN SETTLED THE tray of ham that he'd just sliced in the middle of his parents' enormous dining room table. Adam set the turkey beside it.

"I think that's the last of it," Adam said.

Duncan nodded. As usual, his mother had gone all out. The table was set with her fine china, plus the gold flatware she normally kept in a velvet-lined box in the hutch at the other end of the room. Even the fancy crystal candleholders had been moved from their place of honor on the mantel in the family room to the table, one on each end of a platter of meat. The white candles mixed their vanilla scent with the aroma of an Easter dinner that would see each of them with leftovers for days to come.

The sounds of laughter came through the archway to the kitchen. His father's deep voice rumbled and his mother and Jody laughed in response.

Duncan noted there was an extra chair, as usual.

Adam followed his gaze. "Ever the optimist. When's the last time Ian showed up for a holiday meal?" He shook his head.

"Christmas a year ago," a voice said from the doorway.

They both turned to see Colin step into the dining room from the family room. "But I always show up so you can bask in the presence of the favorite son." He grinned and held out his arms with a flourish, as if bestowing a magnanimous gift on them by simply being there.

Adam and Duncan exchanged a glance and rolled their eyes. "Mom!" they both yelled.

She ducked her head in from the kitchen, wiping her hands on a dish towel. "Inside voices. Were you raised in a barn? I swear I—" She broke off her lecture when she saw Colin, a barely shorter copy of Duncan and Adam, which made him six-two instead of their six-three.

"Ma. I'm home!" He spread his arms again.

"Colin!" She half turned toward the kitchen. "Colin's here!" She ran to him and he wrapped his arms around her, a big grin on his face as he looked at Duncan and Adam and silently mouthed, *"Favorite."*

"About time," Adam complained. "Now we can eat." He softened his words with a smile and headed in for a group hug.

Duncan laughed and clapped Colin on the shoulder, deftly avoiding the group hug and heading into the family room. As soon as he was out of sight of his family, he stopped smiling. Keeping up pretenses of being happy and acting like his world hadn't been ripped apart was taking its toll. If he got through the rest of this smiling, laughing family day with his sanity intact, it would be a miracle.

He lifted his right boot and rested it on the fireplace hearth as he stared into the flames. It had been about two months since Remi Jordan had blown through his life and left him a wrecked man. He'd known he cared about her. But he hadn't known just how much until he'd nearly lost her to a brutal man's knife. And then, after visiting him in the hospital to make sure he survived his injuries from his encounter with Vale, for her to just…leave, to go back to Colorado without a backward glance… He shook his head. Flying there a few days ago and putting the flowers and that note on her sister's grave had been the act of a lovesick idiot. Obviously she didn't feel the same way he did or she'd have responded to his calls or that foolish note by now. Somehow he was going to have to figure out how to go on with his life with a big gaping hole in his chest where his heart used to be.

He just wished he knew how.

The doorbell rang. He frowned and looked over his

shoulder to see if his dad was going to get the door. This was their cabin, after all. And Duncan had zero expectations of his black-sheep youngest brother, Ian, actually showing up. So whoever it was had to be here to see his dad or mom.

It was noisy back in the dining room with the mini–family reunion going on. Colin was in the middle of some kind of secret assignment in his capacity as a U.S. Deputy Marshal. And yet, somehow, he always managed to make it home for holidays. Everyone was obviously too preoccupied to notice the door.

The bell rang again.

Duncan sighed and crossed the expansive family room with its two-story view of the Smokies and opened the door.

He promptly forgot how to breathe.

"Hi, Duncan." Remi gave him a tremulous smile, her brown eyes as warm as honey as she stared up at him. "I hope you don't mind me showing up at your parents' home. I tracked you down through your boss." A light breeze toyed with her dark brown curls, swirling them around her face. She impatiently shoved them back.

"You dyed your hair again." A stupid thing to say, but it was all his shocked brain could come up with at the moment.

Her smile dimmed. "Yeah, well. It's as close to my natural color as I could get. I'm through with dyeing and changing my hair. I quit my job at the FBI. I'm plain old Remi Jordan again." She waited, her gaze searching his.

He stood frozen to the spot, not sure what to say, what to do. He opened his mouth several times, but couldn't seem to make any more words come out.

"Duncan?" his mother's voice called out from behind him. "Who's there?" She pretty much pushed him out of the way and stepped into the open doorway. Duncan saw her smile falter, probably because she'd hoped it was her youngest son. But she quickly recovered and gave Remi a warm, welcoming smile. "Hello there, young lady. Happy Easter."

Remi smiled back, but her smile was much less bright, her expression more guarded now, unsure as she shook his mother's hand.

"Mrs. McKenzie, right? I'm Remi Jordan. Sorry to crash your Easter celebrations. But I was looking for Duncan and I—"

"Remi Jordan?" His mother's eyes widened in surprise. "Oh, my. The FBI agent who…" She faltered, obviously not wanting to bring up bad memories about Becca and what had happened.

Remi took his mother's hands in hers. "It's okay to say it. The FBI agent who came here looking for her missing sister. And found her. Becca's home now, with my parents, and with God. I'm at peace with it."

His mother pulled her into a hug. "You poor, dear child. Come in, come in. You're just in time for dinner."

Remi's eyes widened as she pulled back. "Oh, no. No, ma'am. I couldn't. I really should have waited, but I was, well, I just really wanted to talk to Duncan. If I could." She looked up at him. "Duncan? Can we talk?"

He cleared his throat and drew a ragged breath. Seeing her again had sucked all the oxygen from his brain and made him dumbstruck. Both his mother and Remi were looking at him with concern, or in his mother's case, as if she thought he'd lost every good manner she'd ever taught him. She looked as if she was ready to twist his ear and drag him inside if he didn't speak.

"Give us a minute" was all he could manage, which he knew he'd pay for later. His mother didn't tolerate rudeness.

He grabbed Remi's left hand and tugged her behind him as he headed around the corner of the house.

Chapter Nineteen

Remi allowed Duncan to tow her around the outside of the cabin, using the opportunity to blink back the stupid tears burning her eyes. She'd never felt so humiliated, so ashamed, in all her life. She'd spent a ridiculous amount of money that she couldn't afford to grab a last-minute flight on a holiday and fly halfway across the country to see him. While she hadn't necessarily expected that he'd get down on one knee and pledge his undying love, she'd assumed he'd at least smile at her, hug her, something to let her know that he was actually glad to see her. Instead, he'd glowered at her and hadn't even bothered to introduce her to his mother before yanking her after him like a dog on a leash.

She should have stayed in Colorado.

Instead, she'd built up that stupid note into a fantasy of happily-ever-after, when it had probably just been a colleague paying his respects to her family and wishing her well. The End. Done. Over. She felt so stupid. And hurt. She was surprised her heart was still beating after the huge crack he'd just made in it. All she wanted to do was run back to her rental car and hightail it to the airport to nurse her wounded pride and shattered soul.

They'd just turned another corner around the massive log cabin, into what she supposed would have passed as a backyard if the monstrosity wasn't perched on the edge of the mountain, with a network of stilts jammed into the ground, holding the house up. Her earlier belief that Duncan came from money was definitely spot on. Which just pointed out another big difference between the two of them. She really shouldn't have come. What had she been thinking?

He stopped and whirled to face her. She automatically retreated from the intensity of his gaze and jerked to a halt when the wall of logs pressed against her back.

"Why are you here?" he demanded.

Her face flushed with heat. "Nice to see you, too."

"Remi. You can't expect to just show up out of the blue and—"

"Assume you'd be happy to see me? Let's not belabor that point. I get it. Loud and clear. You're not happy to see me. And this was a huge, ginormous, not to mention expensive, mistake." She stepped to the side to get around him.

He blocked her in, forcing her against the house again. She fisted her hands at her sides and glared up at him. "Okay, this bully thing ends right here. Back off. Now. Before I kick the family jewels into the back of your throat."

His brows rose, then he blinked and did as she'd said, giving her some breathing room. He stared at her, swore, cleared his throat.

"Not much for talking today, I see," she said. "No problem. I think we're done here. Really done this time. Have a great holiday with the family. I won't be bothering you again." She turned to stalk off and could have sworn he growled at her. But before she could even glance his way, he grabbed her.

With one arm around her hips, the other at her back,

he whirled her around and slammed his mouth down on top of hers. She was so startled she didn't have the presence of mind to kick him as she'd warned. But then his mouth and tongue obliterated her capability of thought, and all she could do was hold on and enjoy the ride.

His big, hot, hard body surrounded hers, cocooning her against the house. His kiss tasted of desperation and anger and heat, all at the same time. But there was something else, too, something she couldn't quite define. She was out of breath and gasping for air when he broke the kiss. His shoulders were heaving as he, too, drew ragged breaths. And then his gaze met hers, and the pain in the deep blue depths had her gasping with surprise.

"Why are you here?" he demanded again, sounding more bewildered and resentful than angry this time.

She'd hurt him. Badly. And she hadn't even realized it until this very moment. The proof was staring back at her. The heat was there between them. It always had been. But the emotions rolling off him in waves had nothing to do with lust and everything to do with a man who'd cared about someone, who still cared about her, and was afraid to hope.

Her anger evaporated. Her body relaxed. She smiled and feathered her hands up his chest.

He jerked at her touch. But he didn't move away.

"Thank you for the flowers you sent to my family. I saw the note."

He frowned. "You could have thanked me over the phone."

She hesitated, still feeling like a fool. But she'd gone to a lot of trouble to get here and she wasn't leaving until she told him what she'd come to say. If he didn't want her after that, so be it. She'd go home, lick her wounds and live her life without him.

Somehow.

After drawing a deep breath, she said, "I'm not here to thank you. I'm here to tell you something that I should have told you a long time ago."

His look turned stony, and this time he did step back, forcing her to drop her arms. "Whatever it is, I'm sure you could have used the phone for that, too. My family's probably waiting dinner on me. I'll walk you to your car."

"I love you."

He jerked his head toward her. His throat worked, his Adam's apple bobbing in his throat. "What did you say?"

Determined to give this everything she had, she stepped toward him and then hooked her hands in his belt loops so that if he moved away again, he'd take her with him. "I'm sorry, Duncan. I'm sorry that I left. But as someone I know once told me, if I had it to do all over again, I still would have left. It was something I had to do. I had to take Becca home and lay the past to rest and work some things out in my mind. You have to understand. All my adult life has been geared toward one thing, one goal—find Becca. Once I did that, once we did that, it was like I was floating in space and someone cut my lifeline. I was lost, struggling, didn't know what to do. Nothing felt right or real. I had to sort it all out, find my center again."

"You said goodbye in the hospital, then walked away. I didn't know you were leaving for good. You didn't answer my calls. All you did was text me that you were okay. I deserved better than that."

Her heart squeezed in her chest at the pain in his words. "I know. You did. You do. That was wrong of me, so very wrong. It's no excuse, but I was confused. The words that I wanted to say were right there, on the tip of my tongue, but I couldn't make sense of them. You and me, we don't make sense." She waved at the expensive home and land. "We really, really don't make sense."

She drew a shaky breath and focused on what she was trying to tell him. And hoped it would be enough. "I was worried that it wasn't real, the way I feel about you. How could it be after knowing you for such a short period of time? I wasn't ready for that, for you. There wasn't room in my confused mind to understand it, let alone face it. So, yes. I walked away. But I'm here now. I came back. I came back for you, Duncan. I wasn't ready before. But now I am."

He searched her eyes, then took a step. Toward her. "What are you saying, Remi? What are you ready for?"

"You. I'm ready for you. I love you, Duncan. I want everything you said in the note you sent me. I want a fresh start, a new beginning. I want to be happy. And there's only one thing that will make me happy. You. Always and forever."

He shuddered and reached for her. He didn't kiss her this time. Instead, he wrapped his arms around her, pulling her tightly against him.

"I thought I'd lost you," he said. "I thought I'd lost you."

She wrapped her arms around his waist. "I'm right here."

He drew back and cupped her face. "For how long?"

She blinked, not sure what he meant. "As long as you want me? If you want me, that is. I put my parents' house up for sale. I packed all my clothes, and I do mean all of them. I have four massive suitcases in my rental car. Cost me a fortune at the airport to check those bags."

"Where are you staying?"

He wasn't giving her many clues about how he felt. Her face heated as she put her pride, and her heart, on the line. "With you? I hope. That is, if your cabin's been repaired from the shoot-out and you want me there."

His eyes widened. "If I want you? Seriously?" He reached into his shirt and pulled out a chain that was hanging around his neck, then held it up. A diamond solitaire ring glittered in the sunlight.

"Is that?" She had to clear her tight throat. "Is that what I think it is?" Her voice was hoarse and raw.

He undid the chain and pulled off the ring, letting the chain drop to the ground. He got down on one knee in front of her and held up the ring.

"Remi Elizabeth Jordan—"

"How did you know my middle name?"

He arched a brow. "I'm a criminal investigator."

She smiled.

He grinned. "Remi, I love that sassy mouth of yours, your sexy little body, that gorgeous complicated brain inside your pretty little head. I love everything about you. But mostly I love the idea of having you as my wife, to have and to hold, for better or worse, until death do us part."

Unshed tears clogged her throat. "Shouldn't we save the vows for when we're in front of the preacher?"

"Is that a yes?"

"I don't remember you asking me a question," she teased.

"Nothing's ever easy with you is it, sweet Colleen?"

"Now where would the fun be in that, Irish lad?" She smiled at him through the tears that she could no longer hold back.

"Marry me?" His voice was so full of love and tenderness that she nearly melted into a puddle at his feet.

Unable to speak, she held her left hand out. It shook

so hard he finally had to hold it still so he could get the ring on her finger.

Then he was kissing her, searing her with his heat. And she was kissing him back, trying to show him with actions how much she adored this smart, sexy, wonderful man.

When he finally broke the kiss, a chorus of catcalls and whistles rang out from above. They both looked up. Five happy faces looked down at them, leaning over the balcony railing.

Heat flushed Remi's face as she returned their waves.

Duncan laughed and swooped in for another kiss, much to the amusement of their audience. He pulled back, feathered her face with more kisses as if he couldn't get enough of her. His expression turned serious.

"I love you, Remi."

"I love you, Duncan. More than you'll ever know."

He cupped her face in his hands and stared down at her, his brow furrowed with concern. "You won't ever be alone again. You'll always have your family, the memories, their love in your heart. But you'll have me now, too. And a new family who will learn to love you almost as much as I do, if you want that. But they can be…intense. A lot to deal with. If you need more time, we don't have to stay here today. We can go to my cabin and—"

She put her finger on his lips to stop him. "And miss that mouthwatering dinner I smelled at the front door? Not a chance."

His mouth curved into a sexy grin that had her regretting her offer to stay. Having him at his cabin, all to herself, was more mouthwatering than any food could ever be.

He gently wiped the tears from her cheeks and tucked

her arm in the crook of his elbow. "Come on, future wife. I'll introduce you to your new family."

He kissed her again, a sweet, soft, tender kiss that healed the large crack from earlier, encasing her heart in the warmth and strength of his love. And then he took her to the front of the house, where her new family was waiting to welcome her with open arms.

* * * * *

COMING SOON!

We really hope you enjoyed reading this book. If you're looking for more romance, be sure to head to the shops when new books are available on

Thursday 16th May

To see which titles are coming soon, please visit

millsandboon.co.uk/nextmonth

LET'S TALK

Romance

For exclusive extracts, competitions
and special offers, find us online:

f facebook.com/millsandboon

🐦 @MillsandBoon

📷 @MillsandBoonUK

Get in touch on 01413 063232

For all the latest titles coming soon, visit
millsandboon.co.uk/nextmonth